Riding Blind

by

J.L. Sheppard

Hell Ryders MC Book 3

Riding Blind

Contact Information: info@thewildrosepress.com

Cover Art by *Diana Carlile*

The Wild Rose Press, Inc.
PO Box 708
Adams Basin, NY 14410-0708

Visit us at www.thewilderroses.com

Publishing History
First Scarlet Rose Edition, 2018
Print ISBN 978-1-5092-1884-4
Digital ISBN 978-1-5092-1885-1

Published in the United States of America

**He never knew love,
not until she walked into his life…**

His gaze locked with hers, and because a part of him swore she'd be gone, he held it for longer than he cared to admit. Finally, he tore his eyes away. He couldn't help it, so he trailed them from top to bottom. She wore a black tee with the word "Harley" written in freehand cursive across the chest.

He knew that tee. Not much different than most of his tees, black and it read, "Harley," but it'd been his favorite because all those years ago, she wore it to bed.

The first time he had her, she found it on the floor and put it on. From that night on, she slept with him in that tee. The only nights she didn't wear it to bed, the nights he dealt with club business, and she went to bed without him. On those nights, he stole it back and wore it laced with her scent, so with every breath he took, he'd smell her. After she left, he realized he did it because she wasn't around and he wanted her to be.

When she left, she took everything with her, like she'd been trying to erase the memory of her from him. She was gone, and he didn't know why, and he didn't want her to be. He needed something, anything. He thought he had at least that shirt, so he looked everywhere, tearing his room apart, but he never found it, and now he knew why.

She took his favorite tee.

She stole it and left…

PRAISE FOR AUTHOR

J.L. Sheppard

RUNNING WILD

"If you want a dominant, caring, freakin' awesome hero, an amazing heroine and a hell of a lot of heat. Give this a read!"

~Coffee House Press

~*~

"The author uses a sensitive subject matter to create a beautiful story of justice and love finding the right path. A great beginning to a new MC series!"

~InD'tale Magazine

~*~

"Ready for some hot bikers? J.L. Sheppard has a new series for you!"

~Nightowl Reviews

RUNNING HOT

"Running Hot is impossible to put down! A great read for anytime of the year!"

~InD'tale Magazine

~*~

"[Cuss and Tiffany's] story is epic and thrilling... Running Hot is an amazing second book in a must read series!"

~TBR Pile

~*~

"Strong and slow building storyline, Running Hot was a great MC read..."

~Tome Tender

Dedication

Para Papi:
Seré tu rubia linda siempre.

Author Acknowledgments

A big thank you to my family and friends for their continued support.

To my editor, Sharon Pickrel, I'm forever thankful for all I've learned, your hard work and patience.

To my publisher, including everyone who works behind the scenes: Rhonda, RJ, Diana, and Lisa to name a few, thank you for giving me the opportunity to reach countless readers, and especially, for believing in my stories.

Last but not least, to my readers, it's for you I write. I'm forever grateful.

Prologue

Late and dark, there was no other place he'd rather be than on his bike. The wind beating against his face, the sound and the feel of the engine rumbling between his legs—peace, his peace.

Too soon the ride ended, arriving at his destination, an older-looking home in Santa Rosa, California, just a thirty-minute drive from the Hell Ryders MC's garage and compound. On a Wednesday night, Chip, the president of Chained Disciples MC, was throwing a huge blowout. Since their clubs had joined forces and began working together more than a year ago, making money in illegal and immoral ways, and even though he and Chip weren't as close as his brothers—the men of Hell Ryders MC, he and Chip had become friends, friends who had each other's back during those times they ran drugs and guns across borders, friends who hung out and partied often.

It was his first time visiting Chip's home, but he knew he had the right place. For one, the one-story house was on five acres of land; trees and shrubbery surrounded it and gave the club privacy. It looked like it needed some landscaping and remodeling. A row of bikes parked out front. He counted six in total. Chip and Tracker, Vice President of Chained MC, lived in the house. Two bikers in a home, those two bikers being from a nomad club, they wouldn't be too interested in upkeep. Chained MC being nomads was smart and worked to their benefit considering in their line of work, things could get heated and fast. A home base and roots made it harder to run and hide when need be.

Parking, Ripper hopped off his bike and headed up the stone steps. He knocked and waited. Moments later, Chip swung the door open. Straight away, he handed him a glass of clear liquid. He took it.

Chip tapped his glass against his. "Thanks for comin'. Party's just started." He shot the drink back.

Ripper did the same. The alcohol, vodka, burned down the back of his throat as he strode inside. He glanced around the room taking it all in. Open concept, a big living room, several cream-colored couches that had seen better days surrounded a huge flat screen TV, the only piece of furniture that looked in good shape and new. Ten kegs stood at the end of the room, near a counter lined with bottles of liquor. Several members of Chained MC were already there. As he'd counted six in total, two pounding shots, two others eyes glued to the boxing match on the flat screen, another making out with a tap in the kitchen and Chip. He knew more were en route like he knew several of his brothers were as well. After all, tonight they were celebrating pulling off the biggest gun and drug run in both their clubs' history. Each club had nabbed more than a million on the deal.

As the hours passed, more of his brothers and Chip's joined the party. They laughed too loud, drank too much. Some even fucked in plain sight and passed the leftovers.

Then it happened.

The front door opened, and a girl strode through.

Just the sight took his breath away, so from his seat on the couch, he straightened, gaze deadlocked on her.

Her hair was blonde, not like his, but a light blonde and long enough it reached her mid-back, and her face was flawless, high cheekbones, rosy cheeks, arched brows, and thick lips, so thick he couldn't help but picture them around his dick. Standing at an angle and wearing a pair of skin-tight jeans and blouse, he knew she was lean with a small waist and a hell of an ass.

She wasn't his type. He liked blondes, but he liked boobs more, and she didn't have big ones. Not that they were small, he'd guess a B-cup. She didn't dress like his type either. He liked women who dressed to flaunt, women who didn't mind spreading for bikers, women who knew not to expect a call the next day, women they called taps. He liked those women because he didn't need a hassle and because he didn't like to work to get laid. He liked sex a lot, liked it with different women, and he didn't want those women on his dick getting ideas of the forever kind. That's why he looked for women wearing short skirts he could pull to their waists, women with cleavage, so their tits were in his face when they rode him. Most importantly, he liked women, not girls, and this girl looked like a girl, too young, too clean, and too pure.

Yet she was beautiful, so regardless of all the reasons he shouldn't want her, his body responded too easily, too quickly. Before he thought it through, he stood and strode to her. He didn't make it in time.

Chip did, leaving Ripper standing six feet away, watching as Chip wrapped an arm around her waist, the other around her neck, and roughly hauled her to his chest. Then *she* snaked her arms around Chip's waist for a hug.

At the sight, a deep burn ripped through his stomach.

Chip drew away, his head slanted toward her. Looking straight at Chip, she smiled a gorgeous smile that lit up the whole fucking room.

That deep burn ripping his stomach open rose up his chest.

Chip flashed a grin. "Celebrating tonight, baby. Don't want you cleanin' though."

Baby? Fuck. Fuck. Fuck. That burn reached his throat in the form of bile. He swallowed it down. No denying it now. Young and beautiful, and she was Chip's. He should've guessed. Only taps and old ladies came to biker parties. She wasn't a tap because she didn't dress like one meaning she belonged to a brother and not one of his brothers. Had she been, he would've seen her before now.

"Yeah, right," she shot back with attitude.

Instead of riling Chip's temper like it should've, like anyone would've guessed, Chip threw his head back and laughed like he loved getting shit from her.

If the fact she wasn't his type and the fact she belonged to Chip didn't turn him off, the attitude should've. Worse than a woman who wanted more from him and made him work for it was a woman with attitude. And instead, like everything with the blonde, it had the opposite effect. It made him want her more.

Chip tugged her into him again, kissed her forehead, then said, "Love you, Em," and pulled away.

She quirked a brow. "Don't be dramatic. You just missed me getting you drinks."

Again, that attitude, but Ripper hadn't heard it. His

mind consumed in what Chip said.

Chip wasn't just a biker, and he wasn't just the president of Chained MC. He was a badass, hard, fearless, and fierce enough that he overthrew the last president of Chained with no remorse, no regret to take his shot at leading the club. If the rumors were true, it meant Chip and Tracker eliminated those who opposed him in a way that meant they'd never get back at him. And yet, that same man had so easily admitted he loved the girl. He gave her that in front of his brothers and Ripper's. Shocking, absurd, and unheard of.

Ripper was lost in that, confounded by it, until it hit him—how it made perfect sense. A man didn't keep a girl like her unless he gave that to her. From one look, any man knew she was that type of woman, the type who wouldn't settle for anything less, the type who deserved it.

Those thoughts fled when the sound of Chip's easy laughter rang out. Then Chip turned, leaving one arm draped around her shoulders, and walked toward the back of the house, taking her with him.

No doubt in Ripper's mind where Chip would take her. That thought he couldn't take, so he closed his eyes and angled his head away from them. When he heard his name, he came to and realized he hadn't taken a breath for a while. He'd been standing there motionless for a long-ass time thinking about another man's woman.

"Fuck." What was wrong with him? He'd never reacted to a woman that way. So she was pretty; she was still too young, too innocent. Truth be told, she was too young for Chip too, who was a year older than him. None of that mattered though. As Chip's old lady, even if she and Chip broke up, he couldn't make a move. You didn't fuck with a biker's old lady even if she wasn't his old lady anymore. He had to forget her.

It took him a moment to compose himself, but he finally did, telling himself he didn't really want her, that his reaction had been fueled by alcohol.

He left minutes later.

****

Ripper hopped off his bike, duffle bag in hand, and strode up the familiar stone steps then knocked and waited. It swung open a moment later. She appeared at the other end looking like every other time he'd seen her—too young, too pure, too clean, and too beautiful.

Over the past five months, he'd avoided her the best he could because he'd been wrong. Two weeks after he saw her for the first time, he saw her again, and again, he reacted. He wanted her bad enough he hadn't been able to stop thinking about her, bad enough he'd even dreamt what her skin tasted like, but he couldn't have her, so he avoided her. He wasn't a coward; he was smart to keep his distance.

He scanned her flushed face then helplessly glided his gaze down her body. She wore a blue robe, big on her, so it didn't take a genius to guess it belonged to Chip, and that Rip probably caught them in the act.

Just his fucking luck.

Her brows furrowed. "I'm sorry. I don't know your name."

He snapped his stare from her robe to her hazel eyes. "Bryce," he said too quickly, too harshly, giving her his real name, not his road name, and he didn't know why.

She smiled softly and nodded. Looking at him

6

expectantly but she didn't say a word. After a long moment of silence, she quirked a brow. "Can I help you?"

Right, he hadn't even told her why he'd come, too lost in just looking at her, in looking at her looking at him. Fucking idiot. "Chip told me to meet him here."

"He isn't here, but you can wait inside. I can get you a beer if you want."

Not there? Why then was her face flushed? Why was she wearing a man's robe? Was someone else in the house? Did Chip share her with his brothers? *Her*?

"Track here?" His voice came out gravely.

Her eyes rounded as she shook her head.

"Anyone here?"

She shook her head again.

He took a deep breath and released it. So Chip wasn't crazy, didn't share her. Good thing, too. His instincts would've made him do something stupid like kidnap her and hide her in his room at the compound.

"So are you coming in or…"

Wait, she just said she was alone. Why would she invite any man in when she was alone? Proof of how young and naïve she was.

"It ain't smart to invite a man into your house when you're alone." He hadn't meant to sound so stern but hadn't been able to help it.

Unbelievably, she lifted her chin and smirked. "You're not just a man. You're a biker. That—"

Eyes hardening, body tensing, he cut her off. "More reason—"

She lifted her brows and crossed her arms over her chest. "Are you going to let me finish?"

Shit. She wasn't afraid of him, not even a little bit.

7

He was a scary motherfucker, had always been. He trained himself to be this way. He never had a thing in his life. His own mother abandoned him. His grandmother hadn't cared for him, so he'd turned into a mean, scary SOB. It meant not only did she have attitude, but she was also feisty. It should've turned him off, especially when she directed that attitude at him, but again, because it was her, that attitude had the opposite effect.

His cock twitched. He loved his reaction though it was fucked, and even knowing he shouldn't react at all, he couldn't help but smirk. He then lifted his chin, instructing her to go on.

"Like I said you're a biker. You know who lives here. Not just Chip, President of Chained MC, but Track, the VP. They don't share club stuff with me considering I'm a girl and all, but I'm not stupid either. I *know* you *know* because your club's cool with Chip's, so I know any biker who comes knocking on this door *knows* better than to mess with me because that means messing with Chip and messing with Chained MC."

Damn. He was so hard he swore if she kept talking with that little sharp tongue, he'd blow.

"So, are you coming in or not?"

Because he found her so beautiful, because that was the best conversation he'd ever had with a woman and because he couldn't help it, he grinned. "Thanks, but it ain't right."

She quirked a brow.

"You're right. No one'll fuck with you 'cause of Chip, but I can't take you up on that offer 'cause he isn't home, and it isn't right for me to be in there alone with his old lady."

She threw her head back and laughed aloud, a magnificent laugh, so he watched enthralled. Even though he didn't know why she laughed, he joined in.

When she settled, she looked him square in the eyes. "A gentleman biker? And I thought I'd seen it all." Shaking her head softly, she then added, "You have nothing to worry about, biker. I'm not his old lady. I'm his cousin."

Jaw dropping, he thought back to that first night he'd seen her. She walked in, Chip strode to her, hugged her. She gave him lip, and Chip told her he loved her. Then Chip took her to the back of the house.

"You lyin'?"

Her eyes widened. "Why would I lie?"

He had no clue and said so without words by shrugging.

"I'd kiss you to prove I'm not, but I'm not that type of girl."

With just the thought of her kissing him, his cock jerked.

"So, Bryce, are you coming in or not?"

Alone with her for however long Chip took to get home? Hell, yeah, he was in. "Yeah, babe." He smiled, deciding at that very moment, he'd make her his.

That smirk came again. "Name's Emelia. Everyone calls me Em."

He took a step toward her, stopping an inch from her, so close she had to further angle her head to meet his stare. "Okay, babe."

She shook her head softly and rolled her eyes simultaneously. "That's Emelia to you."

When her eyes met his again, he leaned into her. A breath from her lips, he said, "Okay, babe."

Chapter One

More than seven years later...

Under the hood of a '67 Chevy, Ripper heard the familiar roar of motorcycles.

"What the *fuck*?"

Darting his gaze beside him, he spotted Trick, one of his brothers from Hell Ryders MC, his body tense and ready for a fight. Nothing ever riled Trick, so it caught Ripper's attention.

Ripper straightened making sure he didn't slam his head under the hood of the car, his stare gravitating to the three men who rode up to the lot of Ryders Custom Rides, three men wearing cuts from Chained Disciples MC.

Not good.

The clubs had history and a murky past. Years ago, when the clubs severed ties, Hell Ryders banned Chained from entering their town of Wadden. Though the president of the rival club, Chip, had recently tried to mend fences, Hell Ryders voted against it. One of the brothers who'd been strongly against it was Rip. Three of Chained's bikers, officers no less, showing in their town, driving up to their garage, their compound, was a blatant threat.

Ripper's whole body shot ramrod straight. Fisting the wrench in his hand, he took several steps in their direction eyeing the three officers whom he knew by name, Tracker, Mase, and Till. Tracker, the vice president of Chained, returned his glare. His brothers, about ten of them who'd been inside and around the garage, closed in just as an SUV pulled up behind the bikes. A man, tall, sporting a military-style crew cut, stepped out.

"Doug?" Army, one of his brothers, said, surprise in his voice.

The man lifted his chin in Army's direction. Then the bikes turned off, one by one, and a deadening silence filled the air.

Ripper knew Doug. Army and Trigger, both part of his MC, mentioned him before. Doug served with both in the U.S. Army. Now, he was a private investigator and one of the best. Trigger hired Doug not so long ago to dig up dirt on his old lady's ex. A few months later, Chip, Chained MC's president, requested his number to find his...

Fuck. He closed his eyes tightly trying to erase the image of the beautiful woman who crept into his mind with just the thought of Chip.

Shaking it off, he glanced around wondering where Chip was. It had been Chip who'd wanted the clubs to mend fences. It'd been Chip who so badly wanted Doug's number to find...*her*.

He shouldn't care. The thought of *her* shouldn't fuck with him at all. It'd been more than five years. And still, with just the thought, his heart clenched so hard it made his whole body ache.

"Came to talk to Ripper," Doug said.

That caught his attention, dragging him away from his thoughts. He stepped forward. "Don't know what business you have with me."

Doug's gaze met his as he took several steps in his direction. "I was told to come to you if anything were to happen. Shit happened, so here I am." He paused then explained, "Chip hired me a while back to find his cousin."

Chip's cousin, the beautiful woman he shouldn't give three fucks about, the woman he should've long forgotten by now—Emelia.

Don't think about her. Don't say her name. Clenching his jaw, he shot back, "That's got nothing to do with *me*."

"It does now. My instructions were to give you this information should anything happen to Chip."

He twisted his neck, stare slicing to Tracker. He then looked to Mase and Till and noticed what in the heat of the moment, he hadn't before. Grim expressions, tense, and on alert, only meant one thing.

Directing his attention to Tracker, he asked, "What happened?"

"Shot last night. He's in a coma."

A coma? Ripper couldn't believe it. He and Chip hadn't had a conversation in more than five years, but before that, they'd been friends, good friends. That's how he met Emelia. Honest, one of the things he hated the most after their clubs became rivals was losing Chip as a friend, though he supposed it'd been for the best. He couldn't've handled being around anyone that reminded him of her. He had enough memories in his room, his club, his life. Even still, after so many years, the memories haunted him.

Swallowing the emotion clogging his throat, he told Tracker sincerely, "Sorry to hear that."

He didn't ask who'd done it. He knew. Chained

MC was heavily involved in dealing drugs and running guns. Hell Ryders MC had once been, too. It's why the clubs cut ties. When they had, Chained MC partnered with the Falcons, a California street gang. Chained had only recently attempted to get clean. The Falcons weren't too happy about losing their partners and retaliated, not first time either.

He looked at Doug. "Don't know why he'd send you to me. Tracker's his right-hand man, his VP."

"His request. If he doesn't make it, it means it's his last." Doug handed him a manila envelope.

He hesitated too long before he took it and peeked inside. His heart throbbed at the base of his neck when he spotted a picture—of her, the one and only woman he loved, the one who'd run out on him, the one he'd been trying to forget for more than five years.

He knew what he'd find inside because Chip reached out to Hell Ryders specifically for Doug's number in an effort to find her. Chip hired a series of PIs over the years, and none had been successful. Ripper had to give Chip credit. He never stopped looking for her. For that reason, he shouldn't be surprised to see the picture of her staring back at him, yet he was.

She looked beautiful even after all that time passed. She stood beside a car, that blonde hair still so blonde, still long, reaching mid-back, her lips stained a rose color. Her hips and legs encased in a pair of dark-wash jeans and a white shirt hung off her shoulder giving him a look at her flawless skin.

Without realizing it, he reached into the envelope and pulled out the picture. There were more, a series of them. He didn't want to, and yet he couldn't stop himself. He browsed. Every time he spotted another image, his heart stopped then jump started again.

Over the years, he'd wondered why she left, where she'd gone, how she was. Finally, he had an answer... She was just fine. Eating in restaurants, getting her nails done, working at a small shop, residing in a small house in the suburbs—living, breathing, and doing it all without him. She moved on while he couldn't go an hour without thinking about her.

Chip clung to life and his last wish—for Ripper to get to her, care for her. The reason was clear. The Falcons would start shooting relatives next. Chip knew no one could handle her but Ripper, and he knew, even after all this time, no one would protect her like Ripper.

His job wouldn't be easy. Emelia was feisty, bullheaded, and could frustrate a saint. They fought hard and loved harder—at least on his part. The fights never bothered him. He loved every second of it. Then again, he loved her, loved her more than life itself, and at the end of the day, he knew she could be spitting mad, and he could make it all go away with just one kiss. That wouldn't be the case now. She left him, after all, and moved on.

It shocked him to this day. For a man who'd never known love in his life, he'd loved her so much that when she walked out, he lost himself. He was a man, a biker, and he had pride. It's why he admitted this to himself. Besides, there was no point in lying. Though no one said it, every one of his brothers knew it.

He flipped a picture and caught sight of the only one in the pile of her smiling. The sun shining in her hair making that blonde color seem even more golden. In that split second, he lost track of what he'd been thinking, too captivated by her beauty—petite, long hair, hazel eyes, and the fullest lips known to man.

He was fucked. Not having a choice was messed up, and that's exactly what he had—no choice. Even after all that time, whether or not she screwed him over, he couldn't let her get caught in Chip's club mess. He couldn't let her get killed. He hated that the most. It meant a part of him still cared too much. In truth, he never stopped. Deep down he knew that too because he'd never been able to forget her, no matter how many women he had, no matter how much he drank or smoked.

Finally, he garnered the courage to flip the picture and found a report with the information he needed. Of all the places, she made her new life in Santa Rosa, New Mexico. Their town of Wadden was half an hour away from Santa Rosa, California. His gaze slid to the top of the report. He read her name, except it wasn't right. Emelia Joyce *Knight*. She'd changed her name and took *his*.

Clenching his jaw, his stare, spitting fire, shot to Doug's. Doug smirked then shrugged, looking at him with knowledge in his eyes. The bastard knew, which made Rip think Doug probably knew more than he let on, more than what was written on that report. Rip bet his left nut Doug had done a background check on him too.

Glancing back down at the report, he supposed he had to give Emelia credit. No one would've assumed she moved to Santa Rosa, New Mexico. No one would've assumed she'd taken *his* name, the man she left high and dry five years ago.

He met Tracker's stare. "Don't owe her shit. My

club owes her fuckin' less." He looked away, took a deep breath then met his eyes again. "I'll do it for Chip."

A stupid, futile attempt to hold onto his pride.

He hadn't fooled anyone, least of all himself.

****

"You're such an asshole!"

Ripper sighed heavily. He was tired of fighting. Honest to God, they'd been fighting for so long that he couldn't remember what started this fight. She was pissed in a way only she could get. He had to end this already because he hated fighting with her and especially because his dick was so hard any moment it'd explode.

It happened all the time, early in the mornings, late at night, in the afternoons whether they were cuddling, kissing, or fighting. It was something about her. She was beautiful, yeah, so beautiful even after a year of exclusively fucking her, he still couldn't get enough. Even pissed, she was. Her eyes narrowed, cheeks flushed, and all of it turned him on.

Maybe he knew how to end this fight. He'd never tried it before, so there was a chance doing it would piss her off more.

Fuck it. He'd take the chance.

Smirking, he took a series of menacing steps toward her. She retreated until her back hit the wall behind her. Snaking an arm around her waist, he cupped the back of her neck, trapping her arms against his bare chest.

"Let me go, Bryce!"

Pressing the length of his body against hers, he whispered against her lips, "One kiss, and I'll let you go."

Her eyes further narrowed. "No. I want you to let me go this instant."

The arm around her waist tightened, his fingers digging into her neck. "One kiss, and I'll let you go. I promise."

She scanned his face, seemingly considering the request. Then finally she nodded. He went for the kill, pressing his lips against hers forcefully. She hesitated briefly, but when he buried his tongue in her mouth, kissing her deep and hard, she caved, melting against him like she always did. When he pulled away, she was panting against him. It took her a couple of minutes, but she managed to remember why she'd been so pissed.

Her eyes narrowed. "You don't play fair."

Without bothering to hide his smile, he shook his head. "Not in regards to you, babe."

He didn't have to ask her for another kiss. He didn't have to keep his promise either. A moment later, her lips slammed against his.

"Rip."

He jolted against the seat, his eyes shooting open a second later. The memory fading as fast as it'd come. He was tired, exhausted in fact, but a part of him couldn't sit still, not unless he thought about her.

He peered at Trig, one of the brothers who accompanied him on the trip.

Trig nodded forward, toward the front of the SUV they'd rented at the airport. "We're here."

Without a word, he fisted his hands attempting to hide the nerves, hopped off the passenger seat, and skimmed the small playground in front of him: a series of swings, a sand box, and two slides. His gaze stilled when he spotted her—Emelia. She sat on a bench, her back facing him.

It had been so long, and still, the sight of her even from behind, that flawless golden hair swirling around her, took his breath away.

For the millionth time since she walked out of his life, he wondered why he loved her, a woman cruel enough to leave without a word. He wondered then, too, why still, even after all that time had passed, she had the ability to turn his insides to mush.

He clenched his jaw until it hurt reminding himself he wasn't there for her. He was there as a favor to a man he once called a friend who lay on his deathbed. Holding his breath, he strode toward her so focused on the destination until something crashed into him. Startled, he stopped dead in his tracks, looked down, and spotted a girl with a head of golden curls wearing a colorful flowery dress, her arms tight around his thighs.

She drew away slightly to look up at his face. Smiling brightly, she said, "Daddy! I knew you'd come! I knew you'd come, Daddy!"

Stomach turning, he scanned the beautiful child's face. So familiar, so beautiful… Like the woman he loved so long ago. The same blonde hair, the same oval face, flushed cheeks, and pink lips. Her eyes were different though, an odd blue-green color…

Like his own.

And she called him, "Daddy."

Fuck.

He snapped his head up and immediately met Emelia's ashen face. She'd since stood and turned toward him, a mere twenty feet away. Her hands covered her mouth, tears brimming her eyes, and still as breathtaking as she'd been all those years ago.

Tears… He couldn't believe it. Not once in the years he'd known her had she cried, not even the times she had plenty reasons to. Her watery hazel eyes now pleaded, maybe begging for her life, maybe for mercy. She knew not to fuck with a man like him. She pretended to love him for two years then left. And now, he knew she'd taken something of his—his kid. She hadn't even had the decency to tell him he'd be a father.

His gut knotting, heart clenching, a horrid, burning ache seared his insides alive. He swallowed the bile rising in the back of his throat and came to terms with the truth. The beautiful little girl who looked so much like the woman he loved so long ago, the girl who had *his* eyes was *his* little girl.

He couldn't help the emotion rushing him, welling in his eyes. He had a daughter. He'd had a daughter for a long time, and he hadn't known. She was talking and walking and running, looking to be four. It'd make sense since the last time he saw her mother had been more than five years ago.

He missed so much, her birth, her first words, first steps. Did she go to school? He hoped not. It meant he missed her first day of school, too. Worse, she *knew* him, and he hadn't known about her.

"Daddy?"

His head shot down, gaze hit hers, eyes that strange blue-green color.

He was a daddy. He was this beautiful little girl's father, an absent one, but a father nonetheless, and she didn't seem to mind. She looked so happy to see the man who didn't even know she existed until seconds ago, a man who hadn't been part of her life at all.

His hands went to her shoulders, he tugged her away from him. She released his thighs, her arms falling to her sides, and that beautiful smile lighting her face fell, looking so devastated his heart clenched.

He knelt in front of her. His hand went to her hair. Lacing his fingers through it, he realized it felt like her mother's, thick, silky, and soft. Slowly, he scanned her face trying to memorize it. Then he dropped his head, looking at her from top to bottom, trying to commit to memory every other part of her: shoulders, arms, hands, legs, and small feet.

He met her stare again. Her eyes were wide, watery, and sad. It hurt to see those tears. In a way, he felt like they were his own. He had to do something, anything he could to make them go away.

He opened his mouth to speak, to assure her then stopped short. He didn't know what to call her, didn't even know his daughter's name, so he pulled her small body against his, wrapping his arms tight around her. "It's okay, baby. I'm here, and I'll *never* leave you."

She hooked her little arms around his neck tightly. "I prayed, Daddy. I prayed you'd come. I promised I'd be good, so you'd come. I've been good all this time. I was waiting for you to come, and you came."

His girl praying for him to go to her every night for years? He swore that instant his heart broke, shattered to a million pieces, and it was the reason his whole chest ached. The tears pooled in his eyes, much to his surprise, skated down his cheeks.

He wanted to tell her he'd never left her, wanted her to know he'd never had a choice, but he couldn't force the words out. And he had no clue why nor did he care too much to look into the whys then. He had a daughter, and she was waiting for a response.

Rubbing his palm down her back, he whispered, "You be good or bad, baby. It doesn't matter. I'm not ever leaving you."

"Thank you for coming, Daddy."

Shit. He hadn't come to her. He hadn't even known she existed. Remorse swarming him, he forced out a lie then a vow, "Nothing could stop me from getting to you. Nothing and no one'll ever keep me from you."

Pulling away to look at her face, he paused, so enthralled with the beguiling smile. "You understand?"

She slid her hands against his cheeks rubbing the moisture away. Then her brows drew together. "Do daddies cry like mommies cry?"

Did that mean her mother cried? Maybe now she would because she knew she'd been caught. Never had she before. She was made from stone, and her heart was fucking steel. She *never* cried. Did she? Why would his daughter ask then? Had she seen her mother cry a lot?

She looked down and whispered, "Mommy cries at night sometimes." Then she met his stare. "She doesn't know I know, Daddy, so you can't tell her."

Emelia cried. Why? And why did the knowledge of that make his chest ache more? *You don't care. She's a fucking bitch. She left you, took your daughter. You were a shitty father just 'cause of her.*

"I won't."

"Do you cry at night, too?"

He shook his head. "No, baby, I don't."

He didn't add that the urge would gnaw him raw every time he looked at her. She didn't need to know. His burden and his alone, and no one was to blame but the woman he loved so long ago.

21

"Why do you cry now?"

He cupped her cheeks. "'Cause I'm so happy to see you."

Her smile widened. She wrapped her arms around his neck. "I love you, Daddy."

Four little words said together surged such a blast of emotion that a rush of fresh tears welled his eyes and glided down his face.

When was the last time he heard those words? *Don't think about her. She never loved you. She left you, took your daughter. Think about your daughter.*

Holding his daughter tight against him with one hand on the back of her head and the other around her back smelling the scent of her hair, he swallowed the urge to sob. "I love you more, baby."

He meant it. He loved her from first glimpse, loved her more than she'd ever imagine, more than he ever loved anything or anyone in the world. It made perfect sense that she'd come from the woman he once lived and breathed for, the woman who walked away from him five years ago with his daughter growing inside her.

With every fiber in his body, he should hate her. He couldn't find the strength to because his little girl looked so much like her, because a part of his little girl was her because… Shit. He didn't know. Maybe for all those reasons. Still, he should hate her like he wanted to.

His daughter drew away from him, and reluctantly, he let her go. "Are you coming home with us, Daddy?"

"No, baby." Watching her smile fade, he quickly added, "You're coming home with me."

Her eyes widened, and she smiled a smile that lit

up his whole fucked life. "Mommy and me are going home with you?"

"Yeah."

She jumped in her spot then threw her arms around his neck again. "Thank you, Daddy. Thank you."

Snaking his arm around her waist, he buried his face in her hair and inhaled that sweet scent, a scent he'd remember forever as hers. Putting an arm under her thighs, he stood, carrying his little girl, and strode to the SUV.

Trig opened the back door. He set his daughter inside, strapped her seatbelt on then kissed her forehead. "Be right back."

When she nodded, he turned and strode to Emelia. His gut knotting as he neared. Six feet away, he stopped then finally met her stare. "She's mine."

"Yes."

If his eyes hadn't been glued to her face, he would've missed it since she whispered. Not that he needed a response. It hadn't been a question, more of a statement. Still, she admitted it. Face pale, eyes wet, looking like she was about to faint. After all the messed up shit she'd done to him, it pissed him off. A rage too powerful for words ripened inside him.

Was that all she had to say? Didn't she feel the need to explain? Didn't he deserve an explanation? What had he ever done to her? He treated her like a queen! He loved her so much he would've died for her! No, he loved her so much he died when she left. The God's honest truth because the man she knew died the day she left.

He took a deep breath then released it, deciding he wouldn't flip his lid, not now, maybe not ever. Maybe she thought he didn't deserve a goodbye so long ago. Maybe she thought he didn't deserve to know he had a daughter. Maybe she thought he didn't deserve an explanation. For all those reasons, she didn't deserve any emotion from him, none at all. He'd do to her what she'd done to him—walk away. But first, he needed to know something.

"What's. Her. Name?"

Tears flowing down her too pale cheeks, she said, "Brianna Emma…Knight."

At least she gave her his name. At least she gave him that. Too bad it didn't make up for everything else she hadn't done.

Without another word, he turned and strode away.

Chapter Two

A beautiful day, the sun hung high, not a cloud in the sky. Sitting on a park bench with her eyes glued to her daughter, Brianna, her mind wandered and settled on him. It always did. Honest, it didn't matter what type of day it was. Rain or shine, her mind always drifted and always to him.

What she'd give to rewrite history, turn back time... No, it wouldn't change anything. She had to remind herself time and time again. Too often, she wanted to believe.

Emelia shut her eyes briefly if only to make the image of him dissipate.

"Daddy! I knew you'd come! I knew you'd come, Daddy!"

Her heart pounding a million miles a minute, her eyes snapped open. She stood and turned toward the sound of her daughter's voice, thinking she'd lost her mind, those couldn't have been her daughter's cries.

Brianna stood at an angle. Em couldn't see her face, but she saw her full head of loose, golden curls, her small body pressed against a man's jean-clad legs, her little arms tight around his thighs.

She's mistaken. It's just someone who looks like him. It can't be him.

Em shot her gaze up and locked it on the man's profile. Her heart stopped dead. Her jaw dropped open, and the air in her lungs whooshed out. She blinked then again and again. Only then, she knew. Improbable as it was, it was him, Bryce—the man her thoughts drifted to constantly, the man she loved and lost so long ago. She couldn't clearly see his face slanted down to their daughter, but it was him. She'd recognize him anywhere because she looked at pictures of them every day, and because every time she closed her eyes, she saw his face.

He looked different, yet still handsome, and at six-foot-two, a good nine inches taller than her. The muscles lining his shoulders bigger and broader, clearly defined through the black T-shirt he wore. His blond hair longer at the top and sides; his face, once clean shaven, covered in stubble.

She pressed her hands over her mouth a second before his head snapped up and to *her*, and those strange yet gorgeous blue-green eyes, eyes she loved, eyes her daughter inherited, stared back at her. The question hung in them.

A rush of tears choked her. He didn't need a yes or no. With just one look at her, he'd know it was true.

Brianna was his. Hers. Theirs.

Heart pounding louder and louder, she prayed harder than she ever prayed before, praying he wouldn't turn their beautiful girl away, praying he'd fall in love with her from just one look.

Bile rising in the back of her throat, she watched for what seemed like endless moments, relentlessly repeating her prayer. Finally, his stare sliced down to Brianna. Gripping her shoulders, he tugged their girl away from him.

Her chest tightened painfully, knowing her

daughter's heart too broke.

He knelt in front of Brianna. His hand went to her hair, lacing his fingers through her blonde curls. Emelia watched him stare at Brianna's little face, a face so similar to hers. She watched then as he skimmed Bree from top to bottom. He opened his mouth to speak, shut it, and then, finally, he hauled her small body against his and hugged their girl.

He whispered something in her ear. Emelia couldn't make out the words, but she wondered if he'd fallen. Not a moment later, she had her answer. Tears drifted down his face. She held her breath, shocked speechless and motionless.

He *cared*. He cared about *their* little girl despite everything he'd said, everything he'd believed, everything she knew to be true… Maybe he'd even fallen.

He spoke then spoke again. Her daughter spoke, too. When he drew away from Brianna, their daughter wiped his face, an action so sweet and familiar. She remembered Brianna had once done it for her.

A warmth settled in her chest. Just then, Brianna jumped then threw her arms around his neck. He snaked an arm around her waist, put the other under her thighs, stood, and carried their little girl to an SUV.

Trig, one of the bikers from Bryce's MC, opened the door for them. After Bryce set their daughter inside, he headed in her direction. With each of his steps, her stomach knotted. Looking straight at his handsome face, his arched brows, high cheek-bones, lean nose, and strong jaw, she realized the pictures, her memory, none of it did him justice.

A few feet away, he stopped. Expression ravished,

those eyes, in that strange, ambiguous color, met hers, and they were *dead*. The man she loved, his beautiful eyes, the eyes his daughter inherited were lifeless, and she was the reason. All those years ago, she assumed. She should've told him. Had she, she would've never made such a horrible mistake.

"She's mine."

Another rush of tears swarmed her. "Yes," she managed, barely a whisper. Though she knew it hadn't been a question but a statement.

He took a deep breath then released it. "What's. Her. Name?"

Without blinking, wet stained her cheeks. "Brianna Emma…Knight."

With her response, he turned and strode away.

****

"Go in and get what you need. Then we're out," the dark-haired, tatted man driving the SUV ordered.

Emelia didn't know his name or who he was nor did she know the other man sitting in the passenger seat of the SUV, also dark-haired and tatted, though his hair was long enough he had it tied in a ponytail. She assumed both were bikers from Hell Ryders MC. Neither wore cuts. Still, she nodded in agreement.

She glanced behind her and realized the other SUV, the one carrying her daughter, wasn't parked behind theirs in front of her small, two-bedroom bungalow. Pulse spiking at the base of her neck, she asked abrasively, "Where's Brianna?"

Over the course of her twenty-five years, she grew quite good at discerning moods, a trait she honed as a kid. Even so, it didn't take a genius to figure out neither one of them was her biggest fan, not that she blamed them. Still, their anger aside, she needed to know where her daughter was. She didn't care about riling them. From Bryce's reaction to seeing Bree, she knew he wouldn't hurt his daughter, but it didn't mean he wasn't angry enough to take her. One thing she remembered about Bryce—he never fought fair.

"You'll see her soon."

She released a loaded breath, some of her anxiety dissipating. Still, she didn't know what exactly she needed since she didn't know exactly where they planned to take her. Until then, she hadn't known they'd take her anywhere she needed to pack for, so she tempted both of them again by asking, "What will I need exactly?"

The driver's eyes narrowed. "Fuck if I know. Important documents, clothes, make-up, tampons… Whatever it is you need. Get shit for Rip's girl, too. You won't be coming back here."

This was news to her. It didn't answer another very important question. Why did Bryce show after so long? She would've understood if he'd come for Brianna, but with his actions, he made clear he hadn't known about her.

"Don't got all fuckin' day," the driver barked.

Pushing all thoughts aside, she parted the door, stepped out, and headed into her home, closely followed by the long-haired biker who'd been in the front passenger seat of the SUV. She unlocked her door, skimmed through her small living room and kitchen, and strode into the hallway to her right. Stopping at the linen closet, she grabbed a duffle bag. In Bree's room, she reached into her nightstand, pulled out a shoe box, and packed it. She then packed necessities: clothes, underwear, shoes, and her favorite teddy. Once packed, she dropped the duffle in the hallway and grabbed another. In her room, she went into her nightstand and grabbed another box. After packing it, she packed her own necessities as well as their birth certificates, social security cards, and so on.

As she walked into the living room, she grabbed Brianna's duffle, only to have the biker take both bags from her. In that instant, she decided she liked him. Despite whatever he believed or thought about her, he was nice, taking her bags. A man who did that couldn't be all that bad. Of course, there were exceptions to every rule. But that combined with the fact he wasn't being a dick, unlike his friend, hinted he was probably a good guy.

"Thanks." She headed toward the bookshelf in the living room intent on grabbing two photo albums.

Halfway there, a series of loud bangs sounded making her ears burn. The glass from the windows exploded and shattered. Shoved, she landed hard on her back, knocking the wind out of her.

Not a moment later, she heard a deep voice ask, "You okay?"

Head buzzing, eyes tightly shut, she fought to breathe despite the pressure on her chest.

"Open your eyes," that same voice insisted.

She cracked her lids open and met a set of dark brown eyes only an inch from hers. His full weight on her, the smell of his cologne infiltrated her senses. Recognizing his face, the long-haired biker, she relaxed partially. "I-I can't breathe."

He shifted quickly. The heaviness on her gone, she caught her breath.

"You okay?"

She didn't get a chance to answer. The door into her house crashed open with a loud thud. The man who'd driven them came through.

"Brother, scared the fuck outta me," the biker beside her barked.

She moved her stare to him and realized he held a gun in his hand.

The other's brows rose. "You expected me to knock? The bullets had hit you, no one would've answered."

Bullets? They'd just been shot at. Who'd been the target?

"Where's my daughter?" She talked over the two who she'd since tuned out.

Their heads went to her, but the driver spoke. "With Rip at the airport."

"I need to speak to her."

His eyes narrowed. "What you need is to get your ass off that floor and get in the SUV before they come back."

She should've guessed. Why else would Ripper and the club show out of nowhere unless they'd gotten into some sort of trouble, that trouble, now tracking their relatives and friends intent on getting revenge. Not that she was a friend, just an old flame. Still, they'd go for whoever they could get. She'd lived the MC life, so she knew.

At one point, she couldn't picture her life without the club. She loved it and had been good at it, but all that changed when she found out she was pregnant. She left that life behind and made sure to cover her tracks. Somehow, someway, the club's enemies, whoever they were now, had found her and her daughter. A part of her was surprised. Before she left, Hell Ryders was fighting to get clean. She supposed old habits were hard to break.

"Fuck you," she snapped.

Clenching his jaw, he took a menacing step in her direction.

Perhaps it was stupid and foolish to aggravate a man who wasn't fond of her already. It was that much more stupid and foolish to piss off a biker who didn't like you, but at that moment, she didn't care.

She stood quickly and tilted her chin up defiantly. Though she wouldn't intimidate the more than six-foot-tall biker, she also knew never to show a biker fear. "I'm sure you've convinced yourself you're here out of the goodness of your heart to protect a woman Ripper fucked a long-ass time ago, but you don't really care if your club's blowback gets me killed and neither does *he*. You all couldn't care less what happens to *me*, but I do because I'm the only *mother* my daughter has. She's all I live for. They could've already gotten to *her*!"

Her eyes welled with tears at just the thought. "So, you're going to get your phone, call Bryce, and let me speak to my daughter right this instant, or I swear I'll kill you myself." When she finished, she was panting from the emotion overwhelming her, fighting to catch her breath and hold her tears simultaneously.

He didn't soften, not even a little bit, but after an intense stare down, he reached into his pocket and made the call.

Six years ago, she would've been thrilled she won an argument with a biker. Now, she couldn't celebrate the victory. She still didn't know if her daughter was safe.

****

Ripper's phone vibrated. He reached into his pocket, plucked it out, and brought it to his ear. "Rip."

"You okay?"

The question alone riled him. He just found out the only woman he ever loved fucked him in more ways than he once believed. He just discovered he had a daughter. It didn't mean shit. He was a man, a biker. He didn't need a caretaker, didn't need pity.

"Fuckin' fine."

He tensed when he felt Brianna do the same beside him. She hadn't released him for an instant, not the ride over, not after. Even now, he'd cursed, and she hadn't. He looked down at her. She stood at his side, her hand clutching his tightly, the other wrapped around his leg. Her face angled to his, brows drawn. Damn Hash. Why'd he have to piss him off? He softened his expression, smiled, and laced his fingers through her hair. She rewarded him with a soft smile.

"I meant is everyone okay?"

"Just fine."

"She wants to talk to the kid."

She meaning *Emelia*. That, too, riled him. Did she think he'd hurt his daughter? Did she think he couldn't take care of her? Maybe he didn't know what he was doing because he'd never been given a chance to learn, but that didn't mean he needed her checking on him. It pissed him off more than thinking Hash pitied him, meaning he really wanted to flip his lid. He couldn't though, couldn't afford to lose his cool again in front of Brianna, couldn't say anything snide either. A four-year-old would understand.

"She can talk when she gets here."

"She won't go until she talks to her."

His hand stilled at Brianna's neck. He bit his tongue hard so he wouldn't curse. Still, he knew in about five seconds he'd lose it, flip in a way only he could. It'd terrify Brianna. She'd jumped at his tone only moments ago, and honest to God, sometimes when he lost it, he scared himself. He couldn't risk terrifying her, giving her mother a reason to take her away when he just got her. He had to think fast and act faster.

He lifted his stare. Even among bikers, Strike stood out because the brother was covered in tattoos, the length of his arms, torso, back, and legs. He even had a tattoo on the base of his neck. His little girl was probably scared of him.

His gaze shifted to Trig, short for Trigger, former Army Ranger. A big, ripped, cranky motherfucker, always had been though he smiled more often than ever since he hooked up with Allie, who the brothers called Classy. They'd since married. Before then, Trig had only been in a good mood when he was with his niece, Della.

Bingo.

Della was five or six, and Trig watched her often, had been since she was a baby.

Ripper put the phone to his shirt then met Brianna's eyes. "See him." He nodded in Trig's direction.

She turned and peered at Trig then met his eyes again and nodded.

"That's your uncle Trig. He's got a niece about your age. You'll meet her soon. Trig'll show you pictures while I take this call, okay?"

Her little eyes widened. He looked back to Trig and tried to see him through her eyes, realizing Trig looked pissed. What else was new? Probably because his old lady wasn't around. What a pussy. Not that he could talk. More than once over the years, despite what Emelia had done, he wished she'd come back. He couldn't forget her. Although he didn't know if he could forgive her, having her would make him better than he was—tormented, angry, and bitter.

Pushing his thoughts aside, he glared in Trig's direction then nodded in Brianna's. "*Trig*, got any pictures of Della?"

Trig took the hint, instantly softening his expression and pulling out his phone. Like night and day.

Ripper met his daughter's gaze. "I'm gonna stand over there." He pointed. "I'll be able to see you, and you'll be able to see me."

She nodded, turned, and headed for Trig. He waited until she reached him then walked a good twenty feet away, his stare never leaving Brianna.

"Put her on the fuckin' phone."

"Bree?"

His body tensed, responding to the sweetness in her voice. He clenched his jaw, fighting it. "No, it *isn't* Bree," he snarled. "She's doing fine with her *father*. You've had her for five fuckin' years—"

"I just wanted to make sure… I didn't know—"

"No, you just didn't *think* I could take care of my daughter for an hour."

"Whoever's after you just shot up my house—"

His heart jolted in his chest then started pounding loud. "What… *Fuck.*"

They found her. They'd already struck. And it killed he hadn't been there to protect her. Was she hurt? Was she scared? She didn't sound it, but she hid shit. *You shouldn't give a fuck! Stop giving a shit!* Releasing a breath, he refocused his thoughts. How had they found her? Why hadn't Hash told him? Why let him hear it from her?

Then he remembered what she'd said. *Whoever's after you just shot up my house…* She thought he had something to do with it, made him out to be the bad guy. To her, he was a bad man, bad enough he wouldn't make a good father. Why else hadn't she told him?

She couldn't be more wrong. This shit had nothing to do with him. He'd show her how good of a father he'd be. He'd make himself the best, even if he never had a father, even if he hadn't had a good mother, even if no one had ever taught him how to love.

He bit his tongue until he tasted blood. "Let's get one thing straight. No one is after *me*. No one is after *my club*."

He then ended the call knowing if he heard her voice once more he'd lose his cool, and he couldn't because at that moment Brianna turned to him and smiled wide, looking at him like he made the whole world better by just breathing. His chest filled with the strangest sensation, a heady feeling, so marvelous he lost himself in that, in her, and let everything else fade away.

Walking to her, she met him halfway. "Daddy, Trig says Della's six. He says I can play with her all the time because he says he brings her over our house."

Daddy. He'd never thought being called anything but his name would feel so great, and still, as good as it

36

felt, he didn't know if he'd ever get used to being called that.

"Yeah, baby, and one of your other uncles has a little boy. I think he's a year younger."

Her eyes widened. Then her smile broadened. That feeling filling him, growing, settling a warmth in his middle made him wish he knew what else to do so she'd always smile that way.

Not fifteen minutes later, he spotted Hash, Trick, and Emelia, striding toward them. He scanned her from head to toe telling himself he just wanted to make sure she was uninjured. It backfired. All it did was remind him how beautiful she was, wearing a pair of jeans, a green blouse, and a pair of sandals, so casual yet sexy.

Clenching his jaw as if it'd banish the thought, he cursed himself silently then forced his gaze away, deciding then and there, he couldn't look at her, ever, else risk being reminded again and again.

By the time they closed the distance, he picked up on the smell of her perfume, the same one she always wore. The scent of it hit him square in the chest and took him back. Memories flooded him—her beautifully flushed face after they'd made love, waking up with her legs tangled in his, riding his bike with her cuddled close.

Holding his breath, he decided he needed to stay away from her, too. He didn't want to be reminded. Even without her, even after years, even as badly as he wanted to forget, he remembered it all too well. He *needed* to forget, so he concentrated on the only thing he had for the past five years—anger.

Ripper shot Hash a nasty glare. His brother should've told him they'd been shot at. Hash shouldn't've let him hear it from her. Only briefly did he let that anger dissipate when he looked to Bree and told her, "Be right back, baby. Gotta get you a ticket."

She threw her arms around him, hugging him tightly like he wouldn't be gone for only minutes, making him feel important. Enjoying it, he wrapped his arms around her thinking he could get used to this.

She let him go too soon. He let her.

As he headed for the counter, he plucked his phone out of his back pocket and dialed Tracker. "There's been a change of plans." He managed to keep his voice calm.

"Don't got time—"

"You're gonna fuckin' deal with this shit 'cause I'm not talking to her." He wouldn't talk to her, look at her, or go anywhere near her. That was the plan.

"She hurt your feelings or somethin'? Grow a fuckin' pair, and get—"

"Fuck *you*, asshole. I gotta bigger problem. Her name's Brianna. She's four, and she's my daughter, a daughter I didn't know about until an hour ago. Meaning I'm not wasting the time I got now to tell her mother her cousin was shot for messing with the wrong gang. I don't got the time to pretend I give a flying fuck how she feels about that when she left me five years ago with *my* kid without even telling me I was gonna be a father. I don't got the time to take her to the hospital either. I gotta spend my time getting to know the daughter I didn't even know I had. You don't wanna do it? Then don't, but don't expect me to either."

All of it was true. He'd agreed to this plan for Chip, but shit changed. It changed the moment he realized he had Bree. The way he saw it, now more than ever, Emelia didn't deserve anything from him. And she wouldn't get anything except his protection— Chip's last wish. Ripper kept his word, and he wasn't heartless enough to let her get caught in the crossfire, but also and most importantly, Brianna needed her mom. He knew Emelia was a good one. Way back then, he'd seen her around kids. Though she never said it, a part of him knew she wanted some of her own.

The silence stretched for a long moment until finally, Tracker spoke. "When are you landin'?"

He gave him the time, told him to meet them at the airport then ended the call. He purchased a ticket for Brianna, managing to get her on the same flight then strode toward her. Bree's back facing him so she couldn't see him. Her mother kneeled in front of her offering her a sweater.

"I'm not cold," Brianna said.

"Then I'll hold onto it. You may get cold later."

"Daddy says we're going to live with him."

This caught his attention, so he peered at Emelia wondering and waiting to see what she'd say.

"Yes, we will. I packed some of our stuff."

"Did you pack the box?"

The box?

"Of course, Bree, and I packed your teddy and some clothes. We're in a rush so I couldn't get your toys, but once we settle at your dad's, I'll buy you some clothes and toys, okay?"

Brianna nodded.

Damn. He hadn't even thought about that. His baby girl was leaving everything behind. She needed clothes, toys, a room. He lived at the compound, which was attached to the garage run by his club. There were plenty of rooms unoccupied since some of the brothers had homes off the property, but he didn't think she'd be as comfortable there. He could take them to his house, the home he bought five years ago and never moved into, but it wasn't as safe as living in the compound, and safety was his primary concern. The Falcons had already found Emelia meaning they found Brianna, too. His brothers were at the compound, and it was wired with a state-of-the-art surveillance system. His home wasn't, so he didn't have much of a choice. Still, he felt guilty about it. He wanted to give Brianna the best. The best for her was a stable home with her own room and a yard to play. Only then could he begin to make up for the years he hadn't been there.

None of this mess with the Falcons was his fault, but if it hadn't happened, he might have never known he was a father. He may have never had the chance to be one. Just the thought made his stomach turn.

On instinct, he grabbed Brianna's hand, who instantly shifted to him smiling. "I'll get you all new stuff, Bree."

Chapter Three

Her stomach clenching, Emelia felt bile rising in the back of her throat.

Something wasn't right. Something was very, very wrong. It wasn't just the fact Bryce showed or the fact her house had been shot up. It was him telling her it had nothing to do with him, with his club. In the pit of her stomach, she knew there was much more to this. Logic told her, too. Why else had he come after what he'd done, after five years?

She would've asked except he'd gone from silent anger to visible anger and now moved on to pretending she didn't exist. Out of character for him, he was the type of man you didn't rile. He could flip in a second flat. He also wasn't the type who ignored, and yet he was doing a hell of a job at it.

Apart from her arriving at the airport, he hadn't looked her way again. Even on the flight though they sat only a seat away, Brianna in between them, he managed his charade. The entire time, her nerves got worse. She didn't know what awaited her in California, but she knew something did.

It hurt to be ignored. No point in denying that. Though she preferred the anger, she couldn't blame him for either. He had a reason. She left without telling him about Brianna. At the time, it seemed like the right thing to do. Now, she knew it hadn't been, so she deserved whatever he threw her way. She also knew if she asked what was going on, he'd continue to ignore her. She hadn't asked any of the other four men knowing it'd be pointless too. Not one of them would answer her, even the two she knew from years ago. They wouldn't because Bryce didn't want them to.

As they exited the plane and the terminal, her gaze locked with a set of piercing green eyes she'd never forgotten. Those eyes belonging to Tracker, best friends with her cousin, Chip, and VP of Chained Disciples, the MC she'd grown-up in.

At the ripe age of fourteen, she moved in with Chip and Tracker. Living with two twenty-something-year-old bikers who partook in illegal activities took some getting used to, but it was better than living with an abusive father. As young as she'd been, she knew she'd never be able to repay Chip, but it hadn't stopped her from trying. She cooked and cleaned for them and didn't ask questions. Even so, she'd always been good at observing. To detect her father's moods and avoid him if need be, she honed that trait at an even younger age. That meant though Tracker was a typical biker who never showed weakness, she grew to know him well enough she read the grief on his face with just one glimpse.

Something awful had happened. Quite possibly, nothing would ever be the same, and it had something to do with Chip, her cousin, the man who rescued her fourteen-year-old self from one hell of a messed-up life.

She should've known if whoever shot up her house wasn't after Hell Ryders, they'd be after Chained. All those years ago, she knew Bryce wouldn't look for her, just like she knew Chip would never stop. And Bryce did, meaning he felt he had no choice.

Swallowing the tears flooding her eyes, she turned to Brianna, standing beside her father holding his hand. Em kneeled in front of her daughter. "I'm going to be gone for a little, but I'll see you tonight."

Brianna's beautiful blue-green eyes on hers, suspicion clear in them, she looked to her father as if for reassurance then met her stare again and nodded softly.

"Don't worry. I'll see you later, okay?"

The more she tried to reassure her, the warier Brianna became. Her daughter was too smart and too aware for her age. Further proving this, Bree looked behind her to Tracker. "Who is he, Mommy?"

"He's a friend of your Uncle Chip. His name's Track."

Bree looked at her father again, so she took a chance and did the same. Bryce glared in Tracker's direction, and Bree picked up on it. It didn't help her cause.

She kept staring his way until he finally looked at her. She nodded toward Bree.

He instantly looked down to their daughter then assured her. "Your mom'll be back later."

Brianna's eyes widened a little. "But..."

"There's nothing to worry about. Your dad will take you home and get you settled. I'll be back before you know it."

Finally, Bree nodded softly.

"Maybe your dad can take you out for pizza?"

She smiled then looked to him. "Can we, Daddy?"

The hard lines on his face relaxing, he smiled back. "Yeah, Bree."

When Bree met her stare again, she said, "Be good for your dad, okay?"

Bree nodded. Then Emelia wrapped her arms around her, released her, and headed for Tracker. With her heart in her throat, she stopped feet away and waited.

After several silent moments, he closed the distance between them, snaked his arm around her neck, and pulled her into a hug. "Missed you, kid." He grasped the back of her neck and drew away to look at her face.

He'd always called her "kid," but not once in all the years she'd known him had he hugged her.

Tears welling in her eyes, somehow, she summoned the courage to say, "He's dead." Those tears then streamed down her cheeks.

He wiped them away. "Em cryin'? If I didn't see it, I wouldn't believe it." He shook his head. "He ain't, but he ain't in good shape."

Thank God. He wasn't dead. That meant there was hope.

Fifteen minutes later, she understood why hope sucked. Chip wasn't dead, but he looked it, ashen face, lips tinted bluish purple. The doctor told her what Track hadn't, whether that was because he couldn't force himself to say it aloud, she didn't know.

Chip had been shot five times. One bullet struck his stomach, another his chest, a third was still lodged in his shoulder, and the other two were flesh wounds. Still, by the time someone found him and called police and paramedics, he'd been unconscious and lost too much blood. Despite two surgeries to remove the bullets in his chest and stomach, despite several blood transfusions, he still hadn't woken, and the doctor didn't have much hope he would. The doctor didn't say that outright, but from his expression and tone, she knew.

The only man who'd ever loved her, the man who saved her, the man she owed her life to lay so still on his deathbed, his breathing assisted by a machine. She'd missed out on five years of his life, missed out on five years of everything he had to offer, everything he had given her.

At the time, it seemed like the selfless choice. Now, though, knowing what she did and knowing she also made a mistake with Bryce, she couldn't help but wonder if she should've stayed.

She left Bryce, and she left Chip, too, but for very different reasons. Like she knew Chip would never stop looking for her, she knew he would've supported her decision to keep Bree, knew he would've cared for and loved Bree as if she were his own. What stopped her? She wanted the best for Bree. Giving her an example of a man like Chip would have been great, but Chip came with the club, and the club ran drugs and guns. She wanted Bree as far away from all that as possible.

Deep down, she knew she made the right decision, but guilt ate at her, and it'd eat at her for the rest of her life.

When the doctor left the room, in front of Tracker, Bilk, and Moss, two other bikers from Chained MC, she lost it. Not silent tears, she cried loud, heart-wrenching sobs. She bawled without covering her face or turning away because she didn't even have the strength to hide. She wept so hard she couldn't hold her weight and collapsed on the floor, wailed so hard she didn't recall being lifted and carried to a chair. There, she sobbed until her throat ached, her tears dried, and her eyes swelled shut.

****

"Where's Mommy?"

Ripper's gaze snapped to Bree. God, she was beautiful...just like her mom with those pink cheeks and blonde curls. He was so lost in that thought she had to repeat herself.

"Daddy? Where's Mommy?"

Good question.

After arriving in Wadden, he took Bree to a local Italian restaurant, *Anthony's*. They sat in a booth and ate pizza. Afterward, he took her to the mall. He hadn't stepped foot in a mall in years because he hated even the thought of shopping, but he did it because Bree needed clothes, shoes, toys, and whatever else girls her age needed. It proved to be a herculean task. As it turned out, his daughter didn't just look like her mom but acted like her mom, too.

Like the typical woman, she loved the mall. It wasn't that that reminded him of Emelia, but the fact that he knew she loved going in stores and browsing, but she didn't ask for anything, not a toy, a doll, or clothes, not even after he asked her repeatedly, so he enlisted the help of a sales clerk, who seemed only too pleased to help, who upon realizing Bree needed a whole wardrobe was even more pleased. At the register, as the sales clerk rung up fifteen outfits, five pairs of shoes, three pajamas, underwear, and socks, he looked down at Bree and noticed her gaze glued to a set of barrettes. He picked three packages of them and added them on.

When she saw him do that, her head shot up. She smiled softly, timidly. "Thank you, Daddy."

She thanked him, and she meant it like it wasn't his job to take care of her, and it gutted him. From the detailed report he knew how much Emelia made, how much she paid in rent and bills, so he knew she had trouble making ends meet, and she preferred struggling than asking him for help.

He squeezed her hand. "You gonna prove how thankful you are, Bree?"

She nodded immediately.

"Do you know how I want you to do that?"

Her brows drew together. Then she shook her head, and that beautiful blonde, thick hair of hers swayed.

"I'm gonna take you to the toy store, and you're gonna pick out ten toys, and then, I'm gonna buy them for you, and you're not gonna thank me, 'kay?"

Her eyes widened seeming confused.

He cocked his head. "Bree, do we have a deal?"

She looked to her sides before she met his eyes again and whispered, "Mommy says I'm always supposed to say 'thank you.'"

Damn, Emelia taught her well.

Turning his body to her, he cupped her pretty face with the hand not gripping hers. "Yeah, you are, except I'm your dad. That means I'm supposed to take care of you 'cause it's my job, so you don't have to thank me."

She looked down then lifted her head. "But I don't need toys, Daddy."

What kid didn't want a new toy? A sinking feeling settled in his stomach before it hit him. A really smart kid, smart enough she noticed her mom struggle, didn't want toys. That kid didn't ask for toys either. His little girl grew up worried about shit a four-year-old shouldn't be concerned about.

Why hadn't Emelia gone to him? Why hadn't she told him? He could've made it better, would've made it better. He would've given his daughter everything her heart desired. Then she wouldn't be worried about shit she shouldn't be.

A mixture of anger and sadness tightening his chest, he took a deep breath and bent toward her. "I want to get them for you 'cause I got money to spoil you, so I'm gonna spoil you."

He didn't know if that was the right thing to say. Then and there, he didn't care if it was right or wrong. He wanted his girl to have everything.

After several moments, she whispered, "But you don't have to, Daddy."

He cupped the back of her head, leaned in, and pressed his mouth to her forehead. "I know, baby, but I want to."

She smiled. He straightened, handed the sales clerk his credit card, paid, grabbed the bags, and strode out. He then took her to the toy store and bought her ten toys she picked out. As he paid, she thanked him again, and she did it without thought. When his stare flew to her, he saw something in her eyes, on her face, he didn't like at all. Brows drawn, chin trembling, sad, yes, but disappointed too, looking about ready to apologize.

Before she did, he smiled wide. "You're welcome, baby."

After that, they headed home or to their temporary home, the compound. He dropped off her bags in the spare room across from his, deciding Emelia and Bree would share for the time being. He didn't want Bree alone in a room in an unfamiliar place. Then with the bags of toys in one hand and Bree holding the other, they headed downstairs to the main living room at the compound, which was abnormally quiet. Though he needed to talk to Prez about what happened, the shooting, he couldn't then, not in front of Bree, and he couldn't leave her alone, so instead, he handed Bree her toys and took a seat on the sofa. As he turned on the flat screen TV, she sat on the floor in front of him and unpacked her toys. For a couple of hours, he browsed through the channels flipping aimlessly, watching her more than the TV. He memorized her face, her hands, her hair, her mannerisms, every-damn-thing. As he did, he reminded himself this beautiful little girl was his.

Eventually, she packed her toys in the bags and headed in his direction. Eyes half mast, she rubbed them, sat beside him, and pressed her small body against his side. She then tilted her head to meet his face. "Where's Mommy?"

Good question.

Her mother left with Tracker, who was supposed to explain to her what happened to Chip. It had been hours since then though. Even if Tracker had taken her to the hospital, she should've been back by now. Then again, maybe Tracker finally took his chance.

The VP of Chained MC always had a thing for her. Ripper had known it for years. Something Tracker did not hide even from Chip. Why he never made his move? Ripper could only guess because of his loyalty to Chip.

He shouldn't give a shit where she was or who she fucked, but he did. He cared so much the moment he spotted Tracker at the airport with a set of eyes only for her, he regretted calling him. He cared so much since he and Bree arrived at the compound and he realized her mother wasn't there, a mental image of Tracker holding her and comforting her gripped him and gnawed him raw.

When Bree so sweetly asked was another reminder her mom was being comforted by another man, a man who'd wanted her for years and had probably made his move. Perfect timing since she was vulnerable having just found out the man she admired so much was about to die. It was fucked to take advantage of a woman in Emelia's position, but he wouldn't put it past Tracker. Emelia being defenseless, there was a high probability she'd accept his advances. It meant right at that moment, Tracker could be pulling off her clothes, kissing her lips, and burying himself inside her. All while he took care of their daughter.

He gritted his teeth battling the need to punch a wall or pick a fight with one of his brothers if only so he'd hurt outside like he hurt inside. If he didn't fight back, then maybe he'd get knocked out, and for a little bit, he'd forget too.

Damn, he was fucked in the head. He'd been that messed up for a while…ever since she left.

"Daddy?"

That little worried voice cooled his temper some. He released a loaded breath. "She'll be back soon."

"But I'm tired, and she hasn't told me a bedtime story."

Of course, near midnight, she would be. He didn't know what time she usually went to bed, but it had to be well before midnight. He should've had her in bed hours ago. His first day as a dad and he'd screwed up already.

"How about I tell you a story?"

"Do you know any stories, Daddy?"

No, he didn't. He never had a mom who read to him. He hadn't had a dad at all. He didn't even know why he asked.

Lacing his fingers through her hair, he shook his head. "I don't."

"Can you rub my back until I fall asleep?"

If he needed any more proof she was his, there it was.

"Mommy rubs my back before bed."

She'd done it for him, too. Every night. Never missed one. Then she up and left. For months after, he had to drink himself into a stupor just so he'd sleep. He missed that the most, so he understood why Bree wanted someone to rub her back even though she couldn't get a bedtime story.

"Yeah, baby. I'll rub your back."

She laid her head on his thigh, facing the TV. Just as he placed his rough, calloused hand on the small of her back, she turned her head his way. "Night, Daddy. I love you."

"Love you, too." Just like that, the words he'd never said slipped out, again. "Sweet dreams."

She angled her face away and closed her eyes. He rubbed her back softly shifting his hand lightly over her. In minutes, the daughter he didn't know he had until hours ago fell asleep.

****

One thirty in the morning and she still wasn't at the compound. After Bree fell asleep, he carried her to bed, tucked her in, headed downstairs, and outside. There, he'd been waiting for more than an hour. In the shadows, he stood leaning against one of the metal garage doors. The entire time, the image of Tracker ripping off her clothes flooded his mind. Nothing he did made that vision dissipate.

He was beyond pissed. In reality, he'd been furious all day, with the exception of every time he looked at Bree. No one could stay mad looking at her pretty face, even if that face was identical to her mother's, a woman he should hate. Stewing in anger was the norm for him. Except this time, he had every reason to be.

After the day he had, he needed a long-ass workout to burn some of that fury. A fight would be better. Fights worked miracles. It's why he picked them, even with his brothers, but he couldn't tonight. The brothers he spotted in the compound were, for obvious reasons, keeping their distance. He had to settle for a workout, but the workout he so desperately needed wouldn't come until she came home. The gym was at the far end of the compound. If she knocked, he wouldn't hear. It meant he had to sit around and wait for her before he got a little bit of release.

Sighing heavily so close to losing his cool, he fisted his palms. Five minutes later, he finally caught sight of a pair of headlights. The truck neared, stopped, and parked in front of the gates. He couldn't see inside but knew it was them. Though several of his brothers had trucks, none drove a dark blue GMC.

He waited and waited. Minutes ticked, and each second his mind went there, Tracker taking off her clothes, Tracker kissing and fucking her. And still, nothing. So he waited some more. When the images searing his mind became too much to bear, he took a step toward the truck.

The passenger side door opened and out she came. Without looking back, she pulled the gate open, entered, and closed it behind her. She walked toward the door only thirty feet from him. The entire time, her head slanted down.

When her hand went to the knob to turn it, he said, "You missed her bedtime story." He said it like an accusation, the anger inside so clear in his voice.

Startled, she turned. Her head snapped up to meet his eyes. With the bit of light shining from the overhead lamp near the door, he noticed her face was blotchy. Eyes swollen and still, she looked so beautiful it made his chest burn. Knowing she'd been crying made him regret what he said and the way he said it. Yet *no one* should have such a hold over him. All of it turned his simmering anger to full-blown rage.

His fault. He should've steeled himself to see tears. He should've expected them. Even cold-hearted bitches who never shed tears cried when a loved one was about to die. Too busy wallowing in jealousy, he hadn't prepared or expected them. Even now, try as he may to not give a shit, he cared.

In a soft, solemn voice, she said, "I know. I'm sorry. I was with Track—"

The jealousy that subsided returned, knotting his gut. He didn't need to hear the VP's name, didn't need to be reminded when the image of her and Tracker seared his mind.

In a split second, he closed the distance between them and let his rage speak for him. "Don't fuckin' care what you were doing with him."

She jumped at his tone and took a step back.

He mirrored her, taking one toward her. "What I care about is Bree, and she was worried about *you*, who didn't even call to wish her a good night."

He expected her to snap back, expected her to rant and rave, ask him why he was an asshole. The Em he knew would've, and she had every right. He *was* an asshole. He knew it, and a part of him didn't care. She was the woman who left him, who left with his kid, and who still had so much control over him. Still, another part of him hated himself for being a dick, actually felt remorse.

Her eyes watered, and in that same soft voice, she said, "I'm sorry. I figured you wanted—"

"What I want is for Bree *not* to be worried about shit she doesn't need to be worried about. Among that is you, so get it together."

She didn't snap then either, didn't even speak. Instead, she nodded.

But by then it was too late. He was pissed in that way that scared even him, furious in a way he knew the only way to make it fade would be to make himself hurt outside like he hurt inside. Because he was that angry, he continued to bark, "In case pretty boy was too busy tryin' to get in your pants instead of what he was supposed to be doing, filling you in, I'll tell you. Chained MC is in a fuck of a mess for dealing with the wrong street gang. Don't know how they did, but they found you in New Mexico and shot up your house. Means you're on their radar and so is *my* daughter. You wanna stay alive? Cut out the late nights.

"Another thing, don't even think for a fuckin' second I'm letting you take my daughter anywhere near Chained. You wanna get killed, I don't give a shit. But *my* daughter *isn't* getting caught in the crossfire."

That broke the dam. Tears streamed down her face. She didn't bother to wipe them away. She left them there as if she knew the havoc they wrecked in him. Still, she didn't say a word, so he forced his eyes away, opened the door, and headed inside. She followed behind. He led her upstairs into the room across from his and headed downstairs into the gym.

Without taping his fists, he swung them repeatedly, each punch striking the bag. He did that for hours until he was drenched in sweat, and the bag was stained with the blood pouring from his knuckles. It didn't hurt. He didn't feel physical pain at all. All he felt was the agony tearing his insides apart. It only served to prove what he knew true.

Fights worked miracles. He should've picked a fight instead.

****

"Mommy?"

In the haze of sleep, she heard her daughter's soft voice. Parting her lids, she met Brianna's beautiful blue-green eyes—eyes that reminded her of Bryce. Sitting up in bed, she glanced around the unfamiliar room, white walls, queen bed with blue sheets. Beside the bed, a nightstand, an armoire directly in front of her next to the door, a closet to her right, and a bathroom to her left. Taking all of this in forced her back to reality, her new reality.

Bryce... Chip... Her life was a mess.

Feeling tears prick the back of her eyes, she blinked quickly, forced a smile, and met her daughter's gaze. "Good morning, baby."

Brianna gave her a big, bright smile that reminded

her what she had been put on the Earth for. "I missed you, Mommy."

Tugging her into a hug, she buried her face in her daughter's hair. "Missed you, too, baby."

Her daughter quickly pulled away, leapt off the bed, and headed toward the closet. In front of the door lay a series of shopping bags. Most appeared to be from the same department store; several others were from a toy store.

"Daddy took me shopping. He bought me skirts and shoes and shirts and barrettes," Brianna said excitedly digging through the bags.

When she entered the room the night before, she spotted Brianna fast asleep and still wearing the dress she had on the day before. Bryce hadn't bothered to change her clothes. Then again, she hadn't expected him to. He was new at the father thing and probably felt uncomfortable changing his daughter's clothes, so she did moments before hopping into bed and falling asleep.

"That's great, baby."

"I want to wear the flower dress Daddy got me." Her daughter looked away from the bags and met her gaze. "Can I? Can I?"

She nodded, and since Brianna went back to digging through the series of bags, she added, "Of course."

Finding the dress, white with large pink flowers, Brianna carted it out and handed it to her. She took it and placed it on the bed beside her.

Brianna beamed. "Daddy bought me toys, too, Mommy, and he took me to eat pizza." She paused, looking away from her then met her stare again, and in a soft voice, she said, "He doesn't know any bedtime stories, so he didn't tell me any. Why doesn't Daddy know any bedtime stories? Didn't his mommy read to him?"

Emelia didn't know much, but what she knew— Bryce's mother abandoned him when he was five, leaving him with his paternal grandmother. His grandmother, too old and worn out, hadn't cared for him, not properly anyway. She couldn't say any of this to her four-year-old. "No, she didn't."

Her brows wrinkled. "Why?"

She threw her legs over the bed and stood. "That's a story for another time. Now, it's bath time. Then you'll wear your new dress, and we'll head downstairs for some breakfast."

"Can we eat breakfast with Daddy?"

"We'll go look for him when you're dressed."

While Brianna showered and brushed her teeth, she headed for the phone on the nightstand to make a very important and overdue call to her boss and friend.

Back in New Mexico, she worked at a small antique shop. It was convenient, which for a single mom translated to awesome. The hours were flexible. The pay was good, and when Bree was out of school and on the occasional Saturday she had to work, her boss didn't mind that Bree went with her to work as long as she stayed in the office when customers were around. Her boss, Naomi, turned into her friend, one who knew nothing of her old life including Bree's father.

Emelia should've called her yesterday, explained what happened, and told her she wouldn't return home or to work, but with everything that happened, it had been the last thing on her mind. She had to do it then, an hour before her shift was scheduled to start. She picked up the phone, dialed, and explained the situation. Well, not really, she was vague, telling Naomi she had a family emergency and left town. Naturally, this shocked Naomi as it'd surprise anyone.

"What do you mean you left town?" she shrieked.

"Family emergency. I really can't explain. I'm sorry. I know this is late notice but—"

"When are you coming back?"

A tough question. She was leaning toward never. Not that she wanted to stay in California, not that she wouldn't miss the life she built in New Mexico, but Bryce knew about Brianna now. From what she'd seen, the way Bryce had taken to his daughter, no way she'd take Bree away from her father. And so, she'd live in Wadden, California indefinitely.

"I… We're not going back."

"What?" Another loud shriek.

"Listen, I know this seems crazy, but—"

Naomi sighed heavily then cut her off. "I always figured you were running from something, Em. Guess it was about time you decided to straighten it out."

Her boss slash friend nailed it or part of it anyway. All those years ago, she had run, and she ran intending never to return. Five years later, she had no plans to either, but life happened.

"I…" Her voice trailed off, not knowing what to say.

"You aren't in trouble, are you, Em?"

Yeah, she was, but not the kind of trouble her boss referred to. "No." She didn't explain, and that was okay.

Naomi wouldn't push. In five years, Naomi never pushed, never pried. Exactly the type of friend Emelia needed. The type she shot the breeze with, the type she talked to about the present and near future. Naomi gave her that. It was obvious to her now, Naomi sensed Emelia was running, realized that was the type of friend she needed.

"You'll keep in touch?"

Though her only friend couldn't see her, she nodded. "Yes."

They talked for a couple more minutes. In those minutes, Naomi volunteered to clean out her home and get rid of everything. She hated to make her friend do all that work but agreed because she didn't have a choice, so she told her to sell everything and keep the money. Naomi refused. She insisted and insisted until her friend relented. By that time, Bree walked out of the bathroom, so she said goodbye, hung up, and helped Bree dress. She took ten minutes to get ready herself.

Together, they left their room. Still early, especially for a biker, from what she remembered, Bryce wasn't an early riser. In fact, no one could get him out of bed before noon, ever. Regardless, she headed toward his bedroom door across from theirs, the same room she walked out of five years ago. She did this certain she'd wake him, certain he'd open the door and scream at her, and still, she did this because Brianna wanted to have breakfast with him.

Unbelievable as it was, Brianna was her father's daughter, a daddy's girl. She may have been raised by her mother, and she may have never even met her father until the day before, but Brianna always asked about him. Perhaps, partly the blame was Em's. In some ways, she encouraged it, showing her pictures, telling her stories. How could she not? She wanted the best for her daughter. Even if Bryce wasn't a part of her life, even if he didn't want Brianna, she wanted her daughter to know him.

So as unlikely as it was he'd be awake, knowing that likely she'd wake him, and he'd take the chance to treat her like the scum of the earth, she held Bree's hand and knocked on his door. When he didn't answer, she knocked again with a little more force.

"He's not there."

She angled her body to her right, facing down the long hallway, and met Strike's gaze. "Do you know where he is?"

"Left this morning."

She felt and sensed her daughter's sob before it pierced the air. Immediately, she turned to Brianna and knelt.

Her big eyes filled with unshed tears. Bree blinked then, and those tears trailed down her face. "He left me, Mommy!"

Heart clenching, she cupped her daughter's cheeks. "No, baby, he didn't. He just has to work. He'll be back."

Another wail tore through her daughter's throat. The sound so heart-wrenching she felt it in her bones. Acting quickly, she hauled Brianna close and carried her, pulling her face to her neck, muffling the sound of her sobs.

She needed to get her calm, and it'd take time. Her daughter was a daddy's girl, who thought her father, the father she'd only just met, abandoned her. Emelia couldn't blame her. All her fault, she lied to him, to her, and the lies led to this. All because she'd made a huge mistake.

Guilt clogging her throat, she briskly walked down the hallway and down the stairs, hoping Brianna's cries hadn't woken anyone. She didn't stop until she reached the kitchen. There, she set Brianna on her feet, kneeled in front of her, and tried to soothe her.

Chapter Four

"Brother? You're here?"

Ripper turned and met Strike's stare. Glaring, he barked, "What the fuck does it look like to you?"

God, he was such a dick, all the time. He didn't know how the hell his brothers put up with him. He couldn't blame it on Emelia forever, could he?

Ripper lost her and wanted her back. So many times, he wondered what would've happened if she confronted him back then, if she told him her reason for leaving. He knew down to his bones he would've never let her go, would've found a way to make her stay. He wanted that, another chance, to know why, to make it better, to change her mind. Now, she was back. Instead of trying to do any of that, he was treating her like shit, still being a dick, to her, to his brothers.

Strike laughed. "Looks like you're your usual self, too." He quirked a brow. "Thought you were gone. Your girl's bawling in the kitchen."

His girl? Which one? Which *one?* There was only one—Bree. "Bree?"

"Yeah. Em was knocking on your door. I saw her and told her you were gone. Your girl started sobbing. She thinks you left her. That was like a half hour ago. She's still at it, man. Em's trying to…"

Ripper didn't hear the rest of what Strike said because, on a dead run, he headed inside. Heart lodged in his throat, he slammed open the door leading into the compound then sprinted toward the sound of Bree's sobs, leading him to the kitchen. As he neared, he heard Emelia's voice. For some reason, he froze just out of sight and listened.

"Bree, baby, I promise you your dad is coming back."

"B-but whhhyyyy he leaavvveee meee..."

"Your dad has to work. You know how I used to leave you at school, then I'd come get you?" She paused. "Well, your dad needs to work. It doesn't mean he isn't coming back."

"B-but..." Her breathing hitched. "Before he was away b-because of woooork."

Emelia told her that he hadn't been around because of work? Lying to their daughter when the truth was she hadn't told him about her. If he'd known about Bree, he never would've spent a day away.

Rage pulsing through him, he took a deep breath, and though he never prayed, he prayed then he wouldn't strangle Emelia on sight for making his baby girl suffer, for making him suffer. Yet all that anger faded when it occurred to him... His beautiful Bree, even believing her mother's lies, thinking his work was more important than her, loved him, wanted him around so much she was in tears thinking he wouldn't come back.

His heart clenched so hard he swore any moment it'd explode inside his chest.

Maybe he had a rough life. Maybe Emelia leaving killed whatever good he had, but she gave him something too—his Bree.

"I know that's what I said, but things have changed

now," Emelia said. "Why do you think he brought you here to live with him? It's because he missed you so much because he loves you so much, he wants to see you *every day*, and he wants to spend time with you *every day*."

Her fuck up aside, she was a good mother. Would he ever catch up?

Another sob tore through Bree. He moved, without thought, on instinct, not knowing what he planned to say or do to make her stop crying. At the threshold, he caught sight of Emelia, her back toward him, kneeling in front of Bree, whose eyes were swollen. Still not knowing what to say, what to do, he froze.

Bree's red-rimmed eyes went to him. Her chest rose and fell as she took a deep breath. With her little hands, she wiped her tears quickly. But she didn't go to him, she just stood there, brows furrowed, chin trembling. Emelia twisted, her gaze hit him. He fought not to look her way.

Emelia faced Bree. "See, baby, I told you your dad would come back. Why don't you say good morning?"

Bree's eyes watered again.

Shit. Why was she crying now? What should he do?

Bree's stare shooting to Emelia, she asked in barely a whisper, "Is Daddy mad at me?"

Why would he be mad at his baby girl? He didn't let Emelia speak. "I'm not mad, Bree. I wish you'd stop crying though. Don't like to see my girl cry."

With those words, Bree launched herself at him. He caught her under her arms and lifted her into his embrace. With her small body against his, he pressed a kiss to her forehead and simultaneously laced his fingers through her hair. "Mornin', baby."

"M-morning, Daddy." Her breath hitched on the first word. Her little body jerked against his when she hiccupped.

Drawing away, he met her gaze. "Are you gonna tell me why you think I'm mad at you?"

She hesitated. "...Because I was...crying."

"Let's get a couple of things straight, 'kay?" He kept his voice soft.

She nodded.

"Crying won't make me mad at you. It'll only make me sad 'cause I don't want my girl crying. I want her happy, yeah?"

She smiled softly then nodded.

"Remember what I said yesterday? When I told you I wasn't leaving you?"

She nodded.

"You gotta believe me, baby. You gotta believe I'm not leaving you, *not ever*. Sometimes, I won't be around 'cause I gotta work. Sometimes work'll take me far away. I may be gone for a couple of days, but it won't be like before. I promise you I'll always come back. I'm not *ever* leaving you, Bree, *ever*. You understand?"

Her eyes watered. She wrapped her arms around his neck and pressed her cheek to his chest. Finally, she nodded.

He cupped the back of her head, kissed her forehead, and took a deep breath. God, she smelled good.

Pulling away, she asked, "Do you have to work today, Daddy?"

Yeah, he did. He should. He'd just become a

65

father, meaning he needed extra cash more than ever. Not that he didn't have a bunch in savings, but kids cost or so he heard. He was already five years late saving for her college, and he needed to make some adjustments to his house so by the time the shit storm with Chained and the Falcons was over, he could move her into a real home. For those reasons, he needed to work, but staring into her eyes, eyes that reminded him she was *his* baby girl, he couldn't.

"Today's just for you, Bree."

He had to talk with Prez first, find out how the Falcons found Emelia and Bree, but then, he'd spend the day with her. Deciding this was worth it because Bree gave him this look, like he made the whole world better by just breathing. Then she smiled wide.

****

Angling her wrist to her face, Emelia checked her watch and learned only a couple of minutes had passed since the last time she checked.

After Bree's crying fit that morning, Bryce carried her away. Emelia wanted to give them their privacy, so she hadn't followed. She occupied her time by calling her landlord informing him she had a family emergency and left the state. She only had three months left on her lease, and breaking it meant she had to pay for those three months. That cut into her savings by more than half. Half of the rest of it would go in damages that occurred yesterday when her house was shot up. It sucked, but there was little she could do. She never had renter's insurance, primarily because she couldn't afford rent, her car, gas, food, etcetera for her and Bree on her salary. This meant she had to find a job faster than she thought. That brought another problem. She needed a car to get to a job because she couldn't depend on Bryce or anyone else driving her daily. She had a car in New Mexico. The fifteen-year-old Honda had been close to dying, the reason she'd been saving.

Her landlord also told her she needed to contact the police, so she did. When she spoke to the detective investigating the shooting, she was brief, telling him she and her daughter left town for a family emergency before it happened. Luckily, there hadn't been any witnesses who'd seen them leaving.

An hour later, she left her room, intent on finding Bryce. Strike told her he took off with Bree. That had been around ten in the morning. For nine hours, she hadn't seen or heard from her daughter and Bryce, so she'd been standing outside for close to an hour. She wasn't used to not being with Bree, wasn't used to not knowing where she was. Being the sole provider and caregiver for the last almost five years assured that, so her nerves were expected. So many times, she'd been seconds from asking one of the brothers for Bryce's number to call him. Every time, she stopped herself because he deserved time with Bree alone without her inferring or asking questions, questions that though were asked with good intentions would serve to make him think she didn't trust him with their daughter.

Sighing heavily, she looked down at her feet then heard a familiar voice.

"Scared he ran off with your kid?"

Those words drew her away from her thoughts. She turned and met a pair of light hazel eyes. Bud hadn't changed a bit. Dark hair framed his face and contrasted perfectly against his eyes. He always wore white V-neck shirts. She never asked why. He and Bryce had been close. It sounded odd to anyone else, but that was the way it was. Having seen it in Chained and Hell Ryders, she knew within the club, some brothers got along better than others. Bryce and Bud were best friends, always had been. Their friendship had been forged before they joined the club when they'd just been a couple of kids. They grew up on the same street in a rough neighborhood, so it'd been natural for her to wonder why amid everything that happened yesterday Bud hadn't been with Bryce.

She straightened. "He wouldn't do that."

He laughed aloud though it was humorless. The sound died suddenly when his eyes hardened. "So sure 'bout that?"

She hesitated only briefly then nodded.

Smirking, he shot back, "It's been a long time, Em. People change. He ain't the man you used to know."

The message clear, one Bud didn't need to deliver. The man she loved was long gone. He'd been gone before she left. She didn't know when it happened. In reality, she didn't even know *if* it happened. Maybe the man she fell for never existed. Maybe she lived two years thinking he was someone he wasn't. Eventually, she discovered it, and it was the reason she left.

The difference now, the woman he'd known was long gone, too. Shit happened, and when it happened, it changed you. That's what happened to her.

"I don't think I ever knew him."

She regretted saying it instantly because it didn't matter. She wasn't the first or last woman to be lied to, toyed with, and hurt. A part of her thought she deserved what she got. She *knew* better. Living with Chip and Track, she witnessed the way bikers lived. Rarely if

68

ever did they settle down, and ninety-five percent of the ones who settled cheated, so she should've expected what she got. But she chose to believe the lie, a lie she wanted to believe because it was beautiful. In spite of everything, she *loved* him. It's the reason even knowing everything she knew about bikers, everything she'd seen, she believed the lie until it stared her in the face, laughing.

His eyes widened, brows rose. Taking a menacing step in her direction, the lines of his face hardening, he barked, "What?"

She didn't flinch, didn't respond either, so they stood there in silence until he spoke again. This time, there was much more anger in his voice.

"What the *fuck* is that supposed to mean?"

Again, she didn't answer. She held still, her eyes never leaving his.

After a long moment, seemingly having figured out she wouldn't answer, he looked away, clenched his jaw tightly, and met her stare. "Playing victim ain't gonna work, babe. This is *his* club. We're *his* brothers, and we ain't falling for a bitch's act."

With those last words, he turned and strode inside, slamming the door shut on his way in.

She wasn't insulted in the least. She expected it. Again, everything he said she knew to be true. Brothers in the club covered for each other, no matter the circumstance. She shouldn't have said anything. A slip of the tongue, a glimpse of the woman she used to be that at that moment shone through. Bad timing, they already hated her for leaving the way she had, for taking Bree and not telling Bryce about her, no matter her reasons, so saying what she had only served to infuriate the lot of them.

Feeling like an idiot, she turned just in time to see an SUV drive into the lot. A second later, Bryce hopped out, strode around the car, and opened the back door. He reached in grabbing Bree then began walking toward her with Bree draped across his chest asleep. He had one arm under her butt and the other cupping the back of her head, clutching her to him. His head down, gaze on their daughter, he then lifted his stare, and his eyes met hers. The moment they did, they hardened, his jaw clenching.

He strode past her, releasing the back of Bree's head for a spare moment to open the door. He marched through without bothering to hold the door for her, something he had done all those years ago. The fact he didn't, another bitter reminder of her mistake.

Chest burning, she followed him inside through the garage toward the back door that led into the club's compound. Again, he opened the door and walked through. She followed down the long corridor, past the large living area with several couches, where three others including Bud sat in front of the big screen TV watching a game. The moment they spotted Bryce with Bree, they quieted. Bryce sauntered through without sparing a glance at them toward another hallway. She tailed him, thinking it was nice of them to quiet down for Bree, thinking the bikers she'd known before wouldn't have, thinking, perhaps, another brother had had kids, and it's why they'd grown accustomed to doing this.

Bryce climbed the stairs and continued down another hall until he reached her and Bree's room. Opening the door, he stepped inside and headed for the bed. There, he hovered over the mattress and placed Bree on it gently. Without needing to be told, he removed her shoes, covered her with the blanket, leaned in, and pressed a kiss to Bree's forehead.

Emelia watched, her hand pressed to her chest where her heart clenched. Never in a million years would she have guessed the man who claimed he didn't like kids, the man who claimed he never wanted to be a father, would be so tender.

He turned without meeting her gaze and lifted his chin in the direction of the door. This action, his silent command they talk outside. She shifted and headed for the door. Once outside, she met his glare. His eyes, that strange, beautiful blue-green color, the same that had once looked at her so lovingly, filled with hate, overflowing with anger and *dead*.

Still not used to seeing death in those eyes, she stuttered, "Um, I…"

"Don't got all fuckin' night. Say what you gotta say," he sniped. His voice, too, filled with rage.

She tensed then swallowed. "I have some money in a savings account. Not much, but it's something until I find a job here. I'd need…"

He took a step in her direction and leaned into her, looking so feral she had no choice but to trail off. "You've lost common sense over the last five years?"

She wanted to say no but instead mumbled, "I…"

"What don't you get about the fact a street gang is trying to *kill* you?"

She thought he couldn't possibly get more furious. Wrong. His posture stiff, eyes savage yet lifeless, and that wild look on his face proved it. Still, she went on. She had a daughter to support, couldn't depend on him for everything.

"I have to find a job. I can't just—"

Looking away from her, he muttered, "Fuckin' deaf, too." He then met her eyes. "Shut it, and *listen.* Chip hired a PI to find you, not the first he's hired over the years but the best 'cause the PI found you and *Bree,* and it just so happens the PI sent Chip all that info to his phone an hour before the Falcons found him and shot him. They took his phone. That's how they found *you.* That's why they shot up your house. That means not only do they know about you, but they know about *Bree.* Any way they can find to track you and Bree, they will. That means no cell phone, and especially no leaving this place. I'm not gonna let you get killed 'cause you wanna be stubborn. I gave my word, and most importantly, 'cause my girl needs her mom."

The muscle in his jaw twitched. "That means you aren't working 'cause you aren't leaving this place until this shit with Chained and the Falcons is *done,* so you're not gonna work 'cause you *can't* leave this place 'cause I'm not letting you. Get me now?"

"Okay."

His brows rose, and then, he took a step away and stared, waiting, knowing she wasn't done.

"Maybe there's something I can do around here. Not that I expect to be paid since I'm living here and the club's protecting me and especially Bree, but maybe there's some way I can help out. Cleaning or cooking or whatever... Just talk to the guys and let me know."

The tension leaving his shoulders, he crossed his arms over his chest, making the muscles along his arms bulge.

"And also...Bree needs a booster seat."

Quirking a brow, for the first time in two days, he didn't look angry but confused. It wasn't the way she wanted him to look at her either, but it was way better than livid.

"A what?"

"A car seat."

He leaned in. His face went feral, eyes dead and narrowed, jaw clenched, brows furrowed. "You mean to tell me I've been driving around with Bree when I shouldn't't've been 'cause I don't got a car seat for her?"

Yeah. She would've told him this but hadn't had the chance before now considering they'd arrived just yesterday. She also had no idea he planned on taking Bree anywhere that day, but Em didn't bother explaining. Pointless and stupid, considering he was irate again, and Bryce furious didn't listen to explanations. All it'd do was cause an argument, and the fight she'd had vanished five years ago when she forced herself to walk away from him.

"Are you getting a kick outta making me look like a bad father?"

"No…" she whispered the word. "I know you'll be a great—"

One minute he was feet away, the next in her face. She didn't know how she did it, but she held still, without flinching.

"Don't fuckin' *say* it. Don't you dare say it 'cause I can read through that fucked *lie,* and I'll lose my *shit.* Trust me when I tell you, you don't want to see that. You don't want me to do it 'cause swear to God, I don't know what the fuck I'll do to *you.*"

She hadn't lied. She always knew he'd be a great father because of how he'd been with her. She didn't try to tell him this though, and she wouldn't.

Then and there, it hit her like a sucker punch to the gut what she already knew to be true—he wasn't the man she thought him to be all those years ago. The man she thought he was wouldn't treat her this way, despite the fact she left with his kid because *he knew* why she left and why she had reason to. She wouldn't tell him or remind him of this either. She'd let him take out his anger on her, believing she deserved it. Because the woman he'd known was long gone. With that went what made her *her*, feisty and fearless, a woman who didn't put up with shit, a woman who fought back and dirty. And so, holding his eyes, she forced herself to remain still.

"Anything *else*?"

"Yes, we should discuss getting Bree in school. She's four, but I had her in Pre-K—"

"Haven't had her with me since she was born, so school can wait 'till next week."

She nodded then bracing to feel that vile anger emanating from him again, she blurted, "Her birthday's coming up. It's the Sunday after next."

He didn't say a word. Then again, he didn't have to. The look in his eyes went from dead to deadly. He held so still, hands in fists at his sides, close to losing it and doing everything in his power not to.

"I usually have a small party for her, invite her friends, but we can do whatever you want. I've always made her cake. I'd like to do that again, and if you want to have a small party for her, I can help with the decorations. We can do something simple, or if you want to spend time with her alone, that's fine too. I'd still like to make her a cake. I know she loves them—"

Through gritted teeth, he said, "I'll *think* 'bout it."

She nodded, tore her gaze from his, and strode into her room.

****

Ripper needed sleep and bad. No matter what he did, he couldn't get more than a couple of hours. He tried, but his mind wouldn't stop working, thinking about Bree and all he'd missed.

His baby girl would turn *five* soon, and just two days ago, he hadn't known she existed. He missed everything those five years, and that made the rage inside him so strong it became an ache.

After the conversation with Emelia, he hopped on his bike and rode for hours. He then changed and went for a long run, close to six miles. Even after, he still felt that ache acutely, so he headed to the gym and attempted to further exhaust it out of him by slamming his fists against a punching bag repeatedly. He didn't know how long he'd done that, but it was long enough his legs and arms gave out.

Still, that ache didn't fade.

Still, his mind wouldn't give it a rest.

He showered and trimmed his beard then lay on his bed, eyes wide open, for hours. Finally, he nodded off, only to wake with a start a few hours later when he dreamed a memory he tried hard to forget—the day he came home and found her gone.

Pulling himself out of bed, he headed to the bathroom. Showered and dressed, he walked out of his bedroom and headed to Bree. He didn't bother to knock. Instead, he parted the door slowly and poked his head inside. The moment he did, his gaze locked with a pair of eyes the same color as his.

Bree sat up in bed. Smiling wide, she jumped off, dashed to him, and slammed into his legs. Reaching down, he picked her up and kissed her forehead. "Mornin', baby."

Her cheek pressed against his chest, her arms tightened around him. "Good morning, Daddy."

He couldn't help it. Before he strode away, he spared a glance at the bed where Emelia lay. Seeing that blonde hair of hers sprawled around her, he remembered something he'd forgotten. How often he woke with her thick mass of hair on him, smelling the flowery scent of her shampoo, how often he accidentally pulled on it when he put an elbow on the bed, and how often he threaded his fingers through it mindlessly. He hated the memory came to him, hated remembering.

Clenching his jaw, holding Bree tight, he reminded himself he got something wonderful out of it. He looked to Bree, moved away from the door, closed it, and set Bree on her feet. "What do you want for breakfast, baby?"

She put a finger to her chin. "Um…Pancakes."

He smiled thinking they'd have to go out for breakfast. He didn't know how to make pancakes and wasn't even sure they were stocked for it. The only time he remembered having food at the compound consistently was when Allie, one of his brothers' sister, lived there. She shopped, stocked the kitchen, and cooked for her brother. She always made plenty for the rest of them. Besides that, except once a month when they had the club cookouts, it was hard to find anything but beer and liquor. Allie, who the brothers called Classy, was now married to Trig. Though she often hung out at the compound, she never cooked for them anymore because Trig was selfish and kept her to himself most of the time.

Knowing this added another trip to his list, grocery shopping. Not that he'd cook, he didn't even know how, and he wouldn't test his skills or lack thereof on Bree. But Emelia cooked. If she cooked for Bree and him, maybe it'd keep her busy enough she'd get off his back about working.

"I'm gonna take you out to eat breakfast today. Then we need to get you a booster seat and buy some groceries. You cool hanging out with me all morning?"

She giggled, the sound of it lessening the deep ache that hadn't yet abated.

In between those giggles, she said, "But Daddy, I have to get dressed first."

He quirked a brow, scanned her clothes, noticing the Minnie Mouse PJ's she had on, and smirked. "Thought you *were* dressed."

She giggled some more. "I am, but Daddy, I can't go out in my PJ's."

He hid a smile and cocked his head. "Why can't you?"

"Because PJ's are only to sleep."

"My girl's too smart for me." He grinned. "You need help picking out an outfit, getting dressed?"

She shook her head.

Another bitter reminder of how much he missed. It hurt. No, it killed. Maybe if he'd had her all those years he missed, by now he'd know the rules about girls' clothes, matching shoes, and all of that.

"Right. Then, I'll wait for you here."

He watched her go knowing hearing her giggle

sounded better than anything had in his fucked life.

****

Ripper pulled into the front lot at the garage and parked. His mind on Bree who'd so sweetly announced she wanted to go to work with him and learn about cars and motorcycles. Sparing a glance at his seatbelt and unbuckling it, he did something he hadn't done for ages but had done so often since Bree came into his life, something he couldn't help but do when Bree was around. He grinned. The next minute, he hopped out of the car, opened Bree's door, unbuckled her, and helped her out.

"You'll teach me, right, Daddy?"

Her hand in his, he smiled and looked down at her as he led her toward the garage. "Yeah. I'll teach you 'bout whatever you wanna know."

She stopped mid-stride. "What about the groceries?"

As planned, he took her to eat breakfast first. While they ate, he researched on his phone where to buy a booster seat for a four-year-old and found a store. After breakfast, of which she ate very little, they headed to the store. He didn't say anything about her leaving more than half her food since it was a big breakfast. Honest, he didn't know how much she should eat, something else he needed to find out and soon. Still, it worried him she hadn't eaten as much as he thought she should. After purchasing a booster seat with excellent safety ratings, they went to the grocery store where he let Bree tell him what to buy. He, quite frankly, hadn't been to a grocery store in years.

"Don't worry about those. Boys'll get them."

The garage was busy as expected on a Tuesday

morning. All five large, metal garage doors open, cars and bikes lined inside, worked on by his brothers. Walking through one of the metal doors, he scanned the area looking for the prospects. Spotting Beef striding out the door leading into the compound, he whistled loud. When Beef eyed him, he shouted, "Unload." He nodded in the direction of his SUV and threw his keys at him.

He didn't see if Beef caught them since Bree released his hand. His stare shot down, watching as she ran toward a group of his brothers, Blaze, Cuss, and Army, along with another man he didn't recognize. They stood at the other end of the garage near the office. The man he didn't know looked a lot like a cop. Dark-brown hair styled in a crew cut, clean-shaven, dressed like a detective in a pair of dark-blue Dockers, white button-down shirt, and a sports coat.

Ripper didn't know what it was about cops, though it probably had a lot to do with the fact he spent his life avoiding them, but he could practically smell them. His assumption confirmed a second later when the man pulled his blue sports coat back to set his hand on his hip, giving Ripper view of the badge on his belt.

The cop wasn't local. He knew all the local cops. He didn't care what the cop had come for, and he didn't need to either. His brothers seemed to be handling it just fine. The only reason he strode that way was because Bree was still running in that direction. He made a note to talk to her about running away, about running in the garage at all. He'd been a father for three days, but it didn't take a genius to realize the garage, with so much heavy machinery and tools, wasn't a safe place for her.

When Bree reached for the cop's hand and tugged down, he quickened his pace.

Looking up at the cop as he looked down, his Bree said, "Shawn!" in her childlike exuberance. "Did you come to visit me and Mommy?"

Feet from them, Ripper froze because in that moment, three things became clear. His daughter and Emelia knew the cop. The cop wasn't there by accident, and the cop wasn't just a cop but a staple in their lives.

Rip figured this since a police department wouldn't make a detective travel on their dime to ask a woman some questions about a shooting. They weren't missing or in danger since the cop knew where they were. And so, the cop wasn't just a cop. The cop knew Emelia and Bree well enough he noticed they were gone. He cared enough to find out where they went and paid for a flight to get to them. A man who did this did it because he wasn't just a friend. The man was involved with Emelia and knew his kid better than he did.

Realizing this tore the ache that had begun to fade after spending the morning with Bree wide open. Ripper didn't know how he managed it, but he held still fighting with everything in him not to do what he wanted to—haul his daughter away from the cop and beat the living daylights out of him then find Emelia and lock her in a room for five years. Only then, she'd know what it felt like not to be a part of her daughter's life.

As those thoughts ran through his mind, the cop smiled at his daughter and lightly cupped her face. "Yeah, Bree, I came to visit."

The cop smiled at his daughter. *He* cupped her face, looking at her with familiarity and called her

"Bree."

So fucked. It made another thing very clear. Emelia thought Ripper wouldn't make a good father, so she'd left him without so much as a goodbye, without telling him why, without telling him about his daughter and found herself the complete opposite of him—a cop, a cop she fucked and helped her raise *his* kid.

Just then, Bree turned to him. Releasing the cop's hand, she took three steps his way, grabbed hold of his hand, and said with that same enthusiasm, "Daddy, Shawn came to visit me and Mommy." She faced the cop. "This is my daddy. Mommy and me are going to live with him."

She sounded so excited even as the smile on the cop's face faded. To Ripper, that only further proved what he thought to be true.

Cops were experts with poker faces. They had to be to get people to confess to shit, so his smile fading meant that what Bree said rocked his world. It proved the cop wasn't just a cop, but a cop who was fucking his kid's mother. With that look, the cop confirmed he'd fallen for Emelia. Rip should feel bad for the guy knowing she was stone cold, knowing the cop, like him, was just another man she up and left without so much as a goodbye, but Rip couldn't summon even a little bit of sympathy while his chest burned with envy. The bastard had her as little as three days ago. The taste of her was probably still in his mouth whereas all Rip had were pieces of fading memories. The only lasting ones—the ones that killed to remember.

The cop's green gaze sliced to him.

Ripper saw it then, the pain. It was such a blow the cop didn't have it in him to hide. That was the thing with matters of the heart. No matter how badass or tough you were, that shit got to you. You couldn't hide it, couldn't fight it. It fucking hurt, so no matter how good at poker you were, people read it in your actions and movements and especially, in your eyes.

His brothers, Cuss, Blaze, and Army, closed in around him, probably figuring he was close to flipping his lid. If it hadn't been for Bree being there, he would've already done something stupid like assault a cop.

His gaze still locked on the cop's, he said to Bree, "Baby, go inside with your Uncle Cuss. I need a moment, 'kay?"

Not sensing her move or release his hand, he tilted his head to her. Eyes rounded, a pensive look on her pretty face, she was too smart. Already he knew this, so he lied though he hated to do it. "Everything's fine, baby. Go play. Then we'll get lunch."

Even then, she looked unsure, brows drawn, lips parted slightly, but she was a good kid, proved it when she nodded, released his hand, and took Cuss's, who had his held out to her. Ripper watched them until they were out of ear shot and out of sight.

Turning his attention to the cop, he held his glare.

"Name's Shawn Martin. I came to see Em."

"I know why you're here and what it means 'cause the fact you're here tells me why you're here. What you gotta get is I don't give a fuck you spent your cop salary on a flight here, you ain't *seeing* my kid again. When you leave, you ain't *taking* my kid. Her mom wants to go with you, that's her choice, but *no one* is taking *my* kid. *No one.* I don't care that you're a cop. Don't give a fuck that's her mom. You or her get any bright ideas 'bout involving the law in this shit, I don't give a shit 'bout that either 'cause at the end of the day, my kid's staying with me until she's out on her own."

He further narrowed his eyes. "I lived the past five years without her, not even knowing she existed, so I'll repeat *no one* is taking Bree from *me*."

The cop didn't react, so Ripper had no idea if he knew, if Emelia told him about him, about the fact she left without telling him. Not that it mattered, Rip didn't care. All he cared about was Bree, and no matter how much the cop pleaded, no matter how good the cop gave it to Emelia, how good of a father figure Emelia thought the cop was to *his* Bree, she wouldn't leave. Rip was sure of this. She left men on the drop of a dime, but she wouldn't leave Bree. She loved Bree more than anything in this world. It was clear from just the look in her eyes when she looked Bree's way.

"I gotta say I wanna feel bad for you for getting involved with her. I know what that shit's like. The thing is I *can't*. Piece of advice, make sure she isn't pregnant with your kid too before you take off 'cause you'll miss years you'll never get back, and nothing, not even what you're feeling now, compares to the loss of that."

With those final words, Ripper strode away.

Chapter Five

Emelia bit the side of her lip. She'd done it so often since that morning, it had swelled. Waking to find Bree gone, she had a full-blown panic attack. She dashed out of her bedroom wearing an old Harley tee reaching her mid-thighs, screaming Bree's name at the top of her lungs. Everyone she asked answered with the same lame response, "Don't know." It only made her worry more. Who could blame her? Her daughter was gone. No note, no call, and no one seemed to know where she was.

About to call the police and report her daughter missing, one of the members of Hell Ryders, the same one who treated her like shit the first day, who she since learned everyone called Hash, told her Bree was with Bryce. Even so, after the scare she had, she wanted to speak to Bree. She hadn't spoken to her daughter since the morning before, so she asked for Bryce's cell number. Hash had not only refused to give it to her but informed her no one else would give it to her either.

The minute she saw Ripper stride into the kitchen, alone, where she'd been putting her nervous energy to use by cleaning, she rushed him. As she did this, she took in the angry look on his face, and even so, she treaded forward, her mind on Bree. "You could have left me a note. Where's Bree?"

His jaw clenched, he snapped, "Shut the *fuck* up

before I take my kid and leave."

She stilled and waited minutes while he seemed to fight fury. Fisting his palms, eyes hard, looking like he wanted to rip her head off. She took in his messy, dirty-blond hair, which he hadn't bothered combing that morning. Then avoiding his strange, beautiful eyes narrowed on her, she scanned the stubble marring his chin and cheeks and the rest of him, the muscles lining his shoulders that stretched the black tee he wore, and his large thighs encased in a pair of faded jeans, fitting too well.

"Before you go outside and deal with the fuckin' mess you left and didn't bother to clean up, *again*, get this one thing straight. *I* don't care what promises you made him or what promises he makes you, you aren't taking *Bree*. She's staying with me. You wanna go, fuckin' go. See if I care, but you *won't* take my kid. I missed out on a lot 'cause of you, and I'm done with missing shit."

Having no clue what he was talking about, she began, "I don't know—"

His eyes flared. "I'm done with your *shit*, and I've been done with your shit for five years. Stop trying to play me. You need to get that you're just wasting your time 'cause I'm not falling for your shit. Do me a favor and *stop* trying. Do me and your cop another and go outside and deal with him. I want him off this property in five minutes."

Her cop? She shook her head. "My what?"

Taking a step in her direction, he leaned into her. "Your *fucking cop*! Your *man*! Don't care what his name is. Don't care he's a cop either. I want him off club property *now*."

Watching Bryce turn and storm away, what he implied hit her. The only cop she knew, Shawn Martin, an all-around good guy, sweet, friendly, and handsome. Tall, dark-haired with piercing green eyes, any woman would be lucky to have him, any woman except her. Since he moved across the street from her and Bree back in Santa Rosa, he asked her out several times. She declined every time. Even so, often he swung by her house to chat. A friendship evolved though he made it clear he wanted something more, something she made clear she didn't have it in her to give. They'd never been on a date. Even as friends, they'd never been to lunch or dinner alone, so she didn't know why Bryce thought he was her anything.

Jolting to action, she quickly strode out of the kitchen, down the narrow hallway, and past the door leading into the garage. She scanned it until she found Shawn. He stood at the other end, near the office surrounded by four bikers. As if sensing her, his stare glided around the garage and stopped dead on her. Then his face softened.

She realized, belatedly, she hadn't bothered to call him, tell him despite the shooting, she and Bree were unharmed, and especially, that they wouldn't return. She should've, knowing he'd worry. He was a cop, and his job was to protect and serve, and most importantly, they were friends, and he adored Bree.

She swallowed the guilt choking her and quickened her pace until she stood feet away. Before she spoke, he did.

"Em."

"Shawn." She spared a glance at the bikers surrounding him. Three, she knew. From their stances, they had no plans to give them privacy. She met Shawn's eyes again. "Maybe we can talk outside."

"Office."

She turned and met Bud's gaze. Surprising, he hadn't been there a moment before.

Bud lifted his chin in the direction of the office. "Want privacy, talk in the office."

She nodded, mumbling, "Thanks," then led Shawn up a series of steps, opened the door, and walked into the office.

Hearing the door shut behind him, she faced him. "I should've called—"

The softness in his eyes gone, he shook his head. "Are you here because you want to be?"

Not what she expected him to say. "W-what?"

"Are you here of your own free will or did one or several of those bikers kidnap you and Bree?"

No, they hadn't, but they hadn't given her much choice. She released a breath. "It's complicated."

He took a step in her direction, his face hardening. "It's *not* complicated, Em. It's a yes or no question."

"They didn't kidnap Bree or me."

He scanned her face as if by doing it he could read her expression. He probably could. As a cop, that was an innate talent they seemed to share. One of his annoying cop things he did often. She should be used to it by now but wasn't. Besides, she didn't want or need anyone reading her, not now, not before, and not ever.

"Care to explain who shot up your house and why?" he said, using his hard cop tone, another one of his irritating cop things. He never spoke to her like that, but several times, when he answered his phone, he used that tone.

She didn't need or want to put up with his annoying cop crap. She had enough to deal with, so she snapped, "Are you here on official police business?"

His eyes widened.

Just as he'd never used that tone, she hadn't either. He asked her questions. She avoided them, but even when he pushed, she never lost her cool. Still, it didn't change the fact he'd backed her into a corner. She had no choice but to put a stop to this line of questioning.

She'd been in the biker world for six years before she left and knew the rules. Though she knew the danger she and Bree were in, they were now in the biker world, and in the biker world, cops weren't involved. A club matter would be handled by the club, only. Besides, there wasn't much Shawn, a detective from New Mexico, could do anyway.

"I already spoke to the cops. I doubt they flew you here to question me."

He held her gaze not saying a word until the silence became uncomfortable. Another cop thing, also frustrating even though it was something new she'd never seen him do.

Sighing heavily, he finally spoke. When he did, his voice softened. "No, Em, the department didn't send me here to question you about the drive-by. I took time off work, flew my ass here because I was worried about you and Bree."

What he left unsaid, she understood. He'd made an effort to find out where she'd gone, took time off work, and got on a flight to get to them because she hadn't bothered to call and tell him she moved and had no plans to return. For caring and worrying about her and Bree, she snapped at him.

"I'm sorry. I-I should've called. I—"

"What's going on, Em?"

She shut her eyes tightly. When she parted them, she didn't meet his stare. "It's complicated."

"Kinda figured that. Your house is shot up. You move to another state, take little, tell Naomi to sell all your stuff. You don't even bother to call anyone else. You're gone. Just like that. Like you're running. I traced the number you called her from, flew here, and find out you're living at a garage owned by a motorcycle gang. So I'm left with more questions than answers."

She lifted her head to meet his gaze.

"Want me to take a wild guess?" As if knowing she wouldn't respond, he didn't give her time to. "You're running from the people who shot up your house. I'm thinking it has something to do with this motorcycle gang. And though I want to believe *this* isn't you, I don't know because as it turns out, Bree's father isn't exactly what I thought he'd be like. When I say that, I don't mean the fact he's part of a motorcycle gang."

He shook his head. "You never shared, no matter how many times I asked or how subtly or bluntly I asked. But I've seen you with Bree plenty, heard the stories you tell her, and I've seen the pictures because she's shown them to me in that box she treasures like any girl her age treasures a damn Barbie. I thought it was great you told her about her father and made her think he was a good man. The thing is a woman who does that, does it because she still loves that man and isn't willing to let him go. Knowing he's a biker, I figured the guy was into his biker gang and doing illegal shit, and I figured you didn't want Bree around that, but I was sure that wasn't the full reason he wasn't around because of the way you talked about him."

He paused. Then he hit home with what he said. "You *idolized* him, so Bree did too. Especially because of that, I figured the real reason he wasn't around was because he didn't want a kid. That's why you were raising her alone."

He shook his head. "But I was wrong, so fucking wrong because the man I met, Em, wants his kid. So something here isn't adding up."

She held his stare but didn't speak.

"Tell me it isn't true, Em."

"It's complicated."

His eyes and expression changed in a way she knew the answer she gave hurt him. He further proved it.

"After all this time, don't I deserve an explanation?"

He did. She'd known him for four years. He'd been a great friend and deserved more than an explanation. He deserved the full truth, but she couldn't give him that. A part of that truth wasn't hers to tell, and the other part of it hurt too much to say aloud. Still, because of that, she tried to give him something.

"It's a motorcycle club, not a gang. Hell Ryders is clean. As far as Bryce is concerned, like I said, it's complicated."

"Complicated as in you got pregnant at twenty and took off with his kid without telling him?"

Her eyes filled with so much water she couldn't see through the tears.

Dropping his head, he cursed under his breath.

Blinking, tears slipped out of her eyes. She quickly

wiped them away. "I know it's horrible, but…"

He lifted his head. "Go on."

"I'm not going to give you an excuse. Looking back, I *know* I made a horrible mistake, but at the time, I didn't think I had another option."

He exhaled. "You were young and scared."

"I was young. I was *terrified*." She paused then for some reason, knowing Shawn wouldn't tell anyone, she admitted, "There were…issues between my cousin and him, issues that had been going on for a while. He… I thought he…"

She shook her head trying to gather her thoughts. "He told me he didn't want kids, that he wouldn't make a good father because he didn't have a father or a mother." She stopped abruptly, knowing no way she'd admit the rest aloud.

"And…"

Eyes trailing away, her mind drifted, went there, taking her back to that day. Thinking of it still hurt as much as it hurt to live it. Her eyes welled, and tears fell.

"Did he hit you, Em?"

Her stare pierced his. "No." She said it firmly, holding his gaze the entire time.

"He cheated."

She knew how wrong she'd been when he said it. As it turned out, she didn't need to be the one to say it for it to wound her. Whether she said it or someone else did, she relived it and reliving it hurt her as deeply as it had years ago.

Tears streaming steadily down her face, he grabbed her hand and hauled her to him. Wrapping his arms around her, he held her, resting his chin on the top of her head.

After a long while where he attempted to comfort her in silence, he whispered, "I'm not going to pretend I know why men do stupid shit, Em. What I know is that he cares about you and Bree. I know because he's pissed. If he didn't care, he wouldn't be."

She shook her head. "You're usually right, Shawn, but you're wrong about that. He hates me and has every right to. Obviously, if I'd known then what I know now, I wouldn't have left, and I say that knowing every time I saw him, I'd see…"

Drawing away from her slightly, he met her gaze. She angled her head to him.

"Even after all this time, you can't say it, so I'm going to say this. Then I'm going to go. You need to get past it, Em, because you deserve to be happy. Stop living in the past." He pressed his lips against her forehead. "I'll miss you and Bree. Goodbye." Then he released her, turned, and walked away.

She stayed frozen, gazing at the floor yet not seeing it, thinking her friend and former neighbor had a point.

She needed to move on.

It was about damned time.

****

Bud, eyes glued to the monitor, watched her stare aimlessly at the ground and tried to assimilate what he heard with what he knew to be true. He *couldn't* understand it, rationalize it, or come to terms with it.

He'd known Ripper a long time. They'd been brothers before they joined the club. They grew up together, went to school together, got into too much trouble together. Then right out of high school, they joined the club together. After that, they worked, partied, and played together. Nothing changed until Em came into Ripper's life.

Things changed then, but not for the bad. Bud and Ripper still worked and partied together although Rip partied with an arm draped over Em's shoulders. Rip and Em spent every second together, except while either was at work and while Em was at school. After just four months, Rip moved her in. At the time, Em was the only old lady at the compound and in the club.

Things changed again when she left him and took his daughter with her. That time, everything changed for the worse. His best friend fell apart, and it'd been like watching Achilles fall.

Rip had a fucked upbringing. Because of it, Rip conditioned himself to withstand those hard knocks life threw his way until nothing fazed him. He became the kind of man who, from a look in his eyes, a man grew to fear. Bud thought nothing would break him. But something did.

He fell.

He broke.

Because of a woman.

After she left, Ripper stayed locked in his room for three days. Bud noticed after the second day since even when Ripper was knee deep in a fight with Em, he came out for air. That second day, Bud knocked on his door. Ripper didn't answer. A day and a half later, Bud saw him in the front lot of the garage sprawled on the floor. Chip hovering over him, slamming his fists into Rip's face. Bud and several others hauled Chip away, and they learned why they hadn't seen Rip for days. Em had left him and left Chip. Chip, thinking Ripper was keeping Em away from him, showed at the compound, found Rip, and beat the living daylights out of him. Chip did this even though the clubs were not on good terms. Rip, so broken, hadn't bothered fighting back.

Ripper spent the next week drunk off his ass. After that, he went back to work at the garage, but he wasn't the same. No denying the defeat in his expression and mannerisms, he was better than before, in the sense that Rip was walking, barely talking, but those eyes were *dead*. She'd done that, made him a living, breathing zombie.

Bud did what any man would do. He gave it time, thinking it's what Rip needed. Months passed, but nothing changed. Rip was a different man. No, not a man, he was a shell. After six months, Bud did what he had to do. He attempted to talk to him. Nothing he said, nothing he did made Ripper forget her, nothing soothed him. Relentlessly, Bud kept at it until Ripper got tired of it and flew off the handle. They fought, dirty. Both ended up with cracked ribs, broken noses, and swollen eyes.

After that, things changed again. Ripper walked, barely talked, and picked fights. His eyes still dead and pissed the fuck off. He was a living, breathing, livid zombie.

All of it—her fault.

Bud knew this. He saw it happen. It's the reason Bud stood there, unmoving, staring at her through the monitor, the reason he couldn't assimilate what he heard. It didn't make any damned sense. The man had broken when she left, and a man didn't break like that knowing the fuck-up was his. A man broke like that when the bitch up and left for no reason, leading Bud to conclude either she was one hell of an actress, or she really believed the shit she'd just spewed.

****

"What the *fuck*?"

Startled, Em jolted, slamming the back of her head under the sink.

Shit, she cursed silently, a habit she grew accustomed to once she had Bree. Cupping the back of her head, she pulled herself out from under the bathroom vanity and turned, meeting Bryce's livid, narrowed, dead gaze.

She'd barely seen him over the last day. After Shawn left, she spent the day with Bree. Bryce had been nowhere to be found. Around nine that night, she saw him again when he tucked Bree into bed and wished her a good night. The next morning, she woke again to find Bree gone, but she found a note on the dresser written in Bryce's messy handwriting stating they'd be back later. She made herself some coffee and breakfast then busied herself tidying up their room. It took a half hour. She then decided on cleaning the common areas in the compound, her way of paying back the club. Starting with the kitchen, she moved on to the living room and game room then finally ended with the bathrooms.

On her first bathroom, one of the ones located downstairs near the living room, cleaning the accumulated dust under the mess under the sink, Bryce found her, startled her causing her to hit her head on the bottom of the sink. It hurt in a way she knew she'd nurse a bump for the next couple of days.

Rubbing her head, she released the rag she held in her other hand, turned fully to him, and waited for him to speak.

"What the fuck are you doing?"

On her knees, head under the bathroom sink, a rag in her hand, and several cleaning supplies next to her, it was quite obvious what she'd been doing. Thinking it a rhetorical question, she didn't respond.

He clenched his jaw, taking a step toward her. "Get off the floor, and tell me what the *fuck* you think you're doing."

Releasing the back of her head, she gripped the top of the sink and stood. So much taller than her, she had to keep her head angled. "I'm cleaning."

The vein in his neck began pulsing, and the air around them went electric. "I got eyes. I know that's what you're doing. What I wanna know is why?"

That's not what he asked, and because he'd only get angrier if she pointed this out, she didn't. "I'm helping out."

He took another menacing step toward her. "*Why*?"

"I told you I wanted to help out since I can't work…"

He closed the distance between them. A mere inch from her, so close she almost felt the warmth of his body. Her head tilted back farther, her gaze locked with his dead one that unique color.

"Are you trying to find ways to get me pissed?"

No, but she was tempted to press her lips against his despite…everything.

"You gonna fuckin' answer *me*?"

She jumped and took a step away, trying to remember what he asked. "I just wanted to help out any way I can."

Feeling warm liquid run down the back of her head, she rubbed it away then spared a glance at her hand. Blood, no wonder it hurt so much. She'd broken the skin. "Shoot."

"Fuck."

She looked at him and watched as he ran his fingers through his hair, eyes dead and staring at the blood on her hand. "It's fine."

Bryce grasped her elbow, tugged her to him, yanked a clean towel off the rack next to him, and pressed it to the back of her head. Close enough his body pressed against hers, so close she saw more clearly the beautiful, harsh angles of his face, the angles seared in her mind. She'd burned them there. She took her fill, knowing after all that time, he was still all she wanted, even knowing what he'd done and why they had to end. Taking a deep breath, she closed her eyes and enjoyed the heat of him against her, his hands in her hair.

Then that warmth was gone, so quickly, so swiftly. Her eyes snapped open. He'd put distance between them, a good two feet, and didn't meet her eyes. His hand extended toward her, holding out the towel he'd pressed against the back of her head. She took it.

"You don't clean up after the brothers." He met her gaze. "Club's been meaning to hire a receptionist at the garage for a while. I talked to the brothers. We voted, and the majority agreed. You got the job if you want it."

Her jaw dropped. He hated her and treated her like shit, but he'd gotten her a job? Oh God, it meant she'd have something to occupy her time, her mind, maybe make a little money so she wouldn't be completely dependent on Bryce, on his club. When Chained dealt with the Falcons, she'd get her own place.

"What's it gonna be?"

So excited at the prospect, she stuttered, "I-I... Yes."

"Office is a fuckin' mess. You're gonna have to deal with the customers, the brothers, make orders—"

He started to sound like he was trying to convince her not to take the job.

"That's fine."

"The pay isn't great."

She smiled. "I don't need much."

"Right."

"I'll give you what I make for—"

He narrowed his eyes and barked, "*No.*"

He got her the job, and she wouldn't pay him back by making him angrier, giving him an excuse to rescind the offer, so she said nothing.

"You start Monday, nine to five. You need anything else to occupy your time, you take care of Bree, cook and clean for her, for yourself. You still wanna do more, you can clean up after me. I won't turn away any of your meals either. You do *not* clean up after anyone else. You do *not* cook for anyone else. We understood?"

He was territorial, always had been, an alpha male thing, a biker thing, but also a Bryce thing. That one thing, she learned, hadn't changed, even though he'd done what he had, even though she ran off with his kid. Some part of him still considered her *his property* even if he didn't want her and treated her like shit. Better than nothing, and yet, it wasn't enough, nowhere near. She wanted more, wanted it all, but she'd never get that.

"Tell me you understand."

"I understand."

He held her gaze for several moments. "Are you planning on making dinner?"

She nodded.

"Should start." His brows furrowed. He hesitated before he spoke again. "Bree hasn't eaten much since she got here."

That look on his face, she'd never seen it but knew what it meant—worry, another reminder of the grave mistake she'd made.

She meant to answer quicker, but guilt choked her. When he cocked his head, she found her voice. "She doesn't have much of an appetite. It's nothing to worry about... Well, I mean it is, but it isn't."

His brows went up. "Care to explain that."

"You'll worry about it. As a parent, you can't help it. I've talked to the doctor about it. He says as long as she's eating regularly, she's fine."

"What kinda fucked doctor said that?" His voice rose.

She smiled softly. "He doesn't recommend force feeding her. He did say I should offer her snacks throughout the day."

He nodded. "She's all set to start school Monday." He looked away and ran a hand through his hair. "What does she need for school?"

"Depends on the teacher, but to be on the safe side, I'd buy crayons, markers, paper, pencils, and a couple of notebooks."

"Got it."

"She'll also need a book bag. I can give you—"

With those words, the ease in which they'd been conversing faded.

His body tensed, eyes hardened. "Not takin' any of your money. Stop offering, all you're managing to do is piss me off."

She nodded.

"Dinner." He then strode away.

Chapter Six

Showered and dressed, Emelia headed down the stairs intent on getting dinner started. Clearing the wall leading into the living room, she heard a voice. A woman's, it was unusual to find a woman, any woman, at the compound on a Wednesday especially considering it was barely six.

The brothers liked women and had plenty to choose from especially those who liked bikers and didn't mind being shared. The brothers called them taps, but from what Em remembered, none hung out at the compound or stayed indefinitely. The brothers liked their privacy, so unless there was a party or unless a woman was an old lady, women didn't stick around. They weren't seen or heard at the compound. Plain and simple. Knowing this, Emelia figured either that rule changed or the woman, whoever she was, meant something to one of the brothers.

"Bree," the woman said, softly.

Em stiffened and stayed out of sight. After several seconds, she peeked from behind the wall and spotted a petite brunette.

She knew from one look the woman wasn't a tap. First, the brunette didn't dress like one. Instead of a miniskirt and tiny tank, the usual dress code for taps, the woman wore a pair of well-fitted skinny jeans, peach-colored blouse, and a pair of platform sandals.

Em couldn't see her face because the woman was at an angle, looking down at Bree, the woman's loose, dark hair falling past her shoulder blocking her face. Second, the way the woman spoke to Bree and handed her a bag her daughter opened and pulled out a frilly pink dress, a dress Em knew Bree would love.

Em's gaze veered to Bryce, sitting on the couch a foot away from where Bree and the woman stood. His stare on them, a smile spread across his face, looking proud to have his daughter and the woman making friends.

Chest clenching, stomach tightening, a feeling of lightheadedness came over Em. She couldn't move even if she wanted to, couldn't peel her eyes away from the perfect picture they painted.

She didn't know why she hadn't thought of it before, why it never occurred to her he'd moved on. Maybe her mangled mind protecting her heart refused to acknowledge the possibility.

Five years had passed. At thirty-four, maybe he'd changed and decided to settle down. Maybe he liked to have a steady woman, like he had her, and still liked to party on the side. Or maybe, just maybe, he loved the brunette. Maybe Em just hadn't been enough for him. Maybe the brunette was.

Her heart squeezed so tight she couldn't breathe. Of their own accord, her eyes welled.

The woman shifted. Her head shot up, and her hazel gaze landed on Em. The woman, Bryce's woman, was stunning. Em didn't know why it made a difference, beautiful or not, it wasn't her.

The magnitude of everything Em felt nearly knocked her off her feet. Another slap in the face, another reminder of how much Em cared. Despite what he'd done, despite the fact she left, she still loved him. She never stopped.

"Hi."

Shit. She wanted to disappear, right at that moment. "Hi."

Smiling widely, the woman closed the distance between them until a mere foot away. "I'm Allie. You must be Em."

Allie, the beautiful brunette, further proved she was nice, easy-going, and had confidence, the type of natural confidence that came when a woman had a good life, a good upbringing, and had always felt secure in herself. It's how she'd so easily been able to introduce herself to her man's ex and the mother of his daughter, seemingly without a care in the world.

"Yes."

"Mommy, look!"

Thankful for the reprieve, Em slid her stare to Bree, holding the pretty, frilly dress over herself, the dress her father's girlfriend gave her.

"It's beautiful," she said, meaning it. "Did you say 'thank you?'"

Bree nodded.

"She did, but there's no need."

Of course, the gorgeous, kind woman would say that.

"Allie!"

Allie turned just in time to lean over and catch a small girl around Bree's age as she crashed into her. The girl with dark-brown hair, wearing a pair of shorts, pink T-shirt, and mary-jane's, wrapped her arms around Allie, hugging her tight.

Laughing, Allie did the same. "Hey, Della, how was school?"

The girl didn't get a chance to answer. Trig, one of the brothers, strode into the living room. "Del, you keep running into Allie like that, you're gonna knock her off her feet."

The girl, Della, faced Trig. When she turned back to Allie, her cheeks had gone rosy. "Sorry, Allie."

Allie tucked the girl's hair behind her ear. "Nothing to be sorry about."

Trig closed the distance between himself, Allie, and Della. He then cupped the back of Allie's head, dragged her to him, leaned down, and pressed his mouth to Allie's.

Em's lips parted. Her gaze shifted to Bryce, sitting on the couch. His eyes glued to the TV. She looked at Allie and Trig in time to see Trig trail his mouth down Allie's neck.

"Missed you, baby."

He said it loud enough Em heard, loud enough Bryce had to have heard too, and Trig said it easily like he didn't care who heard.

Allie drew away from Trig and met his gaze. "Missed you, too, honey. How was your day?"

Trig smiled. "Better now."

Oh, God. Thank God. Allie wasn't Bryce's but Trig's. A weight lifted off her chest, Em took a deep breath.

Trig looked down at Della. "You met Bree yet?"

Della shook her head then introductions were made. Em learned Della was Trig's niece, just eleven months older than Bree. Come Monday, they'd attend the same school. Bree, still only four was in pre-K,

Della in kindergarten.

Em's gaze cut to her right as another brunette strode in, taller with green eyes wearing a pair of jeans and a fitted top that accentuated her small pregnant belly. In her hands, she held a casserole dish covered with aluminum foil. Clearly, she wasn't a tap either. Who she belonged to revealed a moment later when a very annoyed looking Cuss appeared behind her, holding another large casserole dish. Five years ago, Cuss had been a prospect along with Trig and Army, and Cuss had a reputation—the biker who could bed any woman with one look. Now, he tailed this beautiful woman, not a tap, and clearly pregnant.

His jaw hardened. "Baby girl."

The brunette stopped abruptly, smiled, and turned to him. "Thomas."

He lifted a brow. "Why didn't you wait for *me*?"

"Because I can carry a tray of lasagna," she shot back. From her voice, Emelia knew the brunette teased.

Cuss, aka Thomas, narrowed his eyes, snaked his arm around the brunette's waist, and tugged her to him until the dish she held in her hands hit his chest. "You're treadin' on thin ice, baby girl."

The brunette got on the tips of her toes and leaned up to press her lips against his. Being too short for his more than six-foot-tall frame, she waited.

Cuss's gaze went from her eyes to her lips then back to her stare. Finally, he slipped his arm from her waist to the back of her neck, clutching her as he simultaneously leaned down and pressed his mouth against hers. A long kiss, long enough he released her neck and removed the tray she held in her grasp. "Don't push your luck, or I'll be carrying your ass home."

The brunette turned and met Em's stare, making her realize she'd been staring.

She closed the distance between them and extended her hand. "Hi, I'm Tiffany."

Em glanced down at it then shook it. "Emelia."

The pretty brunette, Tiffany, smiled. "I know. Nice to meet you."

Before she responded, Tiffany turned and greeted Allie, Trig, Bryce, Della, and finally introduced herself to Bree, making friends with Della.

Taking the chance to leave, Emelia forced a smile. "Nice to meet you both, I should go. I have to get dinner started."

"No need. Tiff made lasagna. Trust me when I say you do not want to miss out on her lasagna. I guarantee it's better than any lasagna you've ever had." Allie smiled.

"I don't know about that, but I do know there's plenty for you, Bree, and Rip," Tiffany added.

Emelia's gaze went to Bryce, staring her way with those dead eyes. He hesitated a moment before shrugged. Losing sight of his eyes, she met Tiffany's. "Thanks. Can I help you with anything?"

"Lasagna's done. I just need to put it in the oven and let it heat, but we're making bruschetta and salad. You're more than welcome to help us with that."

She nodded and followed Allie, Tiffany, and Cuss into the kitchen. Large and open concept, countertops lined the entirety and included a breakfast counter area leading into a dining room.

Cuss loaded the lasagnas in the oven then kissed Tiffany square on the lips before he walked to the fridge and grabbed three beers, presumably for Trig,

Bryce, and himself then left. Em turned to meet Tiffany and Allie's gazes and waited for instruction. She never got them. Instead, she heard a very familiar voice.

"So it's true."

Em closed her eyes tightly and took a breath before turning to meet Mia's gaze. A brunette with curves and spunk, Mia had started dating Stone a few months before Em left, but Stone didn't hesitate to claim her. For those few months, Mia and she had been the only old ladies around. Naturally, they became good friends.

When Em left, not only didn't she tell Bryce or Chip, she never told Mia. She wanted to, but telling Mia or calling her after she settled in New Mexico was a risk, one she couldn't take. Staring at Mia then, she couldn't help but feel guilty. She swallowed to fight the emotion.

"When I heard, I couldn't believe it."

She didn't know what to say to that, so Em said nothing.

"It's been a long time, Em."

Finding her voice, she nodded. "Yeah, it has."

"Met Bree. She looks just like you." Mia's gaze traveled from the top of her head to her toes then back up again. "She's a replica, except, of course, for her eyes."

This, she knew. Again, she said nothing.

"Congrats."

"Thanks."

"See you've met Allie and Tiff."

Em nodded.

"Things have changed quite a bit here. I'll fill you in."

Not what she expected her to say. She expected

Mia to be angry, like Bryce, like the brothers, like everyone except Allie and Tiffany, though she hadn't expected them to be nice to her either. A surprise, a very pleasant one. She meant to say something but then another woman, a blonde with green eyes, wearing a pair of hip hugging jeans and a Harley tank, walked in.

Smiling, the blonde closed the distance between them. "Em, right? It's so nice to meet you. I'm Lynn." Then the blonde, Lynn, did the strangest thing. She hugged her.

Shocking, and nice, so nice, Em couldn't help but return the hug. "It's nice to meet you, too."

Lynn pulled away. "Sorry, I'm a hugger."

"It's…ah…okay."

"Still drinking beer?"

Emelia looked at Mia, now standing by the fridge. She nodded. Mia grabbed four light beers then set them on the counter and uncapped them. She handed them out to Allie, Lynn, and Em, keeping one for herself.

"Thanks."

Mia nodded then shifted to Tiffany, standing by the counter next to the sink chopping romaine lettuce. "You should do that while you're sitting, so Cuss doesn't come in here and bitch."

Tiffany turned then, looking resigned, shook her head and did exactly as Mia suggested.

"Now that we have drinks and Tiff's settled, you and me should talk." Mia's comment directed at Em.

Mia didn't give her a chance to respond. Grabbing her hand, she pulled her to the other end of the room, where the dining room should be, except there wasn't a table or chairs, just several sofas, the same raggedy ones that had been there five years before.

Mia took a seat, tugging her down beside her. "Don't know why you left, but I always assumed it had something to do with Chained and Hell Ryders being at odds."

Just like Mia: no fuss, no muss, and blunt to a fault. Still, Em, wondering why these women welcomed her into their lives as if she hadn't left Bryce and taken his daughter without so much as telling him, hadn't expected it. She appreciated them for it but couldn't confide in them, not even Mia, with her reasons for leaving. Besides, the real reason, she couldn't even say out loud.

After a long moment of silence, Mia shrugged. "Right. Well, I had to try." She took a sip of her beer. "I'm not mad, Em. I'm not trying to play you either. I know why you didn't tell me back then. I also know there's a lot more to the story than meets the eye, and I know this because I know you. Maybe I'm stubborn, but I refuse to believe I was wrong about you. You left. I know you had a good reason even though for the life of me, I haven't been able to figure it out."

God, that made her feel good and sad. She'd left a good friend behind. Not hard to guess then that the other old ladies had welcomed her because of Mia.

"Anyway…" Mia went on as if she'd said nothing significant. "As you can see, things have changed quite a bit around here. I married Stone three years ago now. Lynn and Wild are hitched too. Just recently, Trig met Allie, who's Army's sister. The brothers call her 'Classy,' except Cuss who calls her 'Miracle.' You want a good laugh, whenever he does, look at Trig. It pisses him off. Allie and Trig are married too. Just recent, Tiff and Cuss got hitched. Watch them closely too, and you'll get a laugh because ever since he knocked her up, he's been overly protective…"

Mia lifted a brow. "Well, you know bikers… When they claim a woman, they're a bit overbearing. After finding out Tiff was pregnant, Cuss kicked it up a couple of notches. It's annoying for her, but funny and amusing to the rest of us." Mia chuckled.

Em knew that. Bryce had been overbearing and jealous. She never minded it. It'd been one of the things he did that made her believe he loved her even though he never said the words.

Em took her first sip of beer, wondering if Cuss had ever cheated. Then she wondered if Stone had, if Wild or Trig had. Maybe. Then again, maybe not. After all, they'd married their women, made it official, law-binding. They probably said the words, too.

"Em?"

She'd been too lost in her thoughts. Meeting Mia's gaze, she finally said, "Good to know."

"Hey…"

That simple word, the soft way Mia said it, Em realized she'd let her guard down.

"You need a friend, I'm here."

She swallowed, took another sip of beer, and nodded.

"Come on…" Mia stood from the couch. "You need to get to know the rest of the girls."

Em stood.

"Listen to us talk about crap, and you'll forget whatever's bothering you, even if just for a second."

Turned out, Mia was right. She listened to Lynn, Allie, Tiff, and Mia talk about everything and anything, nothing too important or heavy. She enjoyed the easy camaraderie between the women and partook in the conversations. For a couple of hours, she let herself believe she was just another woman enjoying a drink with friends, and she forgot.

****

"Daddy, what's this called?"

Ripper drew his head from under the hood of a '67 Chevy and met his daughter's inquisitive stare. She sat on a chair he'd pulled out of the office and set just beside him.

Bree wanted to go to work with him. He'd made it happen. Quite a picture they painted with her beside him, wearing a pink t-shirt, jean shorts, and a pair of sneakers, holding a tool in her hand.

He smiled. "It's a wrench."

Her brows drew together. "It's very dirty." She looked at it then back at him. "It's greasy, and so are you, Daddy."

He chuckled out loud. He'd done it and not just imagined it. Several of his brothers, working around the garage, halted and looked his way. Not wanting to get pissed, he ignored them. He didn't hide his amusement after that either. It'd been so long since he'd laughed, he'd forgotten how it sounded, and how good it felt.

"Yeah, baby. Comes with the job."

"Why don't you clean your tools? Then you wouldn't be dirty."

So logical, that got another chuckle out of him. "You're right, but then we'd be spending a lot of time cleaning tools instead of fixing cars."

That seemed to settle her curiosity. As she set the wrench down, he went back to work.

A moment later, he heard, "Can you tell me a story

about you and Mommy?"

He lifted his head so fast he banged the back of it against the hood of the car. Biting back a curse, he straightened and looked her way. "What?"

"Mommy tells me stories about you. Maybe you can tell me stories about her."

Emelia told their daughter stories about him? He could just imagine what stories she told. When they met, Hell Ryders was involved in dirty dealings—running guns and drugs across state borders. They partnered with Chained to do just that. It's how he met Emelia. A couple of years later, the club got clean and severed ties with Chained.

None of this, he was proud of. He'd been one of the brothers who voted to end that shit for good, but it didn't mean Emelia would excuse it. Hell, she ran away and hooked up with a cop because she hadn't thought he'd make a good father. Even if she never told Bree, Emelia couldn't have had anything good to say about him after she left him.

How badly he wished he could hate her.

Fighting anger, he clenched his jaw, took a deep breath then schooled his voice before he spoke. "Go hang out with your Uncle Trig for a sec, 'kay?"

Bree, picking up on the sudden change in him, tensed. He supposed as much as he tried to hide it, he couldn't. Plus, she was a smart kid. He already learned that, which meant he needed to get better at concealing his anger.

Slowly, almost hesitantly, she nodded. He watched her go and waited until she reached Trig, standing near the office talking to Army. When Trig spotted her then him, Rip lifted his chin. Trig nodded, understanding his silent command. Only then did Ripper walk to the back end of the garage through the door leading into the compound and let his fury spill. By the time he searched her room and his, the living room, dining room, kitchen, and found her nowhere in sight, his rage had spiked, making his blood boil. Tearing through the compound on a run, he finally spotted her inside the laundry room. Her back to him, bent over at the waist retrieving clothes from inside the washer. Just the sight of her rear in those tight jeans made him hard.

Seeing red, he fisted his palms until his knuckles cracked. Taking several steps quickly, a second before he reached her, he collided with a mass of muscle.

He sliced his gaze away from her and met Strike's eyes, blocking him from getting to her. "What. The. Fuck. Brother."

Face impassive, Strike took a deep breath. "Gotta calm down, Rip."

Unbelievable. His brother sticking up for her, the woman who left him and took his kid? Why? Was she trying to land another brother? Had Strike fallen for her games? Emelia, the only woman he ever loved, with his brother?

His stomach turned. Clenching his jaw, he narrowed his eyes and shoved Strike off him. Strike stumbled back, almost bumping into Em, now facing them and watching, her body stiff, face pale and growing paler by the second.

"She's off limits, *brother*. Fucked her for a long time means she's off limits. Mother of my kid means she's off limits. She's *mine*."

Strike's face hardened. "Not interested, *brother*."

Thank fuck. He'd have to kill him. No one would

have her, especially one of his brothers. She didn't want him. He'd never have her again, but he had Bree now. Em would never leave Bree, so Em would always be around, and he'd make sure no man ever had her.

"Then get the fuck out of my way."

Strike took a step in his direction. "I will as soon as you calm down."

Mimicking him, he took a step forward. "None of your business."

"It is if you're gonna hit her."

Was Strike out of his fucking mind? He'd never hit a woman. Why his brother thought that he had no clue. *Shit*. He must look enraged, that's the only reason his brother would step in, to prevent him from doing something he'd regret. Still, Strike knew him better than that. Didn't he?

Through gritted teeth, he took a deep breath. "I'd *never* hit a woman."

Strike held his glare for several moments before he walked away. Ripper met Emelia's gaze. Just one look at her pale face and rigid posture and all that fury resurfaced.

The Emelia he'd known hadn't been afraid of anything, not snakes, not guns, not club wars, nothing... And there she stood, trembling, pallid, and terrified. Knowing him, she had a right after all she'd done. But still, it didn't sit well with him. The old Emelia didn't cry, didn't cower, didn't scare. She wasn't meek or soft spoken. She fought back and dirty. This Emelia was a fake, an amazing actress. Trying to save her ass, she put on an act. He had to give her credit. She was good at it.

Closing the distance between them with just one

powerful step, he gripped her arm. "What. Did. You. Tell. Her?"

"I… W-what?" Her voice quivered.

"What did you tell her?"

Her brows furrowed. "Who?"

"*Bree*!"

She shook her head. "I didn't—"

He leaned into her. "She told me you told her stories about *me*. Now, I wanna know what stories you told her."

Her eyes widened. "I…I…"

"Fuckin' tell me!"

"I told her about us, how we met. I told her how you used to take me on rides every Sunday. That we used to eat take-out Wednesday nights and hang out with the club on Fridays. I told her you took me to eat at a fancy steakhouse every anniversary…"

"What *else*?"

"Um…" She shook her head. "I-I…swear Bryce, I didn't say anything bad about you… Why would I?"

Why? Because she fucking left him! Before he pointed this out, she spoke.

"If I had bad-mouthed you, why would she love you so much?"

Shit. She had a point there. He didn't know much about kids, but it didn't take a genius to see how much Bree loved him. He knew that the minute she ran up to him at that park, so excited to see a low-life like him. It wasn't logical that Bree, even after such few days, would be so attached to him unless Emelia talked about him, told her stories. Obviously, she showed her pictures, too. Bree recognized him even though he now sported a permanent five o'clock shadow.

He dropped his head, stare shooting to the laundry basket just behind her. At the top of the pile, the black T-shirt he wore yesterday, the shirt he left lying on his bathroom floor. He'd jumped to conclusions, and she took the time to pick up after him and do his laundry. His gaze snapped up and landed on his hand, gripping her arm. He released her immediately and noticed the red marks he left.

He was a dick. He didn't deserve happiness, didn't deserve shit. Maybe it's why she left with his kid without telling him. Chest clenching, guilt clogging his throat, he didn't bother looking back at her. He couldn't. He just walked away.

Chapter Seven

Emelia didn't start working at the garage until Monday, but that didn't mean she'd wait until Monday to start.

She and Bree had been at the compound for less than a week. During that week, she spent most of her time cleaning, cooking, and of course, taking care of Bree. Bree, though, spent most of her time with Bryce. Bryce didn't mind having his four-year-old daughter follow him and ask questions constantly. Emelia wanted to give them time together and only interrupted them when necessary, like when Bree needed to eat, bathe, or when it was bedtime.

Spending the last several days cleaning not only after herself but Bree and Bryce, she had nothing left to do and wanted to get a head start on her new job. Early that morning after making Bree and Bryce breakfast and cleaning up after them, she headed into the garage and scanned it, looking for Bree. She exhaled heavily noticing Bree and Bryce were both gone.

Over the course of the last several days, he took Bree out often. Never did he find the need to tell her when or where they planned to go or when they'd return. This bothered Emelia. She trusted Bryce implicitly with Bree, but Bryce wouldn't understand her need to know where Bree was at all times. In order to keep the peace, especially after yesterday's incident in the laundry room, she hadn't mentioned this bothered her.

She entered the office through the door leading from inside the garage. The office was quite large and messy. A dark counter divided the room in half. Behind it, a desk and two computers. Behind that, facing a window was another counter with a printer and scanner. In front of the main counter, three fold-out chairs. Windows lined the walls with a clear view of the garage as well as the lot outside. Helplessly, she skimmed the lot but didn't spot Bryce or Bree, nor did she spot his SUV. She tamped down the urge to call Bryce or more likely, pester one of the brothers to give her Bryce's number since she still didn't have it.

Pushing her thoughts aside, she got to work. First, she tackled the mess on the desk, the mass of papers and receipts. Receipts of signed orders delivered, she separated by month. Receipts for food orders and deliveries, she put aside and made a mental note to ask if they were needed or could be thrown out. She also found a series of bills. Some for the garage, others were for customers. She separated those into two piles and made another pile for pay stubs, a separate one for messages—most not dated—and the last one for miscellaneous items. After tidying the desk, she opened the two-drawer file cabinet next to it. Empty, except for an unopened box of file folders. It seemed someone had once thought about filing documents and never got to it. Smiling, she pulled out the box, opened it, and began labeling folders.

Finishing this, she grabbed her phone to check the time. Well past noon, she headed out to the garage, looking again for Bree and Bryce. Still gone. In the kitchen, she made three foot-long subs, one to share with Bree and two for Bryce. She ate her half of one standing over the counter then labeled the others and set them in the fridge.

Returning to the garage with cleaning supplies in hand, she did what she always did, perused the area looking for Bree. No Bree. No Bryce. Back inside the office, she cleaned. It took a lot of time scrubbing to get the grease stains off the counter, computer, and floors, but she managed it. Bent at the waist wiping the door leading into the garage, someone pushed open the front door. Straightening, she turned and found a pair of chocolate dark eyes glued to her ass. Handsome in a not so obvious way, though she knew from just a look at him, he thought the world of himself. His gaze raked her from top to bottom and rested on her breasts.

She cleared her throat and crossed her arms. "Can I help you?"

His stare pierced hers. He took two steps toward her closing the distance between them. In what she assumed he thought subtle, he pushed up his suit jacket to flash his expensive watch. Not like she needed the clue. He looked loaded. The expensive suit, the "I'm-better-than-anyone-because-I've-got-money" look on his face. The not-so-indirect hint didn't do him any good. Maybe if she was that type of woman, the type who didn't care about the character of a man as long as he had money. Maybe if she wasn't still in love with another man.

He took another step, too close for her liking. "Yes, I have a flat tire and need it repaired."

She hated to insult the man, considering he was a potential customer, but she needed space between them.

Granted, if she wasn't in love with another man and had been interested before, she'd be turned off now. Coming on strong and making it obvious he liked what he saw, and all of it made her uncomfortable.

She smiled a fake smile then put down her rag, wiped her hands on her shirt, and turned toward the desk. Behind the counter, she picked up the phone and connected to the garage.

"Yeah?" Cuss.

"There's a customer who has a flat tire. Can you handle it?"

"Give me a couple of minutes. I got it."

She hung up, silently wishing Cuss had been literal when he said a couple of minutes, and met the customer's gaze. "Someone will be right with you."

Smiling a predatory smile, he rested his elbows on the counter and leaned toward her, making it so that he was again too close. "Your name?"

She straightened putting distance between them. "Emelia."

"I'm Rick Grady. You may have heard of me."

No, she hadn't, and she didn't care to hear about him either.

"I own several clubs in Santa Rosa."

She kept her stare level with his, and her face blank, hoping he'd get the hint.

He didn't. He leaned in farther, his gaze gravitating toward her chest. "You know what I'm wondering?"

She didn't respond. First, she didn't care but couldn't tell him. Second, she hoped her silence clued him onto the fact she wasn't interested whether he owned one club or fifty. Last, she really wanted to slap him. He may think the way he checked her out was a compliment, but to the average woman, it made her feel cheap. She couldn't slap him though because she couldn't get fired before she officially started work.

"I'm wondering why a beautiful woman like you is cleaning a garage owned by bikers."

None of his business, but again, she couldn't say this. Instead, she lied. "Because my husband is one of those bikers, I'd rather work here, close to him where I can spend time with him and our daughter."

His eyes widened. When he recovered, he blanketed the shock from his face, smiled another predatory smile, reached into his pocket, and pulled out a card. "A woman like you could get far with just her looks. Like I said, I own several clubs. I'm always looking for beautiful women." He slid the card toward her.

Well, she had to give him credit. He had balls of steel. She'd send him to hell. Screw the consequences. Before she got the chance, the door to the front of the office slammed open. Startled, she jumped, bringing her hand to her pounding heart.

Bryce strode in. His dead, feral eyes glued to them. He looked hot, even furious. His legs encased in a pair of jeans, a well-worn T-shirt tight across his chest. His cut over it. He'd cut his dark-blond hair, faded it on the sides, though still unruly at top. He'd done nothing to the permanent five-o'clock shadow. She was glad. Though he never had it before, it looked good and made her wonder how it'd feel if he kissed her. Of all the things about Bryce, she missed his lips the most. He did wondrous things with them. With the beard, she imagined it'd get better.

The man, Predator Rick Whatever, turned slightly

to look at Bryce and didn't cower. She supposed men with money were used to getting what they wanted and weren't scared of much. It was stupid not to be alarmed though. No one messed with a biker from Hell Ryders, ever. The club may be clean, but that didn't mean the brothers were law-abiding citizens. They may make good money at the garage, but Em doubted there wasn't more going on.

In a little under a week, she'd seen the brothers take off at night and noticed they didn't come back until early morning. A few days ago, she'd been hidden from view, cleaning the kitchen after one of the meals she prepared and overheard several brothers, one of whom she knew, Mellow, talking about a "guard" out of town. Leaving the kitchen only ten minutes later, she caught Marcus, the president, hand over an envelope to Mellow, who opened it just enough to give her a glimpse inside—money, lots of it. She didn't know what a "guard" meant but figured it wasn't entirely legal. No one got that amount of cash for something legal.

Posture tense, eyes glaring, Bryce closed the distance between himself and Rick, coming to a stop a foot from him. "She's off fuckin' limits, asshole."

Rick, still foolishly looking unafraid, straightened and smiled smugly. "No one's off limits."

Shit. That one statement would finally unhinge the anger Bryce tried so hard to control. It did. He snapped, swinging his right fist so fast Rick didn't see it coming. Bryce connected with Rick's jaw. A smack sounded then a thump when the idiot went down.

Just as Cuss, Army, and Trig rushed through the side door into the office, she ran around the counter and looked down at what could've been a customer, his jaw swelling, a bruise starting to show. She didn't feel sorry for him. He kind of deserved it.

Rick planted a hand behind him, sat up with difficulty, and spit out blood. "Are you fucking crazy?"

Bryce went at him again. If Army hadn't stepped in front of him just in time, he would've landed another punch.

Cuss grabbed Rick by the arm and hauled him up. "Gotta go."

"I came for a service."

"And now you're leaving without that service," Trig said.

"What the fuck?" Rick spit out more blood. He rubbed his face then looked around the room. "I see." Glaring at Bryce, he unwisely said, "You can't handle a little competition."

Bryce launched himself again. Army, standing in front of him, took the brunt of the impact. Trig grabbed Bryce around the waist and held him back.

Cuss, shoulders squared, stepped in front of Rick. "Out!"

Stupid, predator Rick said, "I'm pressing charges."

"You aren't pressing shit 'cause you do, you're gonna find yourself in a real shitty situation. *You* don't know who you're messing with. No amount of money can save you from the shit storm we'll throw your way, so take this piece of advice. Get gone. Don't come back. Don't cause more problems 'cause you do, you'll fuckin' regret it."

Rick exhaled. His stare hit hers. "You change your mind. I guarantee you'll—"

The idiot barely got the last word out before Bryce

slammed into him, knocking him to the floor. Trig, who'd released Bryce, allowed this. Bryce landed three punches before Army, Trig, and Cuss hauled him off. By this point, Emelia realized belatedly Strike had walked in and was now helping a bloodied and bruised Rick to his feet. After Strike pulled Rick out the door, she felt it. The air around the room went static making it hard to breathe. She met Bryce's gaze, that strange blue-green piercing, feral, and dead. She didn't know why it shocked her. Maybe a part of her hoped since he defended her, he cared about her a tiny bit. A part of her hoped he would've asked her if she was okay. Instead, she got that fury, that coldness no different from any other time he looked at her.

"*Out!*"

Army, Trig, and Cuss hesitated only a moment before they left, leaving them alone. She held his stare, waited, watching him breathe in and out quickly.

Finally, he walked toward her, closing the distance in two strides. He grabbed her arm, hauled her toward him, and released her. "I'm protecting you. That means your ass depends on *me*. That means what I say, goes, and I'm saying you're off limits so that fuckin' means you're off limits."

"I wasn't—"

"I don't wanna hear your bullshit. I'm protecting you means you belong to *me*. You're *mine*. No one's getting a piece of you. Do *not* tempt me. Do *not* rile me."

She didn't say a word but waited for what seemed like endless moments. The entire time that rage in him strengthening.

"No! Daddy! Don't be mad at Mommy!"

He froze, eyes horrified, face turning into a mask of anguish.

Watching him, knowing he thought he just lost his daughter, the daughter he'd just begun to get to know, her chest tightened. She couldn't stand to see that look, so she tore her gaze away. Her head snapped to her daughter just as Bree barreled into her legs. She wrapped an arm around Bree's shoulders and squatted down to her level. Bree's eyes wide and filling with tears.

"Shh…shh…honey." She pulled Bree in for a hug. When she drew away, she met her daughter's stare. "Daddy wasn't mad at me."

"I…I saw…" Her tears fell.

Tugging her daughter's blonde hair behind her ear, she said softly, "Bree, Daddy wasn't mad at me. He's just angry because someone wasn't very nice to me, so he's angry at the situation."

Bree peered at Bryce. Emelia followed her daughter's gaze. He was still frozen in place, that same anguished look marring his face.

"Daddy?"

Finally, Bryce met his daughter's eyes.

Knowing he hadn't heard what she said, Em repeated it. "Isn't that right, Bryce? You weren't mad at me. You were angry someone wasn't nice to me?"

His face changed, eyes widening. Then his stare hit hers, and for a brief moment, she saw something shine in his eyes, something not dead, something that looked a lot like gratitude.

He cleared his throat. "I wasn't angry at your mom, baby."

She peered at Bree. "See, Bree? Your dad wants to

protect us all the time. He wasn't here when someone wasn't nice so he couldn't protect me, and that made him angry. Do you understand?"

Bree hesitated then looked to her dad. "Did you make it better, Daddy?"

His brows quirked. "Huh?"

"Did you make Mommy feel better?"

"He did." She answered, knowing he wouldn't. Needing to change the subject, she asked, "Did you have lunch?"

Bree nodded. "Daddy and me had pizza."

Bryce often took their daughter out for lunch, usually at a restaurant where they could get a good meal. On a Friday, though, she wouldn't harp on Bryce feeding Bree pizza for lunch. Sparing a glance at her watch, she realized the day had flown by.

The door to the front of the office parted. At the threshold, Strike appeared. "Gotta talk, Rip."

That meant business, her cue to get Bree and go. She hadn't finished cleaning the office, but it looked a lot better than it had. She'd finish the rest tomorrow, a Saturday, but she didn't have much to do anyway.

She stood and grabbed Bree's hand. "Come on, baby. Your dad needs to get some work done."

About to reach the door leading into the garage, Strike said, "Office looks good, Em."

She looked over her shoulder, met his gaze, and nodded, giving him a small smile. Then she and Bree walked out the door.

****

Ripper watched Emelia, her hand in Bree's, stride out of sight, wondering why she lied to their daughter, why she lied for him. She had the perfect chance to do what she'd done once before—tear his daughter away from him. Yet she hadn't.

She was a beautiful woman, a mother but still single regardless of the fact he was protecting her. It'd only be natural for a man to hit on her, and she had the right to flirt with whoever she wanted, except he *couldn't* allow it. Even after all she did to him, he wanted her. He may never have her again, but it didn't make a difference. He was a dick, an asshole, a bastard, and it meant if he couldn't have her, no one would.

He hadn't planned on attacking the rich douche. Obviously, if he thought it through, he wouldn't've shown how much he still cared, the reason he took it out on her too. He hated he still cared so much. He despised he showed her just how much. All of it made him angry, furious in a way he lost all self-preservation and control, forgetting Emelia didn't belong to him, forgetting his daughter stood just outside the door.

All was said and done now though, and still, he wondered why Emelia had done what she had. Since he found her, he'd done nothing but treat her like shit. Maybe she deserved it, yet it didn't mean he didn't deserve her treating him like shit right back.

"Rip, gotta show you something."

Snapped out of his thoughts, he shifted and met Strike's eyes, standing at the threshold leading from the outside lot into the office. Strike didn't wait for him to respond. He strode away, the door slamming shut on his way out.

Ripper followed him into the compound, down two long hallways until they reached the surveillance room, in between the conference room where they held club meetings and Prez's office. A large desk with different pedestals sat in the middle of the room. On those platforms, twenty plus monitors, one larger positioned in the center to review camera angles and video then smaller ones set beside and around it displaying real-time footage of various parts of the compound, garage, and both lots, front and back.

Strike typed on the keyboard. Rip waited. Then without turning his way, Strike stood aside as a video played.

She came to view, bent at the waist in those tiny-ass shorts cleaning the door leading into the garage. What a great view. She had a nice ass, always had. Just one look on a monitor got him hard.

Damn it. He shifted to glare at Strike. Thank God, his brother hadn't been looking at the screen but at him.

"Watch."

He wanted to punch Strike too but knew nothing good would come of it. He held it together by telling himself Strike wouldn't piss him off on purpose. Finally, he focused on the screen just in time to see the bastard walk into the office, blatantly checking her out. He watched the whole thing and watching it made him feel like a bigger dick than he was.

Emelia hadn't been flirting. She didn't want shit to do with the bastard even if the guy had money. The first chance she had, she put distance between them, and then, she lied to him, told him she was married. The jerk just continued to insist. It was irrational, but he was glad he snapped. The man disrespected *her*. It wasn't Rip's job to defend her from rich assholes, from anyone, but he still felt the *need*, as if she never left, as if she still belonged to him.

That was fucked. More fucked, he was

undoubtedly a bigger dick than the rich asshole and deserved to get his ass handed to him too. Maybe it's why Strike showed him the video, to make him realize he needed to stop being a dick all the time, especially to her. What was done was done even if she never apologized, and the way he treated her wasn't helping because nothing would ever change the fact that he lost years with Bree.

For whatever messed up reason Emelia left, she made sure his daughter knew who her father was, which didn't make any sense. Why take Bree away then tell her stories about him? Who knew? But he had Bree now. He *needed* to leave the past behind and move on—for Bree. She deserved parents who didn't hate each other's living guts, a father who didn't treat her mother like shit. Most importantly, he couldn't afford to have Bree catch him being a dick to her mother again.

Past a certain point, Emelia wouldn't continue to lie for him, and Bree, his smart girl, would eventually realize no matter what her mom said, he was a dick, the reason he didn't need Strike to show him the video. Bree walking in on him being cruel to her mother was deterrent enough.

It could never happen again. It could cost him Bree, and he couldn't lose her. Ever.

Guilt clogging his throat, he glared at Strike then without a word, walked away.

****

Friday nights at the compound were party nights. Granted, for some of them, it was a party every day, but Fridays, in particular, all the brothers got together, drank, smoked, and fucked.

He always loved Friday nights. That love started

129

when he was just a prospect running errands. He loved them more when the club made him an official member. When he met Emelia, they got even better. His nights included her, always. He drank, smoked, and partied with her. Because he only wanted her, he never missed the random fucks. That changed when she left.

He didn't party like he used to, didn't have it in him because he couldn't get any fun out of anything anymore. He drank and smoked alone in his room, watching some bullshit on TV. It took him months before he could even look at another woman. No matter how hot, stacked, easy…all he saw—Emelia's face.

He got over that in time then started enjoying his Friday nights a little more. In the sense that he drank and smoked with his brothers and fucked everything in sight, always taps. The average woman was afraid of him. He knew it and figured it was because he wore anger like a shield. He didn't care. Taps were better anyway. He didn't have to try, and they expected nothing. A man like him had nothing to give anyway.

A Friday night, another in the many, and once again, things had changed. He could have a drink or two or ten. He could smoke a blunt to take the edge off, but he wouldn't do any of that because, quite frankly, he didn't feel like it. He wanted to spend time with his daughter, but after what happened that afternoon, he needed to burn off some steam, so he went for a ride.

The ride didn't soothe him, so he went to the gym and worked out his frustration, his guilt on the treadmill. That had been hours ago; now, he knew the truth. He didn't need to burn off steam. He just needed to find the strength to face her—his beautiful baby girl, Bree. A part of him feared she'd figured it out on her own—he wasn't worth her devotion. A part of him thought maybe her mother had finally snapped and taken away what he didn't deserve—a daughter.

Sitting on his bed, his hands in his freshly cut hair, he took a deep breath, stood, strode out his bedroom door, and across the hall. Turning the knob, he walked in closing the door behind him. He hadn't bothered to look up until then, catching sight of her. Not who he'd come for, but his gaze naturally gravitated there. Emelia exited the steam-filled bathroom. Her hair knotted at the top of her head. A towel wrapped around her. His body responded like it always did, tenfold.

She looked stunning, flawless. She didn't even realize it, never had. At least that hadn't changed.

Stare glued to her, body begging for her, he just stood there…like a zombie. He couldn't move, couldn't manage a word. It was too easy to picture her naked, just too hard to stop staring, imagining she was there for him like he'd done so many times over the years.

It was fucked.

He was fucked.

Luckily, in no time, that beautiful face of hers turned his way. The minute she did, his body locked.

"Bryce?"

He didn't respond. Instead, his gaze trailed down her body then back up again coming to a stop on the bruises marring her arm. Had he done that when he grabbed her? So wrong, so messed up.

He knew it, felt the guilt eating him alive. God knew she deserved some pain for what she'd done, but she didn't deserve that, not from a man, especially from him. He'd lost it, but it wasn't an excuse. In fact, to him, the fact that he lost it made it *inexcusable*. He'd been so out of his mind with rage he hadn't realized how he'd hurt her. It could've been worse. *He* could've done real damage.

"Bryce?"

His stare shifted to her face. He knew what he had to do, but doing it meant closing the distance between them, and that, considering she wore a small-ass towel, was a bad idea.

"She's asleep."

He turned his head. On the bed, Bree, her thick, blonde curls sprawled on the pillow. Then he remembered why he'd come—to see Bree. It seemed he'd lost track of time. He messed that up too, hadn't been there to say goodnight. Striding toward the bed, he sat on the edge and pressed a kiss to Bree's forehead whispering "goodnight" as he did.

Then before he thought better of it, he stood and walked toward Emelia. He didn't meet her eyes until he stopped a couple of feet away, close enough she heard what he had to say, far enough he wouldn't smell the scent of her. Still tempting, she had that power over him, probably always would, but then all he had to do was remember what he'd done. He needed that reminder. His gaze went to the bruises on her arm.

Clenching his jaw, he again met her stare. "I owe you an apology. No matter what you did, you don't deserve *that*." He looked at the bruises again then locked eyes with her. "Not from me because I'm not *that* type of man, not from anyone. I don't expect you to forgive me, but maybe for the sake of being better parents for Bree, we can call a truce."

She brought her hand to cover the marks looking every which way but at him. "You know I'm clumsy,

Bryce. I wasn't paying attention and walked into one of those heavy toolboxes in the garage. Not too long ago, I slammed the back of my head under the sink. And yesterday, I slipped in the shower. I have a bruise for that too."

A relief, it hadn't been him. Still, he had to get a hold of his temper.

Impossible for him to ignore, she hadn't met his eyes, and that irked him. He schooled his voice. "Don't know what you've been doing the last five years besides raising Bree. Don't know who you've been associating with either, except, of course, your cop, but the woman *I* knew had the balls to look me in the face."

Her eyes watered. She swallowed. "That woman's dead and gone, Bryce."

Amazing actress. She wanted to throw herself a pity party? Why?

She screwed him over. Just because he apologized for putting his hands on her, just because he wanted to call a truce didn't mean he'd let her drag him around by the balls. Fuck her.

Livid, he forgot why he needed that distance between them. "The man you knew is dead, too, and there's only *you* to blame for that."

He shouldn't have said it, shouldn't have given her that, letting her know how she killed him. A woman like her got pleasure out of the damage she'd wreaked, the reason he regretted it the minute he said it.

Instead of the reaction he expected, her face paled in a way that he knew what he said hurt her, bad. He didn't take any pleasure in it. By that point, the fresh scent of her hit him taking him back. Too soon, he became very aware of how close he stood, of how she had nothing but skin under that towel. The fact he still wanted her and how badly even after everything she did made him angrier. Before he did something he regretted, he walked away.

Chapter Eight

"What the fuck do you mean, I owe two grand?"

Em's first day had been eventful. The weekend came and went without another confrontation with Bryce, but that's where her luck ended.

Monday morning, her first day working at the garage also happened to be Bree's first day of school. She assumed as Bree's mother Bryce would let her accompany him when he took Bree to school. Wrong. The truce he wanted either wasn't really a truce or he decided to take it back after she said the old Emelia was gone. She racked her brain since Friday night trying to figure out why he responded the way he had. She'd changed, a fact. Another fact, he had too.

He ignored her the entire weekend, barely sparing a glance at her. At the time, she figured ignoring her—his version of a "truce." She realized Monday morning this was not the case.

When she followed Bryce and Bree out into the garage, he turned toward Bree. "Need a minute with your mom, baby. Go wait in the car."

Bree did just that.

He faced her, shooting daggers her way. "You're *staying*." Then he turned and walked away.

She did the only thing that came to mind, beg. "Bryce, please...I can't miss her first day..."

Her voice trailed off when he stopped, turned, and

closed the distance between them with three powerful, menacing steps.

Gritting his teeth, his hands in fists, he snarled, "You aren't missing her first day of school. Her first day happened in New Mexico before I even knew I had a daughter."

He had a point, a point he brought up to guilt her, and it worked. She screwed up by leaving, believing he meant it when he said he didn't want to be a father. Didn't he realize he didn't need to remind her every step of the way? Not a second of any day would go by without her knowing the reason her daughter hadn't had a father was *her*.

"But—"

"But some gang is trying to kill you. *You* aren't to be seen with my kid 'cause that gang finds you, means they find Bree. You know what they'll do to you both?"

She had a pretty good idea. Thinking of it, she swallowed and nodded. He made another good point, so she stopped fighting him.

"No, you don't. You can't even imagine the type of sick fucks part of that gang. You can't even begin to imagine what they'd do to a four-year-old. I'm not letting that happen, not to *my* Bree."

With those words, he strode away. She stood there frozen watching him drive away, watching Bree wave at her. He hadn't even given her a chance to say goodbye, to wish their daughter good luck on her first day.

Truce over. Her and her big mouth got her in trouble, again. Bryce was back to being a dick. She deserved it, yes, but he knew why she left, why she had every reason to, so why continue to torture her?

The rest of her day had been hectic. No one thought it important to show her the ropes of her new job, meaning she spent the day trying to figure it out: dealing with customers, placing orders, taking too many calls to count. Added to her workload, the brothers assumed she was their personal secretary, who needed to get them drinks, order food, and so on. She spent an hour ordering lunch alone. By the time she finished, she had yet to place a rush order on parts needed by the end of the week, so she'd skipped lunch.

Before Emelia knew it, Bryce arrived with Bree. Her daughter rushed in to tell her about her first day at a new school. She listened to her daughter in between taking calls. Then the disgruntled customer came in, venting his frustration over the fact he had a two-thousand-dollar bill. If she had a two-thousand-dollar bill, she'd be upset too, but he screamed profanities in front of her four-year-old daughter, hard to miss considering Bree's arm circled her waist in a death grip. She wanted to help him figure out why he owed two grand, but she couldn't, not until he told her his name. She'd asked several times. He ignored her question and continued to rant.

"You care to explain why the fuck I owe two grand? Or you just gonna stand there!"

"I'd be more than happy to help, but I need your name."

"You people think you own this town. You—"

The door to the office banged open.

She hadn't expected anyone to come to her rescue, except maybe Strike because he'd done so once already or Bryce but only because Bree was with her. But they didn't come to her rescue; Bud did.

Her lips parted.

Bud glared. "You got a fuckin' problem, you come to a brother. You don't give a *woman* shit. You don't give our new receptionist shit. What else you don't do? Curse in front of a kid. Now, you're gonna tell me what the problem is, asshole?"

"As your receptionist, she should know—"

"She's new. Even if she wasn't, she can't help you if you're screamin' and not telling her shit besides the fact you owe us two grand. A lot of people owe us two grand."

"She should—"

Bud took a step, getting in the man's face. *"Outside. Now."*

Before either of them moved, Bryce walked in. Being acutely aware of him, she noticed despite the tense atmosphere. His glare dead centered on her. Then again, nothing new. He'd find a way to blame her for this scene too. She tore her gaze away to glance at Mellow, Blaze, and Cuss who walked in. The customer, taking all of them in, did the smart thing. He strode outside. The others followed them, except Bryce.

Avoiding his stare, she tilted her head down and wrapped her arms around Bree. "Learn this lesson, baby. Being rude gets you nowhere."

Bree smiled softly.

She pointed toward the back counter behind her desk. "Sit right there and get started on your homework, okay?"

Bree nodded.

The phone rang, and she answered it quickly. When she looked up, Bryce had left.

****

For some reason, Bud stuck up for her. Bud, the man he grew up with, his former best friend, another thing he lost when Emelia left.

He and Bud grew up on the same block, went to school together, got into too much trouble together, and then became prospects for Hell Ryders together. Bud, like him, didn't like the chase. He liked easy women and took plenty. When Ripper met Emelia, nothing changed except they didn't fuck taps in the same room. Ripper had Em, and she was all he needed. Bud never got it. Bud never said so, but Rip knew. When she left, Bud proved it by expecting him to bounce back. Bud gave him time. The problem—there'd been no bouncing back from her. She was the only woman he'd ever loved, the only woman who'd ever loved him, or so he thought. He came to realize after she left, she'd been the love of his life, and a man lost the one woman for him, he was lost forever.

Bud had never fallen, so he'd never understand, not until he fell too.

Needless to say, Bud wasn't Emelia's biggest fan, yet he'd defended her. A part of Rip was glad Bud stepped in. Bree had been there and that bastard had been cursing and disrespecting her mom in front of her, something Rip hadn't noticed until after Bud involved himself. But Rip also hated it had been Bud and not him who made things better for Bree, for Emelia. That was immature, maybe, but he didn't want Emelia indebted to anyone but him.

This reminded Ripper of a simple truth he knew but still hadn't come to terms with. He still loved her, loved her just as much if not more than he'd loved her then.

Emelia may not be his old lady anymore. She may have left him, but she had once been his. She was the mother of his child, and he was protecting her. In the biker world, the simple fact she had once been *his* meant she was *his*. It meant he made the decisions regarding her, including whether or not to handle a bastard yelling at her. As his brother, Bud shouldn't protect the woman who left him anyway. The fucked part of it, Ripper wouldn't care under other circumstances—if she were really still *his*.

Clenching his jaw until it cramped, he waited until Bud finished with the bastard. It took a good fifteen minutes since Bud had to rearrange the idiot's attitude. Bud ignored his glare and started walking away.

Ripper stepped in front of him. "She's *mine*."

He smirked. "Thanks, but I don't want an old lady. I wanted one, I'd get one that wouldn't run out on me without telling me I'm gonna be a dad."

Exactly what to say to get him to snap. It'd been so long since he had. Since he found Emelia and Brianna, he fought hard to control that anger he lived with. Sometimes, he failed, especially with Emelia but never like this, like he used to after having just lost her. He knew what he was doing, knew it wasn't right, and he knew Bud was trying to rile him like he had the habit of ever since Emelia left him, but Rip couldn't hold back. He lost it.

Launching himself at Bud, the impact sending them both onto the ground, he punched his former best friend right in the middle of his face. He didn't stop, slamming his fist into him repeatedly until Stone and Mellow hauled him off. On his feet, he glared at Bud, nose broken, blood gushing from it, his right eye swelling. Bud sat up, spit, and smirked like Rip's life being shit was funny.

"Fuck you." He pushed Mellow and Stone off him and strode away.

He didn't know how he managed it. Nothing more he wanted than to beat Bud some more, yet somewhere inside, he knew it wouldn't do any good.

It wouldn't turn back time.

It wouldn't change the past.

It wouldn't make her tell him the reason she left or make her want to stay.

And it sure as hell wouldn't make her love him.

****

Em heard the commotion, and without drawing Bree's attention, she neared the window with clear view of the front lot. There, she saw proof of what she'd since figured out.

Bryce and Bud were no longer friends. They went way back and were part of the same club, but what had once been wasn't anymore.

A damned shame, those two had been as thick as thieves. If you asked her, she would've said hell would freeze over before something came between them. Only natural, she wondered what had.

****

Weeks went by, and nothing much changed. Emelia woke early each morning, made breakfast for Bryce, Bree, and herself then got Bree ready for school and kissed Bree goodbye. Afterward, she cleaned a bit and got ready for work. After work, she made dinner. After they ate, while Bryce went to the gym, she spent some time with Bree. Later, after getting Bree ready for bed, Bryce came to say good night. Em then told her a bedtime story. After Bree fell asleep, Em cleaned up some more then showered and headed for bed. When she woke the next morning, she started the process over again.

Good news, last week she received two boxes of her and Bree's belongings sent by Naomi who insisted on shipping them instead of selling the items as Em had asked her to. This meant Em had less laundry to do and Bree had some extra toys to play with. More good news, Em paid off her landlord for breaking the lease, and Naomi told her she got a couple of calls from people interested in buying her car. Naomi was in the process of selling the rest of her stuff, furniture and some other belongings as well. Em insisted Naomi keep the money considering her friend was doing all the work and more for her, but Naomi refused, which meant Em would have some money coming in from the sale of her car that would go into savings.

Another bit of good news, her job got easier as the days passed. That also had something to do with the fact that her third day, the brothers stopped using her as their personal assistant, meaning her work load lessened. She was ninety-nine percent sure that had something to do with Bryce since her second day, he walked into the office while she'd been ordering lunch for Bud, Blaze, and Rake, and he gave her a look she'd become way too familiar with—the look telling her he was close to "losing" it. He hadn't said a word to her. In fact, with the exception of the talk they had about Bree's birthday, he hadn't said more than five words to her at a time. When he said five words to her was usually when he took Bree somewhere. "Taking Bree. Be back later." Bryce barely looked at her either. It sucked. She hated being ignored by him, but she wasn't inclined to do anything about it. She knew any topic opened for discussion had the potential to make him angry and being ignored was better than being his emotional punching bag. She hadn't even mentioned he tell her where he planned to take Bree because she came to the realization she had to get used to not knowing where Bree was at all times. When she and Bree moved out of the compound, Bree would undoubtedly spend whole days and nights with her father, and Em wouldn't know where they planned to go or what they planned to do.

The last bit of good, Bree's birthday went off without a hitch. Five days before her birthday, Bryce told her they'd have Bree's birthday party at the compound. He said she needed to get together with Allie and Mia to help her plan it. He also told her he bought Bree a playground, which he'd assemble in the backlot of the compound. He said the gift was from both of them, and he wouldn't take any money from her for the gift or the party. Then he strode away without letting her say a word. She, Allie, and Mia planned the party, consisting of the club, the old ladies, Della, who had become good friends with Bree, and Cullen, Dodge's son. Bryce had the playground built the day before. Emelia baked the cake. Each old lady brought a side, and two of the brothers handled the grill. Simple, easy, and most importantly, Emelia had never seen Bree so happy.

Bree settled in fine. On weekday afternoons, after Bree got home from school, she did her homework in the office with her. Afterward, she spent time with Bryce until Emelia clocked out at five. Weekends,

Bryce took her on excursions. She only found out where when they came home, and Bree rushed to tell her where her father had taken her, what he bought her, what she ate, and so on.

As for Bryce, besides ignoring her, he took Bree to school, worked at the garage, spent countless hours with Bree, and some nights, he left. Emelia had no idea where he went, but she'd seen several of the brothers leave on what they called "runs."

Once upon a time, those "runs" consisted of running guns and drugs. After the club got clean, it meant something different—their version of cleaning up the streets of Wadden, ensuring no illegal dealings happened in their town. This was what caused Chained and Hell Ryders to come at odds back then since Chained wanted to continue running guns and drugs through Wadden. Bryce said the club was still clean. When the brothers went on runs, they probably did the latter. However, she'd overheard several brothers talk about "guards," and once, she'd seen Prez hand over an envelope with a lot of money to Mellow, meaning she didn't know with certainty if the club was still clean and didn't ask Bryce or anyone else.

She knew club life, and in club life, the brothers shared what they wanted with their old ladies. Before, Bryce had shared plenty though not everything with her. Now, she wasn't his old lady, just the mother of his daughter. Whatever Bryce's reason for protecting her, she appreciated. He hurt her. Absolutely, but after what she'd done, he didn't owe her anything.

She and Bree were both in danger because of Chip. Still, she loved her cousin, always had and always would. She thought about him every hour of every day.

Each time, she prayed he'd get better, prayed to hear some news. She hadn't heard from Track or anyone else from Chained. As bad as she wanted to know, she wasn't stupid enough to call and find out. Calling could lead the Falcons to Hell Ryders' door. She couldn't risk the club that was protecting her and Bree, couldn't risk Bryce, couldn't risk Bree, and so, she'd had no news for three weeks.

Thinking on this, not paying much attention to the order she was in the process of making, she heard a scream pierce the air. She knew that scream, a scream she felt in her bones.

She stood so suddenly the chair she sat on smashed against the back counter. With her heart in her throat, she rushed around her desk and the counter, jogging out the door leading into the garage. The door banged shut behind her. She scanned the area, her stare coming to a stop when she spotted Bree. Only then did she finally take a breath.

At the back of the garage near the door leading into the compound, Bree, butt planted on the greasy floor, cradled her knee. Bryce knelt in front of her, his expression a mixture of horror, concern, and something else she'd never seen and didn't have time to decipher.

Relieved beyond reason since for a brief moment she thought the worst, she rushed to Bree. By the time Em reached Bree, Cuss, Blaze, Army, and several other brothers were huddled around her, making it so that Em couldn't get through. Excusing herself, they made way for her. She immediately knelt beside Bree. Her gaze went to Bree's knee, her little hands covering it.

"Shh...Bree, it's okay," she soothed softly and simultaneously tugged Bree's hands away to get a better look. A pretty bad scrape, bloody, but nowhere near as bad as she'd seen.

"Mommy!" Bree cried. "It huuuurts!"

"It's going to be okay, honey."

She wrapped one arm under Bree's knees, the other around her back, getting ready to lift her when she felt him. Bryce's arms touched hers reaching for Bree. He lifted Bree before she could. She met his gaze. Brows furrowed, grimace in place.

"First aid kit?"

His brows shot up.

"Downstairs bathroom next to the office, under the sink."

She turned and spotted Strike then thanked him and followed Bryce and Bree inside, Bree still crying, her sobs muffled against Bryce's chest.

Reaching the bathroom, Bryce sat Bree on the counter. She searched under the sink. It took her several minutes to find the first aid kit in the mess. Nabbing it, she looked for disinfectant wipes, ripped the package open, and lifted Bree's knee. "This is going to sting."

"No, Mommy, no!"

Bryce wrapped his arm around Bree's shoulders, cupped her cheek, and pressed her against his chest. Leaning into her, his lips on her forehead, he said, "It's okay, baby. Hold on to me. It's gonna be okay."

The way he said it, so soft, trying to comfort her, and so anguished too, like he felt her pain, made Emelia stop what she meant to do to look his way. His eyes weren't dead but pained. Lost in that look, when Bree wailed again and he shifted his attention her, she realized she'd been staring.

Looking away quickly, she said, "It'll be over

soon." She wiped the scrape as carefully as possible.

Bree, her face still pressed against Bryce's chest, sobbed louder.

Done, she whispered, "The worst is over now." She bandaged it then threaded her fingers through Bree's hair. "All better. Now, some ice cream?"

Bree drew her face away from her father's chest, wiped her tears, and nodded. Bryce carried Bree into the living room. She headed into the kitchen and served Bree a bowl of chocolate ice cream, her favorite.

"You can say it. I fucked up."

Her back toward him, but from his voice, she knew he stood a few feet behind her. She faced him, seeing that same look, the one she hadn't been able to put a name to before, guilt. As a new parent, Bryce wouldn't know that guilt was a common feeling. Parents worried. They second-guessed themselves, and when their child got hurt, physically or emotionally, parents felt guilt.

"When Bree was one and a half, she started trying to climb out of her crib. I bought her a toddler bed. It had a rail to keep her from rolling off the bed. Well, she fell any way and bumped her head pretty hard. The sound of her head hitting the floor woke me. It was three in the morning. I was terrified and rushed her to the hospital. She was fine, thank God, but I felt responsible. I still think of that night sometimes. I think about what I could've done to prevent it, and I still remember how scared I was, and I still feel responsible."

His eyes widened as his brows wrinkled.

"This isn't the first time she's fallen. It won't be the last."

His expression changed then. Eyes glowing, he

nodded. "I'm leaving town tomorrow night. Won't be back for several days."

"I'll let Bree know."

He shook his head. "Already told her. Now, I'm telling you. While I'm gone, Strike'll take her to school and pick her up."

She nodded, thinking it made sense Strike drop Bree off and pick her up. Bree had grown fond of the tatted biker, and it was mutual.

Bryce didn't say where he planned to go, what he had to do, or when he'd be back. He just walked away. Then again, she hadn't expected him to tell her.

Before he left the following night, he gave her a cell phone. Only one number programmed in it, his.

****

Ripper had been gone for three days, but it felt like an eternity.

He'd known Bree for a little more than three weeks, and he missed her something awful. He couldn't explain it, didn't understand it, but he felt it. For a man who hadn't known love, he loved her more than anything in the world, a different type of love, love from first glimpse, unconditional love.

How could he not? His own flesh and blood, she was sweet, smart, beautiful, and *his*—his and Emelia's. All of it made him realize what low lives his parents were. More than ever, he couldn't understand how his father walked out, how his mother dropped him off at his grandmother's and disappeared. Granted, he wasn't the best man, father, or role model, but he loved his girl, so he'd turn himself inside out if he had to, to be better for Bree.

Before he left, he knew he'd miss Bree but had no

choice but to go. He agreed to the guard job months ago and couldn't back down when the club had already taken the money. Some of the guard jobs the club provided weren't legal. They got paid to guard, and sometimes, it included beating up assholes who deserved it. The club made sure of it. This one had been an easy one, some dick who wouldn't leave his ex-girlfriend alone and had been borderline stalking her. Her new man had money and paid them to rough up the ex. It took three days. They always stayed behind to make sure they tied up loose ends. He'd made a decent amount of money, enough he could afford to install the high-tech security system he had his eye on and buy some furniture for his home. But he was glad the job was over and done with. He wanted to see Bree, bad. Honest, he wanted to see Emelia too. He called her twice a day to talk to Bree. Also, Strike kept tabs on her and called him daily to report back, so he knew she hadn't bailed with Bree again, but deep down, he wouldn't believe it until he saw her with his own eyes.

The minute he got to the compound, he rushed upstairs, dropped his duffle in front of his door, and headed to their room. He meant to open the door without knocking then thought better of it. The last thing he needed—catch Emelia in a towel again. He knocked twice, lightly. She opened the door. His gaze locked with hers and because a part of him swore she'd be gone, he held it for longer than he cared to admit. Finally, he tore his stare away but only to trail it down her torso. He meant to continue looking down the length of her, but he froze on the oversized black tee with the word "Harley" written in freehand cursive across her chest.

He knew that tee. He remembered it well because it was *his*. Not much different than most of his tees, black and it read, "Harley," but he remembered it because he missed it. He missed it because it was his favorite, and it was his favorite because all those years ago, she wore it to bed.

The first time he had her, she found it on the floor and put it on. From that night on, she slept with him in that tee. The only nights she didn't wear it to bed, the nights he dealt with club business, and she fell asleep without him. On those nights, he stole it back and wore it laced with her scent, so with every breath he took, he smelled her. He did this every time. After she left, he realized he did it because she wasn't around, and he wanted her to be.

When she left, she took everything with her, all her clothes, even pictures like she'd been trying to erase the memory of her from him. She was gone, and he didn't know why, and he didn't want her to be. He *needed* something, anything. He thought he had at least that shirt, so he looked, tearing his room apart, but he never found it, and now, he knew why.

She took it.

She took *his* favorite tee.

She stole *it* and *left* with *his* daughter.

He couldn't lose it like he wanted to, like he should.

The next moment, Bree's little body hit him, her arms circled his thighs, hugging him tightly. "Daddy! I missed you so much."

His arms went around Bree. He tried his hardest to tamp down the too familiar anger. The instant his gaze landed on her beautiful little face and the smile lighting it, the one that made his whole life worth every fucked minute, his rage faded fast. He smiled. "Hey, baby. How's my favorite girl?"

"I'm good, Daddy. Mommy let me stay up because I told her you were coming home."

He spared a glance at the clock on the bedside table, an hour past her bedtime. Emelia was strict about that shit. It was for Bree's own good, so he said nothing. Yet Emelia let it go this one time, giving Bree the chance to see him and give him that smile. Too bad it didn't erase everything she'd done to him.

"Guess that means it's bedtime then?"

Bree looked to Emelia. He refused to look at her, knowing no good would come of it. But he knew she must've nodded since Bree peered at him next and asked, "Can you tuck me in and stay until I fall asleep, Daddy?"

He couldn't say no to that voice, those eyes, soft and pleading. Besides the fact, he wanted to even though he shouldn't. It was just plain stupid to be in such close proximity to her mother, wearing a tee she stole and nothing else. "'Course, Bree."

She grabbed his hand, tugging him toward the bed, where she lay.

He sat on the bedside, tucked her in like he'd seen Emelia do, leaned in, and pressed a kiss to her forehead. "Night, baby." Not knowing what else to do, he pulled away but stayed seated on the mattress.

"You must be tired. You should lay with me, but you have to take off your shoes, so you won't dirty the bed." She made room beside her and in the process undid the sheet he'd so dutifully tucked around her.

He smiled, waited until she situated herself before

he tucked her in again. "I am tired. Didn't realize how tired until I got here." He then kicked off his boots, lay on his side facing her, and wrapped his arm over her head.

She burrowed close, placing her cheek against his chest, her little hands under her face.

It felt good. His little girl seeking comfort in him. Then it got better.

She pulled away from him and tilted her head up. "I love you, Daddy."

In that single moment, he knew why he was still alive—for her. Rip couldn't disguise the feeling, the warmth spreading through him, the emotion welling inside, and he didn't try to. When he whispered, it could be heard in his voice. "I love you more, Bree, and don't you ever forget it."

She smiled wide and tucked her face back onto his chest. In seconds, she fell asleep, and he was left staring at her wondering what he ever did to deserve such beauty.

Chapter Nine

Ripper fell asleep. In fact, it was possible he was still asleep or in an alternate universe. The second his lids parted, he felt it—the heat of a body cuddled close. He saw long blonde hair in his face. Lying flat on his back, he turned his head. That blonde hair fell away, and he came face to face with her, with the beautiful woman he hadn't been able to erase from his mind, not for a single day, not for a single hour. She lay on her side facing him, her head on his shoulder, her arm resting on his stomach.

Just like before.

Except she wasn't pressed against him, no, that was Bree, still burrowed on her side between her mother and him. A dream come true. Crazy, but it felt like heaven. He, her, and their baby girl... Perfect. Except it was a lie.

Emelia hadn't been his for more than five years, and it was possible she'd never been his.

So why had she cuddled beside him? Because he fell asleep, and she had nowhere else to sleep? Because her body had naturally drifted toward body heat no matter who it belonged to? Because she meant to cuddle with Bree not him?

He glanced at the bedside table and realized he slept for five hours straight. Mystifying, it'd been years since he got that much sleep. He hated to admit it, but he knew the reason was *her*. The last time he slept so long, so peacefully—the last night she spent with him.

And there she was, the woman he couldn't have, taunting him with something else he couldn't have. Another something he'd have if she'd never left—sleep, peace. He didn't know if she meant to fuck with him, but it didn't matter. It felt like it because he wanted her, couldn't have her, and had to live with her. *Torture of the worst kind.*

He tore his gaze from her too beautiful face. Then he slowly extricated himself from the bed. Turning back, he peered at Bree. For Bree, the torture was worth it. Shifting, he took a step before he heard a whisper.

"Bryce?"

He held still for endless moments. Without turning to look, he swallowed. "Yeah?"

"H-how was your trip?"

Small talk? He turned so fast it was a wonder he didn't get whiplash. She sat, her hair a mess around her face, making him wish he never left her bed.

"Fine."

"Glad you're back." The blanket she held at her chest fell away.

He darted his gaze down to her chest, that "Harley" inscription blaring, reminding him why he'd been so pissed. "Out. Side. Now."

Her eyes widened. She stood and neared. He followed her out the door and closed it on his way out. Glancing around, a few feet away, he spotted Hash with a couple of taps. One kissing his neck, already topless, the other knelt in front of him unfastening his jeans.

Clenching his jaw, he strode to Hash and hauled the tap kissing his neck away.

"What—" the tap began.

Hash's eyes cracked open. He parted his mouth, no doubt about to protest.

Ripper spoke over the tap. "What the fuck, brother?" His arm shot out. "You realize I got a five-year-old sleeping feet away?"

"She's sleep—"

"Shut. It. Brother." He grasped the tap kneeling in front of Hash by the elbow and yanked her to her feet. She stumbled.

Taking a step toward Hash, inches from his face, he sniped, "She wakes for whatever reason and comes out here and catches you getting a blowjob, I'll have to cut off your dick to make sure it doesn't happen again. What the fuck do you think we got rooms for?"

Hash's jaw hardened. Despite this, he nodded.

Ripper turned, strode toward Emelia, grabbed her hand, and pulled her into his room behind him. He forced himself not to slam the door shut and took a series of steps toward her. She stepped back several times until her back hit the side of the dresser beside the door and behind her.

"Thank you for—"

He shook his head. "Didn't do it for you."

She nodded. "Well, thank you anyway. I was worried about Bree seeing the guys with—"

"*Listen.*" He waited for her to say anything. When she didn't, his gaze snapped down to the tee she stole. After a long pause, he met her stare again. "Take. It. Off." His voice low, deadly.

Her lips parted. "W-what?"

"My tee. You stole it. I want it back."

She looked down at herself as if she hadn't realized

155

what she wore. When she met his gaze again, her cheeks had a rosy tint to them. "You gave it to me."

Yeah, he had, but that was before. "You gave me plenty then took it all away."

Fuck. Rip shouldn't have said that. He should pretend he didn't care. He just couldn't help it, like he couldn't help what came out next.

"You took something else too, something I didn't even know I *had*."

The color faded from her cheeks as she bit the side of her lip and closed her eyes tightly.

"Take. It. Off."

Parting her eyes, she swallowed. "I-I can't. I'm not wearing…any—"

"Not my problem."

Tears filled her eyes. "Bryce…p-please…please, don't."

A fantastic act from an amazing actress, the meekness, the hurt, the tears, all of it took his anger to new heights.

Fisting his hands, he leaned into her. "Seen it before. Wasn't impressed."

Brutal. Strike to the heart. No, she didn't have one in regards to him, anyway.

She wobbled. Without even blinking, tears fell, staining her beautiful face. And still, she made no retort, made no move.

"*Off!*"

Gripping the hem of the shirt, she tugged it over her head. He drew away slightly, giving her room. She extended her hand to give him the tee.

His gaze raked her, except for a thong she was naked underneath. His dick hardened to a painful degree. Stare glued to her chest, her beautiful, plump breasts. She'd never been big, not like he liked them. A B-cup, but the prettiest he'd ever seen, probably because they were hers.

He wanted her, always wanted her. Dreamed of having her again so many times, and there she was nearly naked, and he couldn't have her. He disguised his groan with a growl, realizing then the mistake he made by asking for the shirt.

Like he wanted to continue torturing himself, his gaze drifted down her stomach then traveled to her rounded hips. He wished for a moment she'd turn to give him a view of her perfect ass. *Fuck.* He hissed. The hiss died on his lips when he spotted a horizontal scar a few inches under her belly button.

He looked at her face. Streaks of tears lined her too pale cheeks, and she hadn't made a sound. Crying silent tears, why? Wasn't the point to make him feel bad, manipulate him?

"What the fuck is that?"

She shook her head. "P-please…just let me go," she whispered. "I know I deserve it, but please…"

He studied her, watching for moments too long as those silent tears continued to trail down her face, down her neck. Her expression a mixture of anguish, torment, and *shame.* As the seconds ticked, his chest constricted making it hard to breathe. It took a while, but finally, he realized it.

She wasn't acting. She *couldn't* be. The greatest actress couldn't pull this act. She deserved it. He shouldn't care. The thing was *he did.* He more than cared. It hurt him to hurt her. So, in the end, all he'd done was hurt himself.

The pain of losing her never faded, never dulled. Even now, he had her near, and that agony hadn't ebbed. Why continue to hurt her, hurt himself? When would enough be enough?

Closing his eyes, he endured the searing ache in his chest. "Keep it. Get dressed." He waited. After hearing her movements figuring she dressed, he parted his eyes and met hers. "What happened?"

With trembling fingers, she wiped her face. "Nothing—"

He took a step coming an inch from her. "What happened?"

"I had Bree."

"That scar's from—"

"There were complications."

The breath froze in the back of his throat. "Complications?"

"Yes. It—"

He clamped his jaw so hard he didn't know how it didn't crack. "So what you're saying is, you could've died, and my daughter would've ended up in foster care?"

Tears fell and fell even as she shook her head. "N-no, I swear...I—"

He fisted his hands. "You what?"

Her eyes widened. "I h-had a will. If anything happened to me, you would've been notified."

That, too, didn't make any *fucking* sense. He hadn't been good enough to raise their daughter, he thought that's why she left, so why name him Bree's guardian?

"You're lying."

Shaking her head, she whispered, "No, I s-swear. You would've been—"

He didn't believe her and wanted to get the truth out of her, but he couldn't take the sound of her choked voice, the anguish in her eyes, the tears drifting down her face any more, so he dropped his head and stared at his feet. "Just go."

"What?"

"I said, go. Now. Go."

After she left, he came to realize she hadn't lied. The woman he'd known was long gone. It killed to know that the woman he fell for no longer existed, but it gave him hope. Maybe, just maybe, he was in love with the old Emelia. Maybe knowing the old her was gone, he'd finally get over her and move on.

****

Bryce had been brutal that morning. She took it, but she didn't know how much more she could take. He'd killed her once. With the little left of her, she had the will to raise their beautiful daughter, but if he kept it up, he'd kill that in her, too. At this rate, she'd be gone soon.

"Em? Earth to Em?"

She peered at Mia and forced a smile.

"You okay?"

Nowhere near okay. After Bryce ripped into her that morning, she hadn't been able to get back to sleep. She lay in bed wide awake, crying silent tears until her alarm clock rang. Then she started her day, made breakfast, got Bree ready for school, and headed for work. After work, she checked Bree's homework before Allie and Trig picked her up for a sleepover with Della. She had the night off, the first time in more than five years.

A Friday night at the compound, from her memory,

could get out of hand, so Fridays, she and Bree stayed in their room. That night, though, Mia went looking for her and insisted she needed a break. More than ever, she did and agreed to join her, Lynn, and Tiffany for drinks downstairs.

Now, she sat on a stool in front of the bar toward the back end of the living room with the old ladies.

"Fine." She took a sip of beer.

"You don't look fine to me." Mia smirked. "You know I'm here for you."

She knew. The problem, Mia was part of the club, and she wasn't, not anymore. If push came to shove, Mia's loyalties lay with the club, with Bryce, not her. She smiled softly. "I know. It's just…"

"Doesn't take a genius to figure it out. Trouble in paradise."

She laughed humorlessly. "It hasn't been paradise for a long time."

"Want my advice?"

She lifted a brow, teasingly. "If I say 'no,' you'll still give it, won't you?"

Mia winked. "You know me too well." She took a sip of her drink, vodka rocks, before she spoke. "Talk it out."

Her brows creased. "What?"

"You left. I'm sure you had your reasons, reasons he's been wondering about for years. Hell, everyone has. He's pissed. You're hurt. Talk it out. Air it out. Only then can both of you move on. Together or apart, it doesn't matter, but you need to work together to raise that beautiful girl. Living like you both are, with the ghosts of the past haunting you, you'll never make it."

That made so much sense. She needed to forgive

Bryce for what he'd done, the reason she left. She needed closure. Talking may help. Her problem, it was more than five years later, and she still couldn't talk about it. Even if she could, she doubted hearing his excuses would fix anything. Bryce needed to forgive her, too. Believe it or not, that was a harder feat.

"Where's Jelly Bean?"

She shifted and spotted Strike. The tatted biker wore a pair of jeans and his cut, the tattoos on his chest and arms on full display. Unusual for Strike, he wasn't one to hang around shirtless. Although he was ripped, he wasn't one to show off. Even so, it was explainable. She'd seen him with a tap just an hour ago.

"She's with Allie and Trig having a sleepover with Della."

He cocked his head. "How's that going for you?"

She smiled. "First night away from her ever..." She shook her head. "Not easy."

"She never spent the night away?" He lifted his brows. "Ever?"

She shook her head. "Never trusted anyone that much."

His eyes widened.

She didn't blame him. Hell, it surprised even her to a degree. Bree had friends in New Mexico, whose parents she'd known for years. Even so, she never let Bree stay overnight. With her past, Em had always been too terrified to trust anyone, especially with her daughter. The only person she trusted from a young age—Chip. When he brought her into the fold of the club, she learned to trust others. She knew of two clubs, Chained and Hell Ryders. Both were similar, built on trust and loyalty. Whether or not Trig and Bryce were the best of friends, she knew nothing would happen to Bree in Trig or Allie's hands. Trig was a brother and Allie his old lady/wife. They were family, plain and simple.

"So you're having a drink to relax?"

She smiled softly. "Yeah."

A split second afterward, someone grasped her bicep. Startled, she turned. When her gaze met a pair of dead eyes, the smile faded from her face.

He released her. "Upstairs, *now*."

She set her beer on the bar top and followed him, not having it in her to fight. Before she knew it, they climbed the steps. There, he increased his pace. She stumbled and tripped, caught herself with her hands and a knee. Stifling a groan, she picked herself up and met his eyes, searing her. Endless moments ticked. With each, those dead eyes simmered with fury. Finally, he turned and continued up the stairs, down the hall, and to his room. Opening the door, he allowed her in first then slammed it shut behind himself.

Her heart dropped to the pit of her stomach, hating what she knew would come.

"Haven't you fucked with me enough?"

Em should throw the question back at him, but saying anything of the sort would only make matters worse. Not willing to risk getting him angrier, she did what she had as of late—nothing. It backfired like it usually did. She supposed it didn't matter what she did. Anything she did further infuriated him.

"I don't get what you don't get about what I said."

At this, she had to respond because she had no idea what he was talking about. "W-what?"

He took a deep breath. "Already explained this to

you, but I'm gonna say this shit once more. I'm protecting you. That means your ass depends on *me*. That means what I say goes, and I said you're *off limits*."

Her brows drew together, not understanding why he'd tell her this.

"I get you're missing your cop. I get you're missing getting laid, but I'm protecting you means you belong to *me*. You don't flirt with anyone *especially* one of my brothers."

Jesus. Such an asshole. Why would she flirt with his brothers? Why would the thought even cross his mind? "I've never—"

His arm shot out pointing downstairs. "I fuckin' saw you."

What? Her eyes widened. "I wasn't flirting with Strike—"

All she got out. The next moment, he closed the distance between them, and the words died in her throat.

"That cop must've been giving it to you good. You want it so bad, you know where to find *me*."

A crude invitation, and he was way off base. Shawn had never been hers, and she hadn't had sex for years. Bryce had been her first and last.

She swallowed. Tempting, so tempting to give in. She'd wanted him for so long. She never stopped, but she couldn't give in. Nothing good would come of it. She loved him, but he never loved her. He cheated, destroyed her. She still loved him, but he hated her.

She cast her gaze downward, so she wouldn't have to look at his too handsome, rugged face. "Shawn was never my anything."

"What?" he barked automatically.

Lifting her head, her stare slid to his. "Shawn was just a friend."

"Don't believe you. Either way, it doesn't change shit. You aren't getting it from any of my brothers. So—"

She shook her head. "I wasn't—"

He leaned into her. "Can't hear you. Gotta speak up, *babe*."

Her heart tightened in her chest, something she couldn't have helped after he called her "babe." He used to call her that often. She hated it because bikers used the term loosely. He knew she didn't like it, so whenever he teased her, he called her "babe." He wasn't teasing her now, though. No, right then, it slipped. The look that flashed across his face for a split second proved it. She thought it looked a lot like anguish, but she knew better. It couldn't have been. The man standing in front of her had never loved her. A reminder of the past wouldn't cause him pain. Maybe, she read her grief reflected in his eyes.

With just the thought, tears rushed her.

****

Ripper flinched.

He couldn't help it. First, his slip, calling her "babe." It caused the agony he felt in his very soul, and then, tears wet her eyes.

He'd been crude, but he never thought she'd cry. He hated her tears. He hated the pain he read on her face. He hated he caused it even though she deserved it. He so badly wanted to hate her. He just *couldn't*, no matter what she did to him, to Bree.

The tears flooding her eyes dripped down her

cheeks.

"When did you turn into a woman who just took shit?"

She wiped her face. "That's what happens when you've dealt with so much shit. You just start taking it."

Infuriating. What had she dealt with? Raising a kid on her own? That was her fault, not his. For some reason, he didn't point this out. Instead, he brought up another point. "No, it isn't. That's what happens when you give up."

More tears drifted down her cheeks, a stark reminder of how much she'd changed, how she wasn't faking. He hated that too.

She denied it, shaking her head. "Giving up isn't living. I'm living."

His voice was deadpanned when he spoke. "Stop fuckin' taking it. Be the woman you were."

"I'll never be the woman I was. She's dead, and you're just one of the men to blame."

Jaw dropping, he reared back. When he recovered, he leaned into her until an inch from her face. "Me? You're shitting me! What the fuck did I do? Treat you *too* good? Love you *too* much?"

Her eyes widened then watered anew as wet skated down her pale face.

When she didn't answer, he yelled, "Tell me what I fuckin' did!"

She held his gaze without saying a word. He knew that look. Some things never changed, so he knew she wouldn't respond. Still, he waited and waited and waited and nothing. So he took a chance, a big chance.

He gripped the back of her neck, tugged her to him until her chest crashed against his. Her hands went to his shoulders, the heat of them searing. In case she decided to push him away, he snaked his other arm around her waist holding her to him. Her head slanted up to meet his eyes, her lips millimeters from his. He held her that way for seconds too long.

Then his lips hit hers, and immediately, he swept his tongue inside her mouth. The taste of her slammed him in the chest, burning him like a brand, bringing back all those memories.

He kissed her to prove a point, to piss her off, to give him a glimpse of the girl he once knew, and to win the standoff. He did this knowing he'd risk bringing back memories. He risked it to beat her at her own game, but he fucked up, succeeded in torturing himself more.

Where he went wrong? She didn't get pissed, didn't fight him. Instead, she melted. She *fucking* melted against *him*. Her body softening, her weight resting completely on him, her hands grasping his shoulders later snaked around his neck. She then did the unimaginable. Nails biting into his skin, she tugged him closer. All the while, she kissed him back, just as hard, just as rough.

Just like she used to.

Just like before.

Except it wasn't before, it was now. After she left him. With his kid.

He knew this, so he knew he should stop, but then, she did the damnest of things. With her lips still pressed against his, her tongue in his mouth as she held on to him, she moaned a sweet, soft moan that came from the back of her throat.

The kiss, her reaction, all of it overwhelmed him.

Because it did, he lost the battle. He delved deeper, rougher, choking back a groan. His hand drifted down her front grasping her breast. He trailed his mouth down her jaw then met her lips again. His other hand around her waist tightened as he lifted her off her feet, carried her, and pressed her back against the wall.

The next instant, she slid her hands under his shirt, her touch heating his skin. He trailed his palms down her chest and stomach, reached the top of her jeans, and unbuckled them. Setting her on her feet, he quickly and desperately yanked her jeans along with her panties down her legs. Then he unbuckled his jeans. She helped him, tugging them and his boxers down his thighs. All the while, he never lost her mouth. In one swift movement, he lifted her. Her legs went around his waist, and then, he sunk himself inside her heat.

Buried deep.

In her.

Finally.

After so many years.

Better than he remembered, and he hated that too.

She broke away again only briefly to moan, loud. He heard it vaguely, under the sound of his own groan. Claiming her lips, he pulled out then drove into her again. She screamed so loud it echoed in his ears. Because he loved hearing it, because it had been so long, and it felt so good, because he lost complete control, he drew out then slammed into her again and again, repeatedly.

Slick with sweat, her nails biting into his skin, her cries of pleasure rumbling inside him, she came. Her whole body shook and shivered in his arms.

Just like she used to.

Just like before.

He didn't stop. He couldn't. Against her pants, he claimed her lips, thrusting into her repeatedly. When her moans became more insistent, he slipped his hand between them and pressed his thumb against her clit, like he knew she loved. She came undone, crying out his name.

Just like she used to.

Just like before.

Only then he let go. His orgasm flooded him and went on and on. So powerful, he swore it radiated out of him and left him dazed. With her pressed against his bedroom wall, his face buried in her thick, blonde hair, he held her for a long moment as he fought to catch his breath.

He'd taken her hard and fast and rough. He'd never taken her like that before. Because she was so young, because she'd been a virgin, and because he thought she deserved more than a quick fuck, he always took his time, always went slow.

Things had changed though. She left him, took his daughter, and from what he knew, she'd been with at least one other man. But it's not why he'd fucked her. God knew if he'd planned it, he would've taken his time, if only to savor her, so the next time she left, he'd remember how he had savored her that one time.

Rip fucked her because he hadn't had her for so long, and the last time, he hadn't known it'd be the last. He dreamt of taking her, thought of it unwillingly and constantly. With just one kiss, one moan, he lost it.

It didn't change the fact that it'd been a mistake, giving him a taste of what he missed all those years, of what he couldn't have. She was his addiction, had always been. He'd gone years without and never stopped fiending her. Knowing this, he knew one time wouldn't be enough. With that one taste, he'd crave her more than before. Worse, because now, he couldn't escape her.

Sex with her had always been great, the best he ever had, but this time was the best of the best. He didn't know if it was because he missed her so much or because he now knew just how much he loved her.

She lifted her face buried in his neck, pressed her lips to his jaw, and kissed him there.

Just like she used to.

Just like before.

The moment she did it, he tensed. His chest tightened, and the ache he carried around for more than five years overwhelmed him. Clenching his jaw, he squeezed her and fought the pain, reminding himself what he had to.

It wasn't like before. It'd never be the same again. More than five years down the road, five years after she left him and took his kid. He'd just been an itch she needed scratched. She didn't want him. She wanted her cop.

He gripped her waist and drew away. She stiffened and unwrapped her legs. Then she stood on her feet, unhooked her arms from his neck, and let him go.

Without meeting her gaze, he lifted his boxers and jeans and zipped them. Then he spared a glance at her. "You were always a good lay. Good to know you still got it."

With his heart in his throat, he walked away.

Chapter Ten

Deep agony sliced through her, burning her insides. Emelia thought she could handle it. She resigned herself to it, thinking she deserved it. For weeks, she took his hard knocks. Coming from the only man she ever loved the way she loved him, they hurt as much as she expected them to, but she took them, without snapping back and all the while fighting tears. As it turned out, some things she couldn't take.

You were always a good lay.

Back then, that's all she'd been, and still hearing him admit it broke the little that time had healed. She hadn't thought broken people could be broken again, but with those words, he'd done just that.

Knowing what would come, she did the only thing she could. She grabbed her jeans and panties off the floor, pulled them on, dashed out of the room, down the hall and stairs then outside through the back door of the compound. The cool air hit her arms, face, chest, and legs. She took a deep breath as the first gut-wrenching sob tore through her throat. The sound so familiar, so devastating, anyone who heard it sensed the ache, the pain, the agony as if it were his own.

Then she prayed like she'd never prayed before that no one found her because the dam of tears broke. No holding back now. No fighting it. Last time, she cried for hours. This time would be no different.

****

Ripper was in a foul mood, the worst mood of his life, and that said a lot considering he'd just had the best sex of his life. He didn't want to be bothered. He wanted the tall glass of vodka he just poured, wanted to get rip-roaring drunk until he no longer felt the tightness in his chest, the one he now knew came from making the love of your life feel like a common whore. He didn't want to see his brothers, talk to them, or be looked at. On a Friday night, that was a hard feat.

Since he left her in his room, after pouring a drink, he headed to the only room in the compound he knew would be empty, the room beside Prez's office where they kept the security monitors. He entered, found it as expected, sat in front of the desk without so much as a glance at the monitors, and took a long gulp of his drink. Ready to go for a second swallow, the door behind him parted.

"Not in the fuckin' mood," he barked.

"When are you, brother?"

He didn't hear anything for several moments and didn't know what Strike waited for. If he had to guess, he'd say Strike was trying to piss him off. Out of character for him, but Rip couldn't think of another reason for the pause. Finally, Strike spoke again.

"Know it's none of my business."

He jumped in immediately, snapping back, "It ain't, so don't—"

"Don't know what game you're playing, Rip. Don't care except I'm gonna say something right now, and you're going to listen 'cause I don't think you realize what you're doing. I don't know what happened all those years ago, and I don't care. Though I have to say if you treated her like this, I can't say I blame her for running out on you."

He swiveled the chair he sat on and stood quickly. A foot away, he glared at Strike. "*You* don't know shit."

"What I know is if you want to keep Bree in your life, you better start making amends with her mom 'cause you're giving her plenty reasons to keep you away."

Strike had a point there.

"I *loved* her. I treated her like a queen. She *left* me, *took* my kid without telling me I was gonna be a dad. She *deserves* what she's getting."

Strike crossed his arms over his chest. "You sure about that? I would've believed you a month ago, but now?" He shook his head. "I'm not so sure, Rip. I know a broken woman when I see one. She was broken, and now…" He leaned into him. "She's fuckin' *destroyed*."

Rip didn't know what to think about that. He'd been harsh. She deserved it, but maybe Strike had made another point. She said so herself, she wasn't the woman she used to be. He saw proof of that himself. Unwillingly, she set him off, but only because he loved her, still wanted her, and couldn't have her.

"What do you want, Rip?"

He wanted what he'd always wanted—*her*. He just couldn't have her.

Rip said nothing because he didn't have to say it. Strike knew what he wanted. Everyone did.

"You're never going to get what you want if you keep doing what you're doing. All you're going to succeed in doing is push her away. It happens again, I won't blame her. *No one* will. It happens again, it'll hurt more 'cause you'll lose Bree, too, and it'll be your fault."

He knew this and still couldn't stop making her pay. Why? Because he still didn't know why she left all those years ago? Past time to find out.

"Where is she?"

Strike's eyes widened. "Backlot."

Ripper hauled ass out of the room and to the back of the compound. Once there, he hesitated only for a second before he pushed the door open and headed outside. The minute he did, he heard what he couldn't before—the gut-wrenching sobs, *her* anguished wails tearing through her like she couldn't control them.

Stomach turning, he sprinted toward the sound and found her forty feet away, crouched behind the bark of a large tree, her butt on the ground, hugging her knees to her chest. When he stepped in front of her, her head snapped up to meet his gaze. Her eyes widened, and even then, she couldn't stop the sobs. She tried, slapping her hand over her mouth, trying to muffle the sound, but it didn't work.

Then he remembered something Strike said. He heard him but hadn't listened, probably because he'd been stuck thinking about himself.

I know a broken woman when I see one. She was broken, and now, she's fuckin' destroyed.

The look on her face, the sound of her cries, she *was* destroyed. And he'd done the destroying. The tightening in his chest compounded until it throbbed, until he felt nothing but that ache.

Before he thought of something to say, she spoke. "B-breaking me once w-wasn't e-enough?" Her voice cracked between wails.

He broke her more than once? When? "What?"

Instead of answering, she dropped her head to her knees and sobbed harder.

He grabbed her arms, helped her to her feet, and released her. "What did you say?"

She glared. "You heard m-me."

Just like that, the anger she so easily caused came then. At least this time, he had a reason. Before a month ago, he'd never been anything but good to her. "You're fuckin' kidding me."

Releasing a ragged breath, she side-stepped him.

Before she moved again, he grasped her arm, stopping her, and leaned into her. "Not this time. You aren't taking the easy way out. This time, you're gonna stay, and you're gonna answer my fuckin' question 'cause I got no more patience for your shit, and I'm not taking it anymore."

She wiped her face. "Fuck. You. I *h-hate* you! You'll never touch me again."

Good. Well, a part of it was good. The fact she hated him, the fact he'd never touch her again, not so much. But she'd yelled, and that was great. Emotion, it meant he broke through, made her so angry he got to the core of her, the part of her she'd buried. Proof that beneath the tears was *his Em*.

"*Why?*"

"Because I hate you, and I don't want you touching me ever!"

He flinched, ignoring the sour taste in his mouth. "I wanna know why you left. Why you left with my kid without telling me 'bout her, without telling me I was gonna be a father."

He had an idea why, but he realized it only recently. Before he knew about Bree, for more than five long years, he tormented himself wondering. He thought maybe she left because she wanted more, marriage and kids, the whole package. He hadn't given her any of it. In fact, he told her he wasn't that type of man. The thing was she never asked him for it. After she left, he knew he fucked up. He wanted to go back in time and give it to her, wanted her to come back. He had too much pride to go after her then and refused to because she'd been the one to leave him without so much as a goodbye. His pride only strengthened over the years, and while he wondered the reason she left, he came to his own conclusion—she'd made him think she loved him but never did. After finding out about Bree, he thought maybe she left because she'd thought he wouldn't make a good father, and yet she told Bree about him, made sure Bree knew who her father was, and she claimed she listed him as Bree's guardian in her will. It didn't make sense. It's why he still wasn't sure why she left. It's why he wanted, no, he *needed* to hear it from her.

Tears spilling down her face, her voice solemn, broken when she spoke. "Fuck you, Bryce. *Fuck. You.*"

"I'm not afraid of *you*, babe. You know I can go head-to-head with you for hours, and you know it gets me off, so unless you want me to prove you wrong, show you how easy I can have you again, you'll tell me this instant why you left."

Not for a second did he think he'd have her again. Deep down, he thought he got lucky, that her giving into him had been an aberration. She'd never been one to sleep around, and she didn't want him. She left him after all. Still, he said it to piss her off, so maybe he'd finally get her to say what she fought so hard to hold back.

She pushed at his chest, hard. Her beautiful hazel eyes filled with tears anew. "You want to break me some more? Why don't you just fucking shoot me? It'd be less painful, *Bryce*."

She kept dodging his question, making herself out to be the victim when *she* left *him*.

Eyes hardening to slits, he threatened, "Tell me right now 'cause I swear, I'll get creative to get it outta you."

"You really don't know why I left? Or you just want to hear me say it?" She paused only for an instant before another sob tore at her throat. "Fine! What do you want me to say? What do you want to hear? Do you want the truth or a lie? I'll make up a good lie. I'll say it convincingly, too."

He clenched his jaw as he leaned into her. "Don't mock me, babe. I'm 'bout to lose my shit, and that won't be pretty. You better talk, and you better do it fast. I may not have it in me to hit you, but don't forget I play dirty and fight just as dirty. You ever wanna see Bree again, you'll start talking *fast*."

That he'd never do because he loved her too much, because he loved Bree as much too. But he said it because in saying it, she'd quit the games and tell him.

Her eyes widened, her face paled as fear streaked her frame. When she blinked, thick tears slid out, staining her cheeks anew. "I could tell you I left because the clubs were fighting, the two most important men in my life wanted each other dead. I could tell you I left because I was pregnant, because I loved you so much I couldn't imagine killing something that was a part of you, because you told me you never wanted kids, that you wouldn't make a good father. All of it's true, but none of it would've made me *leave*."

She looked away, took a deep breath, and met his stare again. "With how much I loved you, only *you* had the power to make me go."

Loved. So she had loved him but didn't anymore. He knew she didn't, and yet, hearing it from her lips killed, tearing the wound he walked around with for years wide open.

She shook her head. "I was young and stupid. I was in love, and I thought *you* loved me. You never said it, not in two years, but I felt it. I felt *loved*, and it was enough for *me*."

He never said it, not once, not ever, because he hadn't realized he loved her, hadn't known what it felt like to love. He hadn't even thought he could love, not until she left, and he broke. Only then he realized what he felt for her had to have been love.

Still, because he never said it didn't mean he didn't feel it, didn't mean he didn't show it. For fuck's sake, she said so herself, so it wasn't an excuse. He meant to point this out, but she kept going.

"Then at twenty, I found out I was pregnant, and I was *terrified* because I knew you didn't want kids. I knew you weren't the type to settle down, and I knew I couldn't get rid of *our* baby. But I also knew I had to tell you even if it meant I'd *lose you*."

She swallowed. "That was the plan. Just a day after I found out, I decided to tell you. I was at school, one of my classes had been cancelled. I drove back. It was only eleven. I figured you'd still be sleeping."

Her face changed, anguish streaked it as more tears drifted down her pale face, and still she looked so beautiful. "I was wrong. I knew I was when I saw Lilliam come out of *our* room. I didn't need her to say anything. I knew you'd *fucked* her, but Lilliam being Lilliam did anyway, proving why I felt like I was being gutted alive."

Eyes widening, his jaw dropped.

"I walked into our room and found *her* panties on *our* bed, the bed you bought before I moved in because you said I deserved a bed you hadn't fucked taps on, because you said it would be *our bed*, only ours.

"I realized what an idiot I'd been, allowing myself to fall for you, to believe that because you'd moved me in, that because you bought us a bed, it meant we were exclusive. Little did I know, you just continued to fuck whoever you wanted on *our* bed."

Fuck. Fucking. Shit.

A part of him wanted to continue trying to hate her, wanted to believe this was the new *Emelia,* the fantastic actress making up fucked shit, but the rational part of him knew better. He remembered their last day like it happened yesterday because he'd gone over and over it a billion times in his head since then.

After all that time, he finally had an answer—the reason she left. Through the years, he made himself sick thinking of the why until finally, he came to his own conclusion—she was just a cruel woman who made him believe she loved him when she hadn't. It was so much easier to believe than thinking it was something he did, easier to believe than the truth. The truth was the hardest to take because the truth was utterly devastating.

She'd left, taken his kid, and killed him in the process.

He missed five years with his daughter.

He missed five years with *her*.

He'd spent years alone so had she, but life had played the cruelest joke on him. He'd been without them both.

And all—for nothing.

The sad truth, he didn't know if the reason she left mattered now or if it made a difference because he didn't know if he could forgive her.

She continued to sob, crying those gut-wrenching wails louder than before. He wanted to do something, *anything* to make her stop crying or comfort her. He thought about it for a while before realizing nothing he did or said would make her better. She didn't want him close, wouldn't believe him anyway.

Feeling like he'd been beaten, gutted, stabbed, and shot, he left. Walking away from her then was the hardest thing he'd ever done.

****

"What the fuck, brother?" Dodge, eyes narrowed, jaw clenched, barked when he parted the door to his house, a one-story with a brick, circular drive.

Ripper had been inside several times over the last couple of years, usually to help Dodge remodel it. His brother had reason to be angry. No one liked being woken up in the middle of the night.

"Where is she?"

Dodge's brows furrowed. Cullen, Dodge's two-and-a-half-year-old, poked his head from behind his father's legs, his dark eyes half-mast, hair a rumpled mess.

Rip's stomach turned. Stuck in his own rage, he hadn't thought about Cullen. He woke the kid, probably scared him half to death banging on the door and yelling like he had. If he'd remembered, he would've called Dodge's cell instead. He had to find that bitch Lilliam, and Dodge was technically still married to her, not to mention she was the mother of his kid.

His gaze on Cullen, he swallowed. "Sorry to wake you, bud. Need to talk to your dad."

The boy nodded then tilted his head farther back to meet his father's gaze.

"Back to bed. I'll be there in a few, yeah?"

Cullen nodded and strode away.

Dodge met his stare. "Better have a good fuckin' reason showing up here at this time, Rip."

"Lilliam. I need to find her."

Dodge wouldn't care that he asked for Lilliam. Dodge and Lilliam were through. Lilliam was a bitch, not just because of what she did to Ripper. She started off as a tap around the time he met Em, and she'd banged most of his brothers. It'd been no surprise to him when she made him a proposition, one he refused on multiple occasions. He had Em and wanted only Em. He supposed that's why she'd made Em believe he'd fucked her. Her plan only succeeded in driving Em away and fucking up the last five years of his life. With Em or without, he hadn't been interested in Lilliam. She got the point soon enough and set her sights on Trig. She wanted more from him too. To get that, she started telling the brothers and old ladies Trig planned to patch her. When Trig found out she'd been lying, he stopped fucking her.

She moved on to Dodge after and got herself knocked up. Dodge married her. They had Cullen, but Lilliam wasn't past being a tap. While married to

Dodge, she continued to dress like a tap and flirted with the brothers. She was a shitty mother, too. Dodge had been a single father long before he kicked her ass out months ago. Though Rip couldn't be sure if she stayed gone because it wasn't the first time Dodge and Lilliam called it quits. For some reason—probably the fact they had a kid—Lilliam always found a way back into Dodge's life.

Dodge's eyes widened. "I can't help you there. Don't know where she is."

Rip had been afraid of that. He was glad the bitch wasn't making his brother's life hell, but he needed to find her hours ago.

After Em finally admitted why she left years ago, he hopped on his bike and drove for more than an hour, not knowing where to go. He rode, his thoughts driving him crazy until he decided what to do. The reason it took so long was because a good half hour after learning the truth from Em, he was still in shock. When it faded, he'd been too pissed to make any decisions. No denying he still felt that anger, but at least now, he knew what he needed to do—find Lilliam. He didn't know how he'd get the lying, manipulative bitch to tell the truth, but he'd make her. He needed Em to know what happened. What he'd do after, he had no clue. And for now, he was fine with not knowing. First thing, first.

"What'd she do now?"

Dodge's question drew his mind back to the present. Ignoring it completely, he asked, "Do you know where she's staying?"

Dodge shook his head.

"Her number?"

"Nope."

Nope? Dodge had no way to contact his kid's mother? "You gotta be fuckin' kidding me."

"I'm not. She moved out months ago, called maybe twice to talk to her kid."

His jaw hardened.

"Yeah, you heard right. *Twice.* Though that was just an excuse, what she really wanted was money. I haven't heard from her since I filed for divorce. My lawyer called her, that's when he told me her phone's been disconnected. So if you find her, you let her know I want those papers signed."

Shit. If he didn't find Lilliam, Em would go on thinking he cheated, go on thinking she had every reason to leave him.

"What's going on, Rip?"

He fisted his hands. "Need to find her."

"What'd she do now?"

Eyes hard, he sliced them to Dodge and jerked his head side to side. "It's a small town. You're telling me you haven't seen her?"

"That's exactly what I'm saying. I'm thinking she was staying in town, I'd know."

Fuck.

"The suspense is killing me." Sarcasm bit Dodge's tone. "Are you finally going to tell me what she did?"

He swallowed thickly. "I tell you there's a chance you won't believe me."

Dodge held his stare for a second before he said, "Something to do with Em."

Surprising, Rip didn't know what to say though he supposed he shouldn't be.

"You've got to give me more credit than that, Rip."

Dodge shook his head. "Em... That girl was too in love with you to see straight. Her leaving the way she did never made any sense."

That girl was *too in love with you to see straight.* Another reminder she'd loved him but didn't anymore. He fought the ache in his chest and focused on the present.

Dodge lifted a brow. "Lilliam having something to do with it? That makes perfect sense."

His brother had a point. Em leaving hadn't made any sense. It's why it hurt so much. Who would've thought feisty, bullheaded Em wouldn't have confronted him had she thought he cheated. Why hadn't she? If she had, none of this would've happened. Didn't that make it as much her fault as Lilliam's for believing it?

"Sorry I woke Cullen." He turned and walked away, knowing he had no choice but to find Lilliam and make her tell Em the truth.

****

"Rip."

Having spotted Bud perched outside the door leading into the garage as he drove in, Ripper knew what'd come.

"Don't tell me you believe her."

What the fuck? How did Bud know? "What're you talking about?"

"You know what I'm talking about...her *fucking* sob story."

Taking a step in his direction, he snarled, "*You* listening to my conversations? You grew a pussy in the last five years I didn't know about?"

"I listened to her conversation with that cop. You

wanna know what she told him?"

Shit. Bud had? Why hadn't he? He should've.

"She said you *cheated* on her. *I* know that's a fuckin' lie. *Everyone* knows that's a fuckin' lie. Now, she's been crying her eyes out for hours. You've been MIA for hours, not answering anyone's calls. I *know* she told you some sob story. Pretty sure it ain't the same 'cause no way in hell you'd believe you did something you know you didn't." Bud threw his hands out. "But, brother, if me looking out for you means I gotta pussy, then I gotta pussy."

He didn't say a word.

"She's been here for a month, and you're already her whipping boy: getting her a job, fighting customers who hit on her. But she's Em, so you'd probably sell your soul to the devil if she told you to."

He grinded his teeth. "Fuck you."

Bud leaned into him. "You're the one who's fucked. She destroyed *you*, made you a living, breathing zombie."

His brother had to be kidding—giving him shit after the shit day he had?

"A very *pissed* off, living, breathing, zombie."

"You don't know *shit*."

"I know you—"

"You don't know *shit*."

"I know—"

"You don't—"

"I *know*—"

"She came on to me."

Bud reared back, eyes widening. He shook his head. "You *didn't*—"

"Lilliam had been at it a while. She was fuckin'

relentless. After Em left for school in the mornings, Lilliam would come into our room. As a tap, she wasn't even supposed to be in the compound. I got no clue how she continued getting in, but she did. She got in bed with me a couple of times, so I started getting up earlier."

He released a breath. "That last day...the day Em left, I was in the shower when I heard the door and saw Lilliam, naked. I told her to leave before I got her kicked off club property. She left."

"You *didn't*."

He hardened his jaw. "I *didn't*, but it doesn't make a difference 'cause what I didn't know was that Lilliam left her thong on our bed. I didn't know Em got outta school early and saw Lilliam leave our room. Then Lilliam said some shit to make her think we did."

Bud's gaze slid away. He sighed then finally met his eyes again. "So she's kicking her own ass for believing Lilliam, now?"

He shook his head. "I didn't tell her. What's the point? She didn't believe in me then, why'd she believe what I have to say now?"

"So..."

"So I'm gonna find Lilliam and make her tell Em the truth."

Bud widened his eyes. "You're fuckin' with me."

He glared. "No."

"You just said she wouldn't believe you—"

"She'll believe Lilliam." Then and there, he *had* to believe that.

Bud dropped his head, shook it then met his stare. "After all this time, what difference does it make?"

Ripper didn't know, what he knew—he *needed* Em

to know the truth. "Need her to know."

"Ha," Bud scoffed. "What makes you think she'll believe Lilliam, now?"

He didn't know, but he had to try.

The door to the front of the garage slammed open and out came Strike, shaking his head. His gaze went to Bud's then met Ripper's. "She stopped crying, but she isn't talking."

Before Strike finished the sentence, Ripper headed toward him then past.

"She's still out back."

He stopped dead in his tracks and turned to Strike. "She's been out there all this time?" The question came out in a yell.

Strike nodded.

He cursed. He'd been gone for hours. This time of year, it got cold then colder and colder as the night went on. When he left her, she wore a thin sweater.

Picking up his pace, he headed through the compound, ignoring half-naked taps and his brothers along the way. He went out the back and found her right where he left her, hiding behind the bark of the tree. She sat on the ground with her knees to her chest, head bent, arms resting on the back of her head.

He wrapped one arm around her back, the other under her knees, and hefted her up in one swift movement. Her hands resting between them, her head fell onto his chest. Against the fabric of his tee, he felt her ice-cold cheek.

Clenching his jaw, he carried her inside the compound, up the stairs, and into his room. In his bathroom, he set her on the toilet. There, he got the first good look at her face. Eyes swollen from crying yet unseeing, her expression could only be described as grieved, the type of pain that never went away. It struck him, wounded him, making his heart squeeze tightly in his chest, and it scared the shit out of him too. He hadn't known what to do before, he sure as hell didn't know what to do now.

Turning on the shower, he tempered it hotter than normal. "You gonna take off your clothes?"

She didn't move, didn't blink. He wasn't even sure she was breathing, so he had no idea if she heard him.

He carried her then stepped into the shower, clothes, shoes, and all. As the water sprayed down on them, she gasped. His arms around her tightened, she briefly struggled against him. He kept them under the shower head for several moments. When she stopped moving, he placed her on her feet and wrapped one arm around her waist. Pulling her wet hair from her face, he angled her head to meet his stare. Even with water dripping around them, her eyes brimmed with tears.

"Why'd you do that?"

"W-what?"

"You trying to get yourself sick? You've been out in the cold for hours."

Eyes widening, she hesitated for moments too long. "I'm wearing a sweater."

"That thin-ass sweater isn't gonna do shit, Em. Your cheeks are still ice cold." He wrapped his hand around the back of her neck and pulled her in closer until her chest pressed against his.

She held his gaze without saying a word, her eyes softening more and more by the minute.

He remembered that look. She used to look at him like that a lot. He didn't know why she did it now, but he missed seeing it so much it made him ache at the loss of it.

All because of a lie.

"Can I trust you to warm up by yourself?"

When she didn't say a word, he said, "I can do it for you. Then we'll be doing a lot more than warming up." Just the thought of it had his cock hardening.

She looked away. "I'll be fine."

Shit. He hoped. For a moment there, he thought she might. He'd been lucky once, it could happen again, right?

Pulling away, he stepped out of the shower. "I'll get you a towel."

He took off his shoes, socks, and clothes leaving only his boxers on before he went about finding her a clean towel. After placing it on the sink for her, he walked into his room, took off his boxers, and dried off then dressed.

She took a while, long enough he became impatient and headed for the bathroom door, long enough when he parted it, hot steam hit his face. She'd turned up the heat a lot. He remembered she loved hot showers.

He stepped inside. "Are you about done?"

"W-what?"

Glancing down at the floor, he spotted her wet clothes piled on top of his. Then he shifted his gaze, seeing her shadow through the steamed glass. She stood under the pelting hot water.

"I asked if you're about done."

"I… Yeah," she said but made no move.

He waited for a minute before he lost patience. "Em, unless you want me to go in there and get you out myself, I suggest you start moving."

Turning off the shower, she parted the glass door and poked her arm out. He handed her the towel. She wrapped it around herself then stepped out.

The pale skin on her face, chest, and arms stained red from the heat, her hair dripping wet behind her, she met his gaze. He then noticed her eyes were still swollen and red-rimmed, no longer sightless, just blank. The grief wiped from her face, but it, too, was vacant, like no one was home. He knew that blankness was worse, much worse.

Lost in that look, he didn't realize moments had passed until she shivered, snapping him out of his thoughts.

"It's late. Should get to bed."

She nodded and finally moved. Coming to a stop in front of the sink, she wrung her long hair ridding it of excess water. When she turned again, she stood too close, so he forced himself to move away and out of the bathroom. He reached into one of his drawers and found a tee. By the time he turned to her, she was opening the door to his room. He took several long strides. From behind, he wound an arm around her waist lifting her and pulling her back and away from the door as he simultaneously closed it.

"What are you…" Her voice trailed off when he set her down.

Angling himself so he stood in front of her, he handed her his tee. "Dry up, put it on, and then bed." When he said "bed," he motioned toward his with his chin.

Her eyes widened. The blank look gone for a moment replaced with something that looked a lot like shock…or fear. He didn't know for sure.

Before she said anything, he did. "I'm not leaving you alone." He hardened his eyes, so she'd know he meant what he said. "Not tonight. Tomorrow, you wanna go back to your room, you can. I won't keep you here, but tonight, you're staying with me."

Her eyes rounded and watered. She brought her hands to her chest and clutched his tee.

Terrified. She was fucking terrified, like hurting her wouldn't hurt him too.

"I remember correctly, last time, it was you who jumped into bed with *me*." He leaned into her. "When I woke up, *you* were cuddled close. Just like before. Just like you used to."

Her jaw dropped. Cheeks tinted pink. "I…I…"

Shit. She didn't remember. She'd probably thought he was her cop. He'd just made himself look like an idiot. He was for even bringing it up. It meant nothing to her. He meant nothing to her.

"I'll sleep on the floor. Just sleep, yeah?"

"Why?"

"Why, what?"

"Why can't I just go?"

He was exhausted but too amped up to sleep himself. Still, he knew he'd fall soundlessly if she lay beside him. That wasn't the reason he wanted her in his bed though. She'd been crying for hours out in the cold. He'd left her there thinking she didn't want him near, but now, he *had* to do what he could to make sure she was okay. "'Cause—"

"I'm not leaving. I wouldn't do that to Bree."

"Get in bed, Em."

"I won't—"

"Get. In. Bed."

"Just—"

"Get. In. Bed. Em."

"Please—"

"I need to make sure you're okay, so get in bed before I fuckin' put you in bed. I'm warning you, I put you in, I'm not leaving."

Her eyes widened.

He hadn't meant to admit it, but he didn't regret it since it made her hesitate for a moment too long. In the next instant, he snaked his arm around her waist, bent to wrap the other under her knees, picked her up, and dropped her on the bed then climbed in.

"Bryce, I—"

He lay on the mattress. "Sleep."

She tugged on his tee, only allowing the towel to fall away when it fully covered her. He fought to keep his eyes forward and barely managed it.

"Do—"

She could frustrate a saint, and he was losing the last of his patience. Closing his eyes tightly, he barked, "Sleep. Em. Fuckin'. Sleep."

"The lights."

He shifted to look at her. "Then you'll shut it and sleep?"

She nodded.

He stood, went to the bathroom, turned off the light then headed for the lamp near his bedroom door and did the same. The whole room fell into darkness.

As he got into bed, he warned, "I wake up and you're gone, I'm gonna be pissed, Em." He lay down. "Tell me you understand."

"I understand." She whispered, but it sounded like she'd started crying again.

191

He swallowed and closed his eyes. No way in hell he'd sleep knowing she lay a foot away crying, so he didn't. Within minutes, her breaths evened out, and she cuddled close. Only then did he let himself drift off.

Chapter Eleven

Her head pounded so hard she swore it'd split in two. Eyes swollen, she refused to try to part them. No wonder. Last night, she cried for hours. She'd only sobbed so much once. Still, she knew she had to try. She couldn't stay in bed.

She slid her eyes open and remembered where she was—Bryce's bed. On her side, her gaze landed on the door leading into the bathroom. Her back pressed against the heat of a body. That same warmth snaked around her waist. Carefully, she angled her head to look down and found an arm wrapped around her waist, his arm. One of his legs in between hers, his face at her neck as his breaths heated her skin.

It felt good. She woke up every day for more than five years wishing she had this. It was bittersweet knowing it meant nothing to him and everything to her, and even knowing that, she'd give an arm to wake up like this every day for the rest of her life.

God, she was pathetic. Sleeping beside the man who destroyed her was stupid. Wanting him was weak. Still loving him was pathetic.

He tightened his arm around her waist. Then he shifted. She stilled, holding her breath. He rubbed his face against her shoulder blade inhaling as he glided a hand to her lower abdomen and pressed his hips against her. Feeling the length of his shaft on her butt, she jumped slightly.

A second later, he spoke in his groggy, deep voice. "Fuck."

She held her breath, hoping to God he'd go back to sleep. No way in hell he'd look at her and not know how much she enjoyed waking up like that.

"Know you're awake, Em."

Her chest warmed. He used to call her "Em" all the time. He was never much for pet names, only "babe" when he teased her, but he'd called her "Em" all the time. Even though she'd been living at the compound for close to a month, he never called her Em or by her full name, not until last night. She wasn't that stupid to think it meant something though. He probably felt bad for her. Poor, weak, pathetic Em going all those years still loving a man who never loved her, loving a man who broke her.

She didn't know what she expected. She never imagined seeing him again, never imagined telling him why she left. He made her, and she had. All it cost her—more heartbreak. He'd been shocked. Of course, he never knew she knew and proved it last night. And the fact he didn't have anything to say, not an excuse, not an apology, was because it was the truth. He broke her again, and she had to watch him walk away. Ironic that the last time she'd run away.

That hadn't been enough for him. He forced her in the shower, making her think he cared about her getting sick when he'd been the one to leave her outside for hours. Then he made her sleep in bed with him.

"Em?"

Her chest tightened, this time painfully. She closed her eyes firmly forcing the memory of last night away.

"How're you feeling?"

She should tell him the truth. She felt like she'd been run over by several eighteen-wheelers driven by him. Instead, she whispered, "Fine." The truth. Right then and there, with his arm around her, his breath on her neck, she was just fine.

"Yeah?"

"Yeah."

His hand at her waist gripped her hip. He flipped her until she laid on her other side, her chest to his. Then he scanned her face for endless moments. God help her, but he actually looked worried about her, just like he had the night before.

It's all a lie. Don't believe it. He cheated, broke you.

"You sure?"

She looked like shit, knew it. And he was still looking at her intensely. She should've gotten up while she had the chance even if she'd pay for it. Better than him seeing her looking like shit, right?

God, she was so pathetic!

"You dreaming with your eyes open?" He smiled wide and big and at her.

She'd seen him smile a lot, even recently. For a long time, she thought she'd never see it again. Then she thought she'd never be rewarded with it. And out of nowhere, there it was. He smiled at *her* while he teased *her*.

So shocked by it, she stuttered when she responded. "N-no."

"You sure about that?"

"Yes."

"You sleep good?"

Afraid her voice would betray her, she nodded. "Glad."

Yep, he definitely thought she was weak and pathetic. He slept beside her, cuddled close because he felt bad for her. Could her life get any worse?

"Bree should be coming back soon. We should get up."

Yeah, she just didn't want to. Still, because she had no choice, she nodded and moved.

****

The next several days flew by, Em in a daze, forcing herself to forget—as much as she could—her breakdown. She worked, cooked, cleaned, and spent time with Bree. As for Bryce, something in him had changed that night she told him the reason she left. He didn't seem angry as often anymore. There were times she spotted him in the garage while Bree was at school, and he seemed mad, but he hid it when he spoke to her. The biggest change—the way he treated her. He didn't lose his temper, didn't say mean or crude things, didn't find random excuses to pick fights. Meaning, he wasn't an asshole anymore. Granted, it hadn't been long, but this gave her hope that maybe one day, Bree would have parents who spoke to each other without resentment or anger, that one day she and Bryce could raise their daughter in a healthier environment for all of them.

She and Bree had been living in the compound for more than five weeks. They'd both settled into a routine of sorts, but she had yet to hear about Chip. Thinking on how to broach the subject with Bryce or even if she should broach it, a customer walked in. She greeted him pleasantly and asked how she could help. He gave her his name and handed her his credit card stating he had to close out a bill. She charged him, updated the file in the computer, printing an invoice then had him sign his credit card receipt. She stapled the invoice and receipt copy, handed them to him, and said a quick "thank you" before she went back to work.

"You should smile more."

Her gaze trailed away from the monitor and moved toward him. For the first time, she took a good look at the man standing in front of her. Handsome, a little over six-feet with golden-brown hair gelled back. Eyes a dark-brown shade, he wore a pair of dark pants, a long-sleeved shirt, and tie. The type of man Chip wanted her to end up with.

All those years ago, when she told Chip about Bryce after their third date, Chip hadn't been pleased. He knew about bikers, considering he was one, and he had high hopes for her. He wanted her to end up with a man who made an honest living. Chip lectured her, but she hadn't listened. She'd been so adamant Bryce was different or that he was different about her. Chip gave in eventually, but she never thought it had anything to do with her convincing him. More likely, it had to do with him wanting her to be happy and letting her live her life the way she wanted. Maybe Chip figured when Bryce messed up, he'd be there to catch her fall. If it hadn't been for the fact she'd been pregnant, he would have.

Looking at the handsome man in front of her, she hated to think what would've happened had she fallen for a man like him. Maybe she would've never been hurt. Maybe she would have, but she wouldn't have Bree.

"You've got a beautiful smile. You should smile more."

Times like these she wished she was over Bryce, wished she'd move on. She'd definitely go for a line like that, simple and sweet, a man who subtly tried to find out if she was interested, a man who didn't press her but let her make the next move, so she did.

She smiled softly. "I'll try." Then she looked away, nicely telling him she wasn't interested. Before she did, she caught him smiling.

A loud bang sounded as the door leading into the garage crashed open. Her gaze shot up. The customer's hand on the knob to the other door, leading outside, he stopped mid-stride and turned to the sound. She did as well and spotted Bryce, jaw hard, hands in fists, eyes dead.

She knew that look, knew what would come... Just when things had gotten better between them, a shame. Holding her breath, she steeled herself for the verbal assault.

Bryce glared at the customer then looked at her. "Babe, hungry."

Not what she expected him to say.

He took a step, ending by the window with a view of the garage, and snapped the blinds shut. Walking toward the other side of the office, Bryce made it to the other window and shut those blinds as well just as the customer left. When the door closed, Bryce locked it then strode back to the other door and locked that one as well.

Walking toward her with a hungry yet livid look in his eyes, she spoke quickly, "I'll make you a sandwich."

He strode past her.

She expelled a breath then heard the blinds of the window behind her snapping shut and turned. "I'll make you—"

The next instant, he crushed his lips against hers. His tongue parted her lips, arms wrapped around her back, tugging her to him. And she *didn't* fight. The scent of him around her, the taste of him in her mouth, she *couldn't* fight. She'd wanted him for so long, never stopped, so she couldn't push him away. She gave in just like the last time, and just like the last time, she *encouraged* him, hooking her arms around him, digging her nails into his back. When he trailed his mouth down her neck, she moaned.

"Don't want a sandwich. Want to eat you," he whispered against the skin on her neck.

Goosebumps erupted, her whole body shivered, his heat burning her. The next moment, he pushed her up against the desk and gripped her ass. Lifting her effortlessly placing her butt on the counter, his fingers unfastened the button on her jeans. Before she knew it, he tugged her pants and thong down her legs.

Bare and dripping wet, he knelt in front of her. Her eyes met his, her legs actually widened on their own in anticipation. Wrapping his arms around her thighs, he shoved her forward until his mouth met her core. Then he fed.

The second she felt him there, she screamed a scream that turned into a moan. His tongue lapped against her clit, the stubble covering his chin and cheeks making the pleasure more intense. In seconds, she was there. He knew it, must've felt it because he pulled away just before.

Her legs convulsed. "No... Please..."

"You want it, Em?"

Breathing heavily, she nodded, frantically. "Please..."

"Watch me."

She held his eyes for a long moment. Then he fed from her, again. He did it faster, harder, holding her eyes the entire time almost as if willing her to look away. She didn't. She couldn't. She wanted to watch him there, pleasuring her, wanted to watch his face when he made her come. It didn't take long.

His fingers bit into her thighs as it hit her. Powerful, so mind-numbingly powerful her head snapped back, her whole body shook as she let out a deep moan.

The next thing she knew, he stood, grabbed the back of her neck, and brought her face to his, so she met his strange, beautiful eyes. Those eyes that weren't dead but hungry. For her.

Jaw clenched, muscles on his shoulders bunched, he pressed the length of him into her. She hadn't noticed when he'd dropped his jeans and boxers. Holding her breath, she wrapped her legs around his waist, helping him inside.

Then he was in, stretching her, owning her, and the feel of him...like nothing she'd ever felt.

He held still for an endless moment, eyes holding hers and widening when he let out a groan. "Fuck." His hand at her neck trailed down her side then gripped her hip. He pulled out of her slowly then slammed into her, hard and sudden.

She screamed, and her head flew back, arms went around his shoulders, holding on.

"Look at *me*."

Instantly, she did. She realized in that endless moment and not for the first time just how handsome he was.

His ragged breaths hitting her, he drove into her again and again. Then she forgot everything but the feel of him around her and inside her. He tensed a moment before it hit her again. She was *gone*, but she refused to lose sight of his eyes.

He thrust harder and faster. His cock jerking inside her, he groaned so loud she heard it over her own moans. She couldn't do anything but stare at him connected to her and catch her breath until the high faded. Only then she became very aware of what they'd done, what she let him do to her, again.

He fucked her, hard and rough on top of her desk at work! They hadn't been discreet either. She'd been loud. At least he'd closed the blinds, right?

He had been her first and last, the father of her child, the man she fell for at eighteen and never got over, but he cheated. He never loved her. He destroyed her. She knew all of this, and still, all he had to do was kiss her, and she was spreading her legs?

Feeling her cheeks heat, she tore her gaze from his. Still inside, he hadn't moved. It seemed he didn't have plans to. She should make him. A part of her wanted to, but she couldn't find the strength, which only made her want to cry. She hadn't managed to do anything she should've, so she promised herself in that instant, she wouldn't give him the satisfaction of seeing her cry, again.

He pulled out of her, slowly. Because she was stupid, weak, and pathetic, she missed it, missed him.

She didn't let herself think on that long. Her hands went to his chest, she shoved him hard, hopped off her desk, grabbed her thong and jeans on the floor, and tugged them on quickly. As she did that, her gaze landed on the camera at the top left corner of the room.

How had she forgotten? She noticed it weeks ago, the same week she started working in the office, so she knew they watched her every move.

Oh God, she'd let him film her. Bryce and his brothers would watch how easily he'd taken her on top of her desk at work, how easily he made her his whore. Because having his brothers hear them hadn't been humiliating enough; now they'd get to watch her too, over and over again.

Damn it. Bryce could put that video on the Internet, or he could blackmail her with it, make her do whatever he wanted.

Shit! She'd get fired too, and then, she'd have nothing to occupy her time in between taking care of Bree. She wouldn't be able to save money and would be out on the street as soon as the shit storm with the Falcons ended.

How was it possible she still loved him?

Realizing this, she broke the promise she made to herself a moment ago. Her eyes watered, and tears fell down her face. At least, her voice didn't tremble when she spoke. "Leave."

His eyes went dead when he hardened his jaw. Then he tugged on his boxers and jeans. "Scratched the itch, so you're done with me?"

Her mouth dropped open. "You're unbelievable."

He closed the distance between them. "Gotta speak up, *babe*. Can't hear you."

"You got what you wanted, Ripper. Now, just make it quick and tell me what you want."

Brows furrowing, he cocked his head. "Come again?"

Not in the mood to play his mind games, she shot back, "You got your video." She pointed toward the camera.

He looked to it. Then his body locked.

"Now you can show your brothers how easy I made it for you, how quickly you made me your whore. Though you really didn't need to because I'm sure they heard. Then again, you probably wanted a video for other reasons, right? So you can use it against me?"

She got on the tips of her toes and leaned into him. "Well, do your worst, *Ripper*. Do it. You forget, I'm already broken, and just an FYI, *nothing* will make me give up my daughter."

He just stood there. Body strung tight, looking at her, his eyes dead yet shining. Why the hell? She had no clue. Maybe because she figured out his plan.

He should've said something, anything. He should've at least told her what he wanted, but no, he just walked away. No surprise there, not the first time he walked away without so much as a word, and she doubted it'd be the last.

Thinking this, she inhaled, exhaled, and got back to work.

****

Bree passed out. Thank God. Emelia grew tired of hearing her ask when her father would be home.

Em hadn't seen Bryce since that afternoon. After he had her and walked away, he picked up Bree from school. She caught sight of him when Bree strode into the office. After four, Bryce usually swung by the office for Bree. He took her to the backlot of the compound where he'd built her swing set. Other times, they sat in front of the television and watched a movie or show. But that afternoon had been different. Bryce, it seemed, disappeared into thin air. Bree asked several of the brothers where he went, and no one knew. After work, she took Bree to the backlot herself and let her play for half an hour before she made dinner. She left Bree in the living room watching TV. They ate afterward without Bryce since he was still gone, which in itself was odd. He never missed dinner. In fact, he never missed a meal. When he ate out, he took Bree, always.

Bree asked several brothers again when she spotted them after dinner, and she asked her repeatedly. The brothers didn't know or refused to say. Emelia didn't know what to say. She called him three times. He hadn't answered, so she told Bree Bryce probably had a work emergency.

Finally, Bree fell asleep. She hoped by the time morning came Bryce reappeared. She hated to admit she worried. It wasn't like Bryce to disappear without telling Bree. He spent the afternoons and evenings with her, ate dinner with her, said goodnight, and tucked her in.

With those thoughts on her mind, she headed into her closet to find the Harley shirt she always wore to bed. You'd think after Bryce got so mad seeing her in it, she would've stopped wearing it. She hadn't. She couldn't. She'd worn it for years now. Because he was tall and she wasn't, it hung low on her reaching her mid-thigh. It was also old and raggedly, which made it all the more comfortable. And yes, it had once been his. He gave it to her. She loved it then. She loved it now. She didn't know why he'd been so angry to see her wearing it, didn't know why he let her keep it in the end, but she was glad.

Stripping down to her thong, she donned the tee then stepped out of the closet. The door to her room parted, and Bryce strode in. His stare went to the bed where Bree lay. He released a breath then spared a glance at her tee before meeting her eyes. Instinctively, she crossed her arms over her chest, wishing she waited to dress for bed.

"Lost track of time."

She guessed that much. That or he lay in a ditch somewhere. Bryce didn't miss spending time with Bree, ever.

"Did she ask for me?"

She nodded. "Of course."

"Could've called."

"I did. Three times."

His brows rose. Reaching into his pocket, he pulled out his phone. Looking at the screen, he mumbled, "Fuck." Then he met her stare. "On silent."

"I told her you had a work emergency."

He lifted his chin. "Thanks."

Bryce walked toward the bed, gave Bree a kiss on the forehead as he simultaneously dragged a hand through her hair. Then he straightened and advanced taking step after step toward her. Em fought the urge to back away. Stopping a couple of feet away, his arm sprang forward, holding out a CD. She had no idea why and must've looked confused.

"That's it."

It didn't answer a thing. She quirked a brow and asked, "What?"

Looking down at his feet, he released a frustrated sigh like she should know what he meant. He shifted his hand from the top of his head to the back before he looked at her again. "The video of…today."

Shit. The video. Of them. Not a CD but a DVD, proof of just how easily she became his whore, and he was handing it over. Why? Trying to trick her? Did he have another copy?

He walked a little closer then spoke in a low voice. "I know you probably won't believe me, but I didn't mean to get us on film. I don't want anyone looking at a video of anyone banging my kid's mom even if it's me who's banging her. I'd never even think to use it against you 'cause I couldn't bring myself to share it, 'cause I don't want anyone to ever see it. I acted on impulse, so I wasn't thinking about the camera. Meaning I didn't plan it, and I sure as hell didn't have a motive."

He shrugged. "Yeah, the brothers probably heard you. They heard me, too. I wouldn't care except I wasn't banging some tap. I was banging my kid's mom, so I care they heard you. I care they heard me. We've never been quiet before. The walls here aren't sound proof, so I'm sure they've heard us before. When you were mine, no one said shit to you, so as my kid's mom, no one's gonna say shit to you."

Had he just… Shit, he had. No way in hell she'd hallucinated. Her hand went to her throat, she swallowed thickly. She should say something, thank him at least, but she couldn't put two words together.

"And you aren't gonna be fired."

She didn't know how long she just stood there, looking at him, but it had been a while when he spoke again.

He held up the DVD. "You gonna make me wait all night for you to take this?"

God, he was beautiful, so rugged and handsome with those thick, arched brows, stubble-covered, squared jaw, and unique eyes.

"Em?"

She needed to focus, concentrate. Maybe Em shouldn't believe him. He never said anything he didn't mean though. Yes, he cheated and broke her, but he never said they were exclusive, never said he loved her. He bought a new bed, one he hadn't fucked taps on, but maybe he hadn't had sex with Lilliam there, or maybe he and Lilliam had been more than just meaningless sex.

She believed him, and the fact she did made her feel like shit for assuming the worst earlier and snapping at him.

His eyes hardened to slits. "Fuck it." He turned and stormed off, but before he walked out of her room, he set the DVD on the armoire.

Insane that it made her feel bad for letting him go thinking she didn't believe him. After all he'd done to her, she didn't owe him anything, and still, guilt choked her.

Chapter Twelve

Fuck it.

Fuck her.

Ripper knew it was a long shot, knew it'd be useless, but he did it anyway.

He spent *hours* erasing that video from their system. Ripper didn't know the first thing about computers. Strike did. Since he refused to let Strike know exactly what he wanted deleted or let him do it himself, he demanded Strike teach him how to erase a video, and it took too long. All the surveillance videos were automatically recorded onto DVDs and kept in Prez's office. After finally deleting it from the computer, Ripper took the only copy and gave it to her. He explained himself, how he hadn't meant to record them, how he never wanted anyone, except maybe himself and her, though he didn't say that, to watch that video. She just stood there with her beautiful face and that long blonde hair wearing *his* tee looking at him not saying a goddamned thing.

Now, he was just pissed. He missed lunch because he chose to have her instead. Then he'd been too busy to think about food, picking up Bree while having a panic attack knowing he had to find a way to delete the video from their system. By the time he learned how to delete it, it'd been past dinner. He was starved, and he missed spending the afternoon and evening with Bree.

What the hell did he get out of going through all that trouble—nothing. She didn't believe him. She probably thought he had another copy of that video. Granted, had he been thinking clearly, he would've made a copy. Not to share, never that, but so he could watch it over and over again. God knew he'd probably never get that lucky again. Like the first and last time, he hadn't savored it, her. He should've taken his time, should've made it last longer, much longer.

The realization made him angrier, so revved he wasn't even hungry anymore, just livid. No way in hell he'd get to sleep. Closing his eyes, he released a breath and came to the conclusion a ride wouldn't help cool his temper, only running for miles would. That sucked, big time. The last several days, he'd barely slept. After he tucked Bree in every night, he ran from bar to bar trying to find that bitch Lilliam. All to no avail.

He ripped off his cut and shirt then removed his boots and jeans and donned a pair of athletic shorts and sneakers. With the run on his mind, he pulled the door open and froze.

Em stood there, arms wrapped around her mid-section, still beautiful, still wearing his tee and looking as surprised as he to find her there.

"I...um..." She looked to her right then met his gaze. "Can we talk?"

He looked to his left. Hash and some tap stood ten feet from them making out hot and heavy. The tap nearly naked already, skin-tight shirt, revealing her stomach, skirt hiked up around her waist, Hash gripping her bare ass. Hadn't he just reamed him about this shit?

Ripper whistled loud. When Hash met his stare, Ripper glared. He didn't have to say a word. Hash opened his door and tugged them inside.

Ripper sliced his gaze back to Em. "What?"

He hadn't meant to bark, but seeing Hash getting lucky put him in a shittier mood because Hash was getting some, and he wasn't, because Hash could fuck whoever he wanted, and he couldn't. He wanted Em. No one would do but her, and he couldn't have her.

"I wanted to talk to you."

"Talk."

She looked at his chest quickly, almost like she'd been trying to hide it, but he caught it, and it made him ecstatic. He bit his lip to hold back a smile.

She met his eyes. "I believe you."

Still thinking about her checking him out, he didn't quite catch that. "Say again?"

"I believe you, and I'm sorry I jumped to conclusions and snapped at you, and thank you for giving me the video."

Hearing footsteps coming up the stairs, he grabbed her arm, led her into his room, shut the door, and faced her. "You believe *me*?"

"Yes."

He quirked a brow. "Yeah?"

She sighed. "Yes."

"About what?"

"About the video."

"What about it?"

"I believe you didn't mean to get us on camera. I believe you never meant to use it against me."

He couldn't bite back his smile then. If she believed him, then maybe anything was possible. Maybe she liked what they'd done. Maybe she wanted him again. He should take the chance.

He took a step toward her. She took one back. He took another, and she did the same. He didn't stop though. She didn't either, not until the back of her legs hit the bed, and she fell on her butt.

He knelt, eye level to her. "Would you lie to me, Em?"

She shook her head.

He cocked his. "No?"

"No."

He drew closer, lips an inch from hers. "So I can ask you whatever I want, and you won't lie?"

Her eyes widened. "Not—"

"Did you like what we did, Em?"

Her breath hitched. She put her hands on the bed behind her and leaned away. Positioning himself between her legs, he snaked an arm around her waist, shoved her up, and held her still. Her hands went to his bare chest. That close, her hands on him and feeling her warmth...*amazing*. She liked it too. Her face flushed even as her breaths became shallower.

"Do you want to do it again, Em?"

Her nails bit into his skin. "I...Bryce..."

He rubbed his nose against her cheek then trailed it toward the base of her neck. "You want me, Em?" Moving back up to her ear, he flicked his tongue out licking her lobe.

Her whole body shuddered, legs closing against him instinctively. "Bryce..."

"Gotta answer me, Em."

"Please..."

"Gotta answer me."

He kissed under her ear softly then tasted her and refused to stop. She arched her back as her legs wrapped around him.

"You want me, Em?"

"Always."

Always?

Fuck.

Always?

He reared back, locking gazes with her. She blanched and pushed at his chest. She could do that all she wanted, but she'd get nowhere because he was a lot stronger and no way in hell he'd let her go.

"Please…" She sounded panicked.

"Always what?"

"Stop… Please." She pushed harder.

"Always. What?"

"Stop—"

"Tell. Me."

Her eyes grew wide. Then they watered, so he did something he used to when she got stubborn. He bargained.

"Tell me, and I'll let you go. I promise."

She fought back the tears, but still, two fell out of her eyes and cascaded down her cheeks.

Hating the tears, he shut his eyes. "You always what?"

"I—"

He cracked his eyes open and met hers.

"I always want you." Her voice shook like it hurt her to admit it, like she didn't want to.

Too late though. She had, and he *heard* every word. It left him wondering what she wanted him for? To fuck? To mess with? For keeps? No, not for keeps, she didn't love him, not anymore.

Since he had to keep his word, he had to let her go.

He didn't want to though, and he was a selfish bastard, so he tried to find a way to break his promise. Coming up empty, he had no choice. "I don't want to let you go, Em, but if you want me to let you go, I will."

She didn't say a word, didn't push him away either, so he lay on the bed and tugged her against him. Clutching her to him with the scent of her perfume taunting him, he decided he'd have her. Whatever part of her she'd give, he wanted because he loved her. He never stopped.

Chapter Thirteen

A couple of weeks ago, Emelia admitted something she never should've—that she wanted him, *always*. Since then, she hadn't spent a single night without him. After he tucked Bree in, after Bree fell asleep, he made his move. Because she'd admitted what she had to her first boyfriend, first lover, the father of her child, the man she never stopped loving, she couldn't find it in her to pull away and refuse his advances, which meant they'd had sex, a lot.

The first time she gave in again, just the day after she admitted she wanted him, always. She felt guilty about it, knowing nothing would come of it, knowing she made a complicated situation worse, knowing, in the end, the person who'd suffer the most was Bree. And so, after she gave in, she tried to leave, but Bryce stopped her.

Snaking an arm around her waist, he hauled her toward him until her back hit the expanse of his chest. He then buried his face in her neck. "Get cleaned up, Em, then come right back. We aren't done."

She thought about walking out for about two seconds. Then he pressed a kiss to her temple. Sweet, and also something he used to do before. A warmth spread through her chest. She released a heavy sigh. Her stupid, weak, and pathetic heart for a moment hoped maybe she was more than just sex to him. That thought shattered when her conscience reminded her he'd cheated and broken her, so that heat she felt spread through her faded fast. She realized belatedly—very belatedly—that she had to clean up, and that wasn't good. It was bad news. He hadn't used a condom. In fact, the three times they'd been together, he hadn't used a condom. More bad news. Bryce was a biker and bikers slept around, but aside from that, when they'd been together, he hadn't been faithful. She was not delusional to think Bryce abstained since she left.

"You didn't wear a condom?"

He released her allowing her to turn and face him. "I didn't."

Heat crawled up her cheeks. Her heart dropped to the pit of her stomach. Aggravation, anger, annoyance, and fear… "Why—"

"I'm clean. I got tested after that first time."

He got tested after that first time with her? Why? Because he knew he'd have her again and again? Because he wanted to look out for her? Because, what? Did it matter? He got tested. He was clean, meaning she was too. Some of the tension lining her shoulders melted.

"I can take you to get tested—"

She closed her eyes tightly and shook her head. "There's no need. I haven't been with anyone…but you."

His eyes widened then narrowed. "You're fuckin' kidding me?"

Another admission she regretted the moment she said it. Already she'd handed him too much. Not that it mattered, he didn't believe her. That was heartbreaking because he *knew* her, knew she wasn't like him.

Besides, she loved him and never stopped, so sleeping with anyone else had been out of the question.

She swallowed then lifted her chin. "I have no reason to lie. If you need a reason to believe me, then I'll explain. I was alone in a new city and pregnant. I had to find a job and a place to live. Then I had a baby. I didn't have time to date." She turned, straightened, and stood.

He grasped her hand, tugged her back onto the mattress, and leaned into her ear to whisper, "I believe you."

I believe you. Exactly the words she said to him the night before.

Just then, she wished her chest hadn't tightened like it did, wished he hadn't believed her. If he hadn't, she could hate him and walk away.

He ran his nose along the length of her collar bone. It took a moment to remember what they'd been talking about.

She pulled away, got her thoughts in order, and met his gaze. "Bryce."

His brows creased.

She steeled herself to say what she had to. "I'm not on birth control."

He took this news so easily she convinced herself he hadn't heard her. After a moment, she repeated it. "Did you hear me? I'm *not* on birth control."

He smiled. "Yeah, babe. I heard you."

"The last time...I was on the pill, and I ended up pregnant." Her stomach rolled. She ignored it and went on. "We've had sex three times without a condom. I could be pregnant right now, Bryce. I-I..." *Oh, shit.* "I could be *pregnant*, again." By the time she finished, she sounded borderline hysterical because saying it aloud made it real, and that terrified her.

He chuckled. It wasn't funny, not even a little bit, and the fact he thought it so made her feel like she was in an alternate universe.

He cupped her cheek then trailed his hand backward, his fingers threading through her hair until they reached the base of her neck. "It's gonna be fine, Em."

No, it wouldn't. Bringing another life into the world, another life tied to him wouldn't help. They weren't together. As it was, she stood to get hurt again because he'd break her, *again*. She wanted Bree to have a whole mom. She'd want another baby to have a whole mom too.

Her breaths coming out quickly, she managed to whisper, "What?"

"It's gonna be fine."

Her eyes widened, her voice high-pitched when she shrieked, "Have you lost your mind?"

He quirked a brow. "Naw, Em."

She didn't say anything, but she did stare at him wide-eyed. Thankfully, he took that as the need to explain.

"We made a beautiful, smart girl the first time. I'm sure the second time 'round will be the same."

Her jaw dropped. "You *have*. You have lost your *mind*."

He threw his head back and laughed. Yes, *laughed*, a real laugh, and like everything about him, it was gorgeous.

Lost in the sound, in the fact he laughed with her, it took her a while to say, "I can't believe... I just—"

"It wasn't planned, but that doesn't mean *we* aren't going to deal with it. This time, *we* will deal with it, not just you. You aren't running again, Em, 'cause this time, you run, I'll chase you, and I'll find you and bring you and Bree and anyone else right back," he said this softly, calmly.

A vast change. A few weeks ago, he would've gotten furious, snapped, and said something hurtful. Despite this, she knew he meant every word.

"Get me?"

That he'd chase her shouldn't make her feel good. For some reason, it did. Disturbing, and for good reason. It wasn't a normal reaction. He hadn't said he loved her, hadn't told her they'd be exclusive, hadn't even told her he wanted her. He wanted what was half his—his kids.

He drew closer, grazing his lips against hers, making her breath hitch. With his hand at the back of her neck, he squeezed her gently. "Tell me you understand."

She swallowed. "I understand."

He kissed her. Every thought, every worry faded. They went for round two.

Every night since then, they had sex usually more than once. Every night after they had sex, multiple times, tired and worn out, she fell asleep in his arms. Every morning, she woke around six, left quietly, and headed into her room to wake Bree for school. No one, she knew, had seen her.

The sex was amazing as it'd always been, and as the days slid by, she noticed something—a bigger change in him. It didn't happen overnight, but with the more and more she gave herself to him. He wasn't angry at all anymore. In fact, over the last several weeks, she couldn't recall seeing him upset or annoyed. Before he'd only smiled and laughed with Bree, but now, he did it more so and randomly. Most shocking was that at night with her, he smiled, laughed, and teased her. Like before…

There were smaller changes too. He hardly took Bree out for long periods of time, almost like he was letting her spend more time with Bree. And on occasion when he took Bree out, he made sure to tell her not just where he planned to take Bree but when they'd be back. He also often thanked her for cooking and cleaning.

Still, none of this meant they were in a relationship. Though she doubted he slept around since he spent his nights with her and his days at the garage or with Bree, she couldn't be sure. Nights, they spoke easily and often, and he couldn't keep his hands off her. She fell asleep in his arms and woke in them. But things changed during the day and in front of others. They spoke sparingly; he didn't touch her, hold her hand, pull her into a hug, or kiss her. Showing affection was something he did often when they'd been together because he wanted everyone to know she belonged to him.

So despite the earth-shattering sex, the change in him, and the way he treated her, she knew they weren't in a relationship. He was using her for sex. She had no doubts eventually they'd end, and she'd be further broken. Yet even knowing this, she couldn't stop giving into him. A part of her didn't want to. Because she loved him, definitely, but because those years without him, she'd missed him so much, and now, she had a part of him back. But most importantly, every night, she felt loved, utterly and completely and by him. He took her fast and hard, but he also took her slow and savored her. They didn't just have sex, but they talked and laughed and cuddled.

"Em?"

She straightened and met Cuss's sapphire gaze.

"Parts delivery's here. Can you come out and double check it?"

"Sure." She stood.

Still getting familiar with most of the parts, she had to ask Cuss about a few of them. Distracted mid-way, Bree rushed her. She instinctively looked up and saw Bryce walking inside the garage, looking hot per usual, wearing a pair of jeans and tee with the garage's logo that fit his chiseled frame perfectly, not to mention he had overgrown stubble covering his chin and cheeks and eyes that beautiful-strange color. Though they were sleeping together, and he treated her far better than he had in the past, he never looked her way randomly. This didn't stop her from glancing at him often, and she'd done this since the day he'd moved them in.

As she thought this, his gaze lifted from Bree, locked on her, and heated. Then he lifted his chin, and a shadow of a smile flashed across his lips. Her breath clogging in the back of her throat, her lips parted. The reason her heart beat erratically—that hungry look in his eyes, that small smile he threw her way, and that he'd done it in front of his brothers. In shock, she froze, her thoughts helplessly drifted to the night before.

They had sex three times. After the final time, she collapsed on top of him, and he held her tightly. For a split second, she convinced herself he wanted her for more than sex. With that fantasy, she fell asleep in his arms and woke facing him. Her face buried in his neck, his arms tight around her. Like every other morning, she hadn't wanted to get up, but she did.

"Emelia."

She shifted, her stare locking with a set of hazel eyes identical to hers. Chills ran down her spine. Instinctively and immediately, she wrapped her arm around Bree, pressing her close to her side.

Older, aged by ten years, but it looked more like twenty. Then again, he always looked older than he'd been. Abusing alcohol had that effect on people. His hair was all white now, no blond left, and the wrinkles around his mouth and eyes were more pronounced. He looked like a grandpa. Technically, he was.

As his gaze drifted away from her to Bree, she tightened her hold on her daughter. Then he smiled. She couldn't remember ever seeing him smile. When he peered at her again, the smile didn't fade but softened.

"I'm a Grandpa," he said, almost in awe.

He took a step in her direction, prompting her to take one back and simultaneously tug Bree behind her.

She tilted her head to the side, never losing sight of his eyes and said to Bree, "Honey, go into the office."

When Bree didn't move, she met her inquisitive stare and said more forcefully, "Baby, please, I'll be right in."

Bree did what she asked. Emelia watched her go, fighting the urge to flee herself. It had been eleven years, but the innate urge to run and hide—what she'd learned to do as a child—like the fear, hadn't faded. Not one bit.

****

Ripper didn't know how to describe it, didn't know

how it was possible, but he felt it. Tension so thick, it changed the air around him making it hard to breathe.

He looked up, scanned the garage searching for *them*, Bree and Em. Still right where he left them, just outside one of the metal doors leading into the garage, beside a bunch of parts, Em looking out to the lot.

God, he felt *her*. It didn't make sense, and he couldn't explain it, but he did. The way she held herself, body stiff, shoulders tense, the way she held onto Bree, one arm around her shoulders in a death grip, she wasn't herself. Even for the new Em, it was odd. He skimmed the lot for a threat as he headed straight for them on a dead run. He didn't see anything or anyone but an older man, looking to be in his sixties with white hair. Halfway to them not seeing that man as a danger, he slowed his pace and came to a stop without losing sight of them. He waited. He watched.

"I'm a Grandpa."

So lost in the look of utter awe on the man's face, Rip hadn't fully comprehended what he said. The man took a step toward Em and Bree. Em took one back hauling Bree behind her.

I'm a Grandpa.

Shit. Em's father, the one who spent her childhood drunk off his ass beating the shit out of his baby girl. Just like Ripper couldn't understand his lousy parents, he couldn't understand that "non-threatening" man.

There were different ways to be a shitty parent. Not being around was kind of like a first-degree burn. It stung and hurt, but you got over it and moved on. Having a parent who beat the shit out of you was a third-degree burn. You could heal and move on, but you'd have scars you could never erase that served as reminders, so a part of you would never be the same.

Ripper didn't get how his parents had been able to abandon their own flesh and blood, and he sure as fuck didn't get how a man could beat his child repeatedly, a daughter, nonetheless. Thinking about it then, as the father of a beautiful girl, a girl that looked just like Em, made him sick to his stomach.

Em told him about her father once and never talked about it again. The way she said it with no emotion leaving out details, he figured she was like him. She hardened herself to it, didn't want to talk about it, just wanted to put it behind her, and move on. He never asked. Chip saved her from that. She told him that, too. Still, seeing the man who was supposed to protect her, who hurt her instead for so long, he expected more of a reaction. His Em, the old Em, would've screamed or ranted, or done something, any-fucking-thing. But she just stood there, stiff, still, frozen, not saying anything, not doing anything. Honest, he didn't even know if she'd taken a breath.

His gaze shot to her hands—shaking. Scared, no, *terrified* for herself and especially for Bree, and Em made this clear a moment later when she told Bree to go. If he didn't know Em so well, if he hadn't been so attuned to her, he would've missed it. Still, he didn't know how she could look into the eyes of the man who beat her repeatedly without running or screaming or attacking him.

"Leave." Her voice firm.

The man's eyes widened. "I know it's been a long time, but—"

"Leave."

Rip moved, quick and fast.

"I wanted to…"

He grabbed Em by the upper arm and hauled her beside him.

The man's gaze flew to him. "You're the father?"

Yeah, he was also fucking his daughter every night. She was much more than just sex to him, but he wasn't more than that to her, a realization he came to every morning when he woke to find her gone. So he shouldn't step in, he should let her deal with her abusive father herself, but he couldn't like he couldn't let her father think he was nothing more than Bree's father.

"Yeah, and Em's man."

The man looked from Em to him.

He felt the heat of Em's hand grasp his forearm, tightly. Her palm wasn't just shaky but sweaty holding onto him in a death grip and pulling herself closer. She did this in front of her shit father but also in front of his brothers like she *wanted* him to step in, protect her, save her, like she didn't mind admitting to everyone she *needed* him. And that felt amazing making warmth slice up his stomach.

The man held out his hand to shake his. "Gerard. Em's father."

He looked to the man's hand then further hardened his eyes before meeting his stare again. "Know who you are. What I don't know is what the fuck you're doing here."

Gerard lowered his hand then released a heavy sigh. "Guess you know—"

"Damn fuckin' right I do. Answer the question."

Gerard looked to Em. "I wanted to reconnect with—"

"Eyes up here. She doesn't talk, not to you."

That easiness now faded. Gerard glared at him. "She's a grown woman and can speak for herself." His voice rose.

Em cringed against him, and it unhinged something deep in the middle of his chest.

The need to protect her searing him, he barked, "Yeah, she can, but she *isn't*. I'm not giving you the satisfaction of speaking to *my* woman."

"She's my daughter—" Gerard spoke louder, his tone grew harsher.

Rip could only imagine how many times she heard that tone, too many, probably every time the man beat her. Proving how it affected her, she tightened her hand around his forearm.

He wrapped his arm around her shoulders, forcing her to release his arm. When he tucked her against him so that her chest pressed against his side, she planted the palm of her hand on his stomach. "She's *my* woman, and I protect what's *mine*. Protecting what's mine means she won't be speaking to a man who beat the shit outta her repeatedly."

She flinched against him on the last word then tucked her face against his shoulder.

Her father sighed heavily. "I've been sober for more than a year. I came to make amends—"

"Inside." When she didn't move, he looked down at her to find her staring back at him. "Inside, Em."

Her eyes softened. She did as he asked. He waited until he heard the office door open and close before he spoke. "So your program says you need to make amends, and you come? You fuckin' shitting me?"

"That's—"

He clenched his jaw. "Get the fuck outta here."

"I'm not leaving until I talk to my daughter."

Ripper took a step in his direction then went to take another and felt a hand on his shoulder. He didn't bother to look. He knew when he turned he'd see his brothers at his back, like always. "You will go, asshole, or I'll throw you out. I see you come here again, we're gonna have problems. You come near Em or Bree, we're gonna have bigger problems."

"You can't keep me away—"

"Em's a grown woman. She wants to reconnect with you, she can. That doesn't mean you're ever gonna get near Bree. Em may forgive you, but she loves Bree more than anything, and she'll never let you near her. You talk up her ear and by some fucked miracle convince Em to let you see Bree?" He jerked his head side to side. "That shit still isn't gonna happen 'cause I'm her dad, and I say *hell fuck no*."

Gerard's brows wrinkled. "You—"

"Do the smart thing and leave, man." Cuss now stood beside him.

Gerard hesitated, gaze flying behind Rip. After a moment, he walked away. Ripper watched him until Em's father got into his beat-up truck and drove away. Only then Rip turned and spotted Trig, Mellow, Hash, and Bud. He nodded his thanks. Not in the mood for his bullshit, he avoided Bud's eyes.

Heading for the office, he stopped just outside and pulled the door ajar a fraction of an inch. Em knelt in front of Bree.

"That was my grandpa?"

He wanted to know what she'd say. He kind of needed to know, too, so he stayed just outside the door and listened.

Em's father showing out of nowhere, claiming he was sober and wanted to reconnect worried Ripper more than he cared to admit. He didn't think Em would fall for that bullshit, but he couldn't be too sure. People had a need to ask questions they knew the answers to. When the truth was ugly, people wanted to believe it wasn't the truth, or they wanted to believe there was a good reason for that ugly truth. He'd asked himself time and time again why his mom left. She showed on his door, he may just ask her even though deep down he knew the answer.

"That man was your grandfather, but he's not family... Bree, your family is your dad. It's me. It's *this* club. Your uncles Strike, Trig, Bud, Cuss, Army; your aunties Allie, Mia, Lynn, Tiff; Della, Cullen, and Tina, too, all of them *are* your family. They'll never fail you."

Fuck. He couldn't believe she said it. He never expected her to say it, to believe it, and she thought it true. If she didn't, she would've never said it to Bree. Swallowing thickly, he rubbed his palm over the burn in his chest.

"What about Uncle Chip?"

"Him too."

"Why are you crying, Mommy?"

Damn it. It just occurred to him he hadn't heard about Chip at all. That meant Em had probably been worrying about her cousin this whole time, and she'd never asked.

Em wiped her face. "Your Uncle Chip, he's been sick."

"I'll pray, and he'll get better. I know he will

because I prayed for Daddy, and Daddy came. Remember, Mommy? We used to pray for Daddy."

That ache in his chest compounded and sliced up his throat like a blade, a pain he now felt everywhere.

"Yes, baby. I remember. We can pray for Chip tonight. We'll do it together."

What the hell would happen if Chip died? How would they tell Bree? He didn't know. What he did know—if Chip died, it'd destroy Em. Em had idolized the man ever since he saved her from her piece-of-shit father.

Ripper fully opened the door. Bree looked at him, and a smile spread across her face.

"Time for homework, ain't it?"

She nodded. Em stood and faced him.

"You start while I talk to your mom a minute, yeah?"

Bree nodded again then went behind the desk for her book bag. He held open the door for Em then let it close after he walked out. Just outside the door, they stood barely a foot apart.

"You okay?"

She tilted her head. "Yeah."

"You sure?"

Smiling softy, she nodded. "Thanks for—"

"It's not a big deal, Em."

Her eyes softened. Then she grabbed his forearm and squeezed. "It *is*, Bryce. It so is." She shook her head. "I was…"

Terrified. He knew, and he had a feeling she wouldn't trust him with that. Then again, while he hadn't been a dick to her recently, something she couldn't've missed, he knew he had to gain her trust, something he decided that instant he'd do. He loved her, and though he still didn't know if he could forgive her, he wanted to be there for her however she needed him to be.

"Thank you."

He scanned her face. "Are you buying he's sober?"

She shook her head. "Don't know. Don't care."

He quirked a brow. "Yeah?"

She laughed, humorlessly. "Some wounds never heal."

He agreed but couldn't bring himself to say it, so without another word, he walked away.

****

Ripper's eyes snapped open, and she was still there lying beside him. Her front pressed close to his side, her leg hiked over his, and her face against his shoulder.

Heaven.

That night, he'd gone to her and told her what he found out. Chip was no better, still in a coma. She angled her head away from his, but before she did, he saw her eyes water. He closed the distance between them, put his arms around her, and she let him. She then wrapped her arms around his waist and thanked him for the second time that day. It felt good doing something she wanted or needed, so he swore he'd start doing shit to get her to thank him again and again.

Knowing the real reason she left, he couldn't stop thinking that none of it should've happened. He still didn't know if he could forgive her, but he wanted her, and he made it a point to show her.

He kissed her then, kissed her until she practically begged him for it. He gave it to her hard and fast the first two times. Then he gave it to her nice and slow, just like he used to. He fell asleep moments after her. And now, she was still there, but he was awake, and he had no idea why.

A knock came then, loud and louder.

He looked to Em. Her blonde hair a mess, she hadn't moved. Her eyes still closed. In the process of extricating himself, he heard another knock. He cursed under his breath swearing he'd kill whoever had knocked. They woke Em, and she got up and left, he'd be beyond pissed.

Rushing to the door, he managed to get a pair of shorts and pulled them on a second before he opened it, not caring who saw Em in his bed. He wanted everyone to know. Em was dressed, wearing one of his shirts, so it's not like anyone would see anything they shouldn't.

He met Strike's gaze.

"Daddy?"

His head shot down. Bree's eyes were wide, tears streaked her face, her hand clasping Strike's.

The anger from having been woken faded fast. Deciding to comfort her first, he reached for her and pulled her against him, hugging her tightly. "What's wrong, baby?"

"I-I…" She took a shaky breath.

He wiped her face then threaded his fingers through her hair. Resting his hand on the back of her neck, he angled her face to his. "Tell me, Bree."

"I can't find Mommy. I…need Mommy." She started sobbing.

"Shh…It's okay, baby."

"No, Daddy, it's not. M-Mommy's gone."

He knelt in front of Bree. "Baby, your mom isn't gone. She's with me."

She stopped crying.

He looked at Strike. He hated being jealous his baby girl needed her mom and had gone to Strike instead of him. This, he couldn't show, not in front of Bree anyway. "Thanks, Strike. I'll take care of this."

Strike nodded then peered at Bree. "You'll be okay, Jelly Bean." He rubbed her head softly then strode away.

He waited until Strike was out of ear shot before he asked, "Why didn't you come to me?"

"I did, Daddy, but you didn't answer the door."

Shit. He hadn't heard her knock. It sucked not being there when his baby needed him. He swallowed then said, "I didn't get it 'cause I was asleep, and I didn't hear you knock. I heard it, I would've answered it. Yeah?"

She nodded.

"Next time, Bree, you knock harder, so I hear you. If I still don't answer, you walk right in."

She smiled softly then nodded again.

"If you need your mom, we can wake her, or you can tell me what you need, and maybe I can help."

She took an unsteady breath. "I had a...a bad dream."

He knew about bad dreams, about dreams so bad that you dreaded sleep. Up until a few weeks ago, his were of Em. He still dreamt of her, but now he knew where she was and he had her—a part of her anyway—so the dreams weren't that bad. He didn't know about Bree's bad dreams though, and he didn't know how to comfort a kid who had a bad dream. As a kid, no one comforted him.

His brows furrowed. "Yeah?"

She nodded.

He cocked a brow. "Do you wanna tell me about it?"

Looking away, she shook her head and wiped her face.

"What does your mom do when you have a bad dream?"

Her gaze moved to his. "She sleeps with me."

He smiled. "How about I do you one better. You can sleep in bed with your mom and me."

She smiled and nodded. He picked her up, carried her inside, and tucked her into bed between Em and him.

Sleeping with both his girls close, he fell asleep smiling.

Chapter Fourteen

Em's eyes slid open at the same time every morning, so she knew the most dreaded part of her day had come—getting out of bed, in particular, getting out of Bryce's bed, out of the comfort of his arms. She had to though. Thursday, a school day slash work day, she had to wake Bree and get her ready for school, and she had to get ready for work.

On her side, she faced him, her head close to his. Relaxed in sleep, he looked absolutely beautiful, hair disheveled, stubble overgrown, and chest on display. She should've kept her eyes closed. Now, she really hated getting up.

Feeling movement, she angled her head down and noticed the blonde head of hair snuggled close between them. How the hell? When had Bree joined them in bed? Why would she?

Bree had bad dreams from time to time. When she did, Em let her sleep in bed with her though Bree hadn't had a bad dream for a while, not since moving. Times in the past when Bree had one, she always woke Em, always asked if she could sleep with her. If she had a bad dream last night, Bree hadn't known where to find her since Bree didn't know she left her at night. Bree had woken last night, and her baby had woken alone because she'd been with Bryce. Guilt clogging her throat, she thought back. She would've remembered waking in the middle of the night. She didn't, so she hadn't let her daughter get in bed with her. Had she, she would've put on a pair of undies. And she would've *never* let Bree get into bed with her and Bryce, it'd make her think…

Shit! Bryce was naked!

Gripping the top of the sheet that lay over the three of them, she lifted it. Thank God, Bryce wore a pair of shorts.

"Mommy?"

Her daughter was very inquisitive, too smart. What the hell would she tell her when Bree asked her why Mommy and Daddy slept in the same bed?

She pulled away from Bryce, looked down at Bree, and though her stomach turned, she smiled. "Morning, baby."

Bree returned the smile making her forget what she'd been so worried about. "Daddy said I could sleep with you."

There it was. Sock to the chest.

"I had a bad dream."

She nodded. "You can tell me about it while we get you ready for school."

"Do I have to?"

She nodded. "Yes, you do."

"I do what?"

Her smile widened. "You have to go to school, and you have to tell me about the dream."

"Oh, all right."

"Come on." Em sat up in bed and got to her feet. "Up, slowly, so you don't wake your father."

Bree did as she asked. They left Bryce's room and headed into theirs. Bree went into the closet to pick out her clothes.

Em followed and waited for Bree to set aside a pair of jeans and pink blouse before she spoke. "Bree, tell me about your dream."

Bree turned to face her and sighed. "It was about Daddy."

Brows raised, she nodded. "Go on."

"He was gone…"

She shook her head. "Honey, you know your dad isn't leaving."

Her big, beautiful eyes watered. "Then I woke up, and you were gone."

She knelt in front of her placing her hands on Bree's shoulders. "I wasn't gone, and your dad isn't gone. I am here like I've always been, and your dad isn't going anywhere."

Bree nodded.

"Now, it's time to shower."

She stood and watched Bree go. A moment later, she heard the water run. She turned intent on picking out her clothes for the day when the door to her room parted. She spun.

Of course, Bryce. No one else went into their room without knocking. His chest bare, shorts hanging low on his hips, she was lost in that until she heard his voice.

"Up here."

Her head snapped up, gaze shot to his. She didn't have time to process how she'd been caught ogling him red-handed because he had that look. Shoulders tense, eyes hard and narrowed, the first time she'd seen him upset since the video incident.

He leaned into her, so close their lips were

practically touching. The heat of his body warmed her as the husky smell of him hit her. "This shit's gonna end, and it's gonna end today." His voice firm yet low.

What? Them?

About time, and thank God, he was ending it. No way in hell she ever could. It was for the best, and still, she hated it was over.

"You wanna get your fix, then when I wake up in the morning, you better be next to me."

This time, she said it aloud because she had no idea what he meant. "W-what?"

"I'm good enough to make you come, then I'm good enough to wake up next to."

Again, what? She raised her brows. "What?"

He clenched his jaw. "Em, you're smart, babe. Why aren't you getting what I'm saying?"

She shook her head. "I just don't—"

He grabbed her arms and tugged her body against the length of his. Grip firm, he grazed his lips against hers. Her lids fluttered closed then open.

"You want to fuck, we'll fuck. But from now on, when it happens and I wake up, you better be there, Em. Next time, I wake up and you're gone, I'll cuff you to the bed."

"What?" she said, breathlessly, the meaning different this time. She heard what he said; she just couldn't believe he said what he had.

Eyes widening, he reared back releasing her in the process, so the heat of his body melted away.

"I didn't know you—"

"You thought I wanted to wake up alone? You think I like feeling like you use me to get off?"

Was he serious? That was absurd! If anything, he

used her. "What?"

He cocked his head and further narrowed his gaze. "Stop saying that."

"I'm sorry… I just…" She shook her head trying to gather her thoughts. That didn't work, so she closed her eyes. When she parted them and met his strange, beautiful ones, she repeated, "I didn't realize you wanted me there."

His brows drew together. "You didn't realize I wanted you there?"

"Yes."

"So you left 'cause you thought I didn't want you there?"

She swallowed. "Yes."

His face softened. "That doesn't make any sense, Em, 'cause *you* know if I didn't want you there, I would've made it known. I wouldn't've let you fall asleep next to me."

He made a point, but still… "It makes perfect sense. Besides, I remember you used to like sleeping in."

"So you were letting me sleep in even though as long as you've been here, I've only missed breakfast with Bree a couple of times while I was away?"

"Yes."

One brow raised, he looked like he was mulling over what she said, deciding whether to believe her.

She took the chance to point out, "And anyway, I have to wake Bree and get her ready for school."

His shoulders relaxing, he nodded then looked down at his feet. "Yeah, I guess that's true."

She realized then, belatedly, she had something she wanted to discuss with him, too. "You let her get into bed with us."

He lifted his head. "Yeah."

"I know she had a bad dream, and you were trying to comfort her, but you can't let her do that again."

His brows wrinkled. "So it's okay for her to sleep with you, but she can't sleep with me?"

"It's not that. It's that she shouldn't be in bed with you and me."

He reared back before he asked, "Why not?"

Shaking her head, she attempted to rephrase. "I mean she can. It's just... It's that she shouldn't have been made aware that I was...in bed with you."

He cocked his head. "Again, why not?"

"She's going to wonder why her mom and dad were in bed together. No, scratch that. She's going to think that we're... That you and I are...together."

He quirked a brow. "So?"

Her eyes bulged. "So?"

"Yeah, Em, so what? Why does that matter?"

God, why was he making her explain this? He knew why. Because they weren't. Because he was just fucking her. Because living at the compound, Bree could potentially catch him with a tap, and she'd wonder why Daddy was with another woman. Because their baby girl would get her hopes up only to have them come crashing down when he got tired of her.

"She..." Em shook her head. "She shouldn't think that."

His body tensed a split second before he leaned into her. "Are you fuckin' someone else I don't know about, Em?"

What? Again, was he serious? Besides the fact she was so in love with him she'd never dated or moved on, when would she have the time to be with anyone else? She spent her days at work and with Bree and her nights with him. Because of this, she just looked at him.

"Em? You hear me?"

She took a deep breath and released it before she responded. "Yes, I heard you."

"So *answer me*. Are you fuckin' someone else?"

"No." She kept her voice level. "I haven't ever been with anyone other than you."

"Good." The tension lining his body melted when he smirked. "I'm not fuckin' anyone but you, so we're good."

That didn't mean he wanted her for more than sex. It didn't mean there was a future, and it didn't mean he loved her. But it felt so good to hear she momentarily forgot to breathe.

He smiled wider. "So, we're good?"

She had to think back, remember what they'd originally been discussing—Bree, Bree thinking they were together. No, they weren't good. Because they were exclusively having sex with each other didn't mean their daughter should know they were sleeping in the same bed. Bree thinking her mom and dad were getting back together to have that fantasy shattered when her mom and dad didn't end up together was cruel.

"Morning, Daddy!"

They turned toward Bree at the same time.

"Morning, baby," he said with a smile then threw his arm around Em's shoulders and tugged her close.

It felt good, not just because he felt good and warm, but because he'd been affectionate in front of someone else. That someone else was their baby who shouldn't know about them when nothing would become of them, so she knew she should push him away, yet she couldn't in front of Bree.

Their talk would have to wait.

****

Over the last day, Em hadn't found the time to talk to Bryce about Bree. That's what she kept telling herself, but it was a big, fat lie. The truth was she had chances to talk to him, namely last night before and after they had sex multiple times. While they had talked, she hadn't brought up the reason Bree shouldn't know about them. She also had a chance that morning when he came into her room again with a pair of handcuffs.

He looked at Bree's smiling face and said, "Good morning, baby," then cupped the back of her head and pressed a kiss to her forehead. "Go shower. I'll be right back."

When Bree walked into the bathroom, he laced his fingers through hers and led her out of the room and into his. Before she processed what he intended to do, he'd cuffed her to his bed.

"W-what? Why?"

Leaning into her, her back pressed against the headboard. "I don't talk outta my ass, Em. I do what I say. You *know* this."

Right. He'd threatened to cuff her to his bed if he woke and she was gone. She took the chance to remind him, "I thought we came to an understanding that I have to get Bree ready for school."

He cocked his head. "I thought I told you that shit isn't an excuse since I always have breakfast with you and Bree anyway."

She quirked a brow. "What did you want me to do? Wake you up?"

"Yeah," he said immediately.

That one "yeah" shot straight to her heart making it beat a little faster. "I'll do it tomorrow."

He grinned then uncuffed her.

She could've talked to him then about the many reasons Bree shouldn't know about them. She could've also talked to him about it when he arrived back from taking Bree to school, and he'd stopped by the office and spoke to her briefly about a customer's bill. She just couldn't bring herself to. Maybe she hadn't because of the change in him, the fact he wanted to wake beside her, wanted her to wake him, the fact that when he threatened to cuff her to the bed and when he had cuffed her to the bed, he hadn't been angry or cruel. He treated her with respect, teased her, laughed, and smiled with her, all behind closed doors, but still... All of it made her think things were changing. And maybe she wanted all of this to mean something it didn't, but she didn't want anything to mess that up and possibly revert him to the way he used to be.

The phone rang jolting her to action. She picked it up and heard Allie on the other end. They exchanged hellos. Then Allie asked to speak with Jace, aka Trig, her husband/old man. Allie apologized for bothering her at work but said he wasn't answering his cell, and it worried her. No bother to Em. She put her on hold, went in search of Trig, and found him in the garage talking to Army.

"Trig?"

He turned and met her gaze.

"Allie's on line one for you. She says you aren't

picking up your phone."

He searched his pockets. "Fuck." He glared at Trick, standing beside Army. "You take my phone?"

Trick's dark brow rose. "Why the fuck would I take your phone?"

"'Cause you're always fuckin' playing games."

Trick raised both hands, palms up. "It wasn't me. Maybe you left it at home."

"I didn't—"

"Trig?" She interrupted him. "Allie is on hold, and she's worried."

He ran toward the phone at the back end of the garage near the door leading into the compound. As the familiar roar of motorcycles sounded louder and louder, she turned her head instinctively toward the noise. Three motorcycles, one very familiar since it had been parked outside the place she called home for more than four years.

Tracker sat astride his bike, and she knew what him being there meant. He had news about Chip. It could be good or bad, yet considering the circumstances, she figured it was bad.

Her heart tightening in her chest, her stomach hollowed out as her breaths grew shallow. Before she knew it, she stood feet from him, those green eyes searing her.

"Say it." She had to hear it, just had too. Then she lied. "I can take it."

****

"Rip!"

He turned to Strike.

"You need to get outside. Now."

"Why?"

Shit. Em. Had to be.

Thinking the worst, he dashed toward Strike then past him.

Strike one step behind. "It's Chained. They're here means they have news about Chip, and chances are the shit they came to tell Em isn't good."

That sucked. Chip had been in a coma for weeks, so no doubt in his mind Chip hadn't made it.

He slammed into the door leading to the garage at a run. Scanning the shop and lot immediately, he didn't spot Chained. His view hindered by the cars and bikes lined inside. At one of the metal doors, he spotted her, and his body locked.

Em, the only woman he ever loved, the mother of his child, the woman he pleasured and savored every night then fell asleep beside, *his* Em, had a hand on Tracker's shoulder as she lifted her leg, about to get on another man's bike.

His heart stopped dead. When it started again, he had one purpose and one alone—stop her. Before he knew it, he grabbed her arm, tugged her toward him making her face him.

She stumbled.

He steadied her by releasing her arm, snaking his other around her waist and hauling her until he pressed her to his chest. Staring down at her, he cupped her face. His breaths coming out in gasps, he said for only her ears while he fought to keep the anger out of his voice. "Whose dick was buried inside you not fuckin' eight hours ago?"

Her eyes widened. "You don't—"

"*Whose* dick, babe?"

"Yours." She rested her palms on his sweat-soaked

shirt.

The action alone soothed some of the rage burning his gut. That and the fact she admitted it made him instinctively loosen his hold of her waist.

His blood boiled. He still felt it under his skin burning him, familiar and yet he hadn't felt that fury since she told him why she'd left, since before she'd admitted she wanted him always, since before he bedded her and continued to do it every night. It only proved how far gone he'd been watching her attempt to climb onto another man's bike.

"Who made you come last night?"

"You."

Damn straight. He released a breath, some of the tension lining his shoulders fading. "How. Many. Times?"

"Four…"

Opening his mouth to speak, she spoke over him. "No, five."

He quirked a brow.

She took it as a need to explain and did. "The last one counted as two."

Right, further proving his point. He grazed his lips against hers and said, "That means you're *mine*. You belong to *me*. You don't believe me, I'll prove it to you right here, right now, and give everyone a show. You won't stop me 'cause the second I touch you, you melt. You can't live without me, babe, and you fuckin' know it. What I don't get is you knowing this, you knowing *me* and this *world*, how you'd ever try to do what you just did."

He didn't believe all he said. She melted for him, yes, every time. But she could live without him, she'd done it for a long time. Still, he said it because he wanted it to be true.

"I—"

He clenched his jaw, battling his rage, fighting not to show it to her, take it out on her. "Stop and think before you speak. Come up with a good excuse 'cause I will lose my fuckin' mind if you feed me some bullshit line."

"I'm not going to give you an excuse, Bryce. I'm going to tell you the truth. I didn't think you cared. I—"

His fingers tightened on her jaw. "Told you no bullshit—"

Her hands at his chest fisted. "My turn to talk." Her voice firm. "As of late, you've fucked me a lot. You've also treated me like a tap, so honestly, I didn't think you cared."

He *didn't* treat her like a tap. They had sex, a lot of it. Sometimes, he took her hard, but he made love to her too, something she couldn't have missed. Something else, he cuddled with her, talked to her, smiled and laughed with her, like before, like she hadn't left, like he'd never lost her.

His body vibrated, fury coursing through him too powerful to control. "You've got to be fuckin' kidding me."

Without flinching, she held his stare. A glimpse of the old Em, the feisty one who didn't back down, who didn't cry at every turn. Though still not the same, the old Em would've snapped back, pushed at his chest, or screamed bloody murder until he released her. Still that small glimpse, a reminder the old Em was still in there, elated him.

Not that it mattered, he'd come to the conclusion

Em, old or new, he'd take her any way he could have her. He loved her for more than that temper she once showed so easily and frequently, for more than the meek woman she turned into, and for much more than her beautiful face. He loved her for a combination of everything that made her *her*—the whole package that did him in.

"I'm not fucking kidding you." She cursed, but her voice remained level.

He leaned into her, and again, because he couldn't help himself, he grazed his lips against hers. "Barely come up for air, Em. We didn't have Bree, we wouldn't be getting outta bed. You *know* this."

"That could just be because like you said, I'm a good lay."

He'd lied. She wasn't a good lay. She was the best he'd ever had. Still, she wasn't making any sense.

He released her cheeks, allowing her to look away. One arm curved around her back, he grasped the back of her neck with the other. "We have sex, a lot of it, but we talk and laugh, and…that means something to *me*. You're not a fuckin' tap, not to me, not to anyone. You're just *mine*."

She was *his*, the mother of his child, half of his world, the other half being Bree. He may not mean more to her than sex, but he'd had her every night for weeks, and that meant no matter what he meant to her, she was *his*.

She lifted her head meeting his stare.

"Say it."

"I'm yours."

His muscles contracted. In doing so, he clutched her to him as a heady sensation made his chest clench.

Despite this, he grinned.

A small smile spread across her lips.

He released her waist, slung his arm around her shoulders, buried his face in her neck, and ran his tongue along her pulse.

She melted. Her hands at his chest gripped him tight as her body shivered.

Just above her ear, he whispered, "You're mine. Not gonna remind you again, Em."

Drawing away, he tore his gaze from her and glared at Tracker. "Try that shit again, and I'll hang you up by your balls."

Tracker didn't say anything. He just glared right back. Then again, Tracker knew what he'd tried to do was fucked, a violation of the bro code, a nasty beating or worse in the brotherhood, so there wasn't anything he could do.

Ripper couldn't blame him for taking his chance. It'd been the other way around, he would've done the same just for the chance to feel Em pressed against him on his bike.

Through gritted teeth, Tracker said, "Chip's up and wants to see Em."

Rip darted his stare to Em and let his arm slide across her shoulders and down the length of her arm to grab her hand. Then he led her toward his SUV, opened the passenger side door, and helped her in. Walking around the car, he hopped in, turned on the ignition, waited for Tracker to leave, and waited to gain some of his wits. When he did, he turned to her, swinging his arm around her until his hand grasped the back of her neck. He hauled her toward him. "I let you go once. I'm *not* ever letting you go again."

He said it unwillingly, giving away so much, much more than he ever wanted to. He didn't care.

Her eyes widened, lips parted, and that beautiful face of hers softened.

Just like before. She used to look at him like that all the time. He missed it so much. Watching it then, he decided he'd continue to hand over his balls just to see that look on her face.

"I lied."

That softness faded, fast.

Before she made a move to pull away, he admitted, "You aren't a good lay. You're the best I've ever had."

Then, there it was again—that look.

He wanted to keep it there, so he was tempted to tell her everything: that he never cheated, that he never stopped loving her, that he never could. So he wouldn't, he bit his tongue. He couldn't tell her, not now en route to see Chip, not before he found Lilliam.

He kissed her instead, and she melted against him.

Chapter Fifteen

I let you go once. I'm not ever letting you go again.

Those words kept replaying in Em's mind. Others did too, but those more often than the rest. Enough to say, her thoughts were drowning her. She thought about how much he'd changed, dissected every word, every action, and prayed they meant more, prayed they meant what she wanted them to mean. Though he wouldn't let her go, though he said she was his, he never said he was hers, never said he loved her, never said he wouldn't hurt her again. A part of her was thrilled to be his, to be the only woman in his life at the moment, to have heard him say everything he had, but another part of her was terrified he'd break her again. Em needed to give herself break. The last two days had been a whirlwind, so she had other things to think about.

When Tracker pulled into the garage's lot, she'd been sure the news would be bad. Instead, he told her Chip had woken from his coma and wanted to see her. Doctors said it was rare, but it happened. That said, he had a long recovery ahead of him. He was lucky to be alive. Alive and still, she felt guilty for leaving him, terrified he wouldn't come out of this okay, and nervous to see him after so long.

When she walked into his hospital room with Bryce's strong presence behind her, she took Chip in, all of him. Sitting on the bed, his shoulder-length dark brown hair in a ponytail at his back, face pale, but those chiseled features were still beautiful: strong, square jaw, full lips, high cheekbones. His hazel eyes were warm and got warmer as they came to a stop on hers.

"Em."

She broke down in tears. His eyes widened then softened. She felt the heat of Bryce's hand on her hip for a brief moment before she ran to Chip, sat on the edge of his bed, and wrapped her arms around him.

"I'm so sorry…" Her sob muffled when she buried her face in his neck.

He ran his palms down the length of her back. "Nothin' to be sorry about. Missed you like fuckin' crazy."

Pulling away to look into his eyes, she wiped her face. "Missed you, too."

"Not like I missed you." He smiled. "You know how many drinks I've had to get myself?"

She laughed. It was just like him to tease her, remind her of a time, however brief, when they lived together. He saved her from her father, moved her into his house, and she showed him how much she appreciated that by doing whatever she could around the house, for him and Track. She cooked, cleaned, did laundry, and she teased him constantly, too, to lighten his mood. Being president of a biker club could be stressful.

"I can imagine." She smiled softly. "How are you feeling?"

"Good. Could be the pain meds kickin' in though." He chuckled and cupped her jaw. "You look beautiful, Em."

He always did that. It was like he knew she didn't

see herself as anything but her father's punching bag and knew how badly she needed to feel something other than that. He always let her know how much he appreciated all the things she did around the house and also often told her she didn't need to do all she did. Needless to say, he did everything in his power to make her feel appreciated, needed, and loved.

She shook her head. "No, I—"

"You do…" He dropped his hand, setting it on his lap. "More beautiful than I remember if it's possible."

Her eyes welled yet again, and effortlessly, a tear slipped out and drifted down her face. "You don't have to do that, now. I know why you've always done it, but—"

"'Cause I do it for a reason doesn't mean it's a lie." He wiped her cheek. "Looks to me like you've been in need of it the past five years."

So true. A new wave of tears flooded her eyes. "Enough about me."

He smiled. "Right."

She caught sight of his chipped tooth. Somehow, that small imperfection made him more handsome.

"Tell me 'bout her."

"Brianna. Bree. She's beautiful. She—"

"Looks just like you," he finished for her. His smile widened. "Saw pictures, Em. She's your clone. Except for those eyes." He slid his stare behind her. No doubt to Bryce. For some reason, he then smirked. When he met her gaze again, he said, "I wanna meet her as soon as I get outta here."

"You come to us. You can meet her," Bryce cut in.

A relief, she'd been so sure he'd refuse considering the trouble Chained was in. She twisted to look his way and gave him a small smile. Facing Chip, she said, "She's five now, loves dolls, dresses, and bows for her hair. Daddy's girl all the way."

Chip's stare cut to Bryce for a moment then slid back to her.

"She loves to sit in the garage next to him while he's working. She loves mac and cheese and pizza. Before bed, she needs a bedtime story and her back rubbed."

Chip chuckled. "So to win my niece's heart, I gotta get her dolls, dresses, and bows?"

She shook her head. "You don't have to win her heart. She knows all about you and loves you."

Chip's whole face softened. "Yeah?"

Her eyes watered. She held the tears back. "Of course. She knows what you look like too. I gave her all my old photos. She keeps them in a shoe box and treasures them."

He grabbed her hand and squeezed it. "As soon as I can get outta here, Em, my word."

His word was stronger than steel. She couldn't wait for that day to come, couldn't wait to tell Bree. She hadn't yet but would as soon as Chip was better.

"Em?"

Startled, she turned. There, she spotted Mia looking thoughtful.

It was that special Sunday once a month when the club had a cookout, which meant the brothers, their old ladies, family, and friends were at the compound, drinking, laughing, eating, and lounging around in the backlot. Most of it was grass, except for the basketball court. Right then, several of the brothers were playing a very brutal form of the game. A grill to the left, a few picnic tables scattered throughout. And to her right, a swing set, the one Bryce bought Bree for her birthday.

"Um…yeah," she lied.

Mia took a seat on the picnic table beside her. "I really wish you'd talk to me. I can help."

Turning her head, her gaze gravitated to Bree in the playground sitting on the swing, Bryce behind her, pushing her. "It's nothing."

"I know it's something, so just say you don't want to talk about it."

She swallowed. "You know what it is. It's what it's always been."

"Yeah, Rip, but—"

She peered at Mia. "But you wouldn't understand."

Mia tilted her head as her eyebrows rose. "Try me."

"If I tell you, you have to promise you won't ever tell anyone."

Mia nodded. "I promise."

Her stomach soured. She fought the nausea and whispered, "I left because he…cheated."

Mia's lips parted. After a long moment, she shook her head. "No, he… No."

"I was young and in love with him. I thought we were something we weren't. I let myself believe…" She released a breath. "It was a long time ago."

Mia shook her head. "That's not possible. I remember—"

"It happened, Mia." She dropped her head and stared down at her clasped hands. "How I wish it hadn't, but it did, and that's why I left."

Shots rang out. Loud, fast, seemed like a million of them.

Bree. She snapped her head up, gaze riveted to the swing. "*Bree!*"

Standing, she ran toward the playground and managed four steps before an arm snaked around her waist. Then a body collided with hers. She fell to the ground. Her back took the brunt of the impact, the weight of a mass of muscle and man lying over her making it impossible to breathe.

Back aching, arm burning, lungs fighting for air. "Please! Let me up! I need—"

"Shut it, Em." Bud lay over her, not letting her get to Bree.

"Stop! Please!"

His big hand covered her mouth.

She fought. Her hands gripped his shoulders, pushing, shoving, desperate. Then she fought harder, kicking, hitting, hysterical.

"You're gonna hurt yourself."

Panicked, tears leaked out of her eyes. She continued struggling even knowing if he didn't let up she'd get nowhere, but she had to fight. Seconds, minutes, hours slid by, she didn't know which, but the light around her began dimming as her energy waned.

She gasped. "Can't…breathe…"

Then the world went black.

****

Ripper heard the shots, so loud they vibrated in his chest.

Bree.

His breath froze, stomach hollowed out then knotted, crippling. He didn't let anything settle. Grabbing Bree under her arms, he yanked her from the swing and shielded her body with his as he turned his back toward the sound of the gunfire. He spared a glance behind him, a dark van, side door open, a gun held in a man's grip. Rip ran then dove for cover behind a tree. Finally there, he settled Bree on the ground. Resting his weight on his elbows, arms around her, he laid over her, covering her body with his.

"Daddy! Daddy!"

He cringed at the sound of her terrified voice, buried his face in her neck, ran his hand through her hair, and held her a little tighter. "It's okay, baby. It's all right. I'm here," he whispered and continued to whisper for minutes after the last shot rang out.

Where was Em? He saved his baby girl, but where was her mom?

Heart squeezing, dread settled in his bones. He lifted his head and skimmed the backlot. The dark van was long gone. He didn't know if they'd return, but he made a decision. Swallowing, he drew away from Bree and scanned her for injuries.

"You're okay." Then he wrapped his arms around her, carried her, and sprinted toward the backdoor leading into the compound. Once inside, he set her on her feet. "I'll be back."

Grasping his hand and tugging, she sobbed, "No, Daddy! Don't leave me! Please…"

His heart clenched so tight it left him breathless. "I gotta find your mom, baby. I'll be back. I promise."

"Go, I'll stay here."

He looked up, met Allie's gaze, and nodded. Then with one final look at Bree, he walked back outside.

Chaos. Lynn crying hysterically, her old man, Wild held her close, rushing her inside. Stone, looking frantic, running around, looking for Mia no doubt. A pissed off Army, phone to his ear, yelling something Rip was too in a cloud of haze to decipher. Blaze bleeding from a nasty gash on the side of his face as he cradled his ribs. Hash, Rake, and Strike huddled close. Mellow and Trick headed toward the back fence.

Ripper scanned the lot again and again. Still, he didn't see her. Striding toward the picnic table where she'd last been, he stopped dead. Bud, hunched over someone, looked up and met his stare.

The look on Bud's face and that long blonde hair proved the person lying so still beneath Bud was her, *his Em*. It set in then, terrifying, numbing panic. Pulse racing, a deep searing ache vibrated around his frame.

He gunned for her, made it in no time, sunk to his knees, and cupped the back of her head. "Em! Wake up!"

Swallowing, he skimmed her from head to toe. Face pale, eyes closed, the sleeve of her shirt was soaked in blood. Something else too, he set her head on the ground for a split second to stare at his hand. It dripped blood... A stream of it had pooled behind her head.

He threw his head back and roared, thundered so loud his throat hurt. "Call a fucking ambulance! Call them, now!"

She didn't wake, didn't even stir.

Looking back to her, he put pressure on the back of her head, hoping to stop the bleeding. He cupped her check, lowering himself and pressing his lips to her forehead. "Em! Fuck me, Em. Wake up! Wake up, Em!" He screamed at the top of his lungs the whole time thinking if she died, he'd have no fight left and go right with her. Then Bree would be alone, an orphan.

He could barely see her anymore. His eyes, they weren't working right. Blinking, he felt water stream down his face. "Em! Wake up! Now! Do it! Do it, or I'll fucking... I can't... You gotta help me. You gotta..."

Her lids fluttered.

His breath froze.

"B-Bree..." she mumbled, barely a whisper.

He blinked. Stupid, coward tears drifted down his face.

"B-Bree..."

He glided his thumb against her lips. "She's good, and you're gonna be good, too. Don't go to sleep."

"I can't... I'm..." Her eyes drifted half-mast.

"You can't. You gotta stay with me."

"T-take care of our...baby." Her lids closed.

Someone pushed him out of the way. Too consumed with a multitude of emotions, he couldn't do anything but let them. When he came to, the paramedics had loaded her on a gurney and were pushing her away.

He turned to the first person he saw, Bud. "Strike. Need him to watch Bree." He spun halfway around.

Bud grabbed his arm. "You should stay with Bree. I'll go with Em."

Bud, doing what he did best, trying to keep him away from Em. Any other day, Rip wouldn't let Bud get his way. Right then, she *needed* him, so no one would keep him from her.

Fighting the anger burning his gut, he tore his arm from Bud's grasp. "Two years I knew happiness. All my fucked life, I got two years. That was it, and it was 'cause of her. Now, I got something back. I got Bree. If

I can get more, I'm fighting 'till I get it all."

"You fuckin' blind, brother? You had two years, but it doesn't change the fact that she *left*! She destroyed you. I don't even know who the fuck you are. Haven't known who you are for five fucked years."

He didn't have time for this shit. He had to go. Shooting Bud his deadliest stare, he turned and ran to the ambulance parked just outside the chain-link fence enclosing the backlot.

"Daddy! Daddy!"

He twisted.

Bree, tears streaking her face, rushed him. "Don't leave me, Daddy! Don't…" A sob tore through her, her little body shaking with the strength of it.

He met her halfway and caught her as she jumped on him. Carrying her, he headed toward the ambulance, glaring his way in. No way in hell would he leave Em alone, and no way in hell would he leave Bree.

Over the muffled sounds of Bree's crying, he heard the paramedic say, "Enroute with one GSW to a forearm, laceration to the head, possible concussion."

His heart clenched, pain radiated out of his chest and spread leaving no part of him untouched. If he hadn't been holding Bree close, he would've lost his goddamned mind. His arms instinctively tightened around her. "Gonna be okay, baby," he whispered against her hair and hoped to God he hadn't just lied to his baby girl.

The ride to the hospital seemed endless. The whole way, he held Bree close, whispering reassurances. His gaze on Em, so pale, so still. Then it hit him like a sock to the gut.

What happened to them all those years ago wasn't

anyone's fault but that bitch Lilliam's. If he was wrong, and it was Em's fault, it was his too.

A love like he had for her, he should've chased her.

A love like the one he still felt after all that had happened, he should've fought for.

The thing that stopped him—his pride, the reason he missed out, on her, on Bree, on life.

He was done missing out. It took him long enough to realize it, but now that he had, he'd never forget. He'd make her *his*, fully, completely. Then he'd find a way to make her fall for him, again.

****

God, her head hurt, a lot. Em tried to pry open her eyes. Light, too bright, blinded her. She winced making the pain worse. Pressing her hand to her forehead, a sharp sting shot up her arm.

What the hell happened?

It came to her slowly. Bree swinging, Rip pushing her, laughing. She and Mia talking. Then the shots.

Her eyes slid open. A bandage covered her forearm. That explained why it hurt. She scanned the room and stopped dead when her gaze landed on him sitting at her bedside. Head slanted down, his elbows resting on his knees, hands at the back of his neck.

"B-Bree?"

Bryce lifted his head and moved. Standing, he strode closer, sat on the edge of her bed, and cupped her cheek. "She's safe."

She sighed. "She's safe."

"Yeah. She's worried about you but safe."

"Anyone hurt?"

"Nothing big, except you."

She waited for him to elaborate. He didn't, not

before a man wearing a white coat walked into the room.

"Emelia Knight, glad to see you're up. I'm Dr. Anderson."

She pressed her good hand on the bed lifting herself to a sitting position. Bryce's arm went around her back helping her up. His other hand clasped hers. Then he stood and faced the doctor.

She forced a smile. "Good to be up."

He retrieved a small flashlight out of his pocket and neared. "How are you feeling?"

"My head hurts, a lot."

"That's normal. You have a concussion." He checked her eyes then tucked the flashlight in his pocket. "The head injury caused it and a laceration to the back of your head. It's not deep enough you need stitches. You were also grazed by a bullet on your forearm."

She nodded.

"There's one other thing."

Shit. She knew. She hadn't known for sure, not until she saw the look in his eyes. Then she couldn't deny it. She also knew what had once been was no longer.

"I'm sorry to tell you, you lost the baby."

She lost the baby, her baby, her and Bryce's baby. God, it hurt. It hurt so much she couldn't do anything but feel the ache ripping her insides apart.

Bryce stilled, his hand squeezing hers, the heat of his eyes burning her.

"Were you aware, Mrs. Knight?"

Missus? She let that slide. "I knew it was a possibility, but I wasn't sure."

"I'm sorry for your loss."

Sorry? Hard to believe, he said it so emotionless. Then again, she supposed he had no other choice. Being a doctor meant delivering bad news to people and their loved ones often. He had to find a way to distance himself from it.

Her chest squeezed. She nodded then looked down at her lap and ignored the tears flooding her eyes. When she heard the door open and close, she let the tears stream down her face.

"Em?"

Lifting her head, her gaze cut to his. He settled beside her, wrapped his arms around her, and held her. She let him. His hold gentle and tight, she buried her face in his chest.

"Talk to me."

"I lost our baby."

He released a breath. "We lost him."

"No, I did. It was me who lost him."

He pressed his lips to the top of her head. "We're both missing out, babe, so *we* lost him. It isn't your fault."

"I wasn't sure. I mean…I knew it was possible, but I didn't know, and it…"

Cupping her face, he angled her head to his slowly and gently.

When her eyes met his, she finished, "…hurts."

"We'll make another one."

Her eyes widened. "W-what?"

He smiled. "We can make another one."

She tried to pull away, but his arm tightened around her. "It wouldn't change the fact we lost this one. It wouldn't make the loss of this one hurt any less."

He nodded.

"Besides...we can't. I mean we can, we just shouldn't."

"'Course, we should. We make them pretty and smart and sweet. I want another girl."

What? She thought she was the one who hit her head. "Are you crazy?"

His brows creased. "Why?"

"Because this isn't... You aren't..." *In love with me.* Instead, she said, "We aren't...together."

Eyes hardening, he clenched his jaw. When he spoke, he kept the anger out of his voice. "I thought we went over this. You're mine."

She swallowed. No time like the present to say what she had to. "Fucking me doesn't make me yours. Me letting you doesn't mean you're mine."

His face softened as he leaned to lightly graze his lips over hers. "I'm not with anyone else. You aren't with anyone else. That means you're mine, and I'm yours."

Her head throbbed.

"What else do you want? Do you want a ring? Do you want to go to the courthouse? We'll do it."

Heart pounding too fast and hard against her ribs, she parted her lips then tried to swallow the emotion clogging her throat. A ring? The courthouse? Marriage? Shit, did he just propose? No, Bryce didn't believe in marriage. She forced herself to point this out. "You don't believe in marriage."

"Never said that."

Hard to deny, she was thinking about it, about actually considering his ridiculous proposal. No, it wasn't a proposal. Proposals were planned and romantic, right? What did it matter? Marriage didn't mean he loved her, didn't mean he wouldn't eventually cheat, again.

He closed his eyes and swallowed then asked, "What do you want?"

"What do *you* want?" she returned, instantly.

"I want you."

She wanted him too, more than she'd ever wanted any man, but he didn't love her, and he'd broken her once before. Tying herself to him was much more reckless and stupid than giving herself to him.

She scanned his face for a long moment then whispered, "Like you said, I'm yours."

His gaze trailed to her lips as he slid his thumb across them. Then he met her stare and spoke. "Yeah, but I want you in every way, Em. I want my ring on your finger. I want everyone to know you belong to me. I want it on paper, too. I want it official."

Either he really went crazy, or she hit her head harder than anyone thought and had hallucinated.

"Bryce…" Yes. The word was on the tip of her tongue. A bad idea, bad decision.

Before she said more, the door parted, and Bree and Strike walked in.

Bryce would want a response soon, but for now, she got a reprieve and got to spend some time with her baby.

Chapter Sixteen

Ripper thought long and hard. Sitting at her bedside, he'd thought about Em all night and all morning. He thought about how Em could've been injured worse or killed, thought about how she still managed to look beautiful with dried blood matting her hair, suffering from a gunshot wound and a concussion. Quite frankly, it wasn't fair to other women. He thought about how he'd stupidly asked her to marry him, and the fact she hadn't given him an answer. He knew asking her was a long shot—one he took because he almost lost her, one he took because now he'd fight to get all of her. Though not getting a response made him think he shouldn't have asked.

She kept giving herself to him, but she hid it from everyone, even Bree who'd no doubt be thrilled her parents were together. All those years ago, Em used to be affectionate, touching him, grabbing him, kissing him, constantly. Now, any time they were around anyone else, and he made a move toward her, she looked hesitant, sometimes even scared. There was a time when she should've been afraid. When he'd found her and Bree, he'd been an asshole, but he'd changed his tune that night she told him the reason she left. All of this led him to think she didn't love him, so it'd been senseless to ask her to marry him. He scolded himself all night, all morning while he woke Bree, who slept in a cot in Em's hospital room because she refused to leave them. He scolded himself while he got Bree ready and until he dropped her off at school. Since then, he'd only thought about what Bree said.

Ripper hadn't wanted to leave Em even though she'd still been asleep, even though a couple of his brothers stayed to keep an eye out. But he left because he needed to take Bree to the compound and get her ready. He did amazingly considering Em always handled it. Like usual, he walked her to her classroom, his mind still on her mom. He kissed her forehead and promised to be back to pick her up.

She looked at him, a gorgeous smile in place, and said, "Mommy loves you, Daddy. I know she does."

The breath froze in the back of his throat as his stomach hollowed out then rolled. "W-what?"

"Mommy. She loves you."

He swallowed. "How do you know that?"

"I know, Daddy. I just do."

He knelt in front of her and threaded his fingers through her hair as blonde and as thick as her mother's. "Baby, you're too young to know something like that."

"I'm not, Daddy. I know. Mommy used to tell me stories about you. She told me how much she loves you."

His chest tightened. "She told you she loves me?"

Bree nodded.

It couldn't be, just couldn't. Why didn't she want to marry him then? She must've lied to Bree, must've wanted their daughter to think she loved her dad.

"What's wrong with you, brother?"

Ripper lifted his head and caught Strike's gaze. He didn't know how long he'd been staring at the ground after his set of bench presses thinking about what Bree said.

"Thought you'd be done by now. Saw you come in here a couple of hours ago."

Had it been that long? He ran for a while then moved on to weights, but his head wasn't in it. He lost count between sets more times than he cared to admit.

"Are you about done?"

"Yeah, yeah...I'm done." He might as well be done. It'd be the afternoon before he knew it, and he wanted to see Em again before he had to pick up Bree from school.

Strike laughed. "Are you moving anytime soon, or should I come back?"

He needed to get his shit together, quick. Only normal he felt out of sorts after the drive-by shooting yesterday. Now more than ever though, he couldn't afford to lose focus.

He stood grabbing his towel then wiped his face.

"You okay?"

Ripper shook his head. He hadn't meant to admit it. It'd been so long since he confided in anyone, but he needed to get shit off his chest.

"Want to talk about it?"

He didn't but should. Even though he wasn't one to share, he found himself saying, "I asked Em to marry me."

Strike's jaw dropped. After a moment, he grinned. "She said yeah."

Why did he think that? Ripper didn't respond, just stared back, the question in his eyes.

Strike quirked a brow. "She said no?"

"She didn't say anything, but it was... It was

like…" He gritted his teeth. "I felt like I had to convince her."

Strike laughed. "Are you kidding me?"

Again, why Strike thought this, Ripper had no clue, especially since he wasn't the type to share.

"You must've done it wrong."

His brows furrowed. "How many ways are there to ask a woman to marry you?"

Strike chuckled. "You have to ask that, we have problems."

Was there really more than one way? Would it have made a difference? He was so lost about shit like this. He never had a good mother, never kept a woman but Em, and everyone knew how that turned out.

Strike lifted his chin. "Tell me what you said."

He thought back for a second. "I said she was mine, and if she wanted a ring or to go to the courthouse, we'd go. I told her I wanted everyone to know she was mine."

Shaking his head, Strike released a loaded breath. "I've never asked a woman to marry me, but you can bet your ass I ever do, I'm not proposing like that. I don't even think you can call that a proposal."

His eyes widened. "Why the fuck not?"

"You want her to marry you, you *tell* her you love her then *ask* her to marry you. I think it helps if you do it when she's not in a hospital. Maybe take her to a restaurant or the beach or some romantic shit like that."

Clenching his jaw, he snapped, "She knows how I feel." She had to know. Everything he did, everything he didn't showed it, proved it.

Crossing his arms over his chest, Strike shot back, "Does she? You sure?" He shook his head. "'Cause I'm not. And if I was her, I'd think you hated me."

No, Strike had it wrong. She knew. She had to know. He'd been a dick, but he'd changed the moment she told him why she left. Since then, he'd tried his hardest to show her that he wasn't that man, and he did it by treating her right.

"I haven't…" Shaking his head, he lost sight of Strike's eyes. "I was a dick, but I haven't been that for a while. I've been different, and we… We've been together, a lot. And I've been good to her. I've *shown* her what she means to me."

Strike nodded. "Right, then the only thing I can say is that she's in love with you, always has been, and the only reason a woman wouldn't accept a proposal from a man she's in love with, even if she was asked the way you asked her, is 'cause she thinks he doesn't love her."

In love with him? Was she? Why didn't she act like it? Why didn't she want people to know about them? Why didn't she want Bree to know about them? Why hadn't she said yes? All of it reinforced what he thought—she was using him.

Strike shrugged. "Maybe I'm wrong. Maybe she knows you love her. Maybe she's holding back because she's scared you'll hurt her again. Have you told her the truth?"

Rip met his gaze questioningly.

"Have you told her you never cheated?"

He didn't know how Strike knew, so he was about to ask, but instead, he shook his head.

"I think you should start with that, Rip."

He couldn't, not until he found Lilliam. Em had to hear it from Lilliam. She wouldn't believe him.

"A piece of advice, the best I can give you—talk to

her. Tell her the truth. Tell her how you feel. Both of you need to learn from your mistakes and *talk* to each other."

Strike had a point.

Still, Rip couldn't tell her he never cheated, not yet, but it was about damned time he told her what she meant to him even if he didn't mean the same to her.

****

Emelia didn't know how she'd manage it, but she knew she had to.

Her hair was a mess of dried blood. She felt dirty, sticky, and gross. She hadn't looked in the mirror yet, but she didn't need to. She knew she looked like crap. Hell, she felt like crap. Horrifying to think Bryce had seen her like that and proposed or whatever it was he did. The wound on her forearm and her head still hurt, but she had to shower. She should call a nurse, but she didn't want anyone's help. Doing it on her own would give her something to think about besides the sadness that clung to her since having found out she lost her baby.

Decision made, Em slowly angled herself, so her legs hung off the bed. Even slower, she shifted until her feet touched the cold linoleum floor. Then she stood and moved toward the bathroom. Opening the door, she strode in. Once there, she grabbed onto the metal rail and paused to catch her breath. After, she removed her gown, set it on the rail, strode toward the shower, and turned it on, tempering it just how she liked it, really hot.

"Em?"

She froze. Just like him to show up at the worst time. She didn't get a chance to cover herself before the door to the bathroom parted. She turned toward it. His gaze hit hers, and he exhaled like he was relieved to see her standing there dirty, butt-naked.

She grabbed her gown and brought it to cover herself.

He chuckled. "Seen you naked before, babe."

"Not while I'm sticky, dirty, and gross."

He ignored her comment, not denying she was, in fact, sticky, dirty, and gross. "Don't know what you think you're doing."

"I forgot smelly."

Shaking his head, he smiled. "You aren't smelly, dirty, or gross. Maybe sticky though. I won't know until I taste you."

Just hearing that had her picturing him between her legs, and that made her quiver. Insane, she needed a shower, for God sakes, and he'd sort of proposed.

She took a step away. "I...I need to shower."

"I'll help you." He shrugged off his cut, lifted his shirt, and tossed it aside.

"Wait!" Too late, she got a look at his chest and abs, so she couldn't look away.

"Em?"

Her gaze pierced his.

He grinned, unbuckled his jeans, and kicked off his boots.

She shut her eyes tightly. "Stop! You need..." Exhaling, she met his stare. "You *can't* shower with me."

"'Course, I can." Off went his jeans then boxers.

"No, you can't—"

Naked, he closed the distance between them and gripped her waist. "Em, babe, you're showering, I'm showering with you. You got a concussion, a cut on the back of your head, and a gunshot wound. You need help, and I'm helping you."

"It was a graze, and I can manage—"

Leaning down to her, he pressed his lips to hers softly. When he pulled away, he smiled. "Morning to you too."

Her breath hitched. "I…"

He grabbed the gown she held to her chest and set it on the metal support rail. "Get in, babe."

Shit. She didn't have a choice now, did she? She turned. Before she took a step into the shower, she felt the heat of his firm grip on her waist, holding her, helping her. She walked into the shower, her hands spread holding onto the rails at each side. He stood close behind. Once she felt the water pelt down on her, she grabbed the soap with her uninjured arm while still holding onto the rail with her injured one, wanting to keep the bandage dry.

He snatched the soap away. She turned her head, angling it to him.

"You're too weak. I'm gonna help you."

"I'm not. I can—"

"Let me."

"But I can—"

"I know, Em, you can do it all by yourself. You don't need me, but I want to help you, so let me."

Turning away facing the showerhead, she held still while he lathered her, starting with her shoulders and neck then moving lower.

"I'm fine, you know."

When he didn't respond, she went on. "I know you were probably scared yesterday, but nothing happened.

You don't have to treat me with kid gloves."

His hands, washing her stomach, stilled. "I know I was a dick before, and I know because of it, it's hard for you to trust me. I'm sorry for every fucked-up thing I said and did. I hadn't apologized before. I thought if I stopped being a dick, you'd know I was sorry, but I should've said it, should've apologized, so I am. And I want you to know, I'll never treat you like that again."

Apologizing? Bryce? She spun too fast and immediately got lightheaded. Her uninjured arm went to his chest gripping his skin.

He snaked his arm around her waist, pulled her to him, held her there, and smirked. "I take that back. You do need me."

"I…" For some reason, staring into those beautiful eyes that strange blue-green color, eyes smiling at her, she blurted, "My hair… I need to wash my hair."

"That's next."

He soaped every pore. By the time he finished, she was so heated she had him temper the water cooler. Then he moved on to her hair.

Squeezing a palmful of shampoo in his hand, he hesitated. "Tell me if it hurts, yeah?"

She nodded. He then rubbed it on her scalp, softly and carefully. It felt so good she closed her eyes and rested her cheek against his chest to enjoy it fully.

"What do you think about Friday?"

"Um…" she murmured.

"Friday, what do you think about Friday?"

She had no idea what he was talking about, and she wished he'd stop talking. It took too much of her concentration, and she just wanted to enjoy how his hands moved rhythmically in her hair. "Friday, what?"

"To get married."

The haze of contentment lifted. She stilled, drew away from his chest, and slanted her head to meet his eyes. "W-what?"

Dropping his hands to her waist, he held her stare for several moments. "I think we should give you 'till the end of the week, so you can get better. Then Friday, we can go to the courthouse and get married."

Shit. Why? Why? Why? She was too vulnerable to discuss this right now. Who was she kidding? She was too vulnerable with him period to ever discuss this.

"Em?"

She thought back, remembering what he said, the reason he wanted to marry her—he wanted her, wanted everyone to know she was his. Didn't she deserve someone who loved her? Didn't she want to hold out for that? She needed to speak up. If she didn't, no one else would. "I'm yours, Bryce. Everyone knows. That's not a good reason to get married."

His eyes widened just a bit. "That's not the only reason."

Her heart tightened, hope floating. She held her breath.

"We got Bree."

Stomach turning, her throat clogged. She swallowed thickly and managed to whisper, "That's not a good reason either. We don't have to get married to raise her together."

His jaw went hard. "Wouldn't it make you happy?"

An ache sliced up her chest, making her eyes water. She didn't know how she did it, but she summoned the courage to tell the truth. "Marrying someone who doesn't love me wouldn't make me

273

happy. It'd destroy me."

His eyes darkened a split second before he dropped his head. When he met her gaze again, he swallowed thickly. "You could always see right through me. You knew what I was gonna say before I said it, and here you are telling me I don't love you?"

He gripped the back of her neck and brought her closer, so his wounded, strange eyes were all she saw. "I've always loved you, Em. *Always*."

The breath whooshed out of her as her chest tightened making the pain in her middle compound then compress so she felt nothing but it.

"You *know* how I feel about you."

Shaking her head, she denied, "No. You—"

"I think I loved you the first time I saw you. I'd never felt it, so I didn't know what it was, not until you left. I knew then, and it was too late."

Scanning his gorgeous face, her jaw dropped. Oh, God. He loved her?

Leaning closer, eyes shining, he grazed his lips against hers. "You were gone, and I was *dead*. All those years without you, I tried every second of everyday to hate you, but I couldn't 'cause I still loved you."

Ignoring the roll of her stomach, she swallowed. God, no. Please, no. She never wanted to hurt him. Even if he was the reason she left, even if he destroyed her, she never wanted to do that to him.

"The whole time, I loved you, and I didn't ever say it. I hated myself for that. I couldn't blame you either 'cause I never said it. Then *I* never chased you. I should've found you and told you how I felt, how I *still* feel."

He loved her then? No, that wasn't possible. It

didn't make sense.

"After all this time, I bring you here, and you *see* day in and day out how pissed I am, fuckin' livid. I did and said things I'll never forgive myself for, and it's messed up, but I'll admit it to you. I was a dick 'cause I still wanted you, 'cause I still loved you, and I couldn't have you, 'cause I *should've* chased you, 'cause if I'd chased you, I would've known Bree. And maybe I wouldn't've had you, but I would've had her."

Her hand at his chest tightened into a fist. "Y-you've had me..." Her voice cracked. "You had me, and you kept having me, and you—"

He released her. Feeling the warmth of him gone, she shivered.

"I've had a part of you, yeah, but it's not enough 'cause I want *all* of *you*." He shook his head. "And I tried, Em, I've tried to right the wrong, the way I treated you. Every night, every day, I fight the urge to give into that anger knowing that you're just *using* me."

Her lips parted. "Me using *you*?"

"To fuck."

Her eyes widened. How could he think that? It was so clear how much she loved him, how she never stopped. "Why would you think that?"

Lifting his head, his eyes went behind her. He parted his mouth to speak then closed it without saying a word. After several moments, he spoke. "'Cause you never touch me around other people. You don't want Bree to know about us. You're always saying you aren't mine. You said 'just 'cause I let you fuck me doesn't mean you're mine.'"

"I said you fucking me doesn't mean *you're mine*."

"I *am* yours. I fuckin' told you this." Looking away

from her, he released a frustrated sigh.

In the silence that ensued, everything he said settled. He'd apologized for treating her the way he had. A part of her thought she deserved it. She'd taken Bree, and he'd lost years with her, after all. Even so, he hadn't blamed her and didn't seem mad at her because of that. Instead, he took the blame saying he should've chased her because he *loved* her.

"So you forgive me?"

His eyes widened. After a brief moment, a shadow of a smile crossed his face. "There's nothing to forgive you for, Em. What you did…" He swallowed thickly. "If I was you, I would've left me too. I can promise you though, right here, right now, I'll never hide anything from you. I'll tell you everything. I promise I'll never make the same mistakes again."

Her heart stilled. She parted her mouth to speak then shut it. Without even realizing it, she said, "I love you, Bryce. Always did. Always will."

He stared at her for a long while without saying a word. The expression on his face, she couldn't read.

"I promise too."

He cocked his head. "You promise?"

"I promise I'll never make the same mistakes again."

Finally, his lips quirked up. He smiled big and beautiful. "You love me?"

She nodded.

His stare roaming her face, he pulled her into a hug. "So Friday, then."

Could she? Would he keep his promise?

He drew away yet kept his body touching hers and cupped her cheeks. "I'll *never* hurt you, Em, *ever*. I'll be good to you. I'll take care of my girls, you and Bree."

He meant it. She knew, and she loved him too much to say no.

She smiled softly. "Friday."

That smile that changed his whole face came then. "Tilt your head back. I'll get you cleaned up."

He did. He then dried her, got her into bed, and told her he'd return after picking up Bree. After, he kissed her softly and smiled that big, wide smile. When he left, she let herself drift to sleep and not worry about what she'd just done.

****

"Are we gonna fuckin' start sometime today?"

His brothers turned to look his way. None seemed surprised by his outburst. Some of them looked like they understood or wanted to, but only a few knew exactly how he felt. It could've been a whole lot worse, he knew as did they.

The mother of his kid, his old lady, and soon-to-be wife had been grazed by a bullet. His brothers were shot at too, but no one had been injured like Em. She'd been their target. No doubt in his mind who fired the shots—the Falcons. Desperate to get back at Chained, they made a stupid move they'd soon come to regret. How they found Em, Ripper didn't know, but he needed to keep her safe and make sure that shit never happened again, so they needed to start this meeting and decide.

Prez nodded. "Yeah, we're starting."

"What's the plan?" The looks his brothers gave him made his stomach turn. "Tell me we got a plan?"

It'd been three days since the drive-by. Busy with

Em and Bree, he hadn't been around most of the time. Em hadn't been released from the hospital until the day before, Tuesday. By the time he brought her to the compound and dropped off her prescriptions, he had to pick up Bree at school. After bringing Bree home to keep her mom company, he grabbed Em's prescriptions at the pharmacy. He spent a couple of hours with Bree and Em then headed out to buy dinner. Before he knew it, it was time for Bree to bathe and head to bed. After tucking Bree in, Em decided to shower. He helped her. She hadn't wanted him to, but he did anyway. He fell asleep shortly after with Em tucked close to his side.

Now Wednesday morning, after dropping Bree off at school and checking on Em, who'd get the rest of the week off because he said so, the club met.

Prez shook his head. "No, we don't."

By now, they should've had a plan. While he'd been taking care of Em and Bree, his brothers should've discussed what happened, how to prevent it from happening again, and what they planned to do to avenge Em and themselves.

To fight his annoyance, he gritted his teeth. "What have you guys been doing the last three days?"

Dash held his gaze and calmly spoke. "We know you're pissed about this, but—"

"But nothing. She's the mother of my kid, my old lady, and my soon-to-be *wife*, so something needs to be done and fast."

Every one of them looked shocked, meaning Strike hadn't told anyone.

"We don't know who it was."

Bullshit. They knew. He glared Dash's way, who'd spoken. The brother stood to his left, leaning against a wall. Then Rip snarled, "Yeah, we fuckin' do. We had no beef with anyone but Chained, and that ship sailed a while back. The Falcons want to get back at Chained, so they want Em. We're hiding Em, so they fucked us."

"We got to be sure before we start a war," Hash jumped in.

A war? The club he joined didn't care about starting wars. They made vows to have each other's backs no matter the circumstance. They vowed to protect their club, their brothers, and their family with their dying breaths.

"You're fuckin' kidding me?" He looked around the large room, searching their gazes, trying to find someone, anyone on his side. His stare landing on Wild and Stone, who had old ladies, thinking they'd know how he felt. Nothing.

He slid his gaze to Trig, whose old lady Allie/Classy had been kidnapped; to Army, Allie's brother; to Cuss whose old lady had been attacked in their home. And nothing.

Pulse pounding at the base of his neck, he clenched his jaw fighting to keep composed. "This is fuckin' *bullshit*."

"We gotta talk and discuss," Prez's voice rose.

Bull. They knew who'd shot at them, and they were brothers who'd made vows. Their women, kids, even family were considered part of the club. Untouchable, so there was nothing to discuss but a plan to get back at the Falcons.

"Yeah? Like we discussed beating the shit outta Classy's loaded ex? Like we discussed looking for her ourselves when that asshole kidnapped her? Like we didn't find her and run to her rescue armed and without waiting for the cops? Like we discussed Cuss beating the shit outta that guy for dissing his old lady? Like we discussed Cuss going HAM on that other fucker on his front yard for—"

"That was different, brother."

He turned, took a step in Rake's direction, meeting his gaze dead-on. "Don't call me brother, asshole. She's my woman, the mother of my kid. She could've been killed."

He released a breath, knowing he needed to gather his thoughts and calm down before he lost it. No way. No how. Em could've been killed. Worse, what he hadn't let himself think about, the fact that *Bree*, his baby girl, could've been killed. If one of those bullets... Damn it!

Fisting his hands at his sides, he barked, "You assholes wanna sit around and do nothing to protect her?"

"That's not what we're doing." Mellow shook his head. "We just gotta talk and think real hard before we decide."

His heart pounded so loud, it was almost all he heard. Looking to Trig, Rip said, "That shot could've grazed Allie instead."

Trig's face changed, a ravished look taking hold like he was remembering that day not so long ago when they'd kidnapped Allie, and he'd lost his mind.

Ripper sliced his gaze to Cuss. "You could've lost your baby, instead of me."

Cuss's eyes widened a second before his face blanched.

He struck a nerve. Cuss and Tiff were expecting their first, a boy. Meeting Dodge's stare, he then said,

"Or it could've been Cullen."

Fear so much of it in Dodge's expression, the brother couldn't hide it, the same they probably saw in his.

Spotting movement from his peripheral vision, he shifted. Bud stared straight at him, eyes searing.

Wild cleared his throat. "You're taking this to an extreme. All we're trying to say is we gotta discuss this."

He couldn't believe this shit, couldn't believe he still hadn't convinced them. "They shot at *us*! *All* of us! It could've been one of *us*." He slammed his hand against his chest.

Deafening silence. No one spoke up. No one sided with him.

"We lost our balls over the last five years, that's fine." He spun and headed for the door. Grabbing the knob, he turned it and heard Prez speak.

"We gotta discuss and vote."

Looking over his shoulder, he growled, "You know where I stand."

Chapter Seventeen

"Em."

Shit. Bryce. He sounded surprised, yet his voice had been firm.

After being caught out of bed by Bud, she should've just gone back. In her defense, she figured Bud would run and tell Bryce anyway. She'd already been caught, so there'd been no point in hiding. She expected Bryce an hour ago. When he didn't show, she decided to finish laundry.

Straightening, she turned and met his eyes. He stood at the threshold leading into the room. God, just the sight of him shirtless. Not only shirtless but sweaty, like he'd just finished one hell of a workout.

"What'd I fuckin' say not two hours ago?"

She crossed her arms over her chest. "You said not to get out of bed."

Eyes narrowing, he quirked a brow and stepped into the room. "Are you being a smart ass?"

Totally. She hid a smile. "No."

He nodded. "You're being a smart ass."

She lifted her brows, playing dumb.

"I told you to stay in bed. You know I wanna know what the hell you're doing out of bed, so you're being a smart ass and a pain in my ass, *babe*."

"Just thought I'd finally get around to doing laundry, *babe*."

His eyes widened then narrowed. He moved taking another step inside, slamming the door shut then closing the distance between them. Inches away, as a smile quirked his lips, he leaned into her. "That's my Em, giving me lip and making me wanna do her at the same time." He chuckled. "Where's she been all this time?"

Snaking an arm around her back, he pushed her against him then kissed her, long, deep, and wonderfully. When he drew away, he whispered against her lips, "Fuckin' missed you, *babe*."

Her chest warmed. "Missed you, too, *babe*."

He chuckled then pressed his mouth to hers, soft and slow, and he didn't stop kissing her. One arm firm around her waist, the other moved, gripping her ass and hefting her up slowly until she sat on the laundry machine behind her. Her legs parting, he stood between them.

"Missed your mouth," he said against her lips, his hand now under her shirt, trailing up her back.

"Should've kissed me then."

For days, since she got out of the hospital, he'd only pressed his lips against hers gently, a small peck.

Shaking his head, he chuckled. "You know why I couldn't."

She had an idea. "No."

He unfastened her bra clasp one-handed. Her nipples puckered. Involuntarily, she arched her back, rubbing them against his chest.

"Kissing leads to shit like this…" His hand moved to her front. He cupped her breast then pinched her nipple with his index finger and thumb.

Her whole body shivered, legs instinctively

tightening around him.

"And this…" He dropped his head, kissing her neck. Then he lifted her shirt, trailed his mouth down, and sucked, hard.

She threw her head back and moaned.

He pressed his lips against hers a moment later. "And all that leads to me taking you, and I couldn't do that. We can't do that. Not 'till tomorrow, our wedding night."

No! She wanted him now. Her legs tensed around him, about to protest.

"Plus you're recovering."

What? She was fine and now all hot and bothered. He couldn't leave her like this!

He smiled. "But since you're up and feeling good enough to do laundry, I'm thinking you're feeling good enough to handle me."

Thank God, he'd just been teasing. So mean! It'd been days! Still, she wouldn't tease him back or lecture him about teasing her. She needed him, right now. Not like she could do either with his tongue sweeping inside her mouth.

She hooked her arms around his neck and bucked her hips, stroking against him.

Drawing away from her lips, he smirked. "Guess my babe missed me too."

All she managed to do was nod. Then his mouth hit hers again, kissing her sweetly. He used to kiss her like that all the time.

The next instant, he unbuckled her jeans and gently lifted her off the laundry machine to tug them and her thong off. His mouth lingered down her neck, kissing, licking, suckling, softly and sweetly. He pulled away slightly to undo his own jeans and yank them down along with his boxers. One hand at her waist, the other wrapped around her back, he pressed himself inside and hesitated only for a moment before he began moving inside her.

The entire time, he held her eyes.

He made love to her. Just like he used to.

In that instant, it became clear why she'd thought things between them had been changing. The first few times they'd had sex, he'd taken her rough, and he continued to do that at times, but often, he'd taken her tenderly too. It also became clear why she'd thought he loved her all those years ago even if he never said it. And yet, it still didn't explain why he hurt her.

He stopped. "Em?"

Her legs convulsed, pushing him against her. "Don't stop."

He started moving again, keeping the pace. It built slow but hit hard. As she spasmed, her head flew back, and a scream tore from her throat.

He buried his face in her neck and tightened his arm around her waist. "That's it, babe."

When the high began to fade, she cupped the back of his head and lifted hers. He kept moving. She spotted it before it came. Shoulders bunched, the corded muscles in his neck straining against his skin, his whole face changed, but he never released her, never lost sight of her eyes.

He finished on a groan and stayed buried. Then he released her waist to wrap his hand around the back of her neck. Hauling her against him, he held her tight. Her head buried in his neck, she did something she used to do after every time. She lifted her head and pressed a kiss to his jaw.

He tensed. She drew away slowly and locked gazes with him.

Brows furrowed, blue-green eyes scanning her face. "Love it when you do that, Em. Loved it then and love it now."

Her eyes softened.

"You gonna tell me what's on your mind?"

She quirked a brow. "Um… What?"

"Why there're tears in your eyes?"

Shit. That wasn't a surprise. It took her a spilt second to make a decision, to lie or omit the truth. "It was beautiful."

He lifted his brows. "That's why you're in tears?"

No. She cried because she didn't understand how you could hurt someone you loved. This, she wouldn't admit. She'd made her decision. She loved him, and he loved her. He'd apologized for his mistakes and promised never to hurt her again. She'd leave the past in the past.

"It was beautiful, Bryce, just like before, just like every time."

He squeezed the back of her neck, kissed her forehead, and smiled. "Love you, babe."

She released a breath. "Love you, *babe*."

****

Ripper couldn't believe his luck. No doubt he was the luckiest SOB on the planet. He woke that morning when Em, sleeping pressed against his side, cuddled closer and lifted herself over him. Chest to chest, she kissed him, deep.

"Rise and shine, *babe*," she whispered.

He groaned in protest and parted his eyes half-mast. They landed on her beautiful face, her hazel eyes shining, her hair a mess.

She grinned. "It was your idea to have me wake you, remember?"

Busting his balls, his old Em was back, officially. He loved her either way, but he wanted her to be the woman she was before life got in the way.

He smiled. "Yeah, babe, I remember."

He snaked his arms around her and sat up in bed, bringing her with him. Her legs straddled him, she buried her face in his neck and laughed softly. Then she lifted her head and kissed his jaw.

"Big day today."

She drew away, quirking a brow. "Really? Why?"

Again, teasing him. She *knew* why. It was Friday, the day they'd get hitched. He smirked. She moved off him, threw her feet over the edge of the bed, and stood. He slapped her ass playfully and didn't let her get far. Jumping out of bed, she caught his intent and ran for the door. He reached her just in time, winding an arm around her waist and hauling her backward.

"No!" She laughed. "I have to get Bree out of bed. She can't be late."

He buried his face in her neck. "She's missing school today."

She shifted turning her head to meet his gaze. "No, she can't. She's never missed—"

"Em, her parents are getting hitched. She isn't missing that."

She smiled and nodded. "Yeah, you're right. She shouldn't."

He grinned. "So we're agreeing?"

Her smile widened.

"So you aren't gonna fight me if I drag you in the shower with me?"

She shrugged. "Maybe."

He kissed her then. She didn't protest. He took her to the bathroom. She went willingly. He made love to her then, soft and slow.

Just like before.

Just like he used to.

When he came, he stayed buried. Holding her up, one arm around her back, the other under her butt, his body between her legs wrapped around his waist.

She lifted her head and kissed his jaw. "Love you, Bryce."

Later, they woke Bree and told her she'd miss school since they were getting married. His little girl was so ecstatic she spent the morning telling everyone. After breakfast, they headed to the courthouse. There, he thought, not for the first time, how he never thought that day would come. He looked to Em, standing beside him, wearing a simple red dress, synched at the waist that fell around her ass perfectly. He didn't know if she wore that color knowing it was his favorite, but he'd find out, eventually. Her blonde locks spilling around her, a soft smile in place, she never looked more beautiful. His gaze drifted to Bree, at his other side, her hand in his, also wearing a dress. Hers, a flower print with various colors that had some red in it too.

He looked at the young couple in front of them. The man was in uniform, a marine. His soon-to-be wife wore a white dress and held a bouquet of roses in her hand.

His stomach turned. He should've taken Em and Bree shopping for new dresses and flowers, at the very least. He hadn't even thought about it. Nothing like that to make him feel like a shitty husband before he was a husband.

His stare moved to Em. He leaned in, his mouth at her ear. "Should've got you a new dress."

She angled her head and quirked a brow. "A dress?"

"Yeah, a white dress, some flowers, anything else you wanted."

Her eyes softened that way he liked. "You're all I've wanted for a long time."

His chest tightened, throat clogged as he fought the emotion filling him.

It was their turn soon after. He said his vows first repeating after the officiant. She went next, and as she repeated the words, tears trekked down her beautiful face. Then the officiant asked for the rings. Em tensed and wiped the moisture streaking her face.

He reached into his pocket pulling out two bands. His, a plain, platinum band, hers was platinum too but embedded with fifteen diamonds that went around the length of it, five carats total. He realized then maybe he should've gotten her an engagement ring, too. A ring with a big diamond she'd pair with the band and show off with pride.

"Should've gotten you another one."

She looked from the officiant to him. Then peered at his hand, where he held her ring. Her eyes widened, lips parted. "That's...for me?" She swallowed. "I didn't know... You didn't have to. I..."

"Should've gotten you another one."

"What? Why? No, I-I like it." She shook her head then rephrased, "I love it. I want that one."

He chuckled. "I'm gonna let you keep this one anyway, Em. I meant I should've gotten you another one to go with this one."

Her eyes went wider. They dropped to the ring and met his gaze again. "Why?"

He smirked. "I make good money, babe. My wife should have nice bling."

"That *is* nice bling."

He smiled then nodded toward the officiant, a silent command he continue. A minute later, he slid the band on her finger, and she slipped his ring on his. Then finally, he got to kiss her. And they were married. That easy, that quick, and still, as he left the courthouse with both his girls smiling bright, he thought maybe he should've done more, had a big wedding with the club or anything else Em wanted.

Inside his SUV, Bree sitting buckled in the back, he turned to Em. "We can do this again later."

She tilted her head slightly, her brows furrowing.

"When this shit with the Falcons is over, we can have a real wedding like the one you dreamed of when you were a girl."

She smiled weakly. "I didn't dream of my wedding when I was a girl."

What had she dreamt of? He'd never asked her. Swallowing, he cocked his head. "What'd you dream about?"

Her eyes went soft. She looked away then mouthed, "Bree."

So her dream as a little girl had been something the average girl didn't dream about, something fucked she didn't want Bree to hear. His stomach rolled then hollowed out. Ignoring the sensation, he looked over his shoulder at Bree, smiled then drove to *The Bridge*, the fanciest steakhouse within a hundred-mile radius for lunch. He'd been there with Em before for each of their anniversaries. She remembered. He knew because the moment he pulled up, she looked at him, and her eyes softened that way he liked. That look stayed on her face the whole time. After the hostess sat them, she told Bree that's where they shared their anniversaries before she was born. It brought a smile to his baby girl's face too.

They had a fantastic lunch. He paid a hefty bill, the norm for the place, and didn't mind it one bit. As they left, Bree and Em headed to the ladies' room. While he waited for them, he got a call, the one he'd been praying to get for weeks.

Beef found Lilliam. He'd take her to the compound. That meant soon Em would know the truth.

Best wedding present ever.

****

The best day ever.

Em was *Mrs.* Knight.

She'd been Emelia Knight, Ms. Knight, for a while. When she left him, she'd changed her name. For one, she wanted to stay hidden. She chose his name because she wanted to give their daughter his name, a name she wanted to share. Now, though, she was officially Mrs. Bryce Knight. Maybe it was because she'd been in love with him for years, but it sounded amazing to her. Still, she couldn't believe it.

Em dreamed of being married to Bryce repeatedly over the course of seven years. When she did, she hadn't dreamt about him wearing a tux or in a church. She hadn't pictured herself in a white dress, hadn't imagined a large reception, a reception at all. She dreamt about a simple, courthouse wedding.

She never ever thought that dream would come true. It had, and as it turned out, reality kicked her dream's ass. Because never in a million years had she thought Bryce would buy her a ring, especially not the insanely huge band embedded in diamonds. If it wasn't so beautiful, it'd be gaudy. Not that she'd complain, it was a ring with lots of diamonds and gorgeous, the most beautiful piece of jewelry she'd ever owned. In fact, it was the most beautiful piece of jewelry she'd ever seen. Needless to say, she'd never thought he'd be concerned with getting her a dress or flowers. She'd never even considered he'd wear anything but a plain tee and his cut, yet he had. He wore a black, button-down, long-sleeved shirt and a pair of dark wash jeans, proving he looked handsome even preppy. Last, she never envisioned he'd want to give her a wedding she dreamed of. The lunch at *The Bridge* was just icing on her amazing day.

Now, they were headed to the compound after having just dropped off Bree at Trig and Allie's for a sleepover with Della. They'd get a "honeymoon" night, too. She couldn't wait. Not that it'd be much different from every other night, still, it was nice.

He parked in the front lot of the garage, turned to her, and asked again, "What did you dream about when you were a girl?"

Another thing about today that surprised her—he asked her things he'd never asked before, almost as if he was trying to get to know her better. When they'd been together, they didn't talk about the past. He knew about her abusive father like she knew both his parents abandoned him, and he ended up with a grandmother who didn't care for him like she should, but they never went into details. They never rehashed the past. What for?

She would've answered the first time since she didn't see the point in lying, but she hadn't because of Bree. A part of her figured he'd let it go or forget about it altogether. The fact he hadn't reinforced that maybe he was, in some way, trying to get to know her on a deeper level.

"Getting away."

He cocked his head. "From this town?"

That's what some small-town girls dreamed about she supposed but not her. Shaking her head, she said, "From my father."

His expression hardened, but there was something sad in his eyes. "Never had another dream, Em?"

God, no. That was all she wanted for so long, as a girl anyway. Chip saved her from that. Then she met Bryce, and she'd wanted him, but she hadn't been a girl then.

She shook her head. "No."

"You never dreamed about getting hitched, getting a degree, or having kids?"

That sounded bad, but it was the truth. "I—"

"You were going to college for a while, didn't you want that?"

She nodded. "Yeah, but when I was a girl, I never let myself dream about anything but getting away because I knew I'd never get anything unless I did."

His jaw twitched. "I should've kicked his ass while I had the chance."

She burst out laughing.

His brows furrowed. "Not a joke."

She stopped laughing abruptly, her gaze softening. "I know."

He smiled then. "I gotta surprise for you."

She grinned.

Outside of the SUV, he reached for her hand. Her smile still in place and didn't fade, in fact, it widened, excitement building while she followed close behind him as he led her into the garage and compound. She trailed him down the long, narrow hallway past the living room and kitchen to the back end of the compound. Just before reaching the door leading to the backlot, he turned and opened a door into one of the spare rooms. By this point, her cheeks hurt with how hard she was smiling. When he tugged her inside and beside him, her gaze fell to the center of the room.

Her smile faded. Her chest tightened, and the breath flew out of her. A searing pain that started in her middle spread until she hurt everywhere.

Lilliam sat on a chair in that room. Her legs bare, wearing a mini-skirt, a black shirt exposing too much cleavage, and a pair of stripper heels.

No. Not real. This couldn't be happening, not to her, not on the best day of her life. She shook her head, hating Lilliam didn't disappear, proving it was real and happening. If it wasn't, it wouldn't hurt so bad. It came to her fast. The gut-wrenching realization—this was a joke, a horrible, cruel joke...on her. Get Em to think he loved her, reinforce it by marrying her, giving her a perfect day, only to shove Lilliam in her face on their honeymoon night. Surprise, he's still fucking Lilliam. Surprise, he hated her and wanted her to suffer. How could she have been so gullible to think he loved her?

The room began to spin. Tears rushed her. She needed to get away, fast. Releasing Bryce's hand, she took several steps back.

He moved to face her, blocking Lilliam from her sight. Then he snaked his arms around her back bringing her close. She planted her hands against the expanse of his chest, feeling every muscle, every ridge. It sucked it felt good, so amazing for a split second she forgot what he'd just done to her.

Looking into his eyes as he held her close, the room stopped swirling. A relief, she didn't know if she would've stayed standing otherwise.

The muscle in his jaw jumped. "Don't you trust me?"

She pushed with all her might but only managed to get an inch between them. His arms tight around her wouldn't allow her farther away.

"You trust *me*." His voice firm yet pleading just like his eyes. "You *do*. You said you love *me*. You *love* me, you gotta trust me now."

Trust him? No clue why but even as her breaths came out in gasps, she nodded.

Bryce turned, releasing one arm from around her back yet kept the other firm around her waist. He lugged her to his side pressing her close as if he knew she needed the weight of her body supported.

She swallowed.

"Tell her."

Em realized for the first time they weren't alone. Strike stood to Lilliam's right. Bud to her left, blocking her in. Neither looked happy.

Apparently, Lilliam didn't speak fast enough because Bud barked, "Tell her!"

He screamed it so loud and sudden, she jostled against Bryce. Almost as if instinctively, that arm around her waist squeezed her.

Lilliam's eyes narrowed, glaring at Bud. She threw her fake blonde hair behind her then snapped, "It's been more than five years." Lilliam's head shot forward meeting her gaze. "Looks like she's forgiven him anyway."

Bud ground his teeth then kicked one of the hind legs of Lilliam's chair. It tipped over.

Lilliam caught herself on her hands and knees. "I can't fucking believe you just did that! I'm married to one of your brothers!"

"Not as soon as you sign those fuckin' papers," Strike shot.

Lilliam jutted her breasts forward, stretching the small tank she wore. Then on hands and knees, she turned, put her feet on the ground, giving Em and Bryce view of her bare ass. Lilliam rubbed her knees, stood, and straightened. "Get him *now*. I want to talk to him. When he finds out what you just did to me, he'll—"

"Get him."

Em's head automatically tilted to Bryce. Still trying to process Lilliam being there, and now, the knowledge Lilliam had married one of the brothers, Em didn't notice when Bud and Strike called for him. A minute later, the door behind her opened. She looked over her shoulder.

Dodge, jaw clenched, hands in fists, strode inside. Em knew him. He'd been with the club all those years ago. Since then, he'd had a son, Cullen, who was often at the compound and played with Della and Bree though he was younger.

Dodge's gaze sliced behind her to Lilliam.

Lilliam started talking at him. "They've kidnapped me, and—" Her words died abruptly when Dodge moved.

Standing before Lilliam, Dodge's body tense, anger vibrated from every pore. "I don't give a fuck. I stopped giving a fuck a while back. Just 'cause I stopped giving a fuck didn't mean I expected you to care even less about your kid."

Shit. Lilliam was Cullen's mother? How had Em not known this?

"Though I shouldn't be surprised now, should I? 'Cause you never gave a shit."

"Of course, I—"

"Shut it." Dodge paused for a split second. Then his voice lowered an octave. "Before you fucked with me, you fucked with Trig. Imagine my surprise when I found out before that, you fucked with Rip, with Em. Worse than all that shit is you fuck with..." He slammed his hand against his chest. "*My* boy."

Jabbing his finger in Lilliam's face, he screamed, "*Your* son. In my eyes, you're the worst piece of shit the earth spit out, so I don't give a shit what happens to you. You give Rip what he wants. Then you sign the divorce papers and get gone. By gone, I mean you get the fuck out of Wadden. You go somewhere I'll *never* see your face again."

With those last words, Dodge stormed out of the room.

"Tell her." This came from Bud, his patience fraying by the look on his face.

"Like she'd believe me anyway."

Bud closed the distance between himself and

Lilliam, gripping her arm roughly. His voice deadly, he said, "I think you forgot where you are. I think you forgot what we used to do for a living. Think you forgot you've fucked with a lot of us, and all of us are people you don't fuck with 'cause that punishment is..." He leaned into her. "*Severe.*"

Finally, something sunk in. Lilliam's eyes widened. She turned to Em then reluctantly looked at her. "I made you think I fucked him, but I never did."

Lilliam said it softly. Because she didn't want Em to know, because she wanted to prolong her pain, Em didn't know, but she heard. She heard it clearly, but she didn't say anything. Like everything that happened since she walked into that room and found Lilliam inside, she was still trying to process it.

It took a moment, and when it settled, the magnitude of what Lilliam admitted hit her. Her throat went dry. The room began to twirl, again, this time much faster. Closing her eyes, she swallowed the bile rising in the back of her throat. Her hands went to Bryce, one gripping his stomach, the other his back, nails digging into his skin.

She left him, the man she loved, and took Bree...

Bree had gone without a father...

Bryce missed five years of his daughter's life...

All that time wasted—for nothing. And all because of *her*, because she believed Lilliam. Why had she?

She parted her eyes, realizing belatedly Bryce now stood in front of her, staring down at her. Hands gripping her arms, he'd called her name at least twice.

"Tell me."

His brows furrowed. "What?"

"Is it true?"

He swallowed. "Knew you wouldn't believe me. That's why I've been looking for her for weeks. I'd thought you'd believe her."

A rush of tears came because of what he said, because of what it meant. He hadn't told her himself because he didn't trust her to trust him.

She shook her head. "Why would you think I wouldn't believe you?"

"'Cause you *believed* her."

Shit. She had. She believed Lilliam so easily and never even confronted him. She messed up both their lives and worse, Bree's, by believing Lilliam.

Em caught Lilliam coming out of their room, practically naked. Lilliam claimed she was fucking him. Em found a thong on their bed. It didn't matter. She should've trusted him enough to *ask him*. What had she been so afraid of? Of having him admit it to her face? Of not being strong enough to walk away after staring into his peculiar, beautiful eyes? Of convincing herself she loved him too much to leave even if he'd cheated? Of letting herself settle for that?

"I need to hear it from you."

Gaze holding hers, he released a breath then finally said, "I never wanted her. I never fucked her, not before you, not while we were together, not after you left."

Good God, what had she done? She'd ruined their lives!

Her chest tightened so much it made it hard to breathe. She was hot, sweating, and the tears were coming so fast, she couldn't hold them back. No! She couldn't give that woman the pleasure of knowing how much she hurt.

Her hands firm against Bryce's chest, she shoved

him. Not expecting it, he lost hold of her and stumbled back. She took advantage, side-stepped, and walked past him. Face to face with Lilliam. Even in her position, Lilliam managed to look snarky. Classic bitch.

Em balled her hands into fists then swung. Knocking her to one side, Lilliam fell to the floor. Em pounced, climbing on top of her, punching again and again until she lost count.

An arm tightened around her waist pressing her back to a hard chest. Then he spoke against her neck. "Stop fighting. Gonna hurt yourself."

She caught her breath. Strike and Bud lifted Lilliam and hauled her out of the room. Then everything she held back came crashing down. The magnitude of what an idiot she'd been, the guilt, all she missed, all he and Bree had, the hurt she caused him, herself, and especially Bree compounded until she was gasping. Tears flowed down her face; gut-wrenching sobs tore through her, and the whole time, *he*, the man she hurt, held her close.

His mouth at her ear, arms wrapped around her, he pleaded, "Don't fight me, Em. Don't fuckin' fight me."

She wanted more than anything not to, but she didn't deserve him. So she fought, arms and legs pushing at him, trying to make him release her, struggling to get away. He let her go a split second to make her face him. She took advantage, shoved him, and took a series of steps away.

He rushed her, circled his arms around her back and neck, hauled her to him, and squeezed her. "I'm not letting you go, babe. Made that mistake once, not doing it again. So you wanna fight, fight, but you're not catching me by surprise again, meaning I'm not letting you go. Not for a second."

That slashed through her causing an ache so deep it silenced her sobs.

Cupping the back of her head, he angled her face to his, and his tortured stare locked with hers. "I walked around a long time blind 'cause all I saw was you even when you were nowhere in sight. I'm not doing it again, not letting you go."

Shit. Shit. Shit. She couldn't breathe, couldn't stop shaking, couldn't feel anything but that ache, a pain she felt everywhere but especially her heart.

No way she'd ever doubt him now. In so many words, in actions, he *proved* how much he loved her. Because he wouldn't let her go, because he forgave her, she knew he loved her more, much more than she ever thought possible.

Panting, she shook her head. "Can't b-believe you f-forgive me."

"You'll forgive me too." His hold over her softened though not completely.

"What for?"

"I've had some time to think about this. 'Cause I have, I know if I'd been completely honest with you back then, you wouldn't've believed her." His eyes darkened. "The truth is she'd been trying to get me to fuck her for a while."

She shook her head. "It doesn't make a difference—"

"Yeah, Em, it fuckin' does 'cause you would've known she was making moves on me, and you would've realized she was playing you from the get-go, and you would've never questioned me. You would've never questioned *us*. You would've stayed."

She shut her eyes and swallowed. "Don't do that. Don't blame yourself."

He shook his head. "I'm not. This isn't my fault. It isn't yours. It's hers. Now, we got *us* back, so she loses, not us."

Tears continued to trek down her cheeks. "But—"

"No, buts, Em. It happened. We move on. We *have* moved on. We're married. We got Bree. We're gonna make another baby. We're gonna be happy and make so many good memories, we're gonna forget this shit ever happened."

God, who was this man? Biting the side of her lip, her thought slipped out. "I don't know you at all."

His face softened. "Yeah, you do." He dropped his head resting his forehead against hers. "Proving my point, I never said it, but I've always felt this way about you. If you would've known, you wouldn't't've left."

God, he was killing her. She curved her arms around his neck, pulling him closer. "You showed it. You didn't say it, but I felt it, felt loved."

"I should've said it, babe. Should've said it every day 'cause I loved you every second of every day."

She closed her eyes tightly, feeling too much, some of it bad, most of it good. When she parted her lids, she said on an exhale, "Love you, Bryce."

He grinned. "Love you, Em." His hand slid up her cheek and back into her hair. "We gotta go. I've got another surprise." He turned and glided his hand down her back and side and along her arm to grab her hand. Then he lightly tugged her forward.

"Not sure I want to see it."

Over his shoulder, he asked, "Why?"

She smiled. "You kind of suck at surprises."

His brows furrowed.

"This isn't the kind of surprise you give your wife on your wedding night."

His lips quirked up. "It's a good way to start our marriage, clean slate."

She couldn't argue with that.

He smirked. "'Sides, I guarantee you'll like this one."

Chapter Eighteen

Ripper hadn't lied. He'd stake his life on the fact she'd love his surprise. To get there, they'd ride. It'd been too long since she'd been on the back of his bike.

He led her upstairs and down the hall. Reaching the room Em and Bree share, the room Em still kept most of her clothes in but didn't sleep in since she slept with him, he strode through, pulling her in behind him. He shut the door with his foot then drew her against him as he did. Chest to chest, he asked, "You wear that color for me?"

Eyes red-rimmed and puffy, her cheeks flushed, and still, she looked breathtaking. She smiled and nodded.

"Still my favorite, Em."

Her smile widened.

"Like the dress. Love it on you, but we're gonna go for a ride, so you need to change."

She hooked her arms around his neck, got on the tips of her toes, and tilted her head up for a kiss. He gave in, leaning down to meet her lips. A soft, simple, sweet kiss, he felt it in his bones.

She pulled away. He watched her walk into the closet. Then as he marched out of the room and into his across the hall, he removed the black, button-down shirt he wore, one he bought for the occasion. On his dresser, he grabbed a plain black tee and his cut, donned them, and went back into the room across his. Moments later, she strode out of the closet wearing a pair of jeans, boots, a Harley tank, and a black leather jacket.

He stood motionless staring at her, at that jacket. So familiar, but it couldn't be, it looked new. Closing the distance between them, his stare on the patch on the right, he grabbed one of her arms, turning her. Another patch yet bigger, reading the same, "Property of Ripper, Hell Ryders MC."

She'd kept it, the leather he gave her so many years ago, and it was like new, like she'd treasured it. He swallowed the emotion clogging his throat.

She turned and met his gaze. "Something wrong?"

"Can't believe—"

Lifting a brow, she crossed her arms over her chest. "Haven't we been over this?"

He stilled.

Her face softened, looking at him that way he loved. "Always loved you, Bryce. I couldn't get rid of it. I had to take care of it, even believing what I did."

He looked away then. He didn't, he'd end up kissing her, and then, the ride and her surprise would be long forgotten.

Grabbing her hand, he quickened his pace, led her outside, and hopped on his bike. She planted a hand on his shoulder, swung her leg over, cuddled close, legs tight against his, arms around his waist.

Just like before.

Just like they used to.

He rode off, the wind blowing against them. Her chest pressed against his back, arms tight around his midsection, he finally found what he'd chased for years. He didn't know how to describe it. If he had to, he'd say it was a mixture of a bunch of things he always wanted: freedom, fulfilment, *her*.

At a stop light, Em lifted her butt off the seat and leaned into him. He turned his head, listening over the roaring of the engine, thinking she had something to say. Instead, she pressed a kiss to his jaw.

Just like before.

Just like she used to.

It was only a short ride to her surprise but worth it since Em enjoyed it as much as him. When he drove up to a house with large bay windows, she sighed.

Parking, he cut the engine, grabbed her hand, pressed it to his stomach then slanted his face toward hers. "We're here."

She smiled. "You rented a house for the night?"

He looked to the house she referred to: a big bungalow with four bedrooms, a two-car garage, and a big yard in front and back. He hadn't done much with the yard, the front or back, so it didn't have the curb appeal it should. He'd do something about that next. The inside, he'd remodeled to an open concept, both bathrooms and kitchen had been updated too.

"Naw, babe. It's not rented. It's ours."

She tensed behind him. He let her take in that piece of information as he stood and helped her off his bike.

"It's ours?"

He tugged her toward the front door. "Yeah, it's ours. It's home, or it will be as soon as this shit with the Falcons is over," he added, going up five steps to the porch and door.

"You bought a house?"

He paused turning to her. "Yeah." He didn't elaborate, hoping she'd drop the subject though he knew her well enough to know the chances of that happening were slim.

"I thought you said the club was clean."

"Club is clean, babe."

"I just..." She shook her head, her thick hair swayed. "It doesn't make sense."

She didn't understand how he could afford her diamond band and a house without the club being involved in dirty dealings? The club made good money. What they did wasn't entirely legal, but it wasn't the shit they'd been involved in before. Still, for what they did and what they made, it didn't mean he could afford it all at once unless he'd saved a shit ton of money. He had saved a ton because he had a house he bought years ago he kept rented. He lived at the compound, so most of the money he earned, he saved. Every now and then, between renters, he updated his house, so money went into that. Still, he had a bunch saved. Part of it went to buy her ring. The rest, he put in a college fund for Bree.

As he opened the door and waited for her to enter, he thought of something to say, something that would redirect her attention because he didn't want to admit when he bought the house. He wanted to leave the past in the past and didn't want her knowing anything that could make her feel guiltier than she did already.

"Wow."

He closed and locked the door then looked at her, taking everything in. The room was large and mostly empty, so it made everything look bigger. To their left, a living room with an old brick fireplace he'd refinished. Two large bay windows at each side of the front door. The den at the far end of the house had wall-to-wall built-in shelving. In the middle of that room sat a couch.

To their right, the dining room. Behind it, the kitchen: dark cabinets, white and gray marble countertops that matched the concrete countertop on the massive island and breakfast bar. The back of the house had floor-to-ceiling sliding glass doors.

Between the den and living room, a hallway led to the bedrooms. Off the kitchen and dining room, a door led to the two-car garage and laundry room.

Grabbing her hand, he pulled her toward the hallway and walked until he reached the room before the master. "I thought this could be Bree's room." He painted the walls pink just weeks ago when Bree told him it was her favorite color.

"You painted it already?"

He looked down at her and smiled. "Yeah. She needs furniture though and blankets and..." He shrugged. "...Guess more toys to fill this room up."

Before she said another word, he tugged on her arm, leading her farther down the hall and into the master. An inflatable mattress lay in the center of the room. Aside from that, it was empty.

"It's—"

"Mostly empty now, but we got time before we can move anyway. You can pick out whatever you want, decorate it however you want. Just try not to make it too girlie, yeah?"

Her gaze swept the large room then met his. "The club's clean?"

Right, so it was time to tell her everything the club did. "Remember I went away a while back?"

She released his hand, wrapped her arms around her waist, and nodded.

"I had a guard outta town. That's what we call them, what we do, 'guards,' short for bodyguards. We get paid good money for that 'cause people pay a lot for safety and 'cause we include...extras."

Her eyes went round. "Like?"

"Rough people up."

She didn't even flinch. Then again, he hadn't expected her to. She'd been with him when the club was into running drugs and guns, and before that, she lived with Chip whose club was involved in much of the same. She'd seen worse.

"Like enforcers?"

He shrugged. "Guess it's something like that."

"That's not legal."

"No."

"So technically—"

"We're not gonna get in trouble. We're good at what we do. Besides, the people we rough up are on the wrong side of the law."

She swallowed. "Who pays for something like that?"

"People who're loaded and need protection."

"Like?"

"Like Tiff."

Her lips parted. "Cuss's Tiff?"

"Yeah, Cuss's old lady. Her family's loaded. She was in college in LA and got unwanted attention from a sick loser who'd follow her around and break into her apartment. Her dad paid the club to deal with him."

She quirked a brow. "So, you dealt with him?"

"I didn't. Cuss, Mellow, and Bud did."

She nodded. "Is that how they met?"

He shook his head. "Naw. They go way back, went

309

to high school together from what I heard."

"When you went away—"

He grabbed her arm, tugged it away from her waist, and trailed his hand down her forearm to lace his fingers through hers. "Some dick wouldn't leave his ex-girlfriend alone. Her new man has money and paid us to teach him a lesson."

"How do you know she didn't want him—"

"We check to make sure. We talked to the girl. She was terrified, and cops couldn't or wouldn't do anything. We get that with situations like that, there's not much cops can do but write a report, not until something bigger and worse happens. We make sure it doesn't get to that."

He shrugged. "We're hardly ever asked to rough people up anyway. Mostly just scare them enough they don't think about doing it again."

"So you basically deal with stalkers?"

He squeezed her hand. "No, we deal with all sorts of fucked up people. Not what you're thinking though. We don't get involved with gangs or the mafia or dealers, they handle their own shit 'cause their enemies found out they couldn't, they wouldn't last much longer. Most of the time, we're just providing protection for a short time. For the right price, we provide extras. We work for who we want meaning we don't feel right about someone, we turn them down."

"But you could get hurt—"

He moved closer and cupped her cheek. "You worried 'bout me?"

She rested a hand on his chest then on an exhale admitted, "Always."

He grinned.

She released his hand to wind both arms around his waist tightly. "Bay windows. You remembered I like them?"

He nodded. All those years ago, those windows had been the reason he bought the house. They were also the reason after she left him, he couldn't live in it. Those windows reminded him of her, and he couldn't bring himself to remove them or sell the house, so he rented it.

"I can't believe you found a house so soon. When did you start looking? When did you buy it?"

Drawing away, he grabbed her hand and led her to the en suite bathroom. "Big shower, a big tub for your baths." Then he led her to the closet. "Don't think either of us will ever fill this, but we can try."

"Bryce?"

Having no choice, he met her gaze.

"When did you start looking?"

He turned. "Let me show you the backyard, lots of room."

She tugged on his hand before he took another step. He stilled and faced her but didn't meet her eyes.

"What aren't you telling me?"

There it was. That ability she had, reading him so easily. It seemed she got it back. Too bad it failed her all those years ago. He wished it failed her now instead of then. He didn't want to get into this, not now, not ever. They kept going over the past, they'd never move forward. He wanted her to know he never cheated, never hurt her, but he didn't want her to know this. It'd only wound her.

"Look at me."

He did. He knew the moment she figured it out.

311

Her face changed, a sadness taking hold. "You...bought it before?"

He couldn't bring himself to say it, so he didn't.

"Tell me." She shut her eyes and whispered, "Please, tell me."

He lifted her hand to her face and rubbed the band he placed on her ring finger. "It doesn't change this, so it doesn't matter."

"We're starting over. I need to know."

"For us to start over, you don't need to know. You need to let shit go. Are you saying you need to know before you let shit go?"

She nodded.

He expelled a breath. "I closed on it a week before you left. I was going to tell you about it, and I would've. But at the time, I didn't know when we would've been able to move in because I needed to make some big changes that were gonna have to wait a while."

Her gaze fell from his as tears clouded her eyes.

He lifted her chin with his finger. "It isn't your fault." He shook his head. "I never told you I loved you, but I told you plenty of other shit, how I didn't see myself getting married or having kids, how that wasn't me. I knew you wanted that. So when you left, I kicked my own ass for not giving you that, for not telling you how I felt. I should've."

He drew close until her body touched his. "We've both made mistakes. We both lost years. Now, we got us back, and we got Bree, so Em, we gotta leave the past in the past and start making up for the years we lost, yeah?"

She smiled at that. "Yeah."

"I've never lived here. I've rented it out and fixed it up some over the years. When I found out about Bree, it was good timing 'cause the lease was up, and the tenants hadn't renewed, so I've been coming and fixing some shit here and there, painting mostly. Except for Bree's room, I painted everything white. Now you're here, you can tell me what you like, and I'll paint again."

Her face softened. "I love you, Bryce."

He felt the words in his soul, so he couldn't do anything but stand there looking at her looking at him in that way he loved.

When he managed to move, he did what he'd been dying to do all day. He kissed her deep. The kiss led to other shit that led to other shit that led to him having the best orgasm of his life. It'd be the best until next time. He knew because it got better every time.

****

Her stomach growled. Not a surprise. She and Bryce thoroughly enjoyed their first night as husband and wife. While doing that, they'd skipped dinner.

Close to seven in the morning now, they didn't have to pick up Bree until noon, but hunger woke her, and she couldn't wait any longer. That, in itself, presented a problem, a big one. She didn't think Bryce had stocked the fridge. Not to mention how much she really hated to get up, it was cold, and she was warm snuggled close to Bryce. Her chest pressed against his side, her leg swung over his, her hand resting on his abs.

Slowly, she moved away, first her hand then her leg, and finally, she shifted backward. He didn't stir. She stared at him in sleep for a while, letting the past

313

day flow through her, the best day of her life. A smile spread across her lips. Her stomach growled again loud enough that she thought it'd wake him. She strode out of the master bedroom, where they slept on an inflatable mattress, walked down the hall, through the den and living room until she reached the kitchen. Making her way to the fridge, she parted it. As feared, empty. She then looked inside the cabinets and found those empty too. Her gaze drifted across the kitchen landing on the breakfast bar. Her phone binged, the text message alert sounding. She went in search of it. It didn't take her long to find it right where she left it last night, on the couch. Picking it up, she slid her finger across it and froze.

Got ur grl. U in xchange 4 her. U got a min to decide or she's dead.

It took her less to make the decision. Not much of a decision, she'd give anything for Bree, even her own life.

Without further thought, she ran across the room to the door, unlocked it, and stepped out. A hand grasped her bicep tightly dragging her to her right. She didn't get a chance to see anyone since a second later someone covered her head with a hood.

The heat of a body against her back, that someone's mouth at her ear threatened, "Scream, deal's off."

Another man snickered. Then the person holding her yanked her forward. She went willingly. A short distance later, the man holding her arm tightly released her, and she felt an arm hook around her back and another under her knees. Whoever held her now lifted her and laid her down. Feeling the felt at her back, something slammed down. No doubt, they locked her in a trunk. Where they planned to take her didn't matter. What did—Bree would be safe.

Knowing this, she tried to come to terms with the fact that the best day of her life would be followed by her last.

Chapter Nineteen

The warmth and scent of her gone, he cracked his eyes open and sat up on the inflatable mattress, wide awake.

Any minute she'd walk out of the bathroom. He waited until he lost patience. Annoyed, he groaned his frustration hoping to God she heard him and came before he dragged himself out of bed.

When she didn't, that mild irritation turned to annoyance. He *hated* waking without her. He had the best day of his life yesterday, and he wanted that amazing day followed by one where he woke beside his wife.

Placing his feet on the floor, he stood and drew a hand through his face then searched the floor for his jeans. He found them near the door, his shirt missing since she'd worn it to bed. Pulling his jeans on, his gaze on her clothes beside his, he strode toward the bathroom, smiling with the thought when he found her he'd get to rant and rave, and she'd give him lip.

Finding the bathroom empty, he walked out of their bedroom and down the hall. "Em?" In the living room, he called, "Em?" When she didn't answer a second time, he felt a sinking sensation in the pit of his stomach.

He swallowed then searched the house, front to back, back to front. Everything was as they left it, not that there was much. The place was empty except for his keys, cell, and wallet on the breakfast bar, the couch in the den, and the inflatable mattress in the master bedroom, yet Em was nowhere, her cell gone too.

That sinking sensation deepened like he'd been dropped into the ocean with a ton of bricks tied to him, what people felt when they realized they were about to die, and there was nothing they could do to stop it. Most people never felt it because most people didn't know when they'd die, and yet in one lifetime, he'd felt it twice. The first time—when she left.

Had she *left him*? *Again*?

A memory flashed before his eyes. Em saying her vows, her voice shaking as tears trekked down her face. He remembered something else—how tight she held him last night, how just before she drifted off she whispered, "Always loved you, Bryce. Always will."

She hadn't left. She wouldn't take Bree from him because she loved him, had always loved him, and now, she knew he felt the same. Before he knew what he meant to do, he pressed his phone to his ear. He didn't realize what number he'd dialed until he heard Trig's voice.

"Rip, don't tell me you're coming this early. They didn't get to bed 'till midnight."

"Bree," his voice came out hoarse.

"Sleep—"

"Check. Now."

Silence. Then he heard movement. A moment later, "She's sleeping, Rip."

"She's there?"

"Just checked on them. Bree and Della, they're still sleeping. I just told you they didn't get to bed 'till

317

midnight."

"She's there," he repeated.

"Yeah." A pause. "What's going on?"

If he hadn't known Em hadn't left, there was proof now. Meaning Em was *taken* from their home wearing just his tee while he slept. He knew who took her, and he knew why. His brothers wouldn't help him. He knew who would, but he had to act fast. If they hadn't killed her yet, they wouldn't wait much longer. He didn't let himself think about anything else.

"Get them to the compound. Don't let them go outside," he ordered.

"Why? What the fuck's going on?"

"Don't got time for this, Trig. Get your gun. Get Bree, Della, and Allie and take them to the compound."

He hung up, tugged on his boots and his cut, grabbed his keys, phone, wallet, and headed for the door. There, he turned the knob. Unlocked. No doubt he'd locked it meaning Em had unlocked it, and there was only one reason she would.

Locking the door behind him, he ran to his bike, hopped on, and hauled ass to the compound. Once there, he dug his cell out of his pocket and dialed. He did this while he sprinted toward his room.

"Rip?" Chip sounded like he'd just woken.

"They got Em."

"Fuck."

One word so filled with emotion cut through Rip. No one else in the world except for Bree and him would feel it like Chip. This, he knew.

"How? Never mind, it's not fuckin' important. Where are you?"

"Just got to the compound."

"Meet you there."

He shook his head. "Naw, I'm alone on this. I'll go to you."

"Brothers don't go at it alone."

Rip reached his room, then his closet, opened his safe, grabbed both his guns, loaded them, and tucked them in his waistband. "This one does."

"'Cause of circumstances, we're somewhere new." Chip gave him the address, promised to text it as well then added, "Don't need to tell you we don't got much time."

"No, you don't. I'll be there as fast as I can ride."

He hung up and grabbed a black tee. Heading out of his room and down the hall, he took off his cut, donned the tee then pulled his cut over it. On his way, he ran into Trig, Allie, Della, and Bree. A look at his baby girl, a rush of raw emotion choked him.

Since realizing Em had been taken, he hadn't let himself think she could already be dead. He wanted her alive. It was selfish. A gang like the Falcons didn't have limits on how far they'd go, and there were things far worse than death. Being tortured, beaten, and raped so savagely she'd beg for death. He hadn't let himself think on that either. But now, for the first time, staring at Bree, he failed. He couldn't help but go there, images of Em dead, beaten, tortured, raped seared his mind.

Bree smiled and ran to him, wrapping her arms tight around him. He returned the hug. He wasn't a man of faith, never had been because his life had been fucked, but right then, he prayed he'd bring his little girl's mom home in one piece and alive.

Leaning down, he kissed her forehead. "Gonna be gone for a little. You be good with your Aunt Allie and your Uncle Trig."

"Where's Mommy?"

There it was. And he didn't have a clue what to say. "I'm gonna get her."

The truth. Dead or alive, he'd find Em, and he'd bring her home. He shouldn't've said even what he had to Bree. She was too young to understand, to be worrying.

How would he ever raise her on his own? No, he couldn't think like that. He needed Em. Bree needed her too, so he'd bring Bree her mom. He'd bring back his wife.

Her eyes rounded. He didn't give her time to think, to respond. "You stay indoors. I'll be back with your mom before you know it, yeah?"

Maybe she sensed she shouldn't ask. Maybe she knew he'd lose it because he saw the concern in her eyes, but she just nodded and gave him another hug. "I love you, Daddy."

He threaded his fingers through her hair. "Love you too, baby."

He wanted to run but didn't want to worry Bree more, so he walked away quickly. The whole time, he fought looking back.

"Rip? You gonna fuckin' answer me?"

He turned and met Trig's stare. "Don't got time." Then his gaze flicked behind Trig.

Strike and Prez, both looking like they'd just rolled out of bed. He turned and made it halfway then felt the heat of a hand grasping his shoulder and yanking him back around.

"Where's Em?" Prez asked, eyes narrowed, voice firm.

"Already said I don't got fuckin' time."

Strike dragged a hand through his hair. "Fuck, they took her."

His stare went to Strike then met Trig's and Prez's. He didn't say anything, couldn't force himself to say it.

"Fuck. Fuck. Fuck."

"Call the brothers," Prez ordered.

"Half of them are hung over."

They would be. Friday nights most of them got wasted at the compound.

"Don't give a fuck. Call them."

Ripper didn't get through processing that when he heard Bud.

"What the fuck for? We all know what happened here. She left. Ain't no surprise."

Ripper spun and shot daggers at Bud. Next thing he knew, he was on the floor, straddling Bud, slamming his fists into his face. He got in a few good punches before two brothers grabbed him and hauled him off.

"We aren't helping her this way, Rip," Strike said, standing to his right, holding him back.

He stopped fighting but continued to glare at Bud.

Trig, standing at his other side, hand gripping his bicep, pointed out, "She didn't leave him 'cause Bree's here. She'd left, she would've taken her daughter."

He snatched his arms out of Trig and Strike's grasp. "I already said I don't got time for this shit. You guys wanna talk about this, now isn't the time. Now's the time for me to ride out." He managed a step.

Strike grabbed his elbow.

Taking a deep breath, he turned. "Get your fuckin' hands—"

"This isn't the time to pick fights with your

brothers, either. It's the time you lean on *us*." Strike released him.

They wanted to help now? Now, when there was a chance she was already dead? "Why the fuck now?"

"'Cause now's the time to act," Trig added.

Ripper's gaze cut to Trig's then he screamed, "Should've acted fuckin' days ago, *brother*! Not wait 'till they've taken *my* old lady!"

"They would've expected that, Rip. We needed to regroup and come up with a plan," Strike said.

"While you assholes were regrouping and planning, they took my..." He slammed his palm against his chest. "...*wife*!"

Prez shook his head. "They're desperate. No other reason why they acted so soon."

"They aren't so desperate anymore, are they? They got my woman." Rip spoke, anger vibrating through his voice, making his body shake. He needed to breathe, try to relax. He didn't, he wouldn't be in the condition to talk much less drive. Taking a deep breath, he ran a hand through his hair.

"Tell us how they took her."

Now, he had to relive that? He said it fast. "Woke up, she was gone. Door unlocked."

Strike shook his head. "They must've tricked her somehow. Em's not stupid. She wouldn't've opened the door, not—"

Trig interrupted, "Not unless she thought they had Bree."

Bud and Prez exchanged a look then Prez asked, "Doug find out anything?"

Doug? His brothers hired the PI?

Trig nodded. "He's going to call me with an

address, where he thinks they've been hiding out."

Some of the tension lining Rip's shoulders melted in knowing his brothers hadn't abandoned him. They'd been on his side all along, his and *Em's*. Still, he couldn't breathe right, and he wouldn't, not until he found Em. "Could've told me we were looking into it."

Strike let out a humorless laugh. "So you could go in there guns blazing? No, Rip, we kinda like you, so we're trying to keep you alive."

He swallowed. "What else have you been keeping from me?"

"Doug's guys have been surveilling this place."

He quirked a brow. "That it?"

"Yeah, he's only been on it for a couple of days. We got plenty."

Maybe, but they didn't have Em. He peered at Prez and admitted, "I called Chip. I thought I was alone."

Trick and Rake walked in. Behind them, Army. "They'd give us good numbers."

Rip's phone binged. He spared a glance at it and realized it was the address of the location he was supposed to meet Chip.

Blaze rode in and parked his bike inside the garage. "We're considering teaming up with Chained?"

His brothers kept piling in. All looking like they'd been dragged out of bed, hair a mess, some shirtless. Stone and Hash came next.

Then Mellow, phone to his ear, saying, "Old ladies can watch Cullen, brother. Della and Bree are here too," which meant he was speaking with Dodge.

"Nothing's been decided," Prez answered Blaze's question.

"Told you I don't got time for votes and bullshit,"

Rip growled.

"It'll take a minute," Dash jumped in.

Rip took a series of steps, now face to face. "You realize she could be dead? You realize she could be lying in a ditch in a pool of blood. They could be stabbing the life outta her, or they could be cutting her up, getting ready to dump her in the ocean."

"Can't think like that, Rip." Trig knew what it felt like knowing his old lady was in the hands of an enemy. Not so long ago, his own old lady had been taken.

Solid advice, so Rip knew he should listen, but he didn't because he *couldn't*. The panic and fear searing him was crippling. Standing there talking instead of doing added anger to that deadly mix, making it worse.

"No, you're right. I should be thinking she's alive. She's alive, they could be knocking her around, beating her, *raping* her. *Her!* Is that what you want me to think?"

Trig's jaw went rock hard, but for a moment, he let something slip. A look of utter devastation flashed in his eyes, like in that split second, he'd relived it. "Don't think on it at all."

"All in favor of teaming with Chained?" Dash asked.

Aye's resounded, not one nay.

Prez spoke loud. "Take SUVs. Ride out to Chained." He looked to Rip. "We got an address?"

Rip had his brothers. The relief palpable, but blanketed by the rest. "Yeah," he said, giving the address.

Trig looked to him. "You ride with me."

"I ride my—"

Trig jerked his head. "No, Rip, you won't. You

want to waste more time getting into it about who's gonna drive? Have at it. I'm still fuckin' driving."

He wouldn't waste more time. He hoped Trig drove fast. Otherwise, they'd be getting into it for another reason.

****

Em wished they'd remove the hood draped over her head. Not being able to see made the fear worse. She wanted to orient herself in some way, stare at the men responsible in the face, play it off like she wasn't afraid to die.

Then again, maybe it was a good thing she couldn't see. If she saw them, she could identify them. And if she could, they wouldn't keep her alive. A long shot, she knew, but still, she couldn't help but hope. She had too much to live for.

After they took her and dumped her in a trunk, they drove for a while. When they stopped, they yanked her out of the trunk and dragged her indoors. The blast of air conditioning hit her full force, a drastic change from where she'd been. It was freezing, the type of cold that seeped into her bones, yet she didn't feel it. All she felt—terror. It built while they hauled her farther inside, roughly shoved her into a room, built when she fell face first onto a chilly, hard, tile floor, when they tied her wrists and ankles. It built every second after that too, so now, she could barely breathe. It seemed like it had been hours ago, but it could've just been minutes.

Lying on her side on the floor, she remembered what Bryce told her last night. Just after she'd told him she always loved him and always would, he promised her they'd live the rest of their lives together. She remembered it with such clarity, it was like he'd whispered it in her ear then. And as she heard it, she rubbed the ring finger on her left hand. Bare. Unused to it, she took his ring off to sleep and hadn't put it on that morning. She wished she hadn't taken it off. If she was going to die, she wanted to die with his ring on her finger.

A foot slid up her thigh, up her backside, lifting her shirt, Bryce's shirt, over her butt. Gasping, she jumped. Another thing she hadn't bothered to put on, undies, so whoever lifted her shirt, whoever else was in that room with her, now saw her naked backside.

She should've put on her thong, should've slipped on her ring. Then again, if she could change anything, she wouldn't've been taken to begin with, especially the way she had.

They claimed they had Bree. Panicked, she had no choice. She should've stopped for a second to think about it. While she'd been stuck in the trunk of the car, she overheard the men who'd taken her say their ruse worked, and she heard them laugh about how easy it'd been. It didn't matter. She couldn't change anything now.

That foot, pressing down on her right cheek, nudged her hard enough her whole body shifted until she lay on her chest. With her hands tied behind her back, she couldn't catch herself. Bryce's shirt at her waist, instinctively, she held her legs together. No clue why she bothered, in a room with at least two others, both men from their deep voices, she was at their mercy. They were going to kill her, they'd take whatever they wanted.

"That's a nice fuckin' ass." The man had squatted beside her, his voice too close. With his rough, calloused palm, he groped her ass.

Heart beating too wildly in her chest, she cringed.

"Don't like that?" He spanked her, hard.

She jolted and felt the sting long after.

"Bikers share. He wouldn't mind."

A door opened.

"Get your fuckin' hands off her and cover her up."

She stilled, hearing nothing for several seconds but her pounding heart echoing in her ears.

Movement, then the man who touched and taunted her shouted, "Why the fuck—"

"You remember the plan? We want it to work, she can't be touched, asshole."

More shifting. The man had drawn farther away, when he said, "She'll be alive after I fuck her."

God. Oh, God. Her breaths grew shallow. Bile rising in the back of her throat, she swallowed.

"Both of you can't follow orders, so get the fuck out."

No movement. No voices.

She held her breath, waiting.

"Now!"

She jumped, startled.

Another voice came then, a voice so grim regardless of her situation, hearing it alone would've had the skin on the back of her neck prickle.

"What the fuck's all the screaming about?

"You wanna tell him? Or should I?"

Silence.

"I wanna know what's going on, and I wanna know *now*." That grim voice gave an order she knew they'd follow.

Shifting and shuffling. "You touch her?" That

same grim voice lowered an octave. "After I gave *my* orders?"

A moment later, the voice came again. "Deal with them." A pause. "You're on guard. No *one* touches her."

"But—"

A sound resonated like someone had been punched. A groan then, "Fuck!"

"I said she can't be harmed. That means you don't rape her, you fuckin' idiot." A frustrated sigh then, "Get cleaned up. You're getting blood all over my floor."

The door closed, but she wasn't alone. Someone neared. She felt it in her bones. A hand grasped her shirt. She stilled, holding her breath. That man tugged down Bryce's shirt, covering her bare ass.

Although those men were all responsible for taking her from Bryce and Bree, she whispered, "Thank you."

"I follow orders. Boss orders me to kill you. I'll kill you, so don't thank me."

A tear slipped out of her right eye, all she allowed herself. She couldn't give them anymore, couldn't lose herself in tears. She had to fight, had to find a way to escape. They were keeping her alive and unharmed. Chances were they needed her as leverage. Whatever the reason, she had some time.

Chapter Twenty

Ripper strode into the warehouse outside Santa Rosa, the address Chip texted him, with no reservations.

He scanned the large space, Chained MC's current home base, and ignored everyone's gaze but Chip's.

Face emotionless, Chip spoke. "What do you know?" He didn't blink at the fact Ripper's brothers, all of them, came in behind him.

Not that Chip had anything to worry about. The clubs weren't on bad terms, and Chip, too, was surrounded by his brothers, close to two dozen.

"Got an address."

Chip's eyes widened, a glimmer of hope clouded his face and body for a spilt second before he hid it. "How?"

"Doug."

"Where?"

"'Bout half an hour from here."

"Is he sure they got her there?"

Rip swallowed, hating to admit, "Won't know 'till we go in."

Chip released a breath. "It's a risk. They got her there; they'll kill her when we raid it. They don't got her there; they'll send word to kill her."

This, Rip knew, and yet, they didn't have another option. Ripper advanced. Chip's brothers moved in, flanking their president.

He stopped a foot from Chip. "Your choice. This. *Is*. Mine."

Then and there, for a moment, Rip caught it. Chip's mask slipped, and too many emotions flashed across his face: pain, regret, fear...for Em. Chip loved her like a sister. They were family, so he was hurting but hiding it.

"We need to wait." Chip paused. "I got a call from the Falcons. They got her. They want to trade me for her."

The way Chip said it, Rip knew his choice. Chip would make the trade, himself for Em. A stupid decision, they'd kill him then kill her too.

Chip's brothers protested, several of them speaking at the same time.

Till shook his head. "Stupid as fuck."

"They'll kill you," Mase growled.

"We aren't on board with that shit plan," Cane shouted.

"Fuck," Tracker cursed under his breath.

Ignoring Chip's brothers completely, Rip snapped, "You're *not* doing that. We're raiding the address."

Chip shook his head. "Then what? She ain't there, what the hell are we gonna do?"

"That's what we're doing."

Chip leaned in, eyes hardening. Body vibrating, he shouted, "We do that, they'll kill her! I'm telling you they'll fuckin' kill her!"

Ripper sensed his brothers move in, surrounding him. "We're *not* gonna stand here and debate this shit. I'm her old man. I decide. I've decided we're raiding the address."

Chip clenched his teeth. "I'm her cousin."

"I'm her man."

"I'm the closest thing she has to a brother, a father, a—"

"I'm her fuckin' *man*."

"I'm *family*, the only family she's got."

"She's got Bree, and she's got—"

"Bree's a kid—"

"I'm Bree's father. I decide for Bree—"

"I'm *family!*"

"I'm family, too. I'm her fuckin' *husband*!"

Chip's body rocked.

Rip kept going. "She sleeps in my bed, wears my ring, my cut. She's mine. I'm hers. We got Bree. We *are* family." He stopped to release a breath. "Your plan's stupid as fuck, and I say we aren't doing that 'cause I'm not gonna let you get yourself killed 'cause no way in hell I can tell her I let you trade yourself for her."

Chip's jaw hardened. "Better me than her."

"No offense but agreed. I can't lose her again, but I can't let her lose you either. She couldn't live the rest of her life knowing she lived while you died."

The president of Chained lost his disguise, the charade. He quit hiding behind anger too. Pain streaked his face. "We got no other option. This mess... It's my fault anyway, not hers. She never belonged in any of this shit."

He nodded. "You're right. She doesn't belong in this shit, but you're wrong too 'cause *we do* got another option. We raid the address and pray she's there. She isn't, we make sure no one gets outta there."

Chip cocked his head. "How do you think we're

gonna manage that?"

"There's plenty of us to go in from all angles."

Chip's gaze cut to Prez. "You're all in?"

Prez nodded. "Em's one of us. We're all in."

Tracker jumped in then. "They spot fifty of us comin', they'll alert whoever's got her and—"

"We cut the phone lines and use a cell phone jammer to block the signal."

Chip peered at Army, standing to Ripper's right. "You got one?"

Army smiled and nodded to Strike, who said, "Yep."

Chip released a breath, looked at his VP, Tracker, who grinned. He then met Prez's stare. "You didn't forget who these guys are, did you? It's gonna get bloody. Your club's been clean for years. You sure you want a part of this?"

Ripper turned. His gaze moved around the warehouse, looking at each of his brothers trying to guess if any one of them would back down. He couldn't blame them if they did. They had family. Some had wives even kids. Too much was at stake to lose. He couldn't read them though. Game faces on, showing no fear. Ripper's gaze ended on Prez.

"I already said Em's part of this club. We're in."

Chip nodded. "We go now. This doesn't work, I meet the Falcons. We got 'till one."

Rip nodded and fought like hell not to think about the very real possibility that Em could be dead. Then he spoke to her like she could hear him.

Hold on, Em. We're coming.

****

Ripper took a deep breath, ignoring the knot in his

stomach, the deep burn in his chest. Surrounded by his brothers, surrounded by Chip's, they were inside a home, two houses away from the address Doug gave them, where the Falcons could be hiding Em. Located in a suburb outside Santa Rosa, the houses were large with big lots and shaded by trees.

They arrived in two box trucks, backed into a home with a "sold" sign like they were the new owners moving in. Strike disabled the alarm. They broke in. None of the neighbors seemed to notice. Then again, the big yard and trees surrounding each of the homes made it difficult to, probably the reason the Falcons chose the area.

He stood just inside the front door, out of sight, waiting. He wasn't even sure what he was waiting for, but they'd just arrived.

"You go in last."

Ripper stared to his left, eyes spitting fire locked on Prez. "You're fuckin' high off your ass if you think—"

"You and Chip go in last."

"You're—"

Prez's jaw hardened. "Not a fuckin' request, *brother*. You're too involved. Can't risk you going in the way you are. It could get one of us killed, and I'm not risking one of our brothers. I'm not risking one of theirs. You think on it for a moment, and you'll see I'm right."

He hated it, but Prez had a point. He'd go in there with Em on his mind and miss shit that could get him killed, his brothers killed, Chip, or Chip's brothers killed.

He nodded. "No one touches her."

Prez held his stare for an endless moment then nodded.

They moved, piling out of the house through the backdoor. Their plan: a third of them would enter through the front door, another third through the back, and the last third would surround the home to make sure no one got away.

Ripper headed with the group entering the back. Guns drawn, two by two, they jumped a fence, scanned the area, crossed a neighbor's yard then scanned again. Another fence, this one leading to the backyard of the home the Falcons occupied. Area barren, they neared the sliding glass door.

"Remember no shooting unless absolutely necessary."

Army, the brother, had a military background. How high up the ranks in the U.S. Army his brother had gotten, Rip had no clue, but for the first time in his life, he cared to know.

A shot rang out.

His gut clenched, heart squeezed. Fear streaked every pore, every fiber, every cell.

****

The cold seeped deep into her pores, into her bones. Em didn't feel anything, not her fingers, arms, legs, or toes.

Her hands tied at the wrists, feet tied at the ankles, a hood covering her face. She hadn't heard a word, a sound, not since the warning she didn't take lightly. It was all she thought about, making her more terrified. Sometime after, the temperature got to her.

She released a breath. It came out icy and didn't heat her face. Then she heard it, the shot. She jolted,

334

eyes snapping open. No use, she couldn't see a thing.

A moment later, he grabbed the back of her shirt and roughly yanked her into a sitting position. Then she felt an object against the base of her neck. A gun. No, the barrel of a gun.

She closed her eyes and prayed.

Seconds turned to minutes. More shots sounded then a final one echoed before everything faded away.

****

His heart, Ripper heard it over everything else. It thundered in his chest, rang in his ears. He didn't know how he got to where he was, inside the house, past a bunch of brothers, past the leader of the Falcons lying dead in a pool of blood. It'd all been a blur. Walking by more brothers, he ignored the God-awful pity stares and didn't let himself read into them.

There was still hope. There had to be. He was breathing, his heart pounding, so she had to be breathing, her heart had to be pounding too.

Taking a step into the room where a crowd formed just outside it, his breath stilled in his chest. Two people in the room, a man and a woman.

The woman on the floor, lying on her side, her face covered with a hood. He recognized that black tee she wore, *his* tee. His shirt now hiked up revealing her thighs and hips, naked underneath. Legs cocked to her chest and closed. Under her head, *blood*. It ran in streams away from her.

His Em…with so much blood flowing away. *Dead.*

He'd never get another day, night, minute, second. What he had of her was all he'd ever have.

His heart stopped beating. Breaths slowed. The room spun. One thing became clearer, one thing proved by the way his chest burned, eyes blurred, life leaked out of him…

He'd wasted so much time, never chased her. He should've fucking chased her. He knew by the burn, the blur, the life leaking out of him, he'd never be a man again. The rest of his life, he'd be a zombie. His heart beating, but not pounding, he'd breathe but not live.

Acid rising in the back of his throat, he moved. In a split second, he knelt in front of her in that pool of blood. He reached for the hood covering her face and barely had his hand on it, when it happened.

She screamed and lifted herself from her position on the floor, pushing, struggling, fighting. "No, no…please…"

It scared him. It thrilled him. He took a deep breath, resting his hands firm on her shoulders. "It's okay, Em… It's me."

She let out a sound. Part gasp, part scream, part relief, part joy.

"Hold still."

He released one of her shoulders and tore the hood off her head. When her eyes caught his, they softened that way he loved.

Alive.

Breathtaking.

Beautiful.

A rush of emotion choked him.

Her hair dripping blood, the side of her face and head stained red. The shirt she wore soaked with it. So much blood, he didn't know how she was moving, breathing, talking, fighting.

"Where does it hurt?"

She said one word. "Bree?"

A question. He knew unless he answered, he'd never get anything out of her. "Safe." He shifted his hands over her head, trying to find where the blood came from. "Tell me where it hurts?"

She hesitated a second then shook her head. "Nowhere." Dropping her head, she looked down. "Oh my God."

For the first time, he got a good look at the man behind her. Half his skull missing, blood still oozing out, dead from a gunshot wound to the head. That blood on Em not hers but his.

Catching his gaze, she attempted to turn.

He grabbed her shoulders, holding her still. "Don't, babe. Just don't."

Her eyes rounded. She nodded. "Can you untie me?"

He grabbed a switch blade from his pocket and cut the restraints at her ankles then her wrists. Immediately, she pressed her hands to his chest, her fingers clutching his shirt, his skin.

Wrapping his arms around her, he buried his face in her neck. "Are you hurt?"

She shook her head. "I'm cold."

He felt the cold then. Her hands at his chest like ice, and she wore just a blood-soaked tee.

"I'm sorry."

He drew away from her and watched those beautiful hazel eyes water.

"I'm so sorry, Bryce. I shouldn't have—"

He grasped the back of her neck and hauled her to him as he wound his other arm around her back. Her body pressed close, he hoped absorbing his heat. "Shh…babe, it's gonna be fine. You're safe now, and

I'm gonna keep you safe."

"I …" A sob tore from her throat. "…Thought I was going to die… Thought I'd never see Bree, thought you'd never get to keep your promise…"

He pulled away slightly to catch her eyes.

"Remember…your promise… You promised we'd live the rest of our lives together…"

God, what his Em had been through. He couldn't imagine. Hours held against her will, waiting and waiting to *die*. "I keep my promises, Em. I had to find you, so I could keep it."

Tears streaming down her face, she pressed her cheek against his chest and sobbed. "Always loved you."

"I know," he whispered then released her neck to slide his arm under her. He hefted her up in one swift movement.

Taking several steps until he reached the door into the room, he met Chip's stare. "She's gonna be fine."

Chip didn't look his way. His gaze on Em as he cupped her cheek. "Em?" Voice choked.

She turned her head.

Chip inhaled nosily. "You hurt?"

She shook her head.

"You never forgive me for this, I won't blame you, Em."

Because Em was amazing, she smiled at Chip. "It's not your fault." A chill swept through her.

Chip's arm went over his head, grabbing the back of his shirt. He yanked it off and draped it over her. "Love you, Em."

She pulled away from Rip. Forced, he released her legs and let her stand on her own, yet needing the connection, he kept one hand on her lower back.

She wrapped her arms around Chip. "Love you more."

Chip pressed his mouth to the top of her head. "Go with your man. I'll come see you soon, yeah?"

She nodded, turned to Ripper, and curved her arms around him. A second later, he carried her out.

"My ring…"

He stopped, stare snapping to her left hand on his chest. "They took it?"

She shook her head. "I took it off."

He stopped breathing.

"I don't sleep with jewelry, so I took it off last night."

He started again.

"I put it in my pocket before I went to bed. Do you think… Can we get it?"

"'Course, Em…" He paused for a moment and swallowed. "Promise me you'll never take it off again."

She smiled. "I promise."

Epilogue

Em's eyes hadn't yet drifted open, but she rubbed her thumb along the ring finger of her left hand. Feeling her wedding band, she knew she was safe.

Even so, all of it came back to her in a rush, her wedding day, being kidnapped then rescued. After that, her memory got hazy, probably because by that point the shock had gotten to her. She remembered Bryce taking her into the back of a box truck and falling asleep against his chest with his arms tight around her. She remembered him waking her when they got home. She remembered him helping her shower, placing her wedding band on her finger, and taking her to bed. He laid with her. The minute her head hit the pillow, she passed out. She didn't remember anything after that.

Now, she'd woken. It was dark out. She must've slept all afternoon and evening. Yet, Bryce wasn't in bed. The mattress beside her was cold like he'd left a while ago or never went to sleep. She was still tired, exhausted even, but she didn't want to be in bed without him, didn't want to be without him period maybe because for hours she thought she'd never see him again. Not quite true. The truth—she never wanted to be without him, not for a single day since she realized she loved him years ago.

She stood on her surprisingly steady feet and headed out of their bedroom, down the hallway, and into the living room. He stood by one of the bay windows she loved. Hands on his hips, body strung tight.

"Bryce?" She closed the distance between them.

He turned, and his gaze instantly captured hers. "Why're you outta bed, babe?

She smiled. "Because you are."

She knew that look on his face, the forced smile. When the club had been involved in dirty dealings, he gave her that look and that same forced smile time and time again, so she knew his thoughts weighed him.

She wrapped her arms around his waist, slanting her head to hold his eyes. "Bree?"

"Staying with Trig and Allie again tonight."

Disappointing, she wanted to see her daughter. "I missed her."

He cupped her cheek then swept his hand back threading his fingers through her hair until he grasped the back of her neck. "She missed you, too. Allie brought her around earlier. She went into our room to see you."

"You should've woken me."

"You needed to rest. It's too late to go now."

She quirked a brow. "And you?"

His gaze on her lips, he asked, "What about?"

She narrowed her eyes. "Don't play dumb."

He heaved a sigh as he circled his arm around her back. "Gonna ask you something, and you gotta tell me the truth. It won't change how I feel about you, but I gotta know, so I know how to help you. Yeah?"

She nodded. Even knowing what he'd ask, she waited for him to.

"Did they..." His fingers at her neck spasmed.

"Did they…touch you?"

"One of them touched me."

His jaw clenched, body locked, and those beautiful eyes that extraordinary, blue-green color went dead.

"Not the way you're thinking." Her stare fell from his. "He wanted to…you know, but this other guy, the one in the room with me stopped him. They were ordered not to touch me."

Just before he hauled her against him, his eyes changed—the dead leaving, gratitude shining through. He rested his chin on the top of her head and whispered, "Can't tell you how glad I am, Em."

Pressing his lips against her forehead, his hands went to each side of her neck. Then he tilted her head to meet his face. "I gotta say it again. I'd still love you. I'd still want you. I'd want you any way I could have you. I just don't want that for you 'cause I never want you to suffer like that."

At that moment, it didn't matter that she'd been kidnapped, that she could've been raped or killed. All that mattered—knowing he meant what he said.

She smiled. "I'd want you any way I could have you too."

"They wanted to trade you for Chip."

She closed her eyes tightly, swallowed then parted them.

"He was gonna do it too. I told him he wasn't. We argued about it. Then we did it my way. I'll clarify, we didn't have the address from Trig's PI, I would've traded you for Chip in a heartbeat."

"They would've killed him."

Eyes widening, he scanned her face. "They would've killed you."

"They may have killed me either way."

He clenched his jaw then leaned into her. "I would've tried anything and everything to get you back."

She tightened her arms around his waist.

"After the drive-by, the brothers hired Trig's PI to get dirt on the Falcons. That's how we found you. The PI gave us an address. We're getting ready to go in, and I hear a shot…" He swallowed thickly. "I thought we fucked up, and they spotted us. And I knew if you were there, they were gonna kill you. That first shot was one of their guys, messing with his gun. He accidentally fired it. We didn't know that, so after hearing it, we went in, guns blazing."

He quirked a brow. "More than fifty of us against the ten of them? No contest. But when I went into that room and saw you…" His eyes watered. Voice choked and ragged, when he said, "Lying so still, all that blood… I thought you were dead. Thought I'd fuckin' lost you." He laughed then, but it was forced and sad. "Then you moved… Best scare I ever had."

She hadn't thought of that, of how it must've looked. She heard shots including one close behind her and the commotion and decided to play dead. When someone touched her, she moved on instinct and begged for her life instead. She couldn't imagine what it must've felt like to have been in his shoes.

"That guy in the room with you killed himself. There was a camera outside the door. He saw us coming. He could've killed you but killed himself instead." He shook his head. "I don't know why. Don't care. I'm just glad it was him instead of you."

She knew why or had an idea anyway. He hadn't

been given the order, so he hadn't killed her, but he knew he'd been caught, so he killed himself instead of risk the wrath of bikers.

He pressed a kiss to her lips then pulled away. "I'll *always* come for you, even if after I find you, I gotta spank you." A smile, a real one, spread across his mouth. "Love you, Em. Always will."

"I love you, too, Bryce."

$$****$$

Two days later

The Tuesday after the Saturday she'd been taken, Em was back at work. Bryce told her to take the week off. She took Monday off. She knew Bryce wouldn't be happy when he found out, which would happen in a half hour when he got back from taking Bree to school and saw her in the office, but she couldn't care less. No way she wanted to sit around for a whole week doing nothing but waiting for Bree to get out of school and Bryce out of work.

She grabbed the mess of sandwich wrappers and potato chip bags several of the brothers left on the counter and desk and stilled when she heard his voice.

"Hey."

She lifted her head. Bud stood at the door leading into the garage's office.

Most of the brothers and all of the old ladies had gone up to her at one point or another over the course of the past two days to congratulate her for getting married and to say they were glad she was okay. She expected that from the old ladies and Strike, not from the rest of the brothers. Not that she didn't think they were glad she was alive—for Bryce and Bree's sake at least—but she didn't think they'd make it known to her. She understood by doing that, they were welcoming her back into the fold, expressing in words and actions that the past was just that, and they were moving forward with a clean slate. It was comforting, relieving, and felt damned good.

But Bud hadn't been one of the brothers who went out of his way to talk to her. She hadn't expected him to either. She also highly doubted he was there for that.

"Hi."

"I got something to say. You busy?"

She was, but he'd say what he came to say, and she figured it was better for both of them if they got it over with. The faster, the better.

"No."

He took a step inside, shut the door, and faced her. "I know you think I hate you. I did, and I got my reasons, but I don't anymore."

She didn't know exactly what to say to that, so she said nothing.

"You gotta understand, you left, and he was…" He shook his head. "I got my reasons to hate you, to continue to hate you, but I'm not gonna 'cause I'm not gonna give you another excuse to ride outta here on a whim and take Bree with you."

"I wouldn't. I thought—"

His face hardened. "It doesn't make a difference 'cause it doesn't change what happened after you left."

Right. Well, she knew this. He blamed her even though he wasn't close to Bryce anymore. She guessed he blamed her for whatever happened between him and Bryce, too. Bud wasn't the type of man who wasted time on trivialities. With knowing this, she figured somehow, she *was* the reason Bud and Bryce were no longer friends.

Her stomach turned. She'd not only made herself, Bryce, and Bree suffer, she'd come between two friends. It meant when Bryce needed a friend the most, he hadn't had one.

"I'm sorry."

Bud's eyes widened then narrowed.

"I am sorry," she repeated.

He stared at her for several moments before he said, "Thought it wasn't your fault 'cause you thought—"

"I thought what I thought, and it turns out, I was wrong. Even thinking what I did, when I saw Bryce with Bree, I knew I'd made a huge mistake. So even if I had been right, which I wasn't, I shouldn't have left because I hurt people. One of those people is you, so *I'm* sorry."

Gaze hardening, he shook his head. "It doesn't change anything, but appreciate it the same." He turned and opened the door. Before he stepped out, he said over his shoulder, "Glad you didn't get killed and... Congrats."

She smiled. "Thanks."

****

Later that night

Coming hard and fast, just before she did, he stopped. His tongue tormenting her, gone, fingers at her core, gone.

"Bryce! No! Don't stop! Please..." He had to keep going. She needed him to.

His body covered her a moment later, kissing her in a way that made her melt. She rubbed against the length of him trying to get herself there.

His hands went to her waist, pulling her away. He then sat up. Kneeling between her legs, his fingers tightened around her hips. He lifted her bottom half off the bed and slammed into her. He did it so hard, her overly sensitive clit buzzed. She spasmed, and the most powerful, mind-blowing orgasm of her life hit her, leaving her breathless.

Aftershocks hummed, she watched him pound into her, face a mask of desire, abs tightening with each thrust, chest covered in a wet sheen of perspiration. Beautiful, so stunning, she wanted him closer.

She wrapped her legs around his waist and met his thrusts, adding to the pleasure.

"That's right, Em. Just like that, babe."

Before she knew it, she was breathing in that funny way she did right before she climaxed. Building and building... It hit, so powerful, so much more than the first. She shuddered.

He came a millisecond later. "Fuck," he groaned and collapsed on top of her.

She hooked her arms around his neck immediately, keeping him close.

He trailed his hand up her side and whispered, "I love you, Em."

Chills skidded over her body making her shiver.

"Tell me." He moved, shifting to her side, lying on his. Then he circled his arm around her shoulders and turned her so she faced him.

"What?"

"Haven't heard you say it today."

She smiled. "I love you, Bryce."

****

"What happened between you and Bud?"

347

The wrong time to ask, probably, but honestly, there wasn't a good time to ask, and there was no better time than right after she'd gone down on him.

He cupped her face and pulled her away from his chest. Sprawled on top of him, she went willingly. Lifting herself onto her hands, she met his eyes.

"You trying to ruin the best blowjob I ever got, babe?"

She smirked. "No."

He released her cheeks. Not losing sight of his stare, she rested her chin on his chest, her hands went around the back of his shoulders.

"It's complicated."

"Is it?"

He cupped her cheek then slid his hand until he rested it on the back of her neck. "When you left…"

She lifted a brow. "Go on."

"You left, and I…changed… Like night and day. He didn't get it. He still doesn't."

"I'm sorry."

As he squeezed her neck, his brows drew together. "We've been through this. It isn't your fault."

She nodded. "Yeah, we have, and you said it isn't anyone's fault but Lilliam's. We've moved on, haven't we?"

He grinned. "Fuck, yeah."

"Both of you should too."

He shook his head. "He doesn't get me."

She glided one hand around his shoulder to his chest then his chin. There, she trailed her fingers along his stubble. "No, Bryce. He gets you. He just doesn't get me."

"Same thing—"

"No, it isn't. And it's okay."

His gaze flew behind her, seeming to mull over what she said. She shifted to his side and fell asleep. She woke the same way she had for the past several days: facing him, her arm around his waist, her face planted against his chest, his arms wrapped around her.

****

Two weeks, and four days later

"Surprise!"

Em jumped and gasped loudly. Automatically, she turned to peer at Bryce. Standing behind her, he looked down at her, a wide grin on his face. Her gaze slid from him to Bree at her left. One look and she knew her baby girl had been in on the surprise.

The surprise, the club—all the brothers, old ladies, and kids—at their home, the home they planned to move into that day. Even Tiff, at thirty-six weeks pregnant, showed with her old man, Cuss. It was humbling and overwhelming at the same time.

"I... Wow. I...don't know."

Bryce came to stand beside her, slung his arm around her shoulders, and squeezed. He brought her close, moving her until her chest pressed to his. Then he leaned down. His mouth above her ear, he whispered, "Late wedding bash, babe."

Again, wow.

He drew away. "Everyone chipped in, bought us some patio furniture and a barbeque. We're gonna grill up some steaks. Ladies brought sides. Gonna be a fun day."

"Thank you..."

Over the past two weeks, Bryce had installed a surveillance system. They'd painted, bought furniture for Bree's room, and decorated it. They'd also purchased a large sectional for the den and four stools for the kitchen counter. It'd take some time to fill out their home since it was spacious. She had some money saved from before and from working at the garage but couldn't spend all of it. She needed to start looking into buying a car. Last week, she snuck out during lunch with Mia and bought Bryce a seventy-two-inch flat screen television, which she surprised him with last night.

"Before we start, I got something for my girls."

Bree grinned.

Bud stepped forward and handed Bryce two bags.

"Thanks for picking it up, bro."

That, alone, would've made Em's day. Bryce and Bud had been friendly as of late. The fact Bryce asked Bud for a favor was another move in the right direction. She hoped in time they'd be like before.

Bryce handed one bag to Bree and another to her. She looked to Bree and waited for Bree to open hers first. Bree excitedly pulled out a leather cut. On the back, the club's insignia, and it read, "Daughter of Ripper, Hell Ryders MC."

Bree smiled at her father and wrapped her arms around him. "Thank you, Daddy."

Bryce rested his arms around Bree and grinned down at her. "Love you, baby."

"Love you more," Bree said after drawing away.

He turned to Em. "Your turn."

She smiled, dug her hand into the bag, and grabbed a jewelry box. Inside was a necklace, a simple white gold chain with a pendant of his name written in cursive. She grinned, looked up at him, and whispered,

"Always loved you. Always will."

Then he kissed her.

She barely heard the hollering and hooting.

She did hear him whisper, "Love you, *babe*."

J.L. Sheppard

About the Author

J.L. Sheppard was born and raised in South Florida where she still lives with her husband and son.

As a child, her greatest aspiration was to become a writer. She read often, kept a journal, and wrote countless poems. In 2008, she graduated from Florida International University with a Bachelors in Communications. During her senior year, she interned at NBC Miami, WTVJ. Following the internship, she was hired and worked in the News Department for three years.

It wasn't until 2011 that she set her heart and mind to writing her first completed novel, *Demon King's Desire*, which was published in January 2013.

~*~

Note from the Author:

Thank you for reading *Riding Blind, Hell Ryders #3*. I hope you enjoyed it. To find out more about my releases, including the Hell Ryders Series, visit my site.

Honest reviews are welcome and very much appreciated.

~*~

Visit J.L. at
www.JLSheppard.com
~*~

To chat with J.L. Sheppard and other Wild Rose Press authors of erotic romance, join us at
www.groups.yahoo.com/group/thewilderroses.

Also Available

Running Hot
Hell Ryders MC Book 2
By J.L. Sheppard
http://a.co/dCMXTTT

Thomas "Cuss" Layne has never wanted for anything, except the beautiful girl he saved so long ago. But she's a rich girl, and he's a biker. For years, he hasn't had a glimpse of her. Still, he's never been able to get her out of his mind. When her life's in danger, he rides to her rescue once again. This time, he's determined to do what he should've done long ago—make her his, in every possible way.

Tiffany Hamilton has never gotten over the bad boy with the sapphire eyes and midnight hair, the boy who once saved her. She wants him—a touch, a taste—but he's never wanted anything to do with her. It's past time to move on. When the sexy biker barges back into her life, saving her yet again and making demands, he makes it impossible to say no to his raw magnetism. She'll finally have everything she's dreamed of...but will it be enough?

Also Read

Wicked Dance
Chronicles of a Dancing Heart Book One
By Olivia Boothe
http://a.co/8ZWW5xP

Former dance student Sara Hart had aspired to grace the stage on Broadway, but a reckless decision forced her to renounce that dream. Years later, while struggling with an ungratifying job and an even more unsatisfying love life, she literally stumbles upon a dangerously sexy stranger who sends her heart—and her body—into hyperdrive. His touch makes her feel alive again and sparks a desire to rebuild her dance career. But Sara is still haunted by the demons of her past. One dark lie could cost her everything.

Real estate mogul Tom Wright caters to the rich and famous. He lives the life of the perfect bachelor, partying hard and dating the most beautiful women in Manhattan. But he has one golden rule—no commitments. Ever. Then he meets sexy Sara Hart, and something about her makes him want to throw the damn rule book out the window. Every time she's near, the blood in his veins pulses with a raging fire he can't contain. But Tom's shadowed history is resurfacing, unearthing ghosts he'd rather remain buried.

Will this wicked dance be their last?

Thank you for purchasing this
publication of The Wild Rose Press, Inc.
If you enjoyed the story, we would appreciate
your letting others know by leaving a review.
For other wonderful stories, please visit our
on-line bookstore at www.wilderroses.com.
For questions or more
information contact us at
info@thewildrosepress.com.
The Wild Rose Press, Inc.
www.thewilderroses.com
Stay current with The Wild Rose Press, Inc.
Like us on Facebook
https://www.facebook.com/TheWildRosePress
And Follow us on Twitter
https://twitter.com/WildRosePress

www.ingramcontent.com/pod-product-compliance
Lightning Source LLC
Chambersburg PA
CBHW071513260626
47170CB00002B/357